HER RECOLLECTION
HAD NOT PLAYED HER FALSE

Here, in this perfumed evening garden, he was just as athletic, just as seductively handsome, perhaps even more so. Nighttime felt appropriate, a milieu that suited him, with its promises of dalliance and danger.

She found her voice. "I did not hear you."

He came closer, skirting the edges of light. "Rotten habit of mine, sneaking around. Used it to great effect taking strawberry tarts from the buttery when I was supposed to be in bed."

"So I am the strawberry tart, in this analogy."

He chuckled, warming her. "I'd never call you a tart, my lady."

London wanted to be a little daring, almost as daring as he was. "But if I was a berry, I wonder what kind I'd be," she said with a teasing smile.

"Something sweet and wild," he said, voice low and husky.

London had only just mastered her breath, and his words made it catch again. Her gaze strayed toward his mouth, the mouth that said such wicked things. She made herself turn away, play with her ebony-handled fan. What was wrong with her? All she wanted to do was cross the small distance that separated her from this veritable stranger and pull his mouth down to hers, learning what *he* tasted like.

The Blades of the Rose

WARRIOR

SCOUNDREL

Coming Soon

REBEL

STRANGER

SCOUNDREL
The Blades of the Rose

Zoë Archer

ZEBRA BOOKS
KENSINGTON PUBLISHING CORP.

http://www.kensingtonbooks.com

ZEBRA BOOKS are published by

Kensington Publishing Corp.
119 West 40th Street
New York, NY 10018

All Kensington titles, imprints, and distributed lines are available at special quantity discounts for bulk purchases for sales
promotion, premiums, fund-raising, educational, or institu-
tional use.

Special book excerpts or customized printings can also be created to fit specific needs. For details, write or phone the office
of the Kensington Special Sales Manager: Attn. Special Sales
Department. Kensington Publishing Corp., 119 West 40th
Street, New York, NY 10018. Phone: 1-800-221-2647.

Zebra and the Z logo Reg. U.S. Pat. & TM Off.

ISBN-13: 978-1-4201-0680-0
ISBN-10: 1-4201-0680-5

First Printing: October 2010

10 9 8 7 6 5 4 3 2 1

Printed in the United States of America

For Zack,
who is just enough of a scoundrel

Chapter 1

A Chance Encounter

Athens, Greece. 1875.

The bloody problem with magic was that he wasn't allowed to use it.

Bennett Day ducked as a heavy marble bust of Plato flew toward his head. It smashed into the wall behind him, leaving a sizable hole that could have easily served as the philosopher's allegorical cave.

Bennett tutted. "Not very enlightened of you, Captain. What would Plato say?"

"English swine! I kill you!"

"How un-Platonic." He dodged as the German ship captain, graceful as a drunken bear, lunged for him. Somewhere, Elena screamed. Bennett sighed. She proved herself to be all too typical with her theatricalities, a woman who loved show more than substance.

Bennett easily avoided the German's paws. Yes, things would have been much simpler if Bennett could use an immobilization spell—that one from the Maldives that had been used on him once before and stung like the devil. But he couldn't use that spell or any other. He was a Blade of the Rose. He could only use magic that was either a gift or naturally belonged to him. Which left him with precisely nothing.

Yet, when it came to eluding angry husbands catching him in their wives' bedrooms, Bennett needed no magic. He was well versed in extricating himself from this very situation. He avoided such entanglements, generally, but sometimes it couldn't be helped, especially on assignment.

"Stand still!" roared the captain. "Fight like a man!"

"Like this?" asked Bennett with a neat jab to the German's chin. The heavy captain stumbled back but did not, alas, go down as smaller men would.

Business for the Blades had brought Bennett to Athens, and following a lead brought him to Elena. Her seafaring husband was known as an ally of the damnable Heirs of Albion, and thus a likely wellspring of information as to what the Heirs were doing in Greece, what magical Source they sought. Bennett needed the German's last manifest to know if those pilfering buggers were here, and, if so, which ones had come. Two choices: break into the German's house and steal the manifest; or, and here was the possibility Bennett favored, seduce the captain's wife and nab the manifest along the way. He did so enjoy combining business with pleasure.

She proved herself ripe and eager for seduction. But no sooner had she and Bennett sequestered themselves in her bedroom than her husband had returned at a most infelicitous moment. Ah, well. At least Bennett was still dressed. He didn't want to run through the streets of Athens without any trousers.

Sadly, the captain blocked Bennett's path to the door. Which left him with only one option. Out the window.

"I *am* English," he said to the German, judging the distance. "A little known fact—I'm also one-eighth Greek, on my mother's side. From Olympia. Home of the ancient athletic games."

"Why do you tell me this when I will tear off your handsome, smirking face?"

"One of the events of the pentathlon is—" and here he ran for the window, Elena shrieking, and vaulted over the railing before coming to land lightly in a crouch a story below, "jumping."

He stood and dusted off his palms, grimy from the cobbled street, while the captain shouted the most ungentlemanly epithets from the window above. Elena wept and tugged at her husband's coat. She seemed to be enjoying herself, delighting in the theatrics like a melodrama heroine.

"Come now, sir," Bennett called back to her husband, "you've never *met* my sister, so I strongly disbelieve your assertions about her."

"And your mother is a goat!" With that witty salvo, the captain disappeared from the window, but Bennett knew that, in such situations, husbands seldom retreated to their libraries to indulge in a revivifying and reflective glass of brandy. Sure enough, Bennett heard the captain's pounding steps as he barreled down the stairs. Bennett decided not to wait for the man to make his appearance on the street, even if it was the polite thing to do.

"Another event in the pentathlon: running," Bennett added before sprinting away. He patted his inside jacket pocket, where the manifest rested safe and secure.

Elena and her husband lived in Plaka, one of the oldest parts of Athens, as attested by its narrow, winding streets that seemed to have no reason to exist other than to drive foreigners to madness. White buildings stacked one atop the other like demented sugar cubes. As Bennett sped down these cramped and twisted streets, he deftly sidestepped donkeys laden with baskets of pistachios. The German captain bellowed behind him. Women and men shouted from windows and doorsteps, eager to join in the fun.

This wasn't *exactly* what the Blades had in mind when dispatching him to Greece. A cable had reached Bennett in Bucharest, where he had been returning a Source to its homeland. The Star of David medallion had been used in Mongolia to summon a Golem in a pitched battle between Blades and Heirs. Bennett and several other Blades, including a now-initiated Thalia Huntley and her husband Gabriel, had defended an ancient Asian Source against the Heirs. It had been a tight, tough fight, but the Blades had been successful in their mission. That camel's turd and Heirs operative Henry Lamb had been killed, and his crony Jonas Edgeworth fled back to England and his father. The Mongolian Source was now well protected in a monastery deep in the Gobi Desert.

Bennett wasn't so well protected. The German neared and lunged for him. Nimbly, Bennett ducked under the man's arms, falling behind the captain. Momentum carried the German forward, nicely helped by Bennett's boot planted square in the middle of the man's arse.

Bennett raced past a group of men gathered in a square. One of them held a long walking stick to aid in traversing Athens's uneven streets. Without breaking stride, Bennett grabbed the stick from the man's hand and raced on, ignoring the man's outraged yelp.

Down a set of steep stairs. He paused at the bottom, pivoting on the balls of his feet. The captain ran toward him, panting. With a smooth and easy motion, Bennett hurled the walking stick like a spear at the furious husband, and it smacked the man straight in the chest. The German bent over, gasping, as he lost his air.

"Javelin," Bennett said with a grin. "That's event number three."

But the captain was determined, and, even as he turned

purple, forced himself to straighten up and continue his pursuit. Bollocks. Bennett sped on.

He was a good agent for the Blades, serving as their resident cryptographer. Bennett could unlock nearly any code or cipher, but when he had to, was more than willing to get into a scrap or two. There was something so deeply satisfying about going toe-to-toe against a man, rather than an encoded Aztec manuscript.

If he didn't shake this German, there'd be one hell of a fight. He doubted any of the Orthodox churches he passed would offer him sanctuary. A black-clad priest on a church step shook his head and beard at him. Clearly, the holy man knew that Bennett had broken nearly all of the Ten Commandments. At least Bennett honored his father and mother. He didn't make too many graven images, either. Two out of ten wasn't so bad.

The cheerful din of a daytime *taverna* announced itself before Bennett saw it. Men sat at tables outside, drinking ouzo and nibbling on plates of octopus, palavering. Deftly, Bennett seized one of the empty plates and, glancing quickly over his shoulder, launched the plate at the German's head. It was sheer bad luck that the captain stumbled over a basket in the street, and the plate missed him by a bare inch to shatter on the wall behind him.

"Opa!" shouted the men at the *taverna*.

"Discus, that's four," Bennett muttered. "Damn it. It'll be a complete pentathlon after all."

He rounded a sharp corner, then quickly sprang up to grab the lower bars of a balcony's railing. Bennett pulled himself up, but did not climb inside. Instead, he turned around, heels balanced on the edge of the balcony, hands gripping the railing behind him. Not a soft-bellied, weak-armed nob or an Heir, hiding behind a gun or hired muscle. Working for the Blades kept his body strong. Thirty-two years old, and as fit as he'd been during those two years he spent at Cambridge, before he found his true calling as a Blade.

Judging by the smile of the young woman who was currently sitting on the balcony, she also appreciated his athleticism. She started to speak, but Bennett shook his head and winked. She adjusted her kerchief, giving him a better view of her bosom.

The German stormed down the street, then stopped, looking about in confusion. He didn't see Bennett hovering above him. Then came another lilting melody of Teutonic swearing, a delightful combination of seafaring and Germanic oaths, as the man whirled around, searching for Bennett.

Light as a cat, Bennett launched himself from the balcony and onto the back of the persistent captain. A less bull-like man would have fallen to the cobblestones, but the German only staggered under Bennett's weight. Bennett looped one arm around the captain's neck and held it fast, bracing one arm with the other. The German snarled and choked, spinning around and pawing frantically at the strong arm pressed tight against his throat. Bennett did not relinquish his hold. The captain ran backward and slammed him into a wall. Stars swam in Bennett's eyes, but he didn't let go. Another slam. And another. Bennett held tight. Surely Hercules had an easier time of things with that Erymantian boar.

The captain's movements began to slow, his fingers weakening as they tried to pry Bennett loose. Then the German stumbled and sank to his knees before, at last, growing limp. Carefully, Bennett released his hold. The captain slid in a soundless heap to the ground. Turning him over, Bennett contemplated the man's red face before pressing his ear to the captain's chest.

"And that's wrestling," Bennett murmured. "A true pentathlon. Mother would be so proud."

"Is he dead?" asked the young woman from the balcony in Greek.

"A beauty sleep," Bennett answered, also in Greek.

Standing, Bennett dragged the captain's limp body into an alley. He took a wash line and used it to quickly truss the German up like a chicken. Ready for Sunday dinner. Once the captain woke, it would take a goodly bit of maneuvering before he got free.

Bennett dusted himself off before slipping from the alley. With a wave for the woman on the balcony, he headed west, toward the old market in Monastiraki. He had the manifest, but there was more investigation to be done.

A pity that the captain had to return before Bennett could savor the fruits of his seduction of the man's wife. Elena had held such gymnastic potential.

Cuckolded husbands and thrilling chases aside, he was here in Athens for serious business, and he meant to succeed in his objective. As much as he enjoyed female company, his true purpose was and always would be to find and protect the magical Sources. But when the two coincided, well, that was just good fortune.

To Victoria Regina Gloriana London Edgeworth Harcourt, more familiarly known as London Harcourt, it was a wonderful chaos. After Lawrence died, she had spent her requisite year in full mourning, and then gone through the gradual steps through second and half mourning, which meant that, almost three years later, she was finally free of her somber prison. Now she was out into the larger world. And what a marvelous world it was. Not once in her whole life, not even on her bridal journey, had she left England, but now, to find herself in Athens, in the magnificent anarchy of the Monastiraki marketplace—she felt alive with every part of her being.

Vendors in booths and tents sold every item imaginable. Walnuts, olives, embroidered waistcoats, incense, icons, chips of marble from ancient columns, miniature plaster replicas of the Parthenon, postcards. The hot afternoon air swirled in the square, scented with roasted lamb and frankincense, and filled with a patois of Greek, English, and German. Someone plucked on a bouzouki and wailed a love song. Amidst the mix of traditional Greek dress and more modern Western fashion, English tourists were easily distinguishable by their white cotton parasols, London among them. A lady, she was constantly reminded by her mother, protected her complexion, especially from the burning Attic sun. Certainly, her chic straw hat provided no shelter.

"We should be getting back to the hotel."

London looked back at her exhausted maid, Sally, with a small measure of pity. The whole of the day, London had been dragging the poor woman back and forth across Athens. Already, they had visited the Gate of Hadrian, the Olympium, and the Pnyx, true birthplace of democracy. London and Sally had climbed up the steep mountain to see the Acropolis and marveled at the decayed symmetry of the Parthenon. Or, at least, London had marveled while Sally grumbled about rotten old temples, and why did they have to stomp all over some dirty heathen town when all they had to do was go to the museum back home and see lots of silly pieces of marble, thanks to Lord Elgin.

It stunned London that she truly walked the streets and visited the temples of Theseus, of Pericles. She had read so much about the ancient world, its heroes and tragedies, and to be here now, no longer reading but to stand and breathe the air, dusty as it was, seemed a splendid gift she was determined not to squander. After visiting the site of the Ancient Agora, London wanted to see its modern incarnation, and so she and Sally found themselves in the colorful cacophony of Monastiraki, which was, sadly, thronged with British and German tourists in their white linen suits. At the least, London could purchase a few souvenirs for friends back home, and perhaps something for herself, as well. Once she and Father left Athens tomorrow, he assured her they would be far from anyplace that might sell mementos to travelers. London tamped down her disappointment. They had only arrived in Athens the day before, and too soon they would have to leave.

Yet, she would not complain. It was rather miraculous that she was even in Greece at all, had it not been for circumstance. And her own disobedience.

"Just a little bit longer, Sally," London said. "I promise. And then we'll go straight back to the hotel."

"Your father wouldn't want you out by yourself for too long."

"But I'm not by myself. I have you."

Sally lapsed into another round of muttering, which London decided to disregard. As she wandered between the rows of booths, tempted by bushels of currants and finely woven silk shawls, vendors hailed her.

"Lovely necklace for a lovely lady!" someone shouted in German.

"Wonderful grapes as sweet as your beauty!" another yelled in English.

Everything intrigued her. She didn't know where to begin, her head a whirl from the visual and aural bounty around her. Until something caught her eye. London approached a booth where a vendor, dressed traditionally in a white kilt and short jacket, presided over his wares. Rows of black and red urns, amphorae, kraters, and plates were lined up on tables, all of the pottery depicting classical scenes from mythology.

"Wonderful, ancient vases for you, sir," the vendor said in English to a French tourist. He pushed back his fez. "Each one, priceless relic."

"Priceless, you say?" asked the Frenchman, intrigued.

"All beyond value. All taken with utmost care from earth, where they sleep for centuries, for millennia."

Standing nearby, London considered the amphorae and other pieces of pottery. Some dirt had been rubbed into their surfaces, or a small abrasive pad taken to their paint to give them an antiqued appearance. Though she was no expert in archaeology, even a laywoman such as herself recognized such fraud. "I am surprised there is no paint on your hands," she said, also in English. "For these were made no later than a week ago."

At first, the vendor scowled, but he quickly smoothed over a smile. "My lady is clever. Clever as she is beautiful. Yes, these pieces not old. To weed out ignorants, you understand. I save good pieces, ancient ones, for the sharp-witted, such as yourself and this esteemed gentleman."

"Naturally," London said dryly.

The Frenchman glanced over at her quickly, then took a second, slower look. He was rather handsome and very neatly dressed in a traveling suit. He smiled at London, and she gave him a polite nod.

"Here, I show you." The vendor dove down underneath one of the tables, then reemerged with a small wooden chest. He cleared space between some kraters, shunting the ceramic vessels aside with little care, then opened the box. On the rusty velvet lining lay several shards of pottery. "These are too valuable to simply lay out for any fool to grab. But my lady is wise like goddess Athena, and so I give her this privilege. You both may look, if you like."

London tugged off her cream kidskin glove, which Sally took, and picked up one of the shards. Some writing, faded almost to obscurity, decorated its surface, along with traditional palm-leaf motifs. If it was a fake, it was a kind not so obvious as the vendor's other wares. "What can you tell me about this?" she asked.

The vendor beamed, believing he had an interested customer. "Old, yes, very old. I have on most high authority the piece you hold is from time of Darius the Great."

"Darius the Great!" exclaimed the Frenchman, impressed.

"Are you sure?" London asked.

"Quite, my lady. Papers I have, somewhere, to prove it."

"Sir," she said after a moment, "you are not being honest with me or this gentleman."

The vendor looked offended. "You doubt?"

"I do, sir, very much."

"How do you know he is not speaking the truth, Mademoiselle?" the Frenchman asked with a trace of condescension. London did not bother telling him that she was most definitely a *madame* and not a *mademoiselle*.

"Look here," she said, pointing to the writing. "This form of Greek wasn't in use during the reign of Darius the Great. Here, and here, the wording isn't correct. The vowels, you see. They shifted. It's clear that this piece of pottery came from the era of no earlier than Darius the Third."

The Frenchman gaped at her in disbelief. Sally also looked shocked. But then, Sally had never truly comprehended the depths of London's study of language. London had taken the years of enforced seclusion following Lawrence's death to rigorously apply herself to studying more ancient languages than she already knew, sending servants out to buy dusty, nearly forgotten tomes from the booksellers in Covent Garden and poring over them late into the night. Yet, despite herself and the years of wisdom she had gained since the time of her blighted marriage, London felt her cheeks grow hot. Even here, in Athens, an educated woman was a freakish anomaly.

The vendor scowled. "What do you do? You say I lie and you chase off my customers?"

"No, no," London said quickly. "I merely pointed out that the dates weren't quite—"

"You the one who lies!" the vendor shouted. "No lady knows this language! You make trouble!"

Dozens of eyes turned toward them, drawn by the commotion. People craned their necks to watch as the vendor grew more and more angry. He switched to speaking Greek, a fast barrage of words that questioned London's upbringing and why some rich Englishwoman must ruin his business when he had a wife and dozens of children at home who only wanted a morsel of bread, the pitiful creatures.

The Frenchman slunk away, leaving London alone to face the vendor's verbal bombardment. *This* was certainly something that etiquette training never addressed. She wondered how to extricate herself without getting arrested.

"Save those slurs for your grandmother," said a deep, masculine voice to the vendor. He spoke Greek with an English accent.

London turned to the voice. And nearly lost her own.

She knew she was still, in many ways, a sheltered woman. Her society in England was limited to a select few families and assorted hangers-on, her father's business associates, their retainers and servants. At events and parties, she often saw the same people again and again. And yet, she knew with absolute clarity, that men who looked like the one standing beside her were a rare and altogether miraculous phenomenon.

There were taller men, to be sure, but it was difficult to consider this a flaw when presented with this man's lean muscularity. He wonderfully filled out the shoulders of his English coat, not bulky, but definitively capable. She understood at once that his arms, his long legs, held a leashed strength that even his negligent pose could not disguise. He called to mind the boxers that her brother, Jonas, had admired in his youth. The stranger was bareheaded, which was odd in this heat, but it allowed her to see that his hair was dark with just the faintest curl, ever so slightly mussed, as if he'd recently come from bed. She suddenly imagined herself tangling her fingers in his hair, pulling him closer.

And if that thought didn't make her blush all the harder, then his face was the coup de grace. What wicked promises must he have made, and made good on, with such a face. A sharp, clean jaw, a mouth of impossible sensuality. A naughty, thoroughly masculine smile tugged at the corners of that mouth. Crystalline eyes full of intelligent humor, the color intensely blue. Even the small bump on the bridge of his nose—had it been broken?—merely added to the overall impression of profound male beauty. He was clean shaven, too, so that there could be no mistaking how outrageously handsome this stranger was.

She may as well get on the boat back to England immediately. Surely nothing she could ever see in Greece could eclipse the marvel of this man.

"Who are you?" the vendor shouted in Greek to the newcomer. "You defend this woman and her lies?"

"I don't care what she said," the Englishman answered calmly, also in Greek. "Keep insulting her and I'll jam my fist into your throat." The vendor goggled at him, but wisely kept silent. Whoever this man was, he certainly looked capable of throwing a good punch.

Yet gently, he put a hand on London's waist and began to guide her away. Stunned by the strange turn of events, she let him steer her from the booth.

"All right?" he asked her in English. A concerned, warm smile gilded his features. "That apoplectic huckster didn't hurt you, did he?"

London shook her head, still somewhat dazed by what had just happened, but more so by the attractiveness of the man walking at her side. She felt the warmth of his hand at her back and knew it was improper, but she couldn't move away or even regret the impertinence. "His insults weren't very creative."

He chuckled at this, and the sound curled like fragrant smoke low in her belly. "I'll go back and show him how it's done."

"Oh, no," she answered at once. "I think you educated him enough for one day."

Even as he smiled at her, he sent hard warning glances at whomever stared at her. "So what had his fez in a pinch?"

She held up and unfolded her hand, which still held the shard of pottery. "We were disputing this, but, gracious, I forgot I still had it. Maybe I should give it back."

He plucked the piece of pottery from her hand. As he did this, the tips of his fingers brushed her bare palm. A hot current sparked to life where he touched. She could not prevent the shiver of awareness that ran through her body. She met his gaze, and sank into their cool aquatic depths as he stared back. This felt stronger than attraction. Something that resounded through the innermost recesses of herself, in deep, liquid notes, like a melody or song one might sing to bring the world into being. And it seemed he felt it, too, in the slight breath he drew in, the straightening of his posture. Breaking away from his gaze, London snatched her glove from Sally, who trailed behind them with a look of severe disapproval. London tugged on the glove.

He cleared his throat, then gave her back the pottery. "Keep it. Consider it his tribute."

She put it into her reticule, though it felt strange to take something she did not pay for.

"Thank you for coming to my aid," she said as they continued to walk. "I admit that getting into arguments with vendors in Monastiraki wasn't at the top of my list of Greek adventures."

"The best part about adventures is that you can't plan them."

She laughed. "Spoken like a true adventurer."

"Done my share." He grinned. "Ambushing bandits by the

Khaznah temple in the cliffs of Petra. Climbing volcanoes in the steam-shrouded interior of Iceland."

"Sounds wonderful," admitted London with a candor that surprised herself. She felt, oddly, that she could trust this English stranger with her most prized secrets. "Even what happened back there at that booth was marvelous, in its way. I don't *want* to get into a fight, but it's such a delight to finally be out here, in the world, truly experiencing things."

"Including hot, dusty, crowded Athens."

"*Especially* hot, dusty, crowded Athens."

"My, my," he murmured, looking down at her with approval. "A swashbuckling lady. Such a rare treasure."

Wryly, she asked, "Treasure, or aberration?"

He stopped walking and gazed at her with an intensity that caught in her chest. "Treasure. Most definitely."

Again, he left her stunned. She was nearly certain that any man would find a woman's desire for experience and adventure to be at best ridiculous, at worst, offensive. Yet here was this stranger who not only didn't dismiss her feelings, but actually approved and, yes, admired them. What a city of wonders was this Athens! Although, London suspected, it was not the city so much as the man standing in front of her that proved wondrous.

"So tell me, fellow adventurer," she said, finding her voice, "from whence do you come? What exotic port of call?" She smiled. "Dover? Plymouth? Southampton?"

A glint of wariness cooled his eyes. "I don't see why it matters."

Strange, the abrupt change in him. "I thought that's what one did when meeting a fellow countryman abroad," she said. "Find out where they come from. If you know the same people." When he continued to look at her guardedly, she demonstrated, "'Oh, you're from Manchester? Do you know Jane?'"

The chill in his blue eyes thawed, and he smiled. "Of course, Jane! Makes the worst meat pies. Dresses like a Anglican bishop."

"So you *do* know her!"

They shared a laugh, two English strangers in the chaos of an Athenian market, and London felt within her a swell of happiness rising like a spring tide. As if in silent agreement, they continued to stroll together in a companionable silence. With a long-limbed, loose stride, he walked beside her. He hooked his thumbs into the pockets of his simple, well-cut waistcoat, the picture of a healthy young man completely comfortable with himself. And why shouldn't he be? No man had been so favored by Nature's hand. She realized that he hadn't told her where he was from, but she wouldn't press the issue, enjoying the glamour of the unknown.

His presence beside her was tangible, a continuous pulse of uncivilized living energy, as though being escorted by a large and untamed mountain cat that vacillated between eating her and dragging her off to its lair.

"How did you know I was from England?" she asked. "The vendor was speaking English to everyone."

"Your posture. English ladies have a particular way of holding themselves, as though a disapproving governess was glaring at them."

"Different than, say, a French or Greek lady?"

"There's bundles more self-imposed Anglican morality in an Englishwoman's stance. I am," he added, with a slow, suggestive smile, "an avid connoisseur of the language of the body."

"Of that, I have no doubt," she said, dry.

His chuckle was low and velvet and very, very carnal. If he was unleashed on polite British society, virgin debutantes and genteel matrons would turn into Bacchae, tearing at their clothes and ripping apart anyone foolish enough to stand between themselves and the object of their desire. She felt much the same uncharacteristic urge.

London busied herself with pretending to admire a gold silk scarf at a booth. As she did this, she sent a cautious glance toward the beautiful English stranger. With a small, internal start, she realized that his stance only appeared to be negligent and easy. He was, in fact, vigilant, ready as if poised for movement. And his eyes, though glittering with a secret amusement, were never at rest. He watched the marketplace, keen as a blade. He was looking for someone.

But who? She dared not ask such an impertinent question, and didn't know if she wanted the answer. There was something, the edge of a darkness, in him, or, at the least, a potential for danger. She wondered if he was armed. Travelers to Greece were advised to bring at least a revolver if they planned on leaving Athens. But this man's strong body would be weapon enough.

"Is it within the rules to ask what brings you to Greece?" London asked.

"Never said there were any rules." A small dimple appeared in the corner of his mouth. London wanted to touch it. Or, better yet, feel it with her lips.

"If there were," she said, "you don't play by them."

He gave an unapologetic shrug. "Following rules means there's no fun or pleasure in life."

She was certain he had both in abundance. "And decorum? Responsibility?"

"Decorum stifles. Women, especially."

London picked up the scarf and draped it around her shoulders, as a lady might at the ballet. "That sounds like a libertine's well-practiced speech to lure women into dalliance."

"There's always truth in seduction. That's why it works." He stepped closer and loosened the scarf from her shoulders, then he gently wrapped it around her waist like a sash. She felt it like an embrace. His deft, long fingers tied the fabric into a decorative knot. "Much better. More Greek," he murmured in approval.

London's pulse sped at his nearness, yet she did not step away. "But what of responsibility?"

He gazed at her levelly, and in his clear aquatic eyes, she saw a steadiness of purpose that she had not anticipated. "I take my responsibilities seriously."

"They must be the only things you take seriously," she answered.

No mistaking the way he looked at her, how his gaze flicked down to her mouth and held there for more than a moment. "Try me, little troublemaker."

She felt herself standing above the sea, the warm water beckoning her to plunge into its wet, welcoming depths, frolic in its waves. She wanted to jump. She was afraid of the height. "Sir, you are more dangerous than a Barbary pirate," she said, after a breathless pause.

Again, he laughed, something he seemed to do readily. A bedroom laugh. Teasing. Intimate. And such a laugh made her body respond without thought. Her skin felt sensitive, and a molten heat gathered in her core. Oh, it had been a long time since a man touched her, and not a single half-hearted caress from Lawrence affected her as one laugh from this stranger did. She recalled how, moments earlier, his fingers had brushed her hand, and the strange, intense response even that minor contact had engendered.

"Know many Barbary pirates?" he asked, one eyebrow raised.

"I do, now."

It was then that she realized something. All this time, he had been speaking to her as his equal. Granted, he was a devil of a flirt, but he did not seem to consider her female sex a liability. He talked truthfully, openly, without the polite phrases or evasions so common to the speech of every other man she knew. And when she answered him, it was as if she'd unlatched a little door inside herself and could meet him on the level ground, confident in herself.

"I think *you* are the dangerous one," he said, "but you don't know it yet."

Again, their eyes caught and held. No, she was not imagining it. Something hot and knowing in their shared look. And that other thing, that tie that bound them in ways she did not understand.

"We should get back to the hotel, madam." Sally's voice was sharp. Ah, blast, London had almost forgotten about the chaperoning maid. But it truly was a marvelous thing to flirt with a devastatingly handsome man far from home. To pretend, for a moment or two, that she wasn't esteemed gentleman and governmental adviser Joseph Edgeworth's daughter, a paragon of English virtue.

London sighed and stepped back. As intoxicating as this stranger's company was, she did have to go to the hotel. Father expected her. "All right. We'll go."

"Tell me the name of your hotel," the stranger said. "I'll call later tonight. We'll share some hot . . . tea."

"You know I can't," London said with reluctance. Probably no woman ever refused him. She could not blame them, but London's careful deportment won out. "That would be most indecorous. I don't even know your name."

"Ben Drayton." He took her hand and, like a man at an elegant assembly, pressed a kiss to its back. Even though her glove covered her skin, London felt the warmth of his lips through the thin leather. "Now you give me your name."

She tugged her hand free, though she had an impulse to turn it over so she might feel his lips on the more sensitive flesh of her palm. "I have to disappoint you."

"I'm a man who loves to unlock mysteries."

London was about to say more, when she caught sight of a familiar figure at the other end of the market square. She gritted her teeth. How like Father to send Thomas Fraser out to find her. It was bad enough that Fraser was going to be accompanying them on their journey to Delos, as she had learned to her dismay yesterday when they docked, but now her father's associate was being made to police her. As if London could not be trusted to take care of herself. For goodness sake, she was twenty-six, not sixteen, the naïve days of her youth long passed. At least the English stranger recognized she was a grown woman.

London did not wave to Fraser to alert him to her presence. If he was so determined to monitor her whereabouts, let him earn his duty. It would give her the opportunity to say good-bye to Mr. Drayton.

But when London turned back to speak to him, she found only air. He had vanished.

She blinked in confusion. "Where did he go?" she asked Sally.

The maid shrugged, and sniffed, "I'm sure I don't know, madam. One moment he was here, and the next, gone. Like some kind of phantom."

A chill trickled down London's spine. Mr. Drayton's exit had been positively eerie—soundless and immediate. What kind of man could disappear into the air itself? Certainly no one of good character. Perhaps it had been for the best that London had been so circumspect. Maybe he was a thief, or one of those men who preyed upon traveling women of fortune. Or . . . a mercenary? As she had suspected, a dangerous man. Yet one who attracted her powerfully. Not just for his seductive handsomeness, but the way he made her recognize the capability of herself. She had the feeling that if she had revealed to him her linguistic abilities, he would have accepted and perhaps even admired them. Or were those feelings of trust part of his nefarious arsenal?

Feeling a lingering trace of unease, London turned and waved to Fraser. At once, he began to make his way toward her, showing his usual lack of concern for those around him. A big man, he jostled through the marketplace in his white linen suit, his mildly handsome face looking cross, his pale complexion flushed. Of course, he didn't look cross when he reached her. She was his superior's daughter. London was not unaware of the fact that, as soon as her mourning for Lawrence had been finished, Thomas Fraser had been one of a number of men who paid her particular attention. She did not think they were drawn by her personal charms, but rather by her being Joseph Edgeworth's daughter.

"There you are, Mrs. Harcourt." He took off his hat and fanned himself, strands of wheat-colored hair sticking damply to his forehead. "What an awful din in this beastly market. And deuced hot, too."

"I find it rather comfortable, especially after a gloomy English spring."

"Ah, well." He replaced his hat. "That's a pretty sash you've got there. Quite dashing."

London had forgotten about the scarf Ben Drayton had tied around her waist. She started to untie it, but then stopped. She would keep it as a souvenir of the strange and exhilarating day. Reaching into her reticule, she found a silver fifty-lepta coin with which to pay the vendor, but not before her fingers brushed the pottery shard Drayton had urged upon her. A wicked man, she thought.

After she paid, the very un-wicked Fraser asked, "Would you do me the honor of accompanying me to the hotel? Your father would like you to dress for dinner."

Of course he would, London thought. "Thank you, you're very kind, Mr. Fraser." She took Fraser's offered arm, and they left the marketplace, with Sally behind them. London made herself look straight ahead, as much as she wanted to glance back and see what had become of the mysterious Mr. Drayton. It didn't signify. She doubted she would ever see him again. But she wasn't sure if that should raise or lower her spirits.

That was bloody close. Fortunately, Fraser hadn't spotted Bennett, or else the bastard would have set the usual thugs after him, and that wasn't something Bennett particularly wanted to experience again. Heirs always hired local muscle to do their dirty work. Lucky for the Heirs, greed was universal, so they had a ready supply of desperate, amoral men wherever their searches took them.

As Bennett slid into a nearby alley off the market square, an old enmity seethed back to life. Thomas bloody Fraser. Here in Greece. De-sodding-lightful. Bennett didn't care for any of the Heirs, but Fraser was a particular bane. Especially after Fraser's involvement with the Norway debacle years ago that cost Bennett a piece of his small toe, and nearly his life. Fraser's appearance in the market had made Bennett pull his signature disappearing act. He didn't know what Fraser was doing in the market. Probably the git was performing reconnaissance. Heirs traveled in packs of no less than two, so somewhere out in Athens was at least one other thieving Heir bastard. Who made up the rest of their raiding party, Bennett didn't know.

He would find out soon enough. He'd tail Fraser, maybe find out where he and the other Heirs were staying in Athens.

Bennett took a step from the alley, but a familiar Teutonic voice stopped him. "English dog! Now I break your neck!"

Bennett groaned in exasperation. The captain was awake and untied. And headed straight for him.

No help for it. As soon as the German came within striking distance, Bennett threw out a left jab, connecting solidly with the captain's face and snapping the man's head back from the impact. Quick and sharp, Bennett followed with a hard straight right to the chin. The captain hadn't even the time to make a sound. He collapsed to the ground, unconscious.

Confident that the captain would stay down this time, Bennett ducked back into the marketplace. And swore in several languages. Fraser was gone. With no way to know where he'd gone. The labyrinth of Athens had swallowed up the Heir.

The lady was gone, too.

A damned shame that Bennett hadn't been able to spend more time with that delicious woman. It wasn't a boast that Bennett considered himself something of an expert and a gourmet where females were concerned. And the nameless English lady was indeed a fine specimen that he wished he could explore at leisure. She was beautiful, of that there could be no debate. Thick hair the color of golden brown silk, and eyes the kind of rich chocolate in which a man could lose himself. A wide mouth, ripe and rosy. Her modish light blue day gown set off her slim figure. Not exactly voluptuous, but her curves were honest, her waist small— he knew this from tying the scarf there. He had no trouble picturing his hands at that waist, holding her to a wall as he plunged into her, her moans in his ear. The picture was so vivid, he clenched his jaw and forced himself to walk slowly through the market to cool his heated blood.

The sun began to set. Time to head back to his home base and reconnoiter with his fellow Blade. There was still the manifest to study. Bennett headed north, away from the market, but his thoughts remained behind, lingering over the Englishwoman.

She'd been more than beautiful to look upon. She had a

sharp mind, and that was something Bennett truly appreciated in a lover. There wasn't anything more arousing than a woman applying her intelligence to lovemaking. Such mouth-watering possibility. He'd known many other intelligent women, but something more than her intellect kept Bennett thinking of his unnamed Englishwoman in Monastiraki. Many clever females were satisfied with only their books, preferring a path of the mind.

Lady Troublemaker wanted life, she hungered for it, embraced its messiness and chaos. The world was new to her, and she stood ready to receive it.

How many men had she known? How many lovers? Not many, he'd wager. She had an air of untapped carnal potential, an eager student of sensuality. She could, with the proper guidance, surpass her teacher. And then, what a better world this would be, with such a woman in it.

His cock, disappointed by the interruption at Elena's, appreciated these images and stirred. *Go back to your napping*, Bennett ordered. Still, it was hard to forget her, even harder to ignore that strange, vivid moment when his fingers had touched her hand. In all his years, after countless encounters with a vast array of women, Bennett couldn't recall ever having so visceral, so immediate a reaction to touching a woman. And it had gone beyond the physical, too. A sudden, profound connection with no known origin other than something in his body that recognized her, knew and needed her.

Rot. He simply wanted a fuck, but he wasn't going to get one. Not for a while. He was there for the Blades, which meant carnal appetites would have to go unsatisfied until the mission was complete. That clumsy bull Fraser showing in the marketplace proved that the Heirs were truly in Greece.

Bennett reached into a hidden pocket in his jacket. He pulled out a heavy, old compass and considered its face, four blades marking each direction, a rose at the center.

More than a means of finding direction, it resonated with ancient secrets and sacred promises. All Blades knew one another by this Compass. He used it to guide him back to his home base in Athens. It was time to get down to business. There was dangerous work to be done.

Chapter 2

Unexpected Connections

"I expected you a half an hour ago," Athena Galanos said as Bennett entered the study. She sat at a heavy table, books and papers strewn about in an abstruse system only she could understand. A servant entered the room with Bennett, lighting lamps against the oncoming dusk.

Bennett went to the large pedestal globe in the corner of the room and spun it on its axis. Continents and countries whirled. When the servant came forward with a glass of Muscat, he murmured his thanks and sipped at the wine. Dry and clear, it slid down his throat. Athena always had a fine cellar, but it was to be expected. Her family was one of the oldest and most esteemed in Athens, with a large and elegant house at the base of the southern slope of Lycabettus Hill. The Galanos women had been active as Blades in Greece, well before the country won its independence, in a tradition of honor that passed from mother to daughter. The name Galanos was passed on the female side, since they never gave birth to sons, and saw men merely as means by which the line could continue. Their lovers seldom lasted more than the time it took for the getting of a child. A sophisticated, matriarchal coven on the shores of the Aegean, which Bennett appreciated, being enamored of the whole female race.

"Got a little caught up in something," he said.

Athena raised one dark brow. "And how did the husband feel about that?"

"The usual histrionics. Had a nice little chase through Plaka. Very bracing."

She peered closer at him. "I don't see any wounds."

Bennett placed a hand over his chest. "Just my heart, dear lady."

"Of all your organs," she said, "it is perhaps the most resilient."

"But I did get this," he continued, taking the manifest from his pocket and tossing it to her.

Athena grabbed it from the air, and began to rifle through the pages. "So your appetite for information was satisfied, at least."

He grinned, but decided not to mention the English lady from the marketplace. He wasn't sure what he would tell Athena, anyway. That he'd met an exceptionally pretty, intelligent woman whose simple touch affected him, in more ways than the physical? Athena knew Bennett well and would likely laugh at his description of the encounter. He *did* give his heart easily—though it was nothing compared to the freedom with which he gave his body—yet his heart was boundless and nigh incapable of tapping its supply of affection and desire. He never feared exhausting himself on one woman. True, this meant that he hadn't the capacity for longer, more serious commitments, but this proved no impediment. His lovers always knew he would leave. He was open about this, and they accepted him as he was. Would the English lady from Monastiraki feel the same way?

He found himself revisiting the delicate precision of her face, her musical, slightly husky voice, the combination of freshness and experience that shone in her coffee-colored eyes. Mostly, he was struck by her intense hunger for experience. She was probably a widow, and, if so, then her poor, dead husband was to be pitied for leaving behind so delicious a wife who wanted to devour the banquet of the world.

He grew serious as he focused on more immediate concerns. "Saw Fraser in Monastiraki."

Athena looked up from the manifest. "Who was with him?"

"He was alone, or so it seemed." He leaned against the bookshelves, one booted foot over the other. His and Athena's work as Blades was to protect magic and keep it safe from those sodding Heirs of Albion, who thieved magical Sources from around the world for a nefarious, empire-building agenda. Blades were always vigilant where Heirs were concerned, always dogging their steps to keep the Sources safe.

"And did he see you?"

"No, I got out before he spotted me." Bennett held his glass of wine up to the light, watched it shimmer and glow, before draining it and setting it on a shelf. The spine of one book read, in Greek, *The Practical Art of Spellcasting, or, a Woman's Guide to Thaumaturgy*. Typical reading for Athena.

She nodded. "That is fortunate. We need to keep our presence from the Heirs hidden for as long as possible."

"Wasn't able to follow him, though. The owner of the manifest popped by for a chat."

"And?"

"I let my fist do the talking. That shut him up. But by then, Fraser was gone." And the delectable Englishwoman was gone, as well.

Taking the manifest, Athena pushed back from the table and walked toward the window, with its magnificent view of the Parthenon and the city that shared her name. All women in the Galanos family were named Athena, possessing an aristocratic and dark Greek beauty that rivaled the Caryatides, but to Bennett and the other Blades, this Athena was foremost a capable colleague that should never be underestimated.

"Divine for us, goddess," he said to her. "Urgent matters are afoot."

She peered at the manifest. "I see Fraser's name here. And Joseph Edgeworth."

Bennett swore softly as his eyes met Athena's. "Joseph Edgeworth isn't a field man. He's too high up, too important."

"But now the Heirs have the Primal Source," Athena noted. "With it in their power, all other Sources will be under their control."

"So they're pulling out all the stops. They're even sending one of their most valuable and respected men out in search of more Sources." He shook his head at the implications.

Athena looked back down at the manifest. "I see here that Edgeworth and Fraser are not alone here in Greece. There is another name listed with theirs. L. Harcourt."

"Harcourt," Bennett repeated in surprise, straightening. Harcourt was most definitely dead. Bennett knew that for an indisputable fact.

Athena met his gaze over the top of the manifest. "His brother, perhaps?"

"Better watch my back."

"I think we can find out more." Athena returned to her desk and shoved some books and papers aside to clear some room. From a drawer, she pulled a purple silk scarf, then laid it across the top of the desk. She opened the manifest to the page with the Heirs' names and set it onto the scarf. Then she closed her eyes.

"Need me to do anything?" Bennett asked.

"Just keep quiet."

"Impossible."

She opened one eye to let him know that his humor was not appreciated. Closing her eye, she held her hands above the manifest. "Virgin Mother," she chanted, hushed, "gray-eyed bringer of wisdom and war. Grant your daughter eyes to see and lips to speak. Give life to words, so humbly asks your namesake child."

At first, nothing happened. Then the writing upon the pages of the manifest began to shimmer and sway upon the page. The words twisted like tiny vines. Bennett stepped closer to watch. As a Blade, he had seen much magic, yet it never failed to make his breath hitch with the wonder of it.

He stepped back as the words shivered, then danced up from the page, snaking into the air to hover in the middle of the room. In the lamplight, the writing cast spidery shadows, pulsing, waiting.

Opening her eyes, her hands still outstretched, Athena said in a high, clear voice, "Words, giver of knowledge, we seek your guidance. These men mean to steal magic, and we stand to defy them. What do they seek? Where shall they proceed?"

The writing trembled, then broke apart like a host of moths, fluttering. Bennett kept his arms at his sides as letters flitted across his face and through the room. He could hear them softly beating against each other and the fabric of the curtains. Then they found order, rearranging themselves into sentences in Greek that floated in midair.

The Source is hidden in riddles. To the birthplace of the Sun and Moon, the Heirs advance. Words they possess yet cannot read. One amongst their number shall play Oracle. The words will have meaning.

No sooner had Bennett read this than the words shivered and fell in a cascade back into the manifest. Bennett blinked, and the writing was as it had appeared minutes earlier in some clerk's careful hand.

"My boundless thanks, Chaste Mother," Athena chanted before lowering her hands. The magic-working had drained her, and she sat down heavily in a chair.

Bennett poured her a glass of wine. Handing it to her, he said, "I've a birthday coming up. Will you provide the entertainment at the party?"

"You need a muzzle," Athena replied after taking a sip. She repeated the words, mulling them over. "So, the Heirs are going to Delos."

"An island in the Cyclades."

"Just so." Athena waved a refined hand toward the table. A scroll of paper rose up from it, unrolling itself and revealing it was an ancient map of the Cyclades Islands, which lay past Cape Sounion to the east.

Bennett leaned forward to examine the map as it floated before him. It was true that Blades could not use magic, but only if it was not theirs by right or gift. The Galanos women were not only one of Athens's finest families, they were also witches by birth. Family legend held that the first Athena Galanos, centuries earlier, wielded tremendous power, enough to safeguard the family against the occupying Turks. The centuries, however, had worn gently away at this power, as the city of Athens became more modern and turned from the old ways, leaving the Galanos witches capable of small parlor spells but not much else. The current Athena spent much of her time researching how she and her future descendants might reclaim that which time had taken from them. One had only to look at Athena's library to see her dedication to this cause. Bennett doubted a larger collection of magical texts existed anywhere.

Athena now used her birthright magic to illuminate a small dot of an island on the map.

"This is Delos, the center of the Cyclades," she explained.

"The islands are called that because they spiral out from Delos. It is a tiny place, three miles long and hardly a mile wide, but few other sites hold such mystical power or significance. Even Delphi. The god Apollo and his twin sister Artemis were born on Delos."

"Birthplace of the Sun and Moon. Whatever is there could be very powerful, especially when combined with the Primal Source." Bennett recalled the myths of Artemis and Apollo from his early education, tales told in his boyhood of Greek gods and heroes. At the time, he had believed them to be merely stories, but years with the Blades taught him that a good deal more truth lived in old myths than the ordinary world would have one believe. "Who lives there now?"

"No one. For a time, none could be born nor die on the island. It has been deserted for almost two millennia. Once, it was a thriving center of trade, a holy place for pilgrimage. But no treasure is left, all carried off by pirates. Turks come now to take ancient marble for headstones. There is nothing of what some might call value. Only ruins, most of them buried beneath the rocky soil." With another wave of her hand, the scroll rolled up and replaced itself on the table.

Bennett rubbed his chin thoughtfully, considering this. "So the Heirs have found something on Delos, something they need translated. An Oracle."

"It is the 'who' that we do not know."

"Harcourt's brother, perhaps," Bennett mused.

"We shall see. I've informants on the street to learn where the Heirs are staying whilst in Athens. I am hoping that will help us gather more intelligence."

"You couldn't be more intelligent, my dear Pallas."

Athena dismissed Bennett's easy compliment with a wave of her hand. Yes, they knew each other quite well, enough to render his blandishments nothing more than pretty coins thrown from an abundant pocket. "Even though there is no Blade more capable than you for deciphering and decoding"—she accepted his slight bow of gratitude with a regal nod—"it is very likely that you and I will be unable to read these ruins, whatever they are. You know nearly every code that has been created, but—"

"But I've only the typical Englishman's knowledge of language. Latin, Greek, and French." He smiled. "Such a wastrel."

"None worse," Athena agreed. "Perhaps we can follow the Heirs at a safe distance as they pursue the Source, let them do the work for us."

Bennett paced. His legs were long, and the study was not a large room, so he watched his reflection as he caromed from bookshelf to window and back again.

"I hate the idea of trailing after them like guppies in the wake of a whale," he said. "We should take charge of the situation. God knows what they're after, but whatever it is, once they get their hands on it, hell's going to break loose."

"But what can we do?" Athena asked.

"Find the ruins before they do, translate them ourselves. There isn't much time."

"Even if we got to the ruins before they did, we haven't our own linguistic expert to translate them."

"I'll find a way."

She rolled her eyes. "Spoken like a man. Plow on ahead and damn the details. I need specifics, Bennett."

It was his turn to be exasperated. "You're the most circumspect witch I've ever met."

"All the impulsive ones are dead."

A quiet tap on the study door broke the discussion. At Athena's word, the door opened. Standing there was her mother. A most striking woman, as her daughter was. Generations of strong-featured, genteel women who could slay a man with a look.

"Ah, Athena the Greater," Bennett said, coming forward and taking her cool hands. He kissed her proffered cheek, her skin olive marble. "Your daughter's trying to convince me I'm too impetuous."

"Athena the Lesser can be overly cautious," her mother sighed. "It seems she did not inherit the hot blood of her foremothers."

"Simply because I do not advocate recklessly stumbling around Delos without a plan does not mean I am overly cautious, Mother," Athena ground out.

"And you rein in your powers," Athena the Greater continued. "It is as if you fear them."

"I do not *fear* them," her daughter said through gritted teeth. "But I will not cede control to anything or," she added pointedly, *"anyone."*

Her mother started to speak, but Bennett decided it would be prudent to avoid a familial contretemps, which could last well into the small hours of the following morning. He had a feeling their squabble would be heard throughout the house, disrupting his sleep. Lord knew Bennett and his mother could argue until neither had a voice. Their arguments always centered around her favorite topic, which was also his least favorite: when he planned on marrying. There was something about mothers that brought out the petulant child in everyone, no matter one's age or station. How depressing.

"Much as I revel in your exquisite beauty, Athena the Greater," he interrupted, "was there something you wanted?"

Mother and daughter broke their loving glare. "Indeed, yes. One of the informants is here." She turned to the door and motioned someone in. A barefoot boy, somewhere around ten years old, in clean but threadbare clothing. The child seemed a little awed to be in the presence of not one, but two Galanos women, torn between terror and adoration. Bennett well understood the feeling.

"What is it, Yannis?" Athena the Lesser asked.

It took a moment for the boy to find his voice. "The Hotel Andromeda," he gulped. "That is where the Englishmen are staying. And they leave Athens tomorrow."

The witches looked pleased, a sentiment Bennett shared. "Very good, Yannis," Athena the Greater said. She took a two-drachma coin from a small beaded purse at her waist and placed it in the boy's hand. His eyes widened at the sight, but he recovered himself enough to pocket the coin quickly. At a nod from Athena the Greater, the boy dashed from the room, his bare feet slapping the tiled floor.

Bennett began to follow before Athena the Lesser's voice stopped him. "Going to the hotel?"

He turned to face her. "As you said, I'll grab us more information."

"And then?"

"And then, we'll know what we're up against." He sent Athena and her mother a wink. "Don't wait up."

"I'm going out to the garden before dinner," London said to her father as they sat in the hotel parlor. People were gathering in their evening dress for aperitifs, murmuring pleasantries in English. London had dressed for dinner as well, in a low-shouldered Worth gown of violet gauze over cream satin, her hair pinned up and adorned with silk flowers. She had, in fact, worn that same toilette when having dinner at her parents' house a week before she and her father left for Greece. She had known everyone at the table. Wearing that same gown now, everything in the hotel so proper and ordinary, London half-believed she was back in England rather than thousands of miles from home. "The night is quite lovely and warm. It would be a shame to waste our final evening in Athens inside."

Her father glanced up from a handful of correspondence.

His dark hair and mustache had turned silver over the course of her lifetime, but his eyes were as clear and cutting as ever as he moved his attention from his letters to her. She often thought that Joseph Edgeworth had been born clutching sheaves of letters and reports, for she almost never saw him without bundles of paper in his hands. When she was small, she had asked her father what all those letters meant, why men were constantly writing to him and petitioning him and showing up at his study at all hours with yet more sheaves of paper. He had said he was a very important man of government business and society, which meant others came to him often for direction. When she asked what he did for the government, he patted her on the head and told her to play with her dolls in the nursery, for such things were not the polite affairs of young ladies.

For years, that was all she knew of her father and brother's work—that they, and the men of their circle, did valuable work on behalf of their nation's government. Father refused to tell her more, and Jonas was a dutiful son, keeping silent on that point, at least. Mother was no help, either, insisting that she was just as uninformed as London in the matter, but it was for the best, as her only concern was the home, not what went on past the gate of their house or in the halls of power. And when London asked the wives and daughters of her father's associates, they all said the same thing. Was it not indelicate, they asked, for a woman to ask such questions, to embroil herself in the activities of men?

As a new bride, she waited, seeking the right moment to ask her husband. She had hoped the shared intimacies of the bedroom might form a bond of closeness between her and Lawrence. But what happened in their bed led only to awkwardness, followed by a cold cordiality. When she finally gathered her courage to ask Lawrence about his work with her father, he refused to talk of it. It became, in time, another source of yet more arguments between them.

Whatever it was, it could be perilous, as witnessed recently when her brother had returned from several months abroad. His traveling companion, Henry Lamb, had disappeared. And as for Jonas . . . perhaps it would have been kinder if he hadn't survived. He had been a hale and handsome man. Shortly before leaving, he'd become engaged to Cecily Cole. Then he came home. The burns were terrible, the scars they left behind across half his face almost as bad. Cecily broke the engagement, and Jonas now never left the house, becoming bitter and even more volatile than before. Not a day went by without him smashing some innocent piece of furniture or porcelain to bits. He terrified the servants.

Her dead husband Lawrence had also paid a high price for his governmental work abroad. Paid with his life. But the circumstances of his death were obscure, and her father would not provide specifics. To protect her delicate female constitution from the ugliness of the world.

So, London stopped asking. She would have gone on in complete ignorance, had it not been circumstance that brought her to greater understanding. Father at last revealed more about his work for their government, though grudgingly, and now she was here, in Athens, to finally assist and make herself useful. She hoped she was so useful that she could be a part of his work when they returned home. It sounded far better than endless rounds of paying calls, social breakfasts, regattas and balls, and charity work that did no help at all. And she could apply her knowledge of languages practically, rather than only in theory.

Now she waited for her father's permission to go outside and escape the stifling atmosphere of the hotel parlor.

"Very well," said Father, after a pause, "but take Sally with you."

"It's the hotel garden," London pointed out. "Not a public street. I'll be perfectly safe. You can even see me from the window."

Her father looked over at Fraser, sitting close by in a cane-backed chair. The two men exchanged obvious speaking glances, communicating silently about the frivolity and foolishness of women. London clutched her fan tightly to keep hold of her patience.

"Very well," Father said at last. He actually shook his finger at her. "But, mind, stay within sight of the window."

London dipped into a small curtsey before gliding from the parlor. Honestly, her father and his friends treated women like overgrown infants. It was exceptionally infuriating. But would it be different with other men? She had no basis of comparison, outside of what she read.

Stepping outside from the hotel and walking down into the terraced garden, her exasperation dissipated like mist. Anger and frustration could not stand amidst such loveliness. Abundant oleander glowed in the darkness as it tumbled over walls, and the air carried the richness of its perfume. Little purple cyclamens lined the gravel pathways where torches had been set, should any guest decide to wander out to enjoy the nighttime pastoral. But she was alone, and had the garden entirely to herself. London took advantage of the paths, her dainty satin slippers crunching on the gravel, and wandered slowly down a walkway, always careful to keep herself in sight of the large parlor window spilling its light into the evening. London could even see her father and Fraser in animated discussion, both gesturing toward the papers in Father's hand. Perhaps they were discussing what was to happen once they reached Delos. Neither spoke to her of detailed plans. She had but one function. Beyond that, she needed no other information, so she watched them through the glass, eternally on the outside.

She was mindful of them, but they not of her. They both stood and strode from the parlor, and disappeared somewhere else in the hotel. She blinked. Well. Clearly, Father was not as concerned about her welfare as he professed, or the threat of an evening stroll in a garden was less dire than he would have her believe.

Feeling liberated, London pressed farther into the garden, taking one of the paths off into a pretty little alcove, fragrant with rosemary. It was darker here, and she took a moment to look up at the sky, wanting to see constellations. Now that she was truly in Greece, she might feel more connected to the ancient myths that gave the stars their names. But the city was too bright. Only a crescent moon shone, and a glimmer here and there of a star. It had been better out at sea.

She would be at sea soon enough. And then taken to a completely uninhabited island; according to her father, its only occupants a small team of French archaeologists at a distance from the camp where she and the rest of their party would be based. Though the island lacked for all facilities and comforts, London eagerly anticipated her work on Delos. A little dust and some lizards did not bother her, not when the true experiences of life awaited.

London bent to sniff at the tiny pink blossoms on the rosemary bushes, but a strange awareness prickled along her neck. She straightened and looked around. Everything was silent, save for the chatter of the hotel guests inside, the slight rustle of the tall cypresses in the breeze. The distant nighttime sounds of Athens, too: carts in the street, voices in Greek bidding each other a pleasant evening. Despite this, she could not shake the notion that she was not alone.

"Hello?" she called out. "Father?" Then, "Sally?"

"Never would've forgiven my mother if she'd named me Sally."

London stifled a gasp as a familiar, deep voice rumbled from the darkness. Then the lean, agile form of Ben Drayton half-emerged from the shadows.

"Mr. Drayton," she breathed, pressing a hand to her pounding heart, "you quite startled me."

"My apologies," he said, still keeping largely to the shelter of night. In the dimness, she was just able to make out certain details about him. He wore the clothes he'd had on in the marketplace, definitely not dressed for dinner. Not with those tall boots that had seen much wear, the serviceable fabric of his coat. But London hardly attended to his clothing. She had told herself, in the intervening hours since seeing Mr. Drayton, that she must have embellished her memory. No man was truly that beautifully formed in face and body. A romantic fancy brought about by an exotic setting and too much time reading books at home.

Ah, but no. Her recollection had not played her false. Here, in this perfumed evening garden, he was just as athletic, just as seductively handsome, perhaps even more so. Nighttime felt appropriate, a milieu that suited him, with its promises of dalliance and danger.

She found her voice. "I did not hear you."

He came closer, skirting the edges of light. "Rotten habit of mine, sneaking around. Used it to great effect taking strawberry tarts from the buttery when I was supposed to be in bed."

"So I am the strawberry tart, in this analogy."

He chuckled, warming her. "I'd never call you a tart, my lady."

London wanted to be a little daring, almost as daring as he was. "But if I was a berry, I wonder what kind I'd be," she said with a teasing smile.

"Something sweet and wild," he said, voice low and husky.

London had only just mastered her breath, and his words

made it catch again. Her gaze strayed toward his mouth, the mouth that said such wicked things. She made herself turn away, play with her ebony-handled fan. What was wrong with her? All she wanted to do was cross the small distance that separated her from this veritable stranger and pull his mouth down to hers, learning what *he* tasted like. She never even did such a thing when *married*. She would not now, of course, but the impulse was strong, stronger than she would have suspected in herself.

She had to turn her mind in a less . . . wanton direction. "Are you a guest of the hotel, Mr. Drayton?" she asked.

"No. Visiting someone at the hotel."

She turned back and started. He stood closer so that only a few feet separated them. She did not know any man could move so silently. Perhaps he *was* part feline, after all. Would his body have the warmth of a large cat, as well? It seemed likely. "A friend?"

"Not a friend."

"An acquaintance, then? Who? Perhaps I know them. We may have a friend in common."

"Doubt it. I sincerely hope you don't know them."

"What disreputable company you must keep, sir."

"Those I consider my friends are disreputable in the best ways." He surveyed her with a long, slow perusal that lingered boldly on the exposed flesh of her arms, her shoulders. It was a look like a caress, and her skin responded in kind. No gentleman looked at a woman in such a fashion. But this Mr. Drayton, she was beginning to understand, only spoke and dressed like a gentleman. Underneath the polish he was all rogue. "Sweet and wild, indeed," he murmured. He eyed her formal dinner gown. "A little too much splendor, though."

"Not so splendid that I can't cause a bit of trouble in Monastiraki," she answered with an impish smile. "See what a scoundrel you have turned me into. I still have that piece of pottery." She poked into the small evening reticule that dangled from her wrist, until she produced the shard and held it out to him. "My ill-gotten gains." When he bent closer to peer at the fragment, she said, "Take it. I've had enough of Darius the Third."

He plucked it from her hand, his fingers brushing hers as their eyes held. She felt a hunger low in her belly stir to life.

He held the shard up to read it better in the soft light. "Darius the Third," he repeated. "Really?"

She wondered whether he would dismiss her linguistic skills or condemn them. "I hope *you* don't question me, too," London said with a lightness she did not quite feel. "That's what got me into trouble at the marketplace. I dated it based on the inscription. But," she added quickly, "if someone claims that an antiquity comes from the era of Darius the Great, they oughtn't sell something from Darius the Third's reign."

He lowered the piece of pottery and looked at her, speculative. "You know the difference."

London debated whether or not to prevaricate. She could pretend she knew less than she did, or make light of what was her greatest passion and accomplishment. But the encounter with Drayton in the market square had convinced her that she could free herself, that she had the strength to own herself with pride. And if he did laugh at her or find her unnatural, then she could weather that, too.

"I do," she answered, direct and clear. "I've studied languages my whole life. The more ancient, the better, but I know dozens of modern ones, as well."

"The vendor in Monastiraki insulted you in Greek."

"I understood every word he said, and what you said to him. *Do not doubt me, handsome rogue*," she added in accentless modern Greek. Then, in an ancient dialect he would never know, she said, *"I want to kiss you and see your skin in the moonlight."*

He stared at her, narrowing his eyes. Not contemptuous or patronizing, but something else, as if she were the missing piece to a puzzle he assembled in his mind.

She felt a new kind of unease under that keen scrutiny. "What is it, Mr. Drayton?"

He narrowed his eyes. "Tell me why you're in Greece."

"I shall not, sir," she answered at once. Father had been explicit in his instructions to her. She could not speak to anyone of their purpose. No matter what attraction drew her to Ben Drayton, he wasn't to be let in to her confidence, not about this.

The teasing rogue was gone, and a new hardness entered his voice, his posture. "No husband with you here. A relative, then. Father. Brother."

London stiffened, growing more alarmed. "This conversation is over, Mr. Drayton." She tried to brush past him, but his large hand clamped onto her arm, holding her fast. London's temper and fear spiked. "Release me, immediately."

"What do you know about the Heirs?" he demanded.

"The airs?"

"Heirs," he repeated, positively menacing.

"Whatever you are talking about, it is lost on me. If you do not release me at once, I shall scream." She wished she could do more than scream, but London knew nothing about how to physically protect herself. Now that she faced real danger, she fervently wished she knew how to throw a punch. She very much doubted her feeble efforts would have any effect on the exceptionally strong Drayton.

"London?"

"Mrs. Harcourt?"

The voices of her father and Fraser cut through the heavy garden air, coming toward her. Before London could utter a single word, Ben Drayton was gone, vanishing into darkness noiselessly. She gulped and shivered, feeling the hot imprint of his hand on her arm.

"Here," she called, walking out of the darkness and toward Father with hurried steps. "Did you see him?"

"Who?"

"He said his name was Ben Drayton. . . ." She looked from her father to Fraser.

"A Blade?" Fraser murmured to her father, but Father shook his head slightly.

"Investigate, Fraser," her father barked. Fraser trotted off into the darkness. London could have sworn she saw him take a revolver from his jacket.

Now truly frightened, she turned to her father, hoping to find a measure of comfort in his familiar face. All she saw there was a cold glitter in his eyes, the same look he had given her when he'd discovered her in his study a month ago, rearranging a series of rubbings taken from stone. Her father's jaw clenched. Even though he was a man nearing sixty, regular exercise kept him as hale as a man half his age. Riding, fencing, hunting. Gentlemanly sport. But there was nothing genteel about his sudden and intimidating anger.

"What is it, Father? Do you know Drayton?"

"Not that name. But who knows, maybe he's new," he muttered to himself. Then he directed his attention back to his daughter. "Did he say anything to you?"

"He demanded to know why I was in Greece, who I was traveling with. And he said something about heirs, if I knew about them. What does that mean?"

"Damn and hell," Father growled, shocking London. She'd only heard her father swear in front of her once before. "I knew those bastards would come tailing us."

She gripped the sleeve of his dark evening jacket. "Please, Father, who are you talking about? What is going on?"

"Gone," Fraser said, returning. "Not a sign of him anywhere. Must have jumped the wall."

Her father snarled, "He spoke to her, the bloody rogue. Asked about *us*."

Now Fraser looked at her with icy eyes. "And what did you tell him?"

"Nothing. Nothing." Fear was burning away in the wake of growing anger. No one was giving her any real answers, even though it was clear something was afoot, something that her father and his associate knew about. It had to be about his governmental work. "Please, Father, I'm not a child. You must tell me what is happening. Tell me who that man was."

After sending Fraser a warning glare, her father captured her hand with his and began to lead her toward the hotel. "Some fortune-hunter," he said quickly. "Seeking an heiress to ransom. Do not trouble yourself over it." He patted her hand. "Fraser and I will protect you."

"You must think me a tremendous idiot," London said, halting in her steps. "I want the truth."

Father started, clearly unused to having anyone, especially his dutiful daughter, make demands of him. But she was older now, not as willing to be led where her father wanted her to go. Seeing that she would not be dissuaded, he said, "The work that I do, that Fraser does—it generates its share of enemies."

"What kind of enemies?"

"Enemies against England."

"But Drayton is English."

Her father smiled, but it wasn't at all comforting. "London, I'll not have you upset or overwrought. Go inside now. And believe me when I say that the less you know, the better it is for everyone."

"But—"

"*Now*, London," he said. He spoke as if he were sending her to the nursery to play, out of the way of the adults.

She looked to Thomas Fraser, but he gave her the same bland smile her father handed out like sweetmeats to placate her. Trapped between two men. London had thought, after Lawrence died, that she would have a kind of freedom she'd never experienced before, as a woman of means without a man to whom she must answer. But now, now that dream was slipping away, being lost in the murk of someone else's agenda. What had brought her to this point?

A month earlier, she had been visiting her parents, one of her typical midweek calls. She often saw her mother for luncheon, especially after Lawrence's death, and, though Jonas kept to his rooms, occasionally their father joined them for a meal. He was to eat with them on that day, a rather dreary Thursday in April. London and her mother sat at the table in the dining room, as they did when Father planned to join them. They waited and waited, but Father's seat remained empty. Mother refused to eat until he arrived, but she was too circumspect to send a servant after him. She had even looked longingly at the creamed lobster on toast, yet would not take the smallest bite.

Finally, famished, tired of her mother's unnecessary self-sacrifice, London rose from the table to find her father, herself. She went straight to his study, as he was usually there. Pausing outside the closed door, she had tapped lightly. When there wasn't an answer, she knocked, a little more loudly. Still nothing. London had tried the door, expecting to find it locked as it always was, but this time it wasn't. Slowly, London opened the door and peered inside. It seemed empty. London felt herself drawn into the room. Despite the fact that she was a grown woman, she held her breath as she crossed the Turkish carpet, seeing the shelves of bound volumes, the large maps upon the walls.

Britain. India. Africa. A fire burned in the grate. The smell of tobacco and significance. The Forbidden Kingdom.

The study was the realm of men. At hours early and late, a steady parade of sober-suited men went in and out its door. Jonas had permission to enter. London did not. Even the parlor maids were barred from entrance. Only Slyfield, the butler, had leave to clean the room at Father's explicit order. London never knew what would happen to her if she ever went into her father's study, only that, if she did, something terrible would happen to her. She should not be there. Yet she could not make herself leave.

The massive desk had drawn her like a lodestone. This was the place where her father conducted his business, where he made momentous decisions and shaped lives. London touched her fingers to the surface of the desk, trying to absorb some of its power. She could use more of that in her own life. As she had done this, her gaze fell to some pieces of foolscap arranged in a row. Someone had done rubbings in charcoal on the paper, taken from some stone source. Ancient writings. She frowned. Laid out as they were, they made no sense. London could not stop herself. She rearranged the papers.

"What the hell do you think you're doing?"

London had whirled around at the sound of her father's outraged voice. He stormed into the study, and, for a moment, she actually feared he might use physical violence on her. He had never spoken to her or looked at her this way before, preferring, instead to treat her as if she were made of spun sugar. She didn't care for either form of interaction.

"I'm sorry, Father," London had blurted. She tried to back up, but the desk blocked her. "I was only trying to help."

"Did you touch anything? Read anything?"

"Just these." She gestured to the row of papers. "They were out of order."

"Out of order?" her father had repeated, his eyes straying to the rubbings. Confusion flickered across his face. "You can read this?"

Not knowing whether she was damning herself further by revealing her linguistic knowledge, London decided it was better to openly admit her expertise than revert to a cowering, ignorant girl. "Yes, Father. It is a form of ancient Greek that was only known in the Cyclades Islands. Only a few scholars are even aware of its existence. And me," she had added, trying to keep the pride from her words.

He had scowled, but his temper seemed to be cooling at this revelation. "You?"

"Yes, me."

"Are those other scholars English?"

"One is French, another is German, and the other is Russian. I am the only person in England who knows this form of Greek."

After a moment, he said, almost grudging, "So, what does it say?"

She fought against the fillip of happiness his acceptance brought her. "That's what's odd about it," she had said, turning back to the papers. "Even properly ordered, the words make no sense. There is more, I assume?"

"Yes, much more."

"I would have to see it all, put it in context. Then, I believe, it would become clear."

Her father had paced away from her, then, and finally took a cigar from a rosewood humidor on his desk. Mother didn't like him to smoke in the house, but this was his study and he could do as he pleased in here. After trimming the cigar and lighting it, he had taken a few meditative puffs whilst contemplating the maps. London stood in an agony of worry. What would he do? Disown her? Forbid her from coming back to his house?

"Do you know what I do for the British government?" he had asked, at last.

She had shaken her head numbly.

Carefully, as if he were explaining a complicated scientific principle to a child, he said, "I, and Jonas, and Lawrence and all our associates, are archaeologists. We find ancient objects around the world and bring them back to England, for the glory of England."

That was a surprise. London never would have considered her father nor his colleagues to be men of science or academic learning. But she did not voice this, letting her father continue.

"The rubbings you see here"—he waved toward his desk—"were part of a much larger set taken from a ruin in Greece. Not a man on my team could decipher them. Not a single university professor in the whole of the country could, either. But you"—and here he turned back to her—"a woman, my daughter, were able to do what no one else had been capable of."

"I wasn't able to understand it, though," London felt compelled to add. "Not fully. I would have to see the complete writings to make sense of them."

"Yes," Father had agreed. "It is imperative, for the good of England, that we decipher these writings. Under normal circumstances, I would seek out a British scholar with the proper expertise, but there isn't one. There's only you." He ground out his cigar with a deliberate motion, and watched it smolder for a moment before looking up at her.

"And that's why," he continued, "for the first time in the history of my organization, I must involve a woman in our work, though it pains me greatly to do so." He took from his waistcoat pocket a heavy gold pocketwatch inscribed with symbols London did not recognize. "Today is the twelfth of April. I expect you to have your bags packed and ready for travel by the sixteenth."

London had blinked. "I'm sorry—what do you mean?"

"It means, my daughter, that you are coming with me to Greece."

And so it had begun. Now she was in Greece, being led across a nighttime garden by her father. Enemies, he'd said. Enemies of England. Something else much bigger than simple archeology was happening, and London was in the middle of it, whether she wanted to be or not.

Bennett watched from the shadows of a nearby parapet as London Edgeworth Harcourt was escorted from the hotel garden by none other than the vicious, ruthless, and cold-hearted Joseph Edgeworth, and his blond, hulking toady, Thomas "Never Met a Native I Wouldn't Shoot" Fraser.

Hellfire. And damn. Edgeworth's daughter. Jonas Edgeworth's sister. Harcourt's widow. The Heirs' expert on ancient languages. The enticing woman from the marketplace. All the same. All the bloody same person.

If he'd been at liberty, Bennett would have laughed at the irony of it. But he needed to remain hidden, so he kept his rueful chuckle to himself. Even though he knew magic was real, he wasn't always sure that there was such things as Fate or Destiny. Yet this was proof that the universe had a sense of humor. A very black sense of humor.

Chapter 3

Agendas

"And you are sure?" Athena asked. "Quite, quite sure?"

"Yes. Again, yes. She's Edgeworth's daughter." Bennett walked beside her as they made their way down to the quay at Piraeus, the Athenian harbor town, the following morning. Unlike Athens, Piraeus was laid out with paved, orderly streets that did not drive innocent pedestrians mad with confusion. But that did not make the busy port any less congested. Bennett carefully guided Athena past loaded drays and groups of merchant seamen coming to and from the waterfront.

"And Harcourt's widow. Does she know who you are?"

"Not yet."

"*Theos ka panagea.*" Athena sidestepped around a wagon loaded with currants just shipped in from Zante. "But it cannot be possible. The Heirs are very set against having women in their ranks."

"This one is. In a fashion."

"What do you mean?"

Bennett dodged a crowd of German tourists disgorged from a steamer ship and wagons bearing piles of luggage. "Edgeworth's daughter knows nothing of the Heirs."

"If she is here to translate the ruins, surely she knows what cause she serves."

Bennett shook his head as the scent of seawater washed over him. They had finally reached the harbor itself, where rows of ships of every variety bobbed in the water while gulls shrieked overhead. Fishing boats swayed next to small yachts, pleasure boats for the Athenian elite. Steam-powered freighters and tall-masted clippers were anchored out in the bay, with rowboats going back and forth between the large ships and the quay. Even with such hectic traffic, the water gleamed azure and gold in the morning sun. Bennett breathed deeply and could not stop a grin from forming. He had served the Blades for many years, yet he never tired of the beginning of a mission, the possibility of harbors and ships.

Yet he sobered when he answered Athena. "It was obvious that she'd no idea what I spoke of when I asked about the Heirs."

"You know women, that I'll allow," Athena said. "However, even you can be played false by a pretty face and lovely bosom, Day."

"No doubt I've been lied to," he agreed cheerfully. "'You're only the second man I've ever been with, Bennett,' 'My husband's not at all jealous, Bennett,' 'I like it gentle, Bennett'—the usual games and tricks. Sometimes, I even believe them. But London Edgeworth is as beautiful as she is innocent."

"No woman is truly innocent," Athena said. "Especially not the beautiful ones."

"That's why I love them."

He and Athena skirted along the edge of the harbor, hearing the rough shouts of the fishermen as they called to one another, the ship captains bearing cargoes of figs and olive oil cursing at their crews lazing on deck. It did not matter if Bennett accompanied Athena or not, she was still the object of much male attention, yet she breezed past as serene and aloof as a falcon, not even acknowledging the sailors with so much as a blink.

"I wish we did not have to trust an outsider for this mission," she said to Bennett. "It leaves us vulnerable."

"I sure as hell can't sail a boat," he pointed out. "Neither can you. We've got to get to Delos. Likely beyond, too. Besides," he added, "your contact assured us that this man is trustworthy."

"Or, at the least, is willing to be paid for silence."

"We've abundant coin, if it comes to that. This is it," he said, stopping by a boat tied to the pier. It was a cargo caique, a typical boat of the region, roughly seventy feet long, with a rounded fore and aft and two triangular lateen sails, now furled. Portholes attested to below-deck cabins, though they would not be very large. A loving hand had painted the hull bright emerald, the tiller a vivid yellow, and kept the whole of the boat a sparkling gem, especially compared to some of the shabbier maritime specimens in the harbor.

"You!" Athena called out to one of two seamen coiling rope on deck. "Are you Nikos Kallas?"

"No, captain's below," the man grunted back.

"Then get him," she ordered imperiously. When the man just stared at her, she added coldly, "Now."

Muttering, the sailor slouched off to the quarterdeck house to find his captain.

"Consider being a bit more . . . diplomatic," Bennett suggested wryly.

"Why?" shrugged Athena. "These are rough men. They do not care for social niceties."

After a moment, a man emerged from the quarterdeck house with the first sailor trailing behind him. The captain. He wore the loose blue trousers of a mariner, and a full white shirt with a dark sash wound about his waist. A

small, powerfully built man, he squinted at Bennett and
Athena from behind the smoke of his pipe. "I'm Kallas,"
he called in a gravelly voice. "Who wants me?" He looked
at Bennett with sharp, assessing eyes. Sensing a possible
threat, he changed his stance slightly, a shifting of position
onto the balls of his feet to ready for a fight. This one,
Bennett understood, missed nothing.

"Petros Spirtos sent us," Athena answered.

The sea captain turned his gaze from Bennett to Athena.
For a moment, the two simply stared at each other, each
seemingly unmoved, but Bennett heard Athena's soft inhalation and saw Kallas's hands curl as though trying
to grasp something. *Oho*, Bennett thought. *What have
we here?*

"No shouting across the marina," Bennett said. "We're
coming aboard."

"As you like." Kallas shrugged.

In a moment, Bennett was hopping over the railing of
the boat, then turned to help Athena gracefully descend
onto the top deck. The two crewmen gaped at Athena in
her elegant bronze silk dress and matching parasol, until
Kallas shouted something at them in a dialect Bennett
could not understand. Even though the crewmen were several inches taller than their captain, they hastened to obey
and scuttled off.

"Bennett Day," he introduced himself, "and Athena
Galanos."

"Spirtos told me about you," Kallas said, shaking Bennett's hand, "about what you need."

"So you know everything," Bennett said. When the captain nodded, Bennett said, "Speed and discretion. That's
what we need."

Kallas stroked his full, dark mustache. "If it keeps more
foreigners out of Greece, then my ship and my crew are
yours. No offense to you, Englishman."

"All insults are deserved and well earned. My friend and I have gear we'll need to store in your hold. Some guns, as well."

"Always good to be prepared," Kallas said.

"Do you mind danger?"

The captain grinned, his teeth white and straight in his sun-darkened face. "The Kallas men have pursued many kinds of living on the sea."

"Piracy, you mean," Athena said.

Kallas narrowed his eyes as he moved closer to Athena. Bennett watched her struggle not to take a step back, despite the fact that they were the same height. She straightened her spine as the captain slowly looked her up and down.

"What would a high-born lady like you know of working for your bread?" he growled.

"I find that bread tastes much better if you do not steal it," she answered. "The Galanos women find respectable ways to feed their daughters."

"Fortunate for you, then, that Kallas men are not so respectable. Or I wouldn't agree to hire out myself and my ship. Especially not to aristos."

"A wonderful family picnic," Bennett interjected, stepping between them. "Kallas men, Galanos women. Some grassy hilltop. Ouzo. Walnuts and grapes. We'll plan the menu later. But tell me, how suspect are your morals?"

Kallas turned his attention from a seething Athena. "What did you have in mind?"

"Kidnapping a lady."

"Is she pretty?"

"Very."

Kallas smiled, shaking Bennett's hand again. "Then we'll get along, you and I."

* * *

She hadn't much experience with ships except the one that had brought her to Greece. Departing from Southampton, they'd taken a top-of-the-line triple-masted steamer around the Iberian peninsula, skirting the coast all the way to Gibraltar, to Monte Carlo, then past Sicily, up around Italy to Brindisi, and finally Corfu to Athens. That ship had been surprisingly lavish, with an elegant dining room, two salons, and a card room, plus a host of men and women seated on folding chairs on deck whilst wrapped in flannel.

She knew that their sailing accommodations from Piraeus to Delos would be less opulent. It did not matter to her if the ship hadn't a conservatory. But this . . . this was entirely different from what she had anticipated.

"Do we really need so many guns, Father?" she asked as she was helped aboard by one of the ship's crew. Turning to watch her luggage being hauled up the side of the ship, she found herself staring at the cannons that poked from gun ports like lethal iron fingers. And, on the fore deck, squatted a gun turret and two more cannons, one fore and another aft.

Her father already stood on deck, and surveyed their ship with an approving nod. It was iron hulled with two telescoping funnels and two schooner masts, further powered by a steam-driven wheel at its center. A contradiction between this ship and the others merrily floating in the harbor. The Greek crew, too, looked hardened and intimidating, not returning London's smiles and nods of greeting.

"I know it isn't very luxurious," her father said. "But you must try and bear up, if it isn't too taxing."

"It's not taxing in the least," she said. "But it's the weapons that alarm me."

Thomas Fraser, already turning pink in the late afternoon sun, stood next to her. "We must be prepared," he said. "I'm sure you are familiar with the terrible events five years ago, when brigands captured a party of British tourists near Marathon and demanded a ransom. Many of their captives died during the rescue attempt."

"An awful tragedy," London said quietly.

"And your father has already spoken of enemies, Mrs. Harcourt, of which you may have already met. So the guns are, indeed, necessary."

"I hope we don't have to use them."

Fraser merely shrugged. Then he turned away, and he and her father spoke with the ship's captain. Sally yelped instructions to the men hauling the luggage over the side of the ship. Left to herself, London went to the railing and watched the harbor with its traffic of ships, but her thoughts strayed back to Ben Drayton. Perhaps he truly was one of her father's enemies. She wanted to dismiss the idea outright. They'd shared something, a link or bond that she barely understood but felt deeply. When she was with him, she felt freer, more her true self that had been buried for most of her life. And, it was true, her body wanted him, wanted him fiercely.

Yet she could not dismiss how he had transformed so utterly and quickly in the garden last night from a seductive, charming rake into a flint-eyed man capable of anything. And she recalled his mastery of moving within the shadows as if he were part phantom.

Had it been wrong to find him so attractive, when he could mean her and her father harm? London prayed that she would never have to see Drayton again and test her willpower. Still, she couldn't stop her mind from tormenting her with thoughts of what it might be like to kiss him, to have his hands upon her uncovered skin.

A new voice speaking English behind her caused London to turn around. Standing with her father and Fraser was a tall, skeletal man whose bloodless skin gleamed like hoarfrost in the bright Aegean sunlight. A thin fringe of colorless hair ringed his head, and he was dressed soberly in black and gray. London could not stop herself from staring at the onyx ring glinting on his right index finger. Something cold spiraled through her bones as she looked at him.

"London," her father called, "come and meet my colleague."

With reluctant steps, London went to join the men.

"London," Father continued, "this is John Chernock. He will be accompanying us on our voyage and advising Fraser and I. Chernock, my daughter, London Harcourt."

She gave the man a restrained nod, hoping she could keep her immediate dislike of him hidden. He smirked at her as though reading her mind. "I knew your late husband, Mrs. Harcourt," he drawled. "And I'm sure you do him and your father credit."

"Thank you," London said with a thin smile. "Father, I think I'll find my cabin and settle in."

"Of course. Sally!" her father shouted. "Take your mistress to her cabin."

London was about to state that she could find her quarters on her own, but the maid appeared to provide escort. London gave the men a brief curtsey and then hurried below deck, with Sally scurrying after her. She wanted to put as much distance between herself and Chernock as possible. It would be difficult, though, since the ship was only two hundred and fifty feet long and not, as she hoped, two hundred and fifty miles. She had a feeling that there was no distance far away enough from that walking stalactite her father called a colleague.

As soon as London disappeared into the ship, Chernock addressed Edgeworth. "A pretty young woman, your daughter."

"She's promised to *me*," Fraser grumbled.

"I didn't promise anyone to anybody," Edgeworth said, his voice cutting. "Henry Lamb insisted that he'd prove himself to me in order to win the right to court her, and look what happened to that fool. Killed by Blades in the Gobi Desert. Killed by a woman, for God's sake." Base emotion, which Edgeworth struggled his whole life to contain, clogged his throat. "And his blunder ruined my only son."

Chernock nodded. "Lamb's abject failure forced Jonas to return to England through the Transportive Fire."

"Is such a thing possible?" asked Fraser, aghast.

"No man had attempted it before," said Chernock, darkly, "and now we know why."

Edgeworth growled, "His burns finally healed, but the scarring is abominable. Damn it!" He turned away to rub his stinging eyes on the sleeve of his jacket, trembling with fury. He vowed to himself that the Blades of the Rose would pay for the damage done to his son. Jonas was to have succeeded him as a leader amongst the Heirs of Albion, but that dream died when his son came back from Mongolia a twisted, burnt husk, his mind more damaged than his body.

Edgeworth refused to believe that Jonas's retreat had been anything less than honorable, even though he had heard the whispers. Jonas had fled, it was true, and with terrible haste, but only because Lamb had failed, because the Blades persisted in their foolish, sentimental quest to keep the world's magic from the hands of the Heirs.

"He made a brave sacrifice for his country," Fraser said, placating. "Jonas holds, as we all do, that Britain deserves to command the globe. Its nation, and its citizens, are superior to all others."

"The apotheosis of culture and statehood," Chernock seconded.

Fraser shot Chernock a quick, cutting look. Edgeworth was *his* to appease and flatter, and Fraser wouldn't stand for some skeleton of a man to ride on his coattails. He continued, "The Heirs of Albion willingly give their lives for this belief. I know I would, given the chance."

"It's those Blades that play the gadfly," Chernock sneered. "With their absurd conviction that no nation should rule over another. A mawkish ethos."

When Edgeworth felt he could better suppress his feelings, he turned back to Chernock and Fraser. "We'll have them beaten, soon," he vowed. "Even now, in England, our finest minds are unlocking the secrets of the Primal Source. Between that and the Source here in Greece, we shall finally stamp out the Blades. That's what Lamb was supposed to do."

"Lamb was vain and bloodthirsty," Chernock sniffed. "We are better off without him. He was a liability to the Heirs. We need trustworthy men. Yet," he added, looking pointedly at Edgeworth, "for the first time in our long history, it seems we have a woman in our ranks. I would never presume to question you, Edgeworth, but is this wise? Women are so fragile and emotional. She could be set astray by her feminine sensibilities."

"Don't question her obedience to me. She'll do exactly as she's told. We've only to lead her like a child, keep her sheltered from unwanted influence."

"And if she succeeds in her objective," Chernock persisted, "will the Heirs begin adding women to our confraternity?"

"Of course not," Edgeworth scoffed. "If she makes herself useful, and if this Source is recovered without too much interference from those damned Blades, then I will see her married as soon as we return to England. Yes, Fraser. If you impress me enough on this mission, I *may* reward you with her. You ought to control her better than Harcourt did."

Fraser's meaty face broke into a smile. "Thank you, Mr. Edgeworth."

"Those are numerous 'ifs,'" Chernock pointed out. Fraser glared at him.

Edgeworth's eyes were glacial. "But that's why we have you, my dear sorcerer."

"If the Blades do show themselves," Chernock said with a funereal smile, "then I very much look forward to practicing some of my newer spells on them. There is one, taken from a Hopi shaman I captured, that is most delightful. Giant spiders, you know, with poisoned webs. Exceedingly nasty. Shall I demonstrate?" He lifted his bony hands, the ebony ring glittering like a huge beetle, as Edgeworth and Fraser took a step back.

"Later, perhaps," Edgeworth said quickly. "You both must understand what this mission means to the Heirs, what is at stake, particularly now that we have the Primal Source. I wouldn't have brought a woman, my own daughter, into it without good cause." He turned to the captain, who was shouting orders to his men. "Captain, I want us to raise anchor within the hour. No excuses," he snarled when the captain began to object. "I am not to be contradicted. We sail before five o'clock." With that, Edgeworth stalked below deck, confident that he would be obeyed. No one ever said no to Joseph Edgeworth.

The cities of the world held unending fascination for Bennett. He'd been to many, more than most men could ever claim. The capitals of Europe, and beyond. Moscow. Cairo. Bombay. Peking. Each was a continually unfolding banquet of experience—and women. Yet, for all their exotic and cosmopolitan joys, Bennett never felt as much unfettered joy as he did when presented with the open road. In this case, the open sea.

Nikos Kallas proved himself a sure and able captain as he and his men sailed them away from Piraeus. They nimbly dodged other boats and ships, all coming in and out of the crowded harbor, and moved away from the coast that pushed eastward into Aegean. Cliffs and coastal towns shrank to dark, rocky forms as the impossible lapis blue of water grew and unfolded. Cape Sounion, and its hilltop temple dedicated to Poseidon, glided by as they moved out of the bay into the open sea. The waters were silken calm, and a soft breeze filled the sails, burnished gold by the rays of the sun setting to the west. Anywhere. The sea and the wind could take them anywhere. Limitless freedom. That's why men went to sea again and again. But women, land-bound and earthly warm, brought them back.

It was a woman he followed now. She was on the Heirs' steamship, speeding east. Thank Poseidon that Kallas was a skilled captain. He had to get to London Harcourt before the Heirs reached Delos. Bennett's plan would never work if the Heirs made land before he could reach her.

He urged the caique on, willing it to cut through the waves like an arrow.

Athena had been born and raised in the city that shared her name, and so it took her a small measure of time to gain her sea legs. Bennett watched her walk toward him on deck with the careful precision of a drunkard fighting for balance. Her dusky-fair skin had paled once the caique had reached open water. She came to stand next to him, swaying, as he stood near the bowsprit at the fore.

"Gone a bit green," he commented. "Like an unripe olive."

Athena gave a wan smile. "Always with such flattery. What woman would be foolish enough to let you leave her?"

"*You* did," Bennett pointed out amiably.

"I am better than most women."

"True. Our captain might agree."

Athena made a noise of dismissal, though it proved to be

a bit of a challenge in her compromised state. "Nikos Kallas has made no secret of his dislike of refined, educated women. Which does not surprise me, given his low origins."

Bennett raised his eyebrows, but decided to remain quiet on this point. Interesting, how this might develop, if they were all to share the same, not particularly large boat for the foreseeable future. Instead, he asked, "Feeling well enough for tonight's adventure?"

"Absolutely," she said at once. "Though," she added, "I have never attempted a spell of such size before."

"I've every confidence in you."

"Kidnapping is new territory for me."

"Don't usually dabble in it, myself," he admitted. "Not to worry, though. Blades have 'spirited away' people before. When a powerful Source is at stake."

"And the fact that our intended abductee is, by your own admission, an exceptionally beautiful young woman has no influence on your decision," Athena noted dryly.

Bennett flashed her a grin. "I'm hurt and offended you doubt the purity of my motives."

"Where Bennett Day is concerned, there are no such things as pure motives. But Harcourt's widow will learn, at some point, who you truly are."

"I know," he said flatly. If he had his way, he'd postpone that unpleasantness for as long as possible.

She drew an unsteady breath. "I am going to see if there is a spell for seasickness. I brought several books along for reference."

What would Athena be without her books? *That's* what made your baggage so deuced heavy. Here I was thinking you'd been kind enough to pack a millstone. Should we need to grind wheat."

Athena made a face at him, which wasn't difficult, considering her infirm state, before picking her way back down below the deck. Kallas had ceded the helm to one of his men as he adjusted a sail. She forced herself to walk steadily past him, as genteel as if promenading the elegant Plateia Kolonaki square rather than the tilting deck of a humble cargo caique. Kallas pretended not to notice her, but Bennett saw with a smile the way the captain gnawed on the stem of his pipe once she had passed. Even on the supposed freedom of the sea, one couldn't escape the eternal dance between men and women.

Kallas was a born mariner, that Bennett understood. The captain had kept pace with the Heirs' sleek steamship, staying just out of sight so that none but the most eagle-eyed lookout might detect even a trace of the caique. Athena's spell would—should—take care of the rest.

Bennett turned his face into the wind, watching as the cloak of dusk descended upon the sky and water. Soon, the stars would emerge. He hoped it wasn't a bright night. They would need the shelter of darkness for the plan to run smoothly.

Maybe Athena was right. Bennett would probably be much less likely to abduct the Heirs' linguistic expert if the linguist was a man, particularly a fat man. Hefting such bulk could prove difficult, and on cold nights, Bennett's knees sometimes troubled him. But his interest in London Harcourt troubled him more. He wanted to believe that only her lovely face and slim body drew his attention. She was a woman exceedingly pleasant to look upon. Touching her, learning the secrets of her body with his own—those would be pleasures he greatly anticipated, as he might with any enticing female.

Yet there was something more to her, the fire of intelligence, the gleam of yearning for independence, that drew him in, even in the few minutes they had spent in each other's company. She wasn't a sheltered virgin seeking to lose her innocence. She wasn't a bored, house-bound wife searching for shallow thrills. London Harcourt burned with desire for the world, for visceral experience. As he did. But he had the good fortune to be born male, and so the world opened to him like a feast, while London Harcourt could only look on and starve. What a pleasure it would be to feed her.

If she ever discovered his identity, he would be doing nothing with her.

He shook his head, made himself chuckle as if what he felt were merely pangs of unsatisfied lust. It had been a long, long time since he mooned over a woman. Those he wanted, he got. He could only give his lovers provisional affection, which they accepted, and so he moved on to the next. There was always a next.

Now here was a woman he couldn't, shouldn't have. No wonder he thought himself intrigued. There were more pressing concerns. Foremost was how to sneak aboard the Heirs' ship, past armed guards, the father, and the deuced Fraser, and then steal a whole woman from under their noses.

Thinking of this, Bennett hummed an old sea shanty.

"Considering the certain hell we're going to catch tonight," one of the sailors muttered at him, "you're a calm and cheerful son of a bitch."

Bennett grinned. "I do so enjoy life's little challenges."

"Is there anything else you'll be wanting, madam?" asked Sally.

London looked at her maid's reflection in the mirror propped against a tin cup, a brush midway to her unbound hair. Sally had conquered her seasickness long enough to help London out of her gown before bed, but it seemed, alas, a losing battle for the poor maid.

"I'm all right for the rest of the night, Sally," London

answered. "But is there anything I can get you? I've heard plain water biscuits can help. Perhaps the ship's cook has some."

Sally gulped and gave her head a feeble shake, which made her moan. "I couldn't possibly . . . eat anything, madam. Just a little lie down, I think, and I'll be . . . fresh as Easter morning." That seemed doubtful, considering the waxen, greenish cast to Sally's face.

"Please," London implored, "get to bed. I can put my clothes away."

"Thank . . . thank you, madam." Then Sally dashed from London's cabin to her own across the passageway, slamming her door behind her, but leaving the door to London's cabin hanging open. London rose from the small desk she used as a vanity and gently closed the door, but not before hearing the miserable sounds of Sally surrendering her dinner to a chamber pot. London winced in sympathy, grateful that, landlubber that she was, she somehow escaped the blight of seasickness. Well, it should not last too long for poor Sally. They would reach Delos by late tomorrow morning.

Remembering her father's warnings, London locked the cabin door. She needed to be vigilant. Though it seemed unlikely that anyone could get aboard the steamship. Aside from the cannons that could blast away at any ship foolish enough to get within firing range, armed men patrolled the top deck. London had seen the rifles slung across the men's backs, but the firearms weren't nearly as intimidating as the hard faces and large bodies of the men themselves. They seemed more like hired mercenaries than sailors.

If her father thought them necessary, she could only imagine what kind of threat loomed. Though he often treated her like some fragile hothouse orchid, London knew that in everything else Joseph Edgeworth was exacting and precise, not the kind of man given to wild and fanciful elaboration.

Soon, they would reach Delos, where London's work would begin. Despite the shadowy threat that loomed somewhere out in the world, her excitement could not be tamped down. The mythical birthplace of Apollo and Artemis. And all those writings upon the ruins for her to decipher. How marvelous it was to be.

She turned her attention to the gown laid across her narrow berth and readied it to be put away. London fussed with the hooks, knowing that Sally liked to keep her gowns tidy. It seemed rather unnecessary to maintain fashion out here. This was not a holiday jaunt, and this ship most definitely was not intended for anything but the most rudimentary services besides transportation and, dear Lord, warfare. Though the steamship had cabins for passengers, they were all small and plain. Perhaps the captain's quarters held a little more luxury.

London carefully packed her gown into her trunk, wedged into a corner of the cabin, before returning to her nighttime toilette. She drew her wrapper close over her nightgown and sat back down at the desk. Her dark flaxen hair required thorough brushing, or else it ran the risk of looking like the inside of a mattress. And, as much as she did not want to draw attention to herself as one of two women aboard the ship, she didn't want to resemble bedding.

She drew the boar bristles through her hair, idly watching her reflection in the mirror. Thomas Fraser had been exceptionally attentive tonight at dinner, asking her again and again if she found the food all right, or if it was too simple for her ladylike tastes. Such fawning felt out of character for him, particularly considering the way in which he barked orders at the stewards serving them, as if they were not human beings with thoughts and feelings.

London knew it wasn't polite to be overly solicitous to servants, yet it bothered her to treat them shabbily.

A thought had her brush still in mid-stroke. Good God, she hoped Fraser didn't expect to *court* her. She knew with absolute certainty that he would never approve of her linguistic studies—no doubt he preferred to use books as heavy objects for clubbing people—and she would not marry another man who shared her father's profession. If she married again. There had been little in her own marriage to recommend the state. She still nursed her ideas of love, crafted over years of reading about it, and she did get quite lonely. It could not be denied, as well—she craved a man's touch. Her own had lost its excitement long ago.

Ben Drayton's bedroom laugh tumbled through her mind. Surely that scoundrel understood how to touch a woman, and touch her well. Her eyes drifted shut, imagining such an encounter. Just to think of those clever hands on the curve of her shoulders, the soft flesh of her breasts, sent a thick wave of sensation cascading through her, warming the place between her thighs. She trailed her free hand along her collarbone, back and forth, letting her traitorous mind and body pretend that it was Drayton who caressed her. That he would push down her wrapper, peel away her nightgown and lay her upon the berth before settling his own weight over her, positioning himself between her legs. London's nipples tightened beneath the soft lawn. Her hand began to trail lower to her breasts.

She stilled, sensing another presence in the cabin. London's eyes opened, and she met the hot blue gaze of Ben Drayton in the mirror.

London jumped up from the chair and whirled to face him. The brush dropped from her hand to clatter on the floor. Drayton leaned against the cabin door, arms crossed over his broad chest. He seemed quite at ease, except for the fiery hunger in his eyes and noticeable arousal tenting his breeches.

"Don't stop," he rumbled.

Her heart slammed into her ribs as heat suffused her face. "How . . . how did you get in here?" she gasped. "I didn't hear the door. And . . . it was locked."

"A sorry day when a simple lock keeps me from a lady's bedchamber." He pushed away from the door and took a step toward her, a small smile tugging at a corner of his mouth.

London backed up until she pressed against the cool iron of the hull.

He came nearer. The cabin felt much, much smaller with him in it. He was quite male and quite close. "I haven't much time."

She dare not ask, but couldn't help herself. "Time for what?"

He raised an eyebrow.

"Oh, God," she gulped, her eyes flicking automatically toward the bed.

He laughed quietly. "Not that. Taking my time makes it so much better for everyone, and right now I'm on a tight schedule."

"Well, that *is* a relief," she said tartly, then shut her mouth, shocked by her own brazenness. There was a strange man in her cabin, and she was talking back! What she really should be doing is—

"Don't be tiresome and scream," he said.

That was exactly what London intended to do. She took a deep gulp of air.

He moved like a striking snake, a blur of motion she barely saw. He turned her around and wrapped her in the steel of his arms, one hand covering her mouth. A spike of terror clawed its way up her throat. She tried to scream. His clamped hand stifled the sound. She struggled against him, but he was solid with muscle, immovable. London thrashed about, yet all she managed to do was exhaust herself.

"I'm not going to hurt you," he murmured in her ear. "*We* don't hurt people."

We? Who was *we*? She wasn't soothed at all. She didn't care what Drayton said, she had to get free, had to fight him. Her muscles screamed with effort as she struggled. She couldn't even put her feet down or gain enough space to open her mouth and bite him.

Drayton glanced over at the small brass clock on the desk. "Look at the time. Blast. We've got to go." He didn't sound winded or troubled at all, more like he was mildly concerned about missing a train, whilst London panted for breath.

He loosened his hand from her mouth. Thank God! London gulped in enough air to scream. Before she could, he slipped his cravat from his neck and gagged her with it. She tasted the musk of his skin in the silk. Not that long ago, she would have gladly learned what Drayton's skin tasted like. Now it only reinforced the fact that he completely overpowered her.

He pulled off the belt from London's robe and deftly wrapped it around her pinned wrists before knotting it. She tugged at the belt. It wouldn't give. She was bound, and helpless.

Anger was better than the fear that threatened to swallow her.

"Next time," he grinned as she glared up at him, "I'll let *you* tie *me* up."

Fortunately, she was gagged, otherwise her mother never would have forgiven her for the curses that she tried to spew at him. And then she was easily swung up and slung over his shoulder like a sack of feathers.

"You need to eat more," he said.

She didn't hear him open the cabin door, but suddenly

they were slipping noiselessly into the passageway. He shut the door and fiddled with it for a moment, and she understood he was locking it. If he got her off the ship with no one noticing, they would probably assume she was safe in her cabin. London's absence would only be known in the morning, when Sally tried to come in. Panic fueled her into another struggle. If she could just stay in her cabin, surely everything would be fine. But that feeble hope died as Drayton eased down the passageway.

She prayed they would meet her father, the captain, a sailor, *anyone*, but fortune didn't favor her that night. Once, an armed sailor neared, en route to his duties, but Drayton held back to the shadow of a bulkhead. London tried to shout, despite the gag. Maybe even a small noise could alert the sailor.

"Quiet," Drayton said lowly in her ear. "A peep out of you, and that trigger-eager bloke will fill both of us with bullets. Don't take that chance."

Was he right? London was afraid to find out.

The sailor continued on his way.

Drayton climbed the steep iron stairs that led to the top deck. A peculiar, sweet fog embraced the steamship, rendering everything dreamlike and murky. Sailors patrolled, yet none saw her and Drayton as he slid to the railing. No one was coming to her aid. Drayton was going to abduct her. Off the ship, she would have no chance. *No!* She fought anew, twisting her body this way and that.

Yet she couldn't break Drayton's hold. With one arm clamped firmly around her waist, he grasped a rope tied to a small, thick hook hitched onto the railing, and eased them both onto the other side of the rail. Then he rappelled silently down the side of the ship into the darkness. London could not believe he possessed the strength to hold her and his own weight with one hand, expecting at any moment that they would both go plummeting into the sea.

But hold them, he did, all the way down the rope to a tiny canoe-like boat, anchored to the other end of the rope.

She felt herself lowered to the floor of the boat, and watched as Drayton unhitched the hook with a nimble flick of his wrist. He caught the hook as it sailed down.

"A little gift from our friend Catullus Graves," he whispered at her with a wink.

London had no idea who Catullus Graves was, and didn't much care as the boat, free from its tie to the steamship, glided back and away. London raised her head enough to see the ship steam on into the night, leaving her behind.

Father! her mind screamed.

"Now," Drayton said softly, "it shouldn't be long now before—ah! Here we are."

Appearing from the darkness like a ghost ship was a caique, wreathed in the same sweet fog that had enveloped the steamer. A few dim lanterns hung from the mainsail boom, allowing London to see the hazy shapes of people moving around on deck. She'd been taken. She was alone. Alone with a boat full of strangers. London began to shake. She flinched when Drayton put a large, warm hand on her ankle.

"Don't be frightened," he said with surprising kindness and sincerity. "We truly won't harm you."

London tried to turn away, blinking back tears. She wished she'd never met Ben Drayton. She wished she hadn't seen those blasted writings on her father's desk. She wished she was back in her own home, safely ensconced in her library, reading old tomes in front of the fire and merely dreaming of faraway places.

They were idle wishes. The caique drew up next to the canoe, and London squeezed her eyes shut.

"You certainly know how to treat a lady," a woman's accented voice said dryly. "The poor thing is terrified."

"I know, Athena," Drayton said, impatient. "Give me a hand, Kallas," he added in Greek.

London felt herself picked up and passed from one set of hands to another before being set on her feet. Opening her eyes, London found she was on the deck of the caique. Two Greek sailors stared at her before slinking away, bearing the little canoe. There was another sailor, not particularly tall, but built like a bull, looking at her with an unreadable expression as he worked a pipe stem back and forth in his teeth. A woman, dark and regal, came forward, dressed more appropriately for an afternoon salon than a nighttime kidnapping in the middle of the Aegean Sea. London shied away when the woman reached for her.

"Come now, I only mean to untie you," the woman said gently in English. "But, mind, if I do, do not try and jump over the side. Your father's ship is long gone, and we are far from the shore. You could not swim the distance. Yes?"

Seeing that the woman was right, London nodded. Quickly, the binding at her wrists was loosened until London was able to pull her hands free. She snatched the gag from her mouth, then coughed to clear her dry throat.

Finally, she rasped, "Who are you people? What do you want with me?"

"Everything will be revealed, in time," Drayton said, coming forward. He held up his hands, placating, as London edged back. "All we want is to have a conversation with you."

"A conversation," London repeated in disbelief. She was certain that at any moment she would be assaulted or murdered.

"A conversation," echoed Drayton evenly. "Merely that, and nothing else."

London's fear shifted, reshaping itself. Hot, unchecked anger poured through her. She'd never felt anything like it before, but it filled her with a newfound power. When the woman and Drayton took a few steps toward her, London grabbed a nearby bottle from a crate and brandished it like a club. Miraculously, both Drayton and the woman stopped their advance.

"You abducted me from my cabin in the middle of the night, forced me off my ship, stuck me in a minuscule boat, and then brought me *here*," London said, her voice surprising her with its strength. "If all you want to do is *talk*, then it sure as hell had better be good."

Chapter 4

Mrs. Harcourt's Education

She refused all offers of food and drink. No coffee or wine or figs. She would not sit comfortably inside upon some cushions. She would do nothing except keep her place, clutching the wine bottle, until an explanation was provided as to who these people were and what they wanted with her.

London gave them this much credit. Neither Drayton, nor the woman called Athena, nor any of the sailors brandished any weapons or threatened her. But the night was only just beginning.

Seeing that London was not to be moved except by force, Drayton brought out a folding chair for Athena and, after seating her, leisurely paced back and forth on the deck. The soft lantern light cast him in a burnished glow, illuminating the pristine lines of his face. As he paced, his boots made a soft staccato as they struck the wooden floor, but his step was light and nimble. Now London knew just *how* agile, the proof of which had been her undetected abduction from a ship bristling with armed men. And, she acknowledged in the innermost recesses of her mind, she'd felt the movements of Drayton's body, his strength and ability. Finely wrought, potently masculine.

She chided herself a fool to think of such things when that man had taken her from her ship and was, no doubt, her father's enemy. Which made him her enemy.

"What do you know of your father's work?" Drayton asked her, as if reading her thoughts.

"I know enough," London shot back. She would give neither Drayton nor his refined female companion any true information.

"It's the same work as your brother, and your late husband," he said. "It takes them away and they don't come home for long periods of time."

"*If* they come back," added Athena.

London's gaze flew to the Greek woman. "Maybe *you* have something to do with that," she snapped.

Instead of contradicting London outright, Athena shrugged, her hands neatly folded in her lap. London turned her eyes back to Drayton. He looked uncharacteristically grave.

"Sometimes, it comes to that," he said, a trace of regret in his voice. "But, know that our cause is good. We never want to hurt anyone. Yet there are occasions when there's no choice."

A thrill of newfound fear snaked through London. These people were killers. "Is now one of those occasions?"

"Absolutely not. Mrs. Harcourt," he said sincerely, "you've got to understand that, no matter what your father has told you about us, our goal is to protect life, not harm it or take it away."

"Who is this 'we' and 'our' you keep talking about, Mr. Drayton?" she demanded.

He stopped pacing and dragged his hands through his thick, dark hair. "Firstly, my name isn't Ben Drayton. It's

Bennett Day. And this is Athena Galanos." The Greek
woman regally inclined her head at the introduction.

A small, frantic laugh burst from London's throat. This
wasn't a tearoom. "Very well, Mr. Day," she said, tamping
down her incipient hysteria. She was actually rather amazed
that she had not dissolved completely into crazed tears and
was, in fact, fairly lucid and steady. She clutched the bottle
tighter in her hand. "We've gotten those niceties out of the
way. Give me answers."

He turned to Athena. "Now that she's here, I'm not certain what to say."

"That is because you have to be serious, for a change,"
the woman said dryly.

London smothered a smile. Whomever this Athena
Galanos was, she certainly knew Bennett Day well enough.

"Just begin at the beginning," Athena said as Day hesitated.

"I'll need some visual assistance," he answered.

Athena sighed, then rose to her feet. She closed her eyes
and let her hands drift open, as if she held an invisible
object. Then she began to speak softly in a smooth whirl of
words. London recognized some of them. *Light. Strength.
Goddess.* An ancient language originating from the cradle
of time, nestled in the heart of Assyria.

For a moment, there were only the sounds of Athena
chanting to herself and the slap of the waves against the
hull of the boat, the wind snapping the sails. And then, so
faint as to be almost undetectable, came a trill, like a songbird on a distant tree. London glanced around to see where
the sound came from, thinking, perhaps, that one of the
sailors played upon a pipe, but it was not so. The sailors
clustered in the boat's stern, watching Athena. Day, too, had
his attention fixed on the Greek woman.

A glowing orb formed in the space between Athena's
hands. London gaped. It was small, at first, no bigger

than a croquet ball, but then grew larger and larger, until it was almost three feet in diameter. The deck of the ship was bathed in an amber light, surpassing even the lanterns' illumination.

"What is that?" breathed London.

"Magic, Mrs. Harcourt," Day answered.

She shook her head. "Magic does not exist. That"—she gestured toward the luminous orb—"is some kind of spiritualist trick. Like a false medium at a séance."

"No trick here. Nothing false. See for yourself."

Slowly, London walked toward Athena and the ball of light. As London neared, she felt the air turn warm and alive. Her skin buzzed with a million tiny vibrations, a host of microscopic butterflies beating their wings against her. She reached a hand toward the orb, then hesitated.

"You may touch it," Athena said in a whisper.

London pressed the fingers of her free hand to the surface, then, finding it yielding, pushed them deeper into the globe. It felt like honey, thick and unctuous, but honey made of distilled energy. London pulled her hand back, and small golden droplets clung to her fingers before dissipating into wisps of light that vanished into the starry darkness.

Understanding slammed into her. This was no spiritualist ruse. It was real. Real magic. The bottle slipped from her stunned fingers and rolled away.

She stumbled backward, swung her eyes to Bennett Day. He did not seem at all surprised by what should have been impossible.

"I don't understand," she said. "I don't understand how this can be."

"The world, Mrs. Harcourt, is filled with magic," said Day. "It exists everywhere and in everything. You see—" He waved toward the orb, which shifted into a topographical globe, continents and oceans forming from the energy.

And connecting the land masses and the bodies of water was an infinite lacework of brighter light. "It's been this way since humans formed societies and cultures. With knowledge came magic."

"But I was always taught . . . I mean, everybody learned that it wasn't real, it was for fairy stories and old myths."

"As mankind developed, so did its capacity for destruction and abuse. Magic needed to be hidden to keep humanity from annihilating itself. And so it was sheltered in legend. But that didn't stop others from concentrating it into physical things, tangible objects that hold great power. Those objects are known as Sources."

"Sources," London repeated on a breath. Even saying the word made the shining globe pulse brighter.

"Sources are found all over the world," Day continued. "Most are safely hidden from those that would exploit them. But that doesn't keep people from trying to find the Sources, using them for their own gains."

"What kinds of gains?"

"Some of them small and selfish," said Athena. "Wealth. Love."

Day said, "But there are others, larger organizations, who want the Sources to expand their nation's power to the cost of everyone else. Especially now that the world is expanding, the hidden corners of the planet being forced into the hard glare of an empire's sun. Such organizations can be found in all countries seeking to dominate the globe. They're even found," he added, looking hard at her, "in England."

London swallowed tightly. "And that's who you are."

"No. We're the few who try to stop them. The Blades of the Rose."

The name held a potent resonance. "Only you and Miss Galanos?"

"There are many other Blades, found all over, but there are never enough. Our enemy is large and powerful."

A sudden chill caused London to pull her robe tighter around her body. She felt as though she stood at the very edge of a great abyss. Any moment she could fall into it, disappearing forever. She was afraid to know more. She had to know everything.

She began, "And those people in England, the ones who want the Sources—"

"They call themselves the Heirs of Albion," he said.

London wrapped her arms around herself.

"The name alone gives you an idea of what they believe in," added Athena darkly. She lowered her hands and the luminous orb disappeared. "England first. Above all and any. They do not care who or what stands in their way. They pillage and plunder Sources, eradicating any who oppose them, and subjugate whoever has the misfortune of being left alive."

An awful thought, horrible to contemplate. But, then . . . she remembered hearing her father, her brother, Lawrence, and other men of their circle discussing heatedly how England deserved the greatest share of the empire, that the world was populated by savages and children who needed England's guiding hand. They never spoke this way in front of her, of course, but London caught snippets of conversation as she passed them huddled in groups at parties or gathered in smoking rooms, away from women and frivolity.

Those men. Lawrence. Jonas. Her father. *Oh, God.*

London clutched herself tighter. "I cannot believe you."

"Opium," Day said flatly.

"They didn't invent opium," London shot back.

"No, they didn't," he answered. "But the Heirs helped England develop its crops in India and turn it into profit. The Heirs ensured Britain could peddle opium in China, turn the entire country into a land of poppy addicts. They used Llyr's Might to defeat Chinese ships, and brought the whole of the nation to its knees. The Heirs were there, again, fourteen years later, your father among them."

"I was a child then," London protested. "I can't vouch for the whereabouts of my father when I was only seven years old."

Athena asked, "Do you recall the autumn of 1868? Lawrence Harcourt, your late husband, was away then, wasn't he?"

London nodded slowly, recalling how they had only lately returned from their bridal journey before Lawrence insisted he had important work to do, and was gone for several months. It was the first of what was to be many absences. She remembered how empty and silent their house was, how she'd wandered the rooms like a specter haunting her own marriage.

"He was in India," Day said. "In Tirupati, stealing a Source from a temple dedicated to the god Venkateswara. Later, the Source was used to crush a pocket of rebellion in the Aravalli mountains. Women and babies killed."

"Using India's own magic against itself," Athena added.

"He came home," London said, her mind drifting back, "recovering from malaria. By the time he was fully well, he was gone again." Not before they'd gotten into yet another awful fight, and he'd exercised his husbandly rights only once.

Was it true, what Day and Athena Galanos said?

"Gone to Constantinople," Day said. "He was wounded there, by Tony Morris, a Blade. A cut across his left shoulder."

She knew the scar. "No," London said, her chest constricting.

"Yes," said Day.

"You're wrong!"

He shook his head sadly. London turned to Athena Galanos and saw pity and truth in the woman's eyes. It could not be, but it was, and everything fell to pieces, crashing around London and crushing her beneath the rubble.

"Lawrence?" she asked. "Truly?"

Day nodded, his expression shuttered. "He was one."

"And my father," she choked, "who is he to these Heirs of Albion?"

"He has a seat within the inner circle," Day said. "As his father did, and his father before him. I imagine that Jonas will take over, someday."

London fought back tears. "No. Jonas never leaves the house. Some months ago, he came back from a trip abroad. Burned. Scarred." She and Jonas had never gotten along. He was a bully, stole her toys and tore up her books when they were children. And when they grew older, neither had much to do with the other. Even so, she would not for all the world have wished such a fate upon him.

"From the Transportive Fire," Day said grimly. "In Mongolia. He was with Henry Lamb, trying to seize a Source for the Heirs. The Blades stopped them."

"How do you know this?"

"I was there when it happened."

Her throat felt tight, choking her. She thought she would be ill. "You caused Jonas's burns."

"Your brother fled by jumping into the Fire. None of us touched him."

She barely heard Day, her mind a whirling mass as she struggled to make sense of a world in ruins. "If what you say is true, about my father and Jonas and Lawrence, then this entire time, since I was born until now, I have been living under their roofs, eating their food, wearing their clothes."

"All paid for in blood," Athena said, blunt.

"Mrs. Harcourt," Day began gently, taking a step toward her. "London."

She gazed at him with stricken eyes, stopping him. "I never knew. I don't think any of us women knew." She thought of her mother, all the wives and daughters of her father's associates, shopping, giving parties, paying calls, the girls playing with their dolls in nurseries, later making their society debuts. Each of them culpable by silent consent to rape the world of its magic and profit by its theft. While the dead remained mute but accusing, hovering in the corners of conservatories and over trim green lawns.

"The Heirs do not allow women into their ranks," said Athena. "However, you seem to be an exception."

"Me? I'm not doing anything for them!" She shook her head in denial, even though she knew her protests to be futile, even to herself.

"But that's why your father has brought you here," Day explained. "He needs you to translate the ruins on Delos in order to find a Source. He wouldn't have taken you to Greece, involved you with the Heirs, unless the Source he sought was extremely powerful."

Athena added, "We've learned, recently, that the Heirs have recently seized the legendary Primal Source from Africa."

"The Primal Source is the oldest and most powerful Source of all," Day said, grimly. "No one knows what will happen once the Heirs unlock its secrets. Something incomprehensible. All we can do now is keep them from taking more Sources, including the one here in Greece."

That meant the literal fate of millions could rest on London. It almost made her laugh. She was no one special. Just a well-bred widow who happened to love languages. She had been taught from birth that she should bring honor to her family, a quiet adornment who softened the hard edges of the world. But who had taught her this? Her father. An Heir of Albion. But she could stop him and the Heirs. If she chose.

"And that is why you brought me *here*," she said, waving toward the caique. "Because it is my translation that will guide them."

"Yes." Day came closer, until he stood not a foot away. They stared at one another. Even in the midst of this chaos, London felt it anew, the insistent pull that drew her toward him, itself a kind of spell or charm that possessed no countermeasure. When he reached for her, she did not pull back. And when his fingers lightly brushed over her cheek, the softest, barest touch, she let her eyes close for a moment. Solace. Support. She found them with him in this newly minted world. "The Blades need you, London," he said quietly.

She did pull away, then, turning from him and walking to the rail. A clear and endless night on every side. Water and sky both black and shimmering with stars. She wanted to be swallowed up in the blackness, to disappear, weighted down with secrets. Somewhere out there were her father, Fraser, Chernock. All of them were Heirs of Albion. How long would it take before they realized she was missing? And when they did, what would happen then?

"I don't know what you think I can do for you," London said, still looking out at the sea.

"Join us," he said from close behind her. "Join our fight."

London managed a strangled laugh. "How funny you are, Mr. Day. In case you had not noticed, I'm not much of a fighter. I posed not the smallest obstacle when you took me from my cabin."

"We'll teach you to defend yourself—"

"And I haven't any magical ability."

"Athena is a rarity in the Blades. We hold to a creed whereby none can wield magic that isn't ours by right or gift. She's born into a long line of witches. And I," he said, standing nearer so that she was bathed in the warmth of his body, "am just a man."

With an indrawn breath, London suddenly realized she was wearing only her nightclothes, and nothing underneath them. Only now, with him so close, did she become aware of this, how bare she really was. He might not have possessed true magic, but he commanded his own kind of sorcery over her.

She faced him and had to tilt her head back to look into his eyes. She breathed, "What you ask of me is impossible. I cannot simply turn my back on my father, my family, everything I have ever known. I must give my father a chance to refute these allegations."

Day opened his mouth as if to argue, but Athena's voice cut in. "Bennett, we shall not force her. A Blade must always use their own will and never impose theirs on anyone else. So stop looming over the woman and let her think."

"I'm looming?" he asked London.

"Yes," she answered. "Please. I need a bit of . . . air."

Surprisingly, he complied, though a wry smile curved his mouth. "I am your servant, Mrs. Harcourt. Tell me what you desire, and I'll do everything I can to satisfy you."

Athena made a choked sound of exasperated laughter. Even though she and London appeared about the same age, there was a worldliness about the Greek woman that London could never hope to emulate. No doubt, London seemed very foolish to Athena where Bennett Day was concerned, like a smitten schoolgirl dizzy over her first compliment. But London could prove that she was not a child, and had not been one for a long time. Tonight had aged her by decades.

"Take me back to my father," she said.

A shout from the small Greek sailor—London now understood he was the captain—caught everyone's attention. He yelled orders at his men, who ran to obey, and hurried to the wheel.

"You see?" Day said over the shouting. "All you have to

do is ask and I make your wish come true." He pointed off the port side, where London could just begin to see white columns of smoke heading toward them. "Here's your father now."

The lanterns on the boom flickered out with a wave of Athena's hand. All was darkness. Yet Kallas and his men knew the boat, knew the night, and ran to adjust their course without stumbling. They communicated in whispers. The Heirs' ship had the advantage of steam, however, knifing quickly toward them. Bennett understood little of sailing, and could only shoulder a rifle and tuck a revolver into his belt, should things come to close combat.

"Where's our fog, Athena?" he asked.

Athena looked up from loading a revolver, a difficult task in the dark. "I have never before used the Mist of Thetis. I could not hold the spell for long."

"It served our purposes well the first time," Bennett said, jovial. "Now we get to fight the old-fashioned way." He enjoyed scrapping with the Heirs, giving him the chance to actually lay hands with the bastards. But usually such fights were done without an innocent woman's life in the cross fire.

He glanced over at London Harcourt. Amidst the brisk activity of Kallas and his men, London stood alone at the rail, watching as her father's ship steamed closer and closer. They soon would be within firing range of the cannons.

Bennett went to her, cupping his hand over the gentle curve of her shoulder. He felt the slight start in her body when he touched her, the delicate bones and soft flesh in a minute contraction. This had to be a far cry from anything she had ever experienced. Edgeworth had bred her to be a society lady, not a seafaring adventurer. Nor was she prepared to learn that her father and brother were members of a secret and ruthlessly ambitious society trying to acquire the world's magic for their own dominating agenda. Yet, remarkably, her composure did not waiver. She stood on steady legs to face the oncoming threat.

"They're coming for me," she said, toneless.

"We'll give 'em a good tussle."

"This little boat against heavy guns? I may not know much about warfare, but there is no way this caique can withstand their firepower." She turned to face him, and when she spoke, he heard the resolve fortifying her voice. "I must get back."

"You don't have to," he said. "You can stay here, with us. With me." He tried to take her hand, but she ducked to one side and evaded him.

"Joining the Blades of the Rose is unthinkable. I will lose everything, everyone."

"Consider what you will gain." He couldn't fathom why he wanted her to stay so badly. "You won't be alone." She could provide tremendous help to the Blades, and certainly keeping her linguistic knowledge out of the Heirs' hands was a benefit, but he wasn't thinking only of strategy. He wanted her close by, close to him, a powerful sensation of need he wasn't prepared for.

"I can't," she said. "Don't ask me again."

He stifled the quick, hot cut of disappointment. "So you'll help your father. Translate the ruins for him."

"I—"

"They are aiming the guns," Kallas hissed in the dark.

"Let me go," London said quickly. "Put me in the canoe and send me over to them. They will stop their pursuit if I'm in the water."

"I'm not going to stuff you in some bloody little boat like a mutineer," he growled.

"I'll jump overboard, if necessary."

Bennett swore. London had a spine of steel that even she did not seem to know about.

"She is correct," Athena said. "The Heirs will not give chase if she is out there."

The night tore open as the guns fired a warning shot. Everyone on the caique fell to the deck—the two sailors screaming with panic, Kallas cursing in a dense dialect, Athena muttering prayers to sundry goddesses. Without thought, Bennett covered London's body with his own, shielding her. She felt very small beneath him.

Thank Ares that the Heirs chose only to fire a warning shot. The caique was far enough away that cannonballs might smash into the water and not the hull, but in a few more minutes, they would be a plum ready to be crushed.

"Now," London hissed underneath him. "I have to leave *now*." She shoved at him, and he rolled away.

Hell and damn, there wasn't a choice. Crouching low, Bennett hurried to the canoe leaning against the quarter-deck house. He and Kallas leaned over the rail and eased the small boat into the water. As Kallas held the boat, Bennett took London by her narrow waist and swung her over the rail.

"All right, I'm in," she said. "You can let go of me now."

But he didn't.

He brought his mouth down to hers, his lips against her own. If there'd been time, he would have lingered, studying her, the soft feel of her. He would have brushed his lips over hers, slowly at first, then, unhurriedly, as she opened to him, he would have delved into her in a long, liquid exploration. Stroked the inside of her mouth, brought their tongues together, velvet to velvet. He would learn her tastes gradually, like an unfolding banquet, course by course. He would have discovered what sounds she made in the throws of a deep, endless kiss. All of these things he would have done, had they time.

There wasn't time.

Rough, animal need. A hasty and fierce devouring. Her mouth was warm and silken, and, God, yes, as demanding as his. She clung to his arms, leaning upward, and met him in the kiss with unrestrained hunger. No, she wasn't a civilized lady, not truly, and there wasn't anything that pleased him better. She tasted of cinnamon and oranges and woman, and he wanted her so badly at that moment that he shook with it.

"Bennett," Athena said. She had to repeat his name again before it penetrated the thick fog of desire that enfolded him. "We must leave. Let her go, Bennett."

With great reluctance, he did so, and his hands wanted London back in them immediately. Instead, he curled them into fists.

London gazed up at him, eyes glittering and wide with revelation. Her breath came fast. She collected herself with a shudder. "Please release the boat," London said to Kallas in Greek.

Shouting from the Heirs' ship could be heard, growing nearer, commands to reload the cannons, men running on the iron deck, Edgeworth bellowing over it all.

Kallas relinquished his hold on London's boat. Immediately, the little craft drifted away, toward the Heirs. Bennett could only watch as the white of London's robe and nightgown faded off into the night, like a milkweed puff upon the water. It took everything he had not to propel himself over the side of the caique and swim to her. There was nothing to do but listen to her voice as it floated across the water.

"Father!" he heard her shout. "I'm here!"

"London?" That had to be Edgeworth.

"Down here!"

"Stop the damn ship," Edgeworth yelled.

With a groan, the engines were cut. The steamship

slowed, and sailors ran about the deck as they readied to
pull London Edgeworth from the sea. Free from their pur-
suers, the caique raced off under the expert guidance of
Kallas. He managed their retreat alone, as his crewmen had
not recovered themselves from the cannon fire and still lay
upon the deck, praying and covering their heads with their
arms. Athena stepped over their shuddering bodies to stand
beside Bennett at the rail.

"A surprising creature, that Mrs. Harcourt," Athena murmured. "I did not believe she had the courage to put herself
out into the sea."

"She does astonish," Bennett said hoarsely. He strained
to see her out there, somewhere, in the night, but she was
lost to him.

"Will she help her father, do you think?"

"I think . . ." He might never see her again. Or, if he did,
she might have allied herself with the Heirs, or at least provided the translations that they needed to find the Source.
She would be one of them, the enemy. Then his attraction
to her would become even more problematic than it already
was. One didn't lust after his foe's daughter, his enemy's
widow. Made things deuced awkward.

He still reeled from that kiss, and considered jumping in
the water, anyway, to cool himself off.

Had it been simple lust, then Bennett could have dismissed what he felt for London Harcourt as a simple need
of one body for another. It wasn't simple. Not at all. He felt
it in his body, and saw it in her eyes.

She would ask her father about him. And Edgeworth
would tell her whom he truly was. If he ever did see
her again, those lovely dark eyes of hers would be clear
and glittering with hate. He knew it had to be, and yet
couldn't stop from wishing otherwise. He would have
even preferred indifference, that enemy of lovers. But hate
him, she must. And with just cause.

"I think . . . that I need a drink." He wandered off in search of a bottle of ouzo.

Swaddled in a blanket, London sat in her father's state-room, a snifter of brandy cupped in her hands. His cabin was larger than hers, but it was only when London observed the nautical charts and equipment scattered about the room that she realized her father had commandeered the captain's stateroom. Presumably the steamship's captain had been relocated to another cabin, the first mate's perhaps, and that sailor was forced somewhere else, and so on, until the entire ship's crew had been displaced. For some reason, she found the whole idea funny, imagining everyone struggling into clothes that didn't fit and assembling on deck in too-large pants or too-small shirts.

"I don't see what's so humorous about the situation," her father said with a confused frown. "These are serious circumstances we're in."

London carefully controlled her smile. "Sorry, Father. Just strained nerves, I suppose."

At once, he became contrite, solicitous. "Yes, yes, you've been through a terrible ordeal. What else do you need? Shall I fetch Sally? I'll get her." He strode to the door of the cabin.

"No, please," London said, stopping him. "I'll be all right soon."

"I should dismiss that maid at once," he grumbled. "Across the passageway from you the whole time, and not a peep from her when you were taken."

"Sally is very sick, Father," London pointed out. "And there were men all over the ship who didn't help, either. Will you dismiss them, as well?"

He lowered himself into another chair with a mutter. "Everyone's gone tense. By God, those rogues have some audacity, to take you right out from our very noses! Next time, we shall be better prepared."

"Next time?" London repeated. "Will they come back?"

"Their kind never give up," her father said blackly. "Only death stops 'em. But you needn't worry," he continued in a reassuring tone. "We'll find those bad people, and put an end to them for good."

The image of Bennett Day lying cold on the deck of the caique made London shiver. She took a warming sip of brandy, hoping to quell her thoughts. But they would neither disappear nor sit quietly in her brain. Everything that Day and Athena Galanos had told her rioted in her mind. Her father. A merciless villain intent on dominating the world. Jonas, Lawrence, even Thomas Fraser, all part of the same merciless cabal. When she had been aboard the caique, listening to the even words of Day and Athena, it seemed almost possible. But now, sitting with her father, his face so familiar to her, his gestures the same she had known her whole life, it all seemed unreal, impossible. Magic? Truly? And her father in the middle of it? And, if what Day said was true, what was London to do about it? Sudden weariness weighted her shoulders.

"I think I should like to go to bed," she said, setting the glass on a nearby table.

"Very soon, London. But before that, I must ask you some questions. Regarding your abduction. This may be difficult, but try to bear up, there's a good girl." He grew sharp and serious. "It was the Blades, wasn't it? They took you." His words sent fiery ice all throughout London's chest. So—it was true, not a collection of stories and tricks. Hearing her father even say the name of the Blades made it all so much more real.

"Yes," she said quietly.

His gaze turned shrewd and penetrating. "What did the Blades want with you?"

London hesitated. She did not know what her father might do if she told him that she had been asked to join the ranks of the Blades of the Rose. He might view her with suspicion, curtail her movements, even keep her guarded by armed men. Caged.

"They only wanted to know what I knew," she finally said. "Which was nothing. Until tonight."

"Did you get their names?"

London hesitated. "No. But, Father," she said, focusing on the coarse weave of the blanket gripped tightly in her hands. "They told me things," she said quietly. "About you and Jonas and Lawrence and, and everybody. They said . . . you were monsters."

Instead of being angry, her father was amused. "There's no such thing as monsters, London." He chuckled. "I'm sure to the Blades, the Heirs are fiends. But only because we do not share their naïve idealism."

"But to take things from their rightful owners," London objected, "at the cost of many lives. Surely that cannot be right."

Again, he gave a little laugh, as though entertaining a child's fancies. He gestured toward the maps piled on the table. "The world is changing, London, whether one wishes it or not. It would be pretty to think that the savage and heathen peoples of the world exist in some prelapsarian paradise where there is no greed, no hate, no sin. Yet we know that isn't the case. Those godless savages live in misery, deprived of all the good things that English civilization and society can provide. Do you know," he continued with the air of a schoolmaster, "that the Hindus burn their women? When a husband dies, the wife must throw herself onto a pyre and burn herself alive! Just think, if we practiced suttee in England, you would have been set on fire when Lawrence died. Now, you wouldn't like that, would you?"

"What does that have to do with stealing magic?" London wondered.

"It has everything to do with it," he said, his tone growing slightly impatient. Clearly, her objections and questions were both unanticipated and unwelcome. "The more Sources the Heirs of Albion acquire, the more powerful they become. The more powerful *England* becomes. With such tools at our disposal, the Empire can defeat her foes and flourish. Enlightenment and the English way of life will spread like a blaze, illuminating the world."

"And those that you trample in your quest for power, do they not matter?"

Her father waved his hand in airy dismissal. "The lives of a handful of ignorant brutes are nothing compared to the needs of millions. Would it not be better to kill a few men in order to preserve the welfare of entire nations? It is simple arithmetic. Even a woman can understand that," he said, smiling at her with fond indulgence.

She was windswept, barren. It seemed so simple from her father's point of view. England was right. Everyone else was not. Yet nothing existed in uncomplicated binary systems, she was learning. There were many shades of gray. Unfortunately, London was now so mired in gray that there was no color anywhere, especially not within the reaches of her soul. After a moment, London asked, "Does Mother know?"

"Only what I tell her, which is not much. She isn't like you, London," he added in a confiding, flattering tone. "I know you're a clever young woman. Smarter than poor Jonas, too, I'd wager. Even Harcourt hadn't the intelligence that you have. And that is why the Heirs need your help."

"To translate the ruins and find a Source."

"Exactly!" He patted her knee. "Come now, won't you tell your old father how you escaped from those horrid Blades? Hm? Were you a clever girl?"

London had no desire to tell him what transpired on the caique, and nothing could get her to relate the kiss she'd shared with Bennett Day. Even thinking of it now made her pulse speed. "I think I was allowed to leave, when they realized I wasn't useful."

He nodded, satisfied. "Without your understanding of language, they'll be running around blind. But we can't expect them to tuck their tails between their legs and run home. Blades stick like leeches. Until we burn them off."

More gruesome images flitted through London's mind, images that left her rather ill. She pushed the blanket off, then rose to her feet. Her father followed suit. "I really do need to go to bed, Father."

"Of course," he said with a paternal chuckle. "You aren't used to such activity. Women are fragile flowers."

"I don't feel very floral right now," London said flatly.

He had no answer for that, so instead, he tucked her hand in the crook of his arm and led her out of his borrowed stateroom and down the passageway to her cabin. London was reminded of when she had made her debut, in her frothy white dress, entering a ballroom for the first time. And then she thought of her wedding day, being led down the aisle by her father to her waiting groom. She had been so eager, so afraid, close to asphyxiating in her tight corset, but believing it would all be worth it once Lawrence took her as his wife.

Where was her father leading her now? Into the world of the Heirs of Albion?

Lawrence had been an Heir. He'd scoured the globe in pursuit of Sources. That was why he was never at home. London was more used to having their town house to herself than sharing it with her husband. During the few weeks that he'd be at home between assignments, things always started out well between them, and, at first, London truly believed they could be happy together, true husband

and wife. But after the first few days . . . it was best not to
think of it. After a while, London no longer believed she
would find pleasure and joy in her married life. Yet divorce
was impossible, and she could not bring herself to take a
lover. So she continued on, thinking that this was how
things were to be.

Until Lawrence died. An accident abroad, she was told.
The carriage tipped over a cliff on the rocky southern coast
of France. There was no body, and the headstone marked
an empty grave. She had to mourn.

"What happened to Lawrence, Father?" she asked as they
neared her cabin. "I assume it wasn't a carriage accident."

"It wasn't," her father said, grim. "A Blade killed him on
assignment near Marrakesh, but we got the Source, after
all. Day's victory was hollow."

London froze. She pressed her hand to her throat. "Day?
What is that?"

"Not what, but who," her father said, his voice icing with
hatred. "Bennett Day. The Blade who killed Lawrence."

Chapter 5

In the Ruins

No good. It was no good. She failed.

She was glad. And bitterly disappointed. It freed her conscience, but not her pride. For years, she nursed her secret love, believing with quiet arrogance that few men and no women possessed her linguistic knowledge. All those volumes on her bookshelves at home, the sheaves of paper upon which she'd transcribed translations of little-known texts—they meant nothing. She was in the world, at last, in the ruins at Delos, and all she had produced was nonsense.

London, squinting in the unrelenting light, studied the inscriptions on the columns for the hundredth time. She glanced down at the papers she held, shuffled them. Yet it did not matter in what order she placed the inscriptions. She'd tried every combination. None worked.

The ruins stood on the southern tip of the island, centered in an excavated pit roughly thirty feet wide. A tumble of gneiss and granite surrounded the pit where members of the Heirs' archaeological team had uncovered a series of flat-sided columns. The columns lined up in three rows of three, forming a square. Each side of the Parian marble

columns bore inscriptions in an ancient dialect, and, at
first, London felt she would have no trouble deciphering
them. That belief did not last beyond her first few hours
on Delos.

"Any progress?"

She turned as her father and Fraser climbed down into
the pit. Both men's faces shone with perspiration. Even the
armed Greek sailor who guarded her had stained his shirt
with sweat. A rocky, barren dot of land, Delos offered no
shade, no relief from the blazing sun of its patron god, as
if Apollo leveled any and all things that distracted from
his presence. It did not matter that it was late afternoon.
Everything roasted. The scouring northern wind offered
no solace.

"I am still working on it," she answered, which was true
enough.

"Make sure you get out of the sun," her father cautioned.
"We don't want you getting overheated or fainting."

Fraser quickly took off his hat and began fanning her
with it.

She waved him off. "I'm fine, thank you. And I have
never fainted in my life. I doubt I will begin now." In her
white cotton shirtwaist and navy blue serge skirt, she felt
the heat radiating from the sky above and the granite below,
yet her wide-brimmed straw hat kept most of the glare from
burning too harshly.

"You are a long way from the comforts of home," her
father pointed out. "And we do not want you overtaxing
yourself and falling ill. Fraser, take her back to her tent so
she can get some relief."

"That really is not necessary," London objected, but her
father refused to hear her. Her father and the guard remained behind, while she found herself being lifted out of
the pit and escorted across the stark island. Fraser corralled
her to the Heirs' encampment.

For that's what it was: an encampment of the Heirs of Albion. Now that London knew their name, their purpose, her father, Fraser, and Chernock all spoke more candidly about their organization. Not full disclosure, of course. They still withheld the identity of the Source they sought—what it was, the power it contained. She was fed carefully worded explanations, certain details elided or eliminated, to protect either her delicate feminine sensibilities or the Heirs' agenda. It mattered little. London sensed the men's prevarication in the slight pauses, and the shared, knowing looks. She might not have noticed, before.

Now her eyes were open, and she saw more than she wanted.

"A pretty dreary place, don't you think?" Fraser asked her. "Nothing but rocks, weeds, and half-buried ruins."

They picked their way over uneven ground. Wild thistles and barley grass brushed at the hem of London's skirt, and the hard northern wind tugged at her hat. The only shelter was to be found in the lee of Mount Cynthus, the island's lone geographical feature. Once, Delos had been a place of pilgrimage and wealth. Now, it was harsh and lifeless, blasted by sun and time into a ghost of former glory.

"We share a kinship, this island and I," she murmured.

"What's that?" Fraser blinked at her.

"I rather like it here," London said. "It has a kind of sterile elegance that strips away everything extraneous and false."

He dabbed at his forehead with a linen pocket square. "Uh. Yes. Quite." He tucked the square back into his jacket pocket. "Nearly there. Then you can cool off, get some rest. And when you're feeling better, you can try again with the inscriptions."

London kept silent. The Heirs grew restive, but would not speak to her of their impatience. Instead, both her father and Fraser danced in attendance, proffering folding camp chairs, canteens of water, even peeled apricots. They brought her offerings as if she were a temperamental, sulky goddess in need of appeasement. The Heirs waited with barely contained eagerness for her to divulge the ruins' secrets.

They had arrived at Delos yesterday morning, and, while the camp was being set up, her father and Fraser took her to the ruins located far from the French archaeological team's explorations on the western side of the island.

"No one else knows of this site, yet," her father had informed her. "Only the Heirs, who discovered this place just a few months ago. We've taken pains to keep those Frenchmen away and ignorant."

She could only speculate what those "pains" might have entailed. Bribes, perhaps. Threats of violence. Everything seemed possible to her.

She'd spent the whole of that day and this at the ruins, studying the inscriptions. And as the words revealed themselves to her, everything became less and less clear. Now, on this sun and wind-scoured speck of an island, she was trapped in a miasma of uncertainty and doubt. Loneliness assailed her, as cutting as the wind.

"Here we are," Fraser said. The Heirs' encampment clustered on the southwest edge of Delos, a group of a dozen canvas tents and three wooden tables that all seemed pitifully temporary compared to the worn marble dotting the island. From their camp they could sometimes see the islands Paros and Naxos to the south, depending on the clarity of the air.

At the approach of London and Fraser, armed men from the ship halted in their patrols of the encampment, brandishing their rifles. "It's Fraser and Mrs. Harcourt," Fraser announced in English.

The guards were satisfied, and resumed their sentinel. London's gaze danced toward the weapons. The men held them with confidence and familiarity. They were there to protect her, or so Father and Fraser claimed. But to her, they were prison guards.

And Fraser was taking her back to her cell. London shared her tent with Sally, and, as she and Fraser neared, the maid darted out. A worried frown nestled between Sally's eyebrows.

"Is everything all right, madam?" she asked nervously. Sally had recovered from her seasickness long enough to receive a blistering lecture from London's father about dereliction of duty, and now the maid was as much London's guard as the rifle-toting men.

"Everything is fine," London began, but Fraser cut her off.

"Mrs. Harcourt is overheated. She needs refreshment and rest."

Sally immediately produced a canteen of drinking water and gave it to London with a curtsey. London took a small sip, clearing the dust from her mouth. There was no water on Delos, and if they ran out, the steamship would have to be dispatched to Mykanos to the east to get more. Aside from the weeds, the only life on Delos were the lizards scuttling over rocks and staring with blank, knowing eyes.

"I've got your cot all ready for you, madam," Sally trilled, waving London inside. London stepped across the threshold, pulling the hat from her head.

Fraser stopped at the front flap of her tent. "This is as far as propriety will allow me." He grimaced apologetically.

London nearly laughed. This large, pink-faced man spoke of propriety when he had no compunction robbing magical Sources from across the globe. He killed those who stood in his way.

So did Bennett Day.

"Sally is tending to me," London said, suddenly weary. "Thank you for your consideration, Mr. Fraser."

"Will you . . ." He cleared his throat. "I would like it if you called me by my Christian name, Mrs. Harcourt. London." His skin flushed deeper.

Oh, God. Here was a complication she did not want. She smiled weakly. "That's very . . . sweet of you. It is a little soon, however."

He nodded. "Of course. Of course. Forgive me if I overstepped my bounds."

"There is nothing to forgive. However, if you do not mind, I need a bit of solitude. The heat, you know, makes my head pound." As she said the words, an actual headache began to throb behind her eyes.

"I'll be with your father at the ruins, if you need *anything*." Then he lumbered off, as quickly as a man his size could manage. He had none of the grace and economy of motion that Bennett Day possessed. Thomas Fraser would be a clumsy lover, too. Unlike Day.

No. She shoved him and hot, vivid memories of his kiss from her mind as she set down the stack of papers she carried. They, and her white cotton gloves, went onto a portable desk that held several books, a lantern, and a letter to her mother that London couldn't finish. What could she say? *Having a wonderful time in Greece. Father is responsible for the deaths of thousands. I'm besotted by a man who killed my husband. Wish you were here.*

London sank down into the folding chair set up in front of the desk. She spread out the papers and stared at them, her head cradled in her hands. Behind her, Sally fretted and fussed. A dreadful rock, this Delos, she clucked. Rough men with guns all around. Not a drop of water or life anywhere, and it wasn't fit for ladies to be in such a place. How's she to arrange for a bath for her mistress?

"Sally, where is my edition of Covington's *Dialogues on Hellenic Morphology*? I can't find it in any of these books." The maid stopped her monologue and looked alarmed.

"Perhaps in your luggage, madam." She hurried to the trunk and rifled through it.

London knew Sally wouldn't find the book there.

"It's not here, madam," the maid said, wringing her hands.

A stab of guilt pierced London for what she was about to do. "I really need that book. And I think I left it on the ship. Will you fetch it for me?"

"But," Sally stammered, "that means I'll have to get someone to row me out to where the ship's anchored. Then I have to find the book. And then I have to be rowed back. It could take hours."

"I am sorry," London said sincerely. Then she said with less sincerity, "But you know what a terrible time I've been having with these inscriptions, and I'm certain the Covington will help. It's very important to my father."

"Mr. Edgeworth said I wasn't to leave you alone, not for a moment!"

"There are armed guards everywhere. Not even Zeus himself could harm me."

Sally twisted her apron in her hands, wavering. Finally, she nodded. "I'll go. But, please, don't leave the tent, madam," she pleaded.

"I will stay right here." Which was the truth.

With another nod, Sally hurried from the tent. London heard her yelling in English at one of the guards, and the man's answering grumble, then their receding footsteps as they walked toward the beach.

Alone, at last. Somewhat. There were still guards outside. London marked their boots on the rocky soil as they patrolled. At least she had some moments of privacy in her tent. Ever since her abduction, London hadn't a second to herself. Someone always stood nearby. Sally. Father. Fraser. And the guards. Her only relief was that Chernock made himself absent, spending hours in his tent, muttering about things that London did not care to know, though she was fairly certain he was chanting spells in Ammonite.

In her solitude, London took the pins from her hair and let it tumble down over her shoulders. She rubbed her tight scalp with her fingertips. Looking around, she made sure that the tent flap was down and she was truly alone before unfastening her shirtwaist and revealing her lightweight traveling corset. She slackened the front fastenings, then took a deep breath, as deep as she could allow. Even with her corset loosened, she was still being squeezed.

London picked up one of the sheets of paper and considered the writing upon it. Technically, she had already translated it. But the words themselves made no sense.

Her headache grew like a titan struggling to be born from her skull. She was trapped. If she did manage to decipher the ruins and passed her knowledge on to her father and the Heirs, she colluded with men whose goals she despised. She could try to feed them false information, but eventually they would learn she deliberately led them on a fruitless quest. Then her life was in their hands, and she could only pray that her blood ties to her father would prevent harsh retribution. Up to now, he shepherded her around as if she were a soap bubble, liable at any moment to pop. But the Heirs' agenda might take precedence, and her actions perceived as treason.

She could, as Bennett Day offered, join the Blades, join him. That was outright betrayal. Everything in her life would be lost. She had no idea where he was, anyway, not having seen a trace of him since the night of her abduction. Perhaps it was enough for him to plant the idea of her defection and leave her to play the saboteur, his own hands remaining unsullied.

If she could, she would run away. There was no way off Delos without a boat. Even though London knew how to swim, she hadn't the strength to get far enough to the nearest islands. She would drown, or the Heirs would get to her before she made land. She could go to the French archaeologists. But they either could not or would not help her.

London abruptly rose from the desk and went to her cot. She sat down upon it, her shoulders slumping. How tired she was. She hadn't slept much since her abduction, and when she did manage to sleep, dreams of Bennett Day tormented her. In dreams, he seduced her with honeyed words and caressed her with hands stained in Lawrence's blood. And in those dreams, she laughed at the red prints his hands left on her nude body, laughed because she was free, he had freed her from her marriage. Then guilt and horror and desire woke her and she would lay in bed, shivering.

The headache and heat pressed down on her. She could barely keep her eyes open. London stretched out on the cot, slipping off her shirtwaist. Only Sally would come in, and Sally had seen London in all states of undress. The minimal air in the closed tent cooled the skin of her arms, her upper chest. If only she had true privacy, she'd strip off her clothes entirely and feel the afternoon heat on her bare skin. She saw herself clambering naked over the rocks of Delos, an Oread, free from everything but her connection to the earth.

London watched the roof of the tent bellow and collapse in the wind. How wonderful to be blown away, blown out to sea, lost like a windflower upon the waves, leaving behind Heirs and Blades and shame and responsibility and desire. A small, rueful smile curved her mouth. Back home in England, she had wanted to experience the world, to come out from the protective cocoon that had been spun around her. Now she was exposed and buffeted on all sides, even from within.

When the gods want to punish you, they answer your prayers.

* * *

He'd snuck into better-guarded places. Even though the Heirs had a dozen men patrolling their camp, they were only mercenaries, taking whatever coin offered them to perform a multitude of crimes. No one had any expertise. No pride in their work. Pitiful, really.

All Bennett had to do was wait until dark. From his vantage behind a granite boulder, he watched, learning the guards' patterns. The maid left the tent for the first time since he'd begun his surveillance. He wondered how London had managed that. It was clear London was precious cargo to the Heirs. At all times she was watched. And his eyes were yet another that followed her wherever she went.

As difficult as it had been to put London on that boat and send her back to her father, having her so close by but unreachable systematically drove him mad. It wasn't like him. He generally enjoyed prolonging his gratification. Not indefinitely, but enough to make the consummation that much sweeter.

Ever since he'd kissed her—and, holy God, did she kiss him back—he'd become a man on the verge of obsession. He wanted her mouth again, to touch her beneath the fabric of her clothing. He needed to hear her voice, low and melodious. Even stranger, he wanted to *talk* with her. He enjoyed pillow talk and flirtation as much as the next libertine, but nothing communicated so well as two bodies. Yet, the times he'd conversed with London Harcourt brought him a kind of pleasure he had never experienced, not from talk alone.

By now, she would have learned the truth from Edgeworth.

He'd concern himself with that later. Night fell. No lantern went on inside London's tent, but she did not leave.

She must be asleep. The maid hadn't yet returned when Edgeworth and Fraser came into the camp. After Edgeworth poked his head into London's tent and was assured she was still in there, the Heirs, including their loathsome sorcerer, gathered around a table for their evening meal. Their voices drifted up to him over the sounds of cutlery on enameled tin plates. He heard his own name, the names of several other Blades, but little he could distinguish, not without help. Catullus Graves was tinkering on a listening device back in Southampton, and Athena's magical skills were in use camouflaging their boat as it lay in anchor nearby. So there was nothing for him to do but wait for the perfect moment.

Bennett deciphered both codes and darkness. He had a way with shadows, ever since he was a boy, completely at home within them, while most others embraced bright daylight. In darkness, he found pockets of space, niches through which he fit himself like a key into a lock. Perhaps it was its own form of magic. He didn't question it. When the time was ripe, he moved forward, dissolving into the night.

His boots made no sound as he edged closer to London's tent. The guards paced back and forth, rifles ready, eyes piercing the darkness. Only a breath of a moment, the smallest lacuna as the guards passed, and Bennett crept past them. Under the heavy canvas of the tent. He slid inside, exhaling, then smiled. Almost as delicious as easing into a woman.

The close air inside the tent smelled of sleeping woman, of London. Sweet and spicy. His body tightened, knowing she was near.

His eyes had already adjusted to the dimness, so he could see everything plainly in the tent. The desk, the trunks and books. Two cots. One empty. London lay across the other.

Soft and low, she breathed in the rhythm of slumber. Bennett stole his way to stand beside her, gazing down at her. She dreamt, the fans of her eyelashes gently flickering as she moved through the space of dreams. Her mouth pursed, released. His throat constricted. He was a lucky, lucky son of a bitch. He'd done nothing in his life to earn the privilege of seeing London Harcourt sleep, for she was as lovely and seductive as a sylph.

Bennett sank down to his knees.

She lay on her back, her hair loose about her shoulders in waves of silk, one arm upraised and curved around her head in a gesture of unconscious grace. Upon her stomach curled her other hand, rising and falling with her breath. The forms of her legs shifted underneath the fabric of her skirt. In the quiet of the tent, the intimate sound sent excruciating pleasure shooting through him.

Her shirtwaist had been cast off. Above the waist, she wore only her chemise and a lightweight corset. His mouth watered. He wanted fiercely to lick the skin of her bare, pale shoulders, the honeyed expanse of flesh above the chemise's neckline, delve his tongue into the shadowed valley between the small, perfect rounds of her breasts. His fingers twitched, desperate to finish unfastening her corset, peel it away to reveal the woman underneath. She would be warm and pliant yet firm.

He could take her, now, as she slept in this tent. Slip his hands up her skirt, between her legs, tease her into slick readiness before he slid his aching cock into her. Her orgasm would wake her just in time for his release.

You're a bastard and a cad, Ben, he thought. *And you picked the worst time to cultivate scruples. Idiot.*

Instead of putting his lips to hers, he covered her mouth with his hand. Her eyes opened immediately, her body tensing.

"They're just outside," he whispered.

When she nodded, he removed his hand and craved the feel of her lips against his palm again. He moved back slightly as she swung her legs around, sat up, and looked at him. For a moment, they each did nothing but stare at the other.

"I am surprised to see you here." Her words were barely audible.

"You thought I'd toss the world's problems into your lap and skip away to my next seduction."

When she did not answer, he knew she entertained that very possibility.

"Think what you like of me as a man." He eased from kneeling into a ready crouch. "But I'm also a Blade. We have codes and honor."

"Honor enough to kill."

So. She knew. He refused to look away. "If we must. The Blades hold life sacred, but there are times when we've no choice."

"The needs of the many, et cetera." Even in a whisper, her voice cut. There was a new hardness in her that hadn't been there a few days ago. "When did you know?" she asked. "Was it in the marketplace in Monastiraki? The garden of the hotel? Did it amuse you to flirt with the widow of the enemy you had slain?"

"After I left you in the garden," he said. "I heard you with your father and Fraser. That's when I knew."

She tipped up her chin. "On the caique. You said nothing about it. You . . . kissed me, knowing." She neared a shattering point, her words were so brittle.

"We made the gods jealous with such a kiss." And carved him apart, but he hadn't minded the sacrifice, not at all, and that surprised him.

"You killed Lawrence."

He nodded.

"Why do you not defend yourself?"

"Because it's done. And it had to be done."

London glanced down and noticed she wore no shirt. She quickly stood and grabbed the shirtwaist. She tightened the fastenings of her corset, then slid her arms into the sleeves, saying, "What a wonderful thing it must be, to be a man. To act and damn the consequences." She began to button the shirt with quick, precise fingers.

He also rose to his full height and stalked to her. "Every day I live with the consequences."

"While women like me live without their husbands, their fathers and brothers." Finished buttoning, she tucked the shirt in, sealing herself off.

"That's right," he answered, clipped. His anger surprised him. He never got angry. "And you're right in the middle of them, giving them a soft place to lay their heads after a hard day of thievery and subjugation and murder."

She turned away. A palpable hit. Yet he took no pleasure from it.

He saw, draped over a corner of the desk, the gold scarf he'd tied around her waist in Monastiraki. She'd kept it, and kept it close.

She saw the direction of his gaze, and flushed.

"London," he said.

"They were wrong, you know." She fiddled with the books on the desk, aligning them. "They believed I could translate the ruins, brought me all the way to Greece. But I can make no sense of them." She waved at the laid-out papers. "The words have come, yet they tell me nothing." She gave a harsh rasp that might have been a laugh. "So the joke is on everyone, especially me."

He suppressed the urge to put his hands on her shoulders, comfort her. Instead, he said, "Show me."

She pushed the papers into his hands, then crossed her arms over her chest and leaned against the desk, facing him.

For some moments, the only sounds came from outside the tent as his most hated enemies ate their supper of roast lamb, laughed, and talked of astronomy. A revolver was holstered on Bennett's belt. He could simply walk outside and start shooting. The guards would kill him, of course, but not before he took out at least Edgeworth and Fraser. Without them, especially Edgeworth, the Heirs would be crippled, giving the Blades a much-needed advantage.

But he'd spoken the truth to London. Blades had a code. And it did not condone deliberate, callous murder. No matter what London Harcourt believed.

He studied the papers and her feminine but purposeful handwriting. What she had translated created sentences, yet they were as opaque as ebony. *Voices split cypress. Old chorus grasps water. The dolphin pathway sings.*

"A riddle," he said. He handed her the papers. "Blades see them often, searching for Sources. Damn ancients loved their riddles. Nothing better to do with their time."

"Then perhaps the Blades can solve this riddle, for I cannot." She set the papers down, and her expression was closed off as she turned her eyes to Bennett. "You can't stay. Sally will be back any moment. She'll alert my father if she finds you here."

"Take me to the ruins," he said.

Her eyes flew to his. "Why? You've seen everything."

"I need to see the ruins, themselves."

She stared at him, shuttered and unreachable. He suspected she would refuse him. Then, after a pause, she said, "Guards are everywhere. I don't know how you got here, but it's impossible for two of us to get by unnoticed."

"I accept your challenge." His smile had no warmth, but it proved to him that he was still himself, the man who smiled at impossibilities.

* * *

He was confident, she less so. London donned her dark gray jacket to hide the whiteness of her shirtwaist. She denied him the intimacy of watching her put up her hair, leaving it loose around her shoulders and down her back. She had long passed the point of decorous behavior—it mattered not at all, not out on this lonely scrap of rock, surrounded by murderers and scoundrels.

They hunkered together in the darkness of her tent. Day turned his head to the side, as if listening to the night, his eyes far off but focused. To signal readiness, he held up a hand. She remembered the feel of it against her mouth, the rough palm to her lips as she woke. She had not been afraid, for she knew his smell and taste at once, and thought herself a fool for the comfort his presence brought. Now she crouched with him, waiting to spring from her prison, waiting for a moment of opportunity that only he could sense.

Something changed. London could not tell the difference from one second to the next, but suddenly Day nodded at her and held up the canvas wall, ushering her out. Her father, Fraser, and Chernock sat around a campfire, smoking cigars. The fire flickered gold and red light over the rocks, casting long, demonic shadows. A nightmare landscape in which she would surely be caught, if not by her father, then by the men with rifles who never seemed to tire. But Day took her hand, lacing his long fingers with her own, and drew her away into the night like Hades claiming Persephone as his netherworld bride. No one heard them leave. She let out the breath she held.

A crust of moon turned the rocky plains of Delos into the bottom of the sea. She and Day swam quickly through the silvered air, and he held her tight when she misjudged a distance and stumbled in her dainty, useless lady's boots. His grip was strong, sure, deceptively trustworthy. Without him, she felt sure she would drift into the current, but she wanted her own ballast.

She whispered direction, expecting at any moment the sounds of the Heirs shouting, gunfire, pursuit. Yet Day had taken the night for his own, possessed it, and they slipped through hollows of time toward the ruins. Here and there lay scattered relics of ancient holy temples, a statue's dismembered torso, a cluster of stones marking a long-vanished road.

"This is it," she whispered when they reached the ruins.

Within the excavated pit, the columns gleamed white as bones. Day leapt down into it, then reached up to help her. His hands clasped her waist as he easily bore her weight. Her body slid against his on her descent. He was as solid and lean as she remembered, yet she felt as though she'd barely comprehended its potential. His eyes gleamed in the darkness, fastening onto hers.

She pulled away when her feet touched the ground. Every space felt too close, even this one.

"Have you a lantern?" she asked.

"Better," he said.

From inside his jacket, he produced a small brass cylinder. In the dimness, London saw two little glass compartments within the cylinder, and a tiny knob between them. The glass compartments held some kind of liquid, and, when Day turned the knob, a few drops from one compartment dripped into the other. He tightened the knob, then shook the cylinder. The liquid within one glass compartment began to glow an eerie green.

London marveled. "Magic?" she asked quietly.

"All science. I can't claim ownership of the idea. It's the work of Catullus Graves."

"Another Blade?"

"Our genius in residence."

In the cylinder's light, the pit gleamed acidic green, otherworldly, and the columns seemed luminescent. Spectral light turned the precise planes of Day's face into a warrior's mask. She felt herself in some faerie king's derelict palace, and Day the deposed ruler come to claim his birthright. She shivered, then reminded herself he was only a man.

He stepped toward the columns, holding the brass cylinder aloft. "The writing's on every side." His hands gently touched the marble, feeling the inscriptions.

"Yes, but no matter how I've arranged the sentences, they make no sense."

Day stepped back, his eyebrows in thoughtful downward angles. Backing farther away, he slowly circled the columns, edging sideways in a clockwise direction. His movements held an animal fluidity that was impossible not to watch. She almost believed he had been created as a torment just for her.

"What are you doing?" she asked.

"Finding the viewing point."

"The what?"

His words punctuated his movements. "Damned ancients." He edged farther. "Always putting in some little catch. Can't make it"—another shift to the side—"easy on a fellow. They especially loved. Tricks of the eye. Wait. Yes. There!" He stopped, standing on the other side of the columns. "Come and see."

London hurried over to him. She stood beside him and stared at the columns. She expected revelation, but was disappointed. "They look the same as before."

He put his hands upon her shoulders and pulled her closer. She stiffened. "Easy," he murmured. "I'm not going to ravish you." Then he added in an undertone, "Yet." He positioned her so she stood in front of him, though he kept his hands upon her shoulders, and his body warmed hers through the layers of her cotton clothing. "Now, look."

She did. And could not stop her slight gasp.

The words had arranged themselves.

"I didn't think you could read this dialect," she said.

"I can't. But I know a deciphered code when I see one. Tell me what it says."

She read, *"Upon the island in the form of a dolphin, find there the stream that sings. Its voice will guide you farther to the terrible waterborne gift of the golden god."*

"'Terrible gift,'" he echoed, wry. "Of course. They're never happy little trinkets."

"It was there the whole time," she said in wonderment. She turned slightly to consider him and knew she looked reluctantly impressed. "You're much cleverer than you look."

"I hear that often." He chuckled, then grew more contemplative. "But it was you who unlocked the words. A capital partnership, you and I."

That was true. Even beyond him discovering the ruins' viewing point and her translation, they shared an even exchange of ideas, neither in command of more than the other. Unlike her father and Fraser, Day did not treat her like a breakable bauble, nor did he consider her gift with language to be an unearned aberration. But she did not feel he respected her. He hoarded knowledge. He'd known the truth about Lawrence's death and had said nothing to her. And, there was no way around it: he was a killer. A man who killed other men.

"Sometimes," was all she allowed him.

Day suddenly frowned. He took a piece of heavy cloth from his pocket and wrapped it around the brass cylinder, cutting off its light. London's eyes could not adjust fast enough. Darkness swallowed them. She felt his hand on her wrist, pulling her somewhere, and she had no idea what was happening.

Then she heard it. A man's footsteps running in their direction. The glow of a torch dawned over the lip of the pit, and then there was Thomas Fraser, a burning torch in one hand, a revolver in the other.

"London! We've been looking everywhere for you!" Fraser glared at Bennett Day. "So it's you, Day," he sneered. "Might've known if there was a woman involved you'd come sniffing around." He aimed the gun at Day.

London tried to pull Day toward the nearest wall of the pit so he might climb to safety, but he abruptly released her wrist. She lunged for him and grabbed only air. He wove through the columns toward Fraser. Fraser fired at him, and chips of marble from the columns and granite from the pit flew into the air. She clapped her hands over her ears from the awful sound of the gunshots, so different from the muffled pops of hunting rifles she'd heard before on her family's Somerset property. A whiz and pop next to her head had her crouching low, shielding herself. Gravel rained down on her.

"Watch the ricochet, idiot," snarled Day. He drew his revolver and fired back, causing Fraser to duck and hold off his own gunfire. Day ran straight for the pit wall at Fraser's feet, and, in motion too quick for her to see, leapt up the wall and grabbed Fraser's ankles. Before Fraser could kick him away, Day pulled on his legs and the other man tumbled into the pit. His torch and gun followed.

Flickering torchlight revealed the forms of Day and Fraser locked in combat. They struggled for Day's revolver, and it went spinning away. Each man threw punches, drove elbows into stomachs, and struggled for dominance. London gaped. She'd never before seen two men fight, not like this. Once, she'd spied upon her brother training in pugilism, but that seemed genteel compared to what she saw now. This meant death. Vicious, deliberate death. And Fraser and Day knew what they were doing, both were skilled fighters. Clothing ripped. They swore. They drew blood.

Fraser was bigger than Day, but Day had speed and precision. They pummeled each other without mercy, scrabbling in the dirt, grunting in pain and anger. One of them would die if something wasn't done.

Locked together in combat, both men froze when they heard the sound of a revolver's hammer being cocked. Looking up, they saw London with the gun in her hands, pointing it in their direction. She'd never held a firearm in her life, and hadn't counted on how heavy it was. She struggled to keep her hands steady. The heaviest thing she'd ever held was a huge seventeenth-century tome on Parthian.

"Stop," she said.

Fraser smirked, while Day looked grim and taut, knowing it was very likely she might shoot him, her husband's killer.

"Very good, London," Fraser said. "Your father should be here in a moment. We'll hold this bastard until he gets here."

Yet when Fraser pushed away from Day, London kept the revolver trained on Fraser.

A minute easing of Day's expression, but something black and horrible twisted Fraser's face as realization dawned.

"You little bitch," he spat.

Day's fist into Fraser's face stopped the words and sent Fraser sprawling back into the dust. Fraser flopped back, motionless, while blood from his mouth spattered onto his grimy shirtfront.

London lowered the revolver, shaking. Day found his gun and holstered it. He kicked dirt onto the torch, extinguishing it, then appeared at her side. It took him a moment to pry her fingers loose from the handle of the weapon. He tucked it into the other side of his belt. Before she could breathe, he pressed a hard, fast kiss to her mouth.

"Brave Amazon," he murmured.

Sounds of more footsteps and voices shouting sliced the air. Men from the ship. Her father.

"Come on," Day said. He sprang up the side of the pit and quickly pulled her up after him. As soon as her feet touched the ground, he took her hand, and they ran.

"London!" her father roared behind them.

She did not stop. That volume of her life was over, the covers closed and the book burnt. An unknown fate yawned before her in the darkness. With Bennett Day at her side, she kept running into the blank, unwritten future.

Chapter 6

At Sea

Bennett ran through the small waves that lapped the rocky beach, London Harcourt in his arms. She had her own arms loosely, impersonally around his neck, and kept her gaze fixed firmly ahead. The caique bobbed at anchor. Bennett could not actually *see* the boat, thanks to Athena, but he knew where it was supposed to be. Shouts and the sounds of pursuit neared.

The water splashed around his boots, then up to his thighs, and the back of London's skirt grew soaked despite his efforts to keep her dry.

"You can't carry me and swim," London said with a surprisingly level voice. "But I don't think I can get very far on my own."

"Not swimming," he said.

"Then where the hell are you going? There's nothing out there but water."

He smiled grimly to himself at her coarse language. It didn't take much to strip away the ladylike polish to find the wicked woman beneath. But what such a woman might be capable of, he didn't know. He expected at any moment that she would turn on him like a cornered cat, raking him with her claws.

"Don't trust appearances," he advised. He ran a little farther into the water, then, with a small *oof*, they knocked into the hull of the caique, or where Bennett assumed the caique was supposed to be. It certainly felt like it.

"Brought some friends, I see," Athena's voice said from somewhere above them. "Always so popular. Come, I will help."

London started when Athena's hand appeared from the air. Her surprise did not last long, and she took the offered assistance to clamber over the rail of the cloaked boat. Bennett watched her disappear into the shielding magic, her trim ankles vanishing last into the middle of the air. He did so love his work.

The calloused hand of Nikos Kallas emerged to help pull Bennett aboard. Bennett grasped the captain's hand, using it for leverage as he climbed on board, and he felt a buzzing in his head and bones as he crossed the border of Athena's magic. Once on the boat, the caique became visible to him, with London, Athena, and Kallas standing on deck. Athena looked pale from holding the spell for so long.

"You know how to sail?" demanded Kallas.

"Only a bit," answered Bennett. He glanced around. "We lost our crew?"

Athena said, "They fled to the Frenchmen on the island while you were gone."

Kallas spit over the rail of the boat. "Cowards. Couldn't handle a few crumbs of cannon fire. When I see them again, I'll flay them, use their hides for sails. Now, you and the women must serve as crew." He turned to Athena with a scowl. "Or are your noble hands too soft to tighten a line?"

Loftily, Athena said, "I am not afraid of hard work."

"Good—then make ready to come about," ordered

Kallas. "Day, hoist the mainsail. Sheet it flat. Then I'll raise the foresail."

"Tell me how to help," London said, stepping forward.

"When I say, you'll hoist the jib, but keep them slack," Kallas answered, pointing to the foremost triangular sail. She immediately went to stand ready. Bennett, hoisting the sail, shook his head slightly in amazement. Here she was, on a boat with the man who'd killed her husband, fleeing her family and the only life she had ever known. All done for a good cause. She was poised to work, watching Kallas for his signal.

She did turn when her father's voice boomed from the beach. "What the bloody blazes happened to them?" he bellowed to the men with him. "They were just here! Day took my damned daughter, you sods! I want her back!"

A film of pain glazed her eyes as she stared at him. Bennett started to go to her, but stopped when she steeled herself and turned back to her task. Edgeworth didn't know of his daughter's willing defection, but he'd learn of it soon enough, as soon as Fraser came to. Edgeworth and his minions couldn't see the caique just fifty feet in front of them. Or, at least, they couldn't as long as Athena's magic held.

Chernock stood beside Edgeworth, panting with exertion. The sorcerer peered into the darkness, then smiled coldly. He picked up a rock, muttered something over it, then threw it hard toward the boat. The rock hit the caique's hull with a thud. Athena cried out as if she'd been punched, and Kallas leapt to her side, supporting her as she sank down to the deck. The air hummed, and the caique shimmered.

"There," Chernock crowed. "Simple schoolgirl magic."

He'd broken Athena's spell, and now they were visible. Gunfire split the air, and chips of wood flew from the masts and rail. Bennett dove from his position to grab London, shielding her from the flying bullets.

"Just get us out of here," Athena gasped to Kallas beside her.

He tore himself away to hoist the anchor. As soon as it was raised, he ran to the wheel. "Man the jib!" he shouted to Bennett.

Bennett unfolded himself from around London to grab the sail's line, and she quickly rolled away from him as if to escape his touch. The wind caught in the unfurled sails, pushing the caique out to sea. A bullet tore through the foresail as they came about.

"Careful, you swine!" Edgeworth shouted. "My daughter is somewhere on that boat."

The gunfire slowed, then stopped. Bennett, pulling hard to secure the sails, could only watch as London stood and revealed herself to her father. She solemnly gazed at him from her position at the rail, her hands gripping the wood.

"London!" Edgeworth strode into the surf, but he'd never catch them. They were already making for open water. "Jump, London!"

She stared at Edgeworth, as if memorizing him. She raised a hand. "Good-bye, Father."

Silence. Edgeworth gaped. Confusion creased his face before anguish took its place. Bennett actually pitied the man. Betrayed by his child. The moment stretched out, tight and piercing, as father and daughter held each other's gaze over the surf. Bennett wondered if London might actually jump from the boat and go back to her father, back to the familiar and safe.

London turned away from her father. Tears glistened on her cheeks, yet she did not falter as she helped Bennett with the sails. In the shimmer of night, hair wild, face sparkling with tears, she looked like a heartbroken angel, and Bennett's heart broke with hers. She slipped away from his comforting hand on hers.

Kallas guided the caique deftly through the shoals and

rocks surrounding Delos. Despite the darkness, the captain knew these waters, and soon the deep navy velvet of the sky met the inky black sea uninterrupted, the only sounds from the snap of the sails and the waves slapping against the bow. A strong, fresh breeze gusted, taking them away.

Dawn over the Aegean. It began pearl gray, then the sun broke the eastern horizon, gilding the sky and sea into a white-gold luster. Wisps of coral clouds surfed the bowl of heaven before the air shifted blue and clear. Far-off crests of islands broke the mirrored water like tawny dolphins surfacing, playful and serious. All around was the scent of brine and wind.

And coffee. As Bennett manned the wheel, Kallas brewed strong, bitter coffee over a bronze brazier, using a long-handled *briki* pot to boil the water. He stirred in spoonfuls of ground coffee with the austere ceremony of a high priest. Athena, sitting nearby, couldn't quite hide her approval of his methods or the dark, rich foam that formed in the pot as the coffee brewed. As soon as the foam rose to the top of the *briki*, Kallas divided it into four waiting cups, then poured the coffee itself. He disappeared into the quarterdeck house, then emerged with a painted tin, which he opened and handed around.

"My mother's *koulourakia*," Kallas said as Bennett helped himself to a few buttery pastries. "Good with coffee."

After yielding the helm to Kallas, Bennett moved to take a cup of coffee to London, but Athena intercepted him. She plucked the cup from his hand and gave it to London, casting him a warning look. The witch cautioned him with her eyes. *Stay back.*

An animal is never so dangerous than when wounded.

With a small nod, Bennett paced away, taking his own cup of coffee. He leaned his back against the rail while munching on the pastry and sipping the wonderfully punitive coffee. The morning came to life all around him. A breakfast at sea. Life was full of many small pleasures.

But it was a hard pleasure, darker and more bitter than the coffee. He glanced over at London, seated on the deck with her back against the railing. She stared down at the cup in her hands, swirling the coffee, before taking a sip. She choked, coughed.

"You like it?" Kallas asked.

"It's very . . . assertive," she gasped.

Athena's soft laugh joined Kallas's chuckle before they realized they were laughing together. Each busied themselves with the suddenly complex task of drinking coffee.

Bennett watched London as she nursed her coffee. He wished he hadn't kissed her. He knew now what he was missing, and, having tasted her once, burned to do it again. He had a sudden wish to go back to that moment, when she didn't know who he was and all that had been between them was desire. Now, her anger and uncertainty were palpable things that crouched on the deck, snarling and snapping at any who dared approach.

Yet he couldn't stop himself. He crossed the deck to stand near her. In the dawn light, her hair became caramel and her skin pink-hued ivory. When she turned her eyes up to him, he saw that they were not merely dark brown, but a shifting mosaic of hues, chocolate and amber and even flecks of gold and green.

"Come to pay your respects to the bereaved?" she asked.

He resisted the urge to strike back with his own cutting words, but it was hard. He was used to defending himself against assaults—the physical kind, anyway.

"I will tell your fortune in the coffee grounds," Athena said quickly. She walked over to them and held out her hand. "Finish your cup."

London shut Bennett from her sight as she downed her

coffee in one swallow. She shuddered, then gave the cup to Athena. The witch went into the quarterdeck house, then reemerged with a saucer. Athena placed the saucer over the cup and handed them both back to London.

"Move them both counterclockwise," the witch advised. "Close your eyes and concentrate. Open your mind."

London shut her eyes and followed Athena's guidance. Bennett stared at London, wondering where her mind was taking her, wishing he could be there, in her thoughts.

"Now, flip the cup and saucer over," Athena instructed. "Wait a few moments, but keep your mind focused. Shut out everything around you."

Ideas and feelings flickered across London's face, and, even silent, she radiated a complexity Bennett might never decode. He glanced up to find Athena watching him with something very like pity, making him scowl.

"Open your eyes and turn the cup over again," said Athena. "Remove the saucer."

London did so. Both she and Bennett gazed down into her cup, where thick coffee grounds formed swirls and patterns along the white ceramic. Athena took the cup back from London and stared intently at the inside of the cup. The witch started in surprise.

"What does it say?" London asked.

Even Kallas at the wheel leaned closer to hear Athena's divination.

"Many knots, like the branches of a tree," Athena murmured. "You are deeply enmeshed in a tangled problem. The branches form a bridge, saying that you must make a difficult decision. And I see a man. He beckons to you, he will give you something, something important, but his hands are empty."

"So he has nothing to offer," said London.

Athena shook her head, then gazed directly at Bennett, staking him with a look. "He has more than he realizes."

"Is this a prophecy?" asked Bennett.

"It is what may be."

"And what of certainty?" London asked.

"Nothing is ever certain."

London tipped her head back so she could watch the sky. The sorrowful loveliness of her face hurt Bennett in the center of his chest. "I'm learning that," she said softly.

He ached to touch her, even for a moment. He began to reach for her.

She straightened, drawing about her the mantle of propriety, and he dropped his hand. Then she looked down and saw saltwater whitely drying on her navy skirt. "One thing is certain, my clothes are a disaster. Yet I haven't anything else to wear." Clothing, it seemed, was easier to contemplate than figuring out how to untie the knots tangling her life.

"You are welcome to whatever I have," Athena said.

London gave her a nod of thanks. "That's kind of you. But there's no way for me to pay for anything. I do not have any money." Realization dawned, and it pained Bennett to watch it in her face, the accompanying bleakness that hollowed her out like a glacier's path. "I have . . . nothing."

He tried to bring her back from that abyss. "The Blades take care of their own. We provide whatever's needed. Even clothing."

Her eyes flew to his, and instead of despair, they were filled with a sudden anger. "Including widows' weeds?"

He felt the stab of her words, as much, if not more, than the curved Moroccan knife her husband had tried to gut him with. That wound had faded into a pale line across his right side. Sometimes he forgot about it altogether. He knew just then that London's wounds would last much longer.

"She knows," said Athena.

"She knows," London snapped. "Apparently, she is the last

to know about her husband's murder. And who committed it."
She glared at Bennett, but he refused to back down.

"Me," he said.

"It was not murder," Athena said gently. "It was not deliberately or maliciously done."

London's hurt gaze turned to Athena. "So, you were there, too?"

"No, but I know Bennett and I know our cause. We are soldiers, not murderers. One kills in the heat of battle. The other coldly destroys life."

"Have *you* killed?" London asked Athena.

The witch shook her head. "Thank the Fierce Maiden I have not had to, not yet. But I know it is not lightly done by the Blades. It is not lightly done by Bennett."

London looked away. The ghost of Lawrence Harcourt lingered, hovering over the deck. After a moment, she said in a low voice, "The Heirs will be coming for us, won't they? Fraser. Chernock. My . . . father."

Bennett was glad that, at the least, Harcourt's death could be momentarily overshadowed by more immediate threats. "We'll stay ahead of them," he vowed. "Kallas's boat is a fleet little thing."

"Only Hermes flies faster," Kallas said with a raffish grin from behind the wheel.

"Even so, they will come," said London.

Bennett knew she spoke the truth, but he wasn't deterred. Being a Blade meant living cheek by jowl with the enemy. He was used to it. "Which means we'll find the Source first."

"You're so cocksure," she said.

"Always." That wasn't entirely true—not where she was concerned. With most women, he knew exactly what he wanted from them and usually got precisely that, no more, no less. He might desire their bodies, their company. Sometimes he played the seducer to gain information for the Blades. And when his desire had been met, he could continue on his way and think of each woman as a fond, often salacious, memory. They would take other men into their beds after he had gone, sometimes their husbands, sometimes new lovers. None of which troubled him.

London Harcourt proved to be much more complicated than this. He'd killed her husband. She wasn't a Blade. She wasn't an object of simple lust. She turned him into a walking nerve, aware of her every movement, every emotion. He wanted her, his enemy's widow.

He needed to focus, had to be sharp. He could exert discipline over himself. Hadn't he nearly been starved out when holed up in an abandoned nunnery in Sicily, protecting a Source from the Heirs and their mercenaries? By the time he, Catullus Graves, and Michael Bramfield had killed or chased off the attackers, Bennett had lost almost a stone and was half-dead from thirst. Surely he could handle the torment of having London Harcourt nearby, close but unreachable. But he felt like Tantalus. The kiss he and London had shared had been revelatory, and he wanted more. Wanted and couldn't have, not again. For a handful of moments, she'd been his, and now she was lost.

"We don't even know what we are looking for," she pointed out.

"What did the ruins on Delos tell you?" Athena asked.

London recited what she had translated from the columns: *"Upon the island in the form of a dolphin, find there the stream that sings. Its voice will guide you farther to the terrible waterborne gift of the golden god."*

"Something borne upon the water," Bennett mused. "If the Heirs want it, it must be powerful, and can be used as a weapon."

"What weapon can be carried on water?" London frowned in thought. "Perhaps a ship of some kind."

"Or a machine of war," suggested Kallas. "Like the Trojan Horse."

They all fell silent, considering the multitudes of possibilities. Those ancients never made the journey a smooth one, not where Sources were concerned. Bennett might have appreciated their foresight if he wasn't in a sodding life-or-death race.

Suddenly, Athena jumped to her feet, startling everyone. "Virgin Mother! A weapon of that awful power in the hands of the Heirs . . . they would be invincible. The Blades could do nothing to stop them."

"Athena, you're starting at the end," Bennett said. "Begin at the beginning so we know what the hell you're talking about."

Athena looked horrified. "Greek Fire. That is what the Heirs are after."

Bennett cast back in his mind to the stories of his youth, the tales of adventure his father spun when he'd come into the nursery. "A very old seafaring weapon. It could burn on the water's surface, and couldn't be extinguished."

The witch nodded. "A liquid fire. Used for generations—the Romans had heard of it, and it was said that Greek Fire defended Constantinople from Saracen ships. Then it disappeared."

"I've read of it," London said. "The theory is that it was invented by a Syrian, Callinicus. Many have speculated about its chemical composition. Some said naphtha, resin, burning pitch, quicklime. It is science, not magic."

"That's how Sources hide," Bennett said, "shrouding themselves in easily accepted fact. If the truth was known about such things, like the origins of gunpowder—"

"Gunpowder isn't magic!" London exclaimed.

Bennett said, "Tell that to the Chinese wizard who created it from a Fire Demon."

Her eyes widened in surprise, and a smile tugged at

her mouth as she looked up at him. "I had no idea. It's like another Earth has been found existing just beneath the surface of this one." For a fleeting moment, Bennett and London shared the wonder of discovery, the sheen of adventure, and a reckless happiness careened through him.

Then her smile faded. She remembered who he was, what he'd done. Collecting herself, she asked Athena, "Are we then to believe that this Greek Fire is a Source?"

Bennett wouldn't let himself be shut out so easily. "Makes sense," he said. "*A terrible waterborne gift.* The Heirs would certainly want such a weapon."

"Control of the sea is everything," Kallas added. "If the oceans are yours, the world is yours."

"Then we'll stop them now," Bennett said. "We'll find it first."

"Where?" asked Athena.

"The island in the form of a dolphin," Kallas repeated. "I know this place. On the shore, there is a small church and a tiny village. Mostly goats and rocks. It is a day's sail from here, to the east."

Athena challenged, "Does it have a stream that sings?"

"If it does," Kallas shot back, "it is inland, where I never go. The sea is my home. I haven't got a landlocked palace full of servants and costly baubles, Lady Witch."

Athena's fingers twitched as if she meant to cast an unpleasant spell on the tormenting captain.

"Take us to that island," Bennett said quickly. He didn't want a mollusk for a captain.

Kallas nodded. "I will need help with the sails."

Bennett straightened to give his assistance, but Athena surprised everyone by stepping forward.

"*This* palace-dweller can do it," she sniffed.

Kallas scowled. From a pocket in his vest, he took his pipe and stuck it between his teeth. "Follow me," he growled. "Day, you take the helm. Steer us east by northeast, and mind the wind." Then the captain strode aft with Athena at his heels, mariner and lady determined to show their indifference to each other. It made Bennett smile despite the continued sting of London's anger.

Bennett did as Kallas ordered, manning the wheel. From his jacket, he pulled out the Compass.

"I have to plot our direction, so I'll need you to hold this," he said. When London rose and came to stand beside him, he kept his eyes ahead on their course, but felt her there, just the same. Sharp, pained desire flared in him, their fingers tangling as she relieved him of the Compass. The tips of her fingers were already growing more resilient from use, not quite as soft or pampered as they once had been.

He glanced down at the face of the Compass, marking their position and adjusting the wheel, but it was her hand and her fingers that captivated him.

"This is beautiful," she said, after examining it. "It feels old, weighty."

"All Blades carry a Compass. It's our most precious belonging. We'll defend them to the death."

The implications of London being allowed to even touch such a prized object were not lost on her. "I shouldn't be holding it." She held it out to him.

"The Compass isn't just beautiful. It works, has a use and function. If I kept it closed up all the time, it wouldn't fulfill its purpose."

She was silent for some time, studying the Compass.

"It was him or me, London," he said, his eyes on the horizon. "I picked myself, and the Blades."

"Is it so easy a choice?"

"Never easy."

"You didn't tell me."

"So I was supposed to pay a call on you in your cabin

and say, 'I'm the bloke that killed your husband. Let's have a cup of tea.'"

"Don't be flippant about this," she said, eyes sharp and glittering. "Not this." She began to walk away.

"I need you next to me," he said. At her hard, questioning look, he said, "To hold the Compass."

Slowly, she walked back to him, the open Compass in her hands. Her lips pressed tightly together as she deliberately kept her eyes on the horizon and away from him.

He was not used to apologizing. "I'd never hurt you."

"That would be pleasant to believe."

Anger erupted, barely checked. "Better that you should be a widow than three hundred Nubians should lose their lives," he growled. "That's what your husband did. He killed a whole village for a Source. That Source was used to slaughter thousands in China."

Color drained from her face, leaving her ashen. "I—"

"And you know what's the bloody icing on the biscuit?" His laugh felt like a fist as he pushed it from his lungs. "Even though I had to kill Harcourt in Morocco, the Heirs *still* got their hands on Aisha's Tears and wiped out half the damned populace of the Gold Coast. Your husband died, but his mission was a success. So take some comfort in that, Mrs. Harcourt."

He couldn't look at her, almost afraid of what he'd see.

After a moment, she said, "Hate is such an uncomplicated word. This," she said, gesturing to the air between them, "is much more tangled." She closed the Compass and put it into his hand. "I'm sure you can find your own way."

She went below, leaving him.

Bennett's knuckles whitened on the wheel. He said nothing when Athena approached him.

"Have you considered a career in diplomacy?" she asked.

He shot her a look, but she did not shrink away.

"She will need some distance," Athena said, more gently. When Bennett did not answer, she eventually drifted away to help with the sails.

Bennett opened the Compass and stared down at its face. No matter how long he looked at it, he felt himself utterly lost.

Edgeworth kicked his way around the camp, shattering chairs and tables, throwing the cooking pots, scattering ashes from the fire. The imbecile maid bawled from inside her tent, partly from fear, partly from the slap he'd given her. He'd pawn her off on the French archaeologists later. How the maid returned back to England was not Edgeworth's concern.

Chernock and Fraser stood nearby, as did the guards, all watching him with carefully blank expressions. Edgeworth wanted to smash their faces in with a rifle butt. But he needed men for the mission, so he corralled his rage and unleashed it on inanimate objects. It wasn't very satisfying.

He was being punished. For that's what it was, a punishment, to see the child of his flesh, his lifeblood, who wore short skirts until she came of age, and then white ball gowns and, finally, a wedding dress. He'd coddled her, kept her sheltered from the viciousness and brutality of the world. She had been given more toys and dolls and dresses than any girl could ever need, her whims and fancies indulged—to a point. She wanted to go to university, but she had a governess instead, long past the age that she might learn anything useful. He'd taken great pains to raise her as a model Englishwoman, to instill in her the values of the nation and shape her into Britain's feminine ideal.

He still saw London, her mother's plaything, standing upon the deck of the Blades' boat, not only standing there, but her hand up to bid him good-bye as one might from the compartment of a train sliding out of the station, until noise and smoke carried them away to their destination. In London's case, her destination was betrayal, and he was at the platform knowing that he'd bought the ticket for her journey.

By involving a female, he'd violated the sacred principle of the Heirs of Albion, and now punishment had been meted out. He deserved it.

But he couldn't believe London had betrayed him. It was impossible. He was Joseph Edgeworth. She was his child. Anything other than perfect obedience from his daughter was unthinkable.

Edgeworth stood, panting, in the midst of the wreckage. Finally, Chernock picked his way to him, around the destroyed furniture and shredded tents.

"Day is a Lothario," the sorcerer said. "He obviously seduced the girl. It was no fault of your own."

Edgeworth seized upon this. "Yes—seduced. That has to be the reason. The female will is feeble, no matter her intellect. Even my own daughter is just a woman. Her emotions led her astray." Grim but comforted, Edgeworth felt the cloud of rage dissipate. "Day is a master at manipulating females. Who knows what kind of nonsense he's put into her head?"

Fraser, his face bruised and blood-crusted, grunted. "Next time I see Day, I'll cut his fucking balls off." There were probably scores of men across Europe who'd gladly queue up for the same privilege.

"I could summon a storm," Chernock offered. "Cripple their boat."

"No," Edgeworth said. "I won't put London in peril. I'm certain that if we take her back from Day, away from his influence, she'll see how she had been misled."

Edgeworth did not see the quick, exchanged glances between Chernock and Fraser.

"We need to find out where they're going," Edgeworth continued. "London said she couldn't decipher the ruins, but likely Day had convinced her to lie."

"But what if the Blades get to the Source first?" Fraser asked, plaintive. "The Heirs need it. It took us years to decipher the tablet that led us here."

"*Greek Fire is born of the sun*," Chernock recited. He'd read the tablet, too, many times, and none of the Heirs had been able to determine its significance. Not until the discovery on Delos. Then the pieces began to fall together.

"Greek Fire will give the British Navy unlimited power on the sea," Fraser said. "But without a means to understand the Delos ruins, we're running blind out here trying to find it."

Chernock gave one of his awful smiles. "Gentlemen, don't concern yourself. I've a reliable method of tracking them. All I'll need," he added, drawing a wicked, black-bladed dagger from his belt, "is a little blood."

It was easier to focus on learning to sail than how to live her newfound life. As soon as London began to contemplate what this meant—homeless, friendless, virtually orphaned—she felt a gaping chasm open inside her, and, rather than tumble down into it, she kept herself busy throughout the day. If she could not walk steadily on land, then she vowed to conquer her place on the sea.

The steamships she'd taken from England to Greece, even the smaller ship on which she'd traveled from Athens to Delos, had been noisy machines belching smoke, riding high in the waves. She had thought the sea pretty before, but now, on the elegant caique skimming across the surface of the Aegean, London felt herself tumble into a kind of desperate, lonely love with the glittering sapphire water, the pellucid sky, the white and green islands in scattered handfuls, thrown by an indulgent god. Out here, she could pretend that she was a creature of the elements and nothing else mattered but sun and wind and water. The sea gave her complete freedom, and yet, its endless expanse made her small. She was herself an island, alone in vast, empty waters. This was a new life, and it was sweet and bitter.

Everything would have to be learned. Yet she commanded one realm, that of language. Words in their many shapes and sounds were hers, their power was hers, and she held it tightly as one might clutch at unstrung pearls, hoarding and proud.

Nikos Kallas was a gruff little bull of a man, but an able teacher. He showed them all the parts of the sails and masts, the multitude of ropes and lines, how to judge a good wind and the best ways to ride it. They each took a turn at the wheel, even Athena and London, but it was the captain's privilege to man the helm, for he loved his boat with an intractable pride and would suffer few to tame her.

In the bright glare of the day, Kallas and Athena squabbled over the god Zeus. Athena considered him a remorseless philanderer whose peccadilloes cost untold human suffering. Kallas insisted the god had a natural right to share his divine glory with as many women as he liked, and Hera's demands for fidelity were too great. Neither the lady nor the captain seemed willing to concede.

London listened to them as she practiced tying knots with a length of rope she'd begged from Kallas. Figure eights, monkey fists, Turk's heads. Hitches and splices, each with their own personalities. She worked, cross-legged on the deck, until her hands turned red and throbbed, but she would not stop, not for a moment, because to stop meant being alone with her thoughts.

"Be careful of your hands, or they'll turn to pulp."

She looked up at Day, then back down at the rope in her hands, feeling burned by his image as he stood close by. His jacket and waistcoat were gone in the heat of the afternoon, so he wore only snug trousers, braces, tall boots, and a shirt, open-necked and sleeves rolled up, revealing the lean muscles of his throat, the planes of his upper chest, powerful forearms. The wind tousled his dark hair like a paramour.

"The knots have their own language," she said. "And I will learn it." She hoped he would mistake the flush in her cheeks for the effects of the sun.

He took the rope from her and began to coil it the way Kallas had shown them. She could not stop watching the movement of Day's long, nimble hands, those hands that were so deft but also potently masculine.

"Can't see Joseph Edgeworth encouraging and overseeing his daughter's linguistic studies," he said. "I thought the Heirs liked their women strictly decorative."

"They do. I am . . ." she began, then corrected herself, "*was* an anomaly. No one knew. It was my secret. I taught myself."

"How?"

"It started as an accident. I found a Latin book belonging to my father—must have been about five or six. Tacitus's *Annales*. That's where it started."

"Bloody hell," Bennett swore. "When I was five, I was busy putting snails down my brother's collar. Not reading Roman historians."

London could not stop the smile that curved her mouth, but she did not let it live long. She focused on the red flesh of her palms. "I scrounged for more books and moved on to Greek, ancient and modern, then the usual assortment. French, German, Italian, Spanish. But I liked the ancient languages best. As soon as I got pin money, I'd spend it on books, even send away for them. I told my mother and Lawrence they were etiquette manuals."

"And no one ever found out."

"Not until a month ago."

"Your father."

She nodded. "He said it was for archaeology, and I believed him." The clarity of loneliness surrounded her, made her tiny and lost.

"It *is* a kind of archaeology," Bennett said, and his voice anchored her before she drifted away entirely. She wondered if he knew that, if it was deliberate, but didn't want to think so. "The Heirs search out and dig up the world's magic, and the Blades try and stop them, keep the magic safely hidden."

She unfolded her legs and stood, putting her face into the wind, glad that she was ruining her prized porcelain complexion, a relic of her old life. "Magic truly exists. It's still so difficult to believe. I'd never seen it before I came to Greece."

He let the rope unwind, then began to coil it again. Somehow, it comforted her to know that he needed to keep busy, just as she did. "You've seen magic before, everyone has."

"Of course I haven't," she said at once.

"That's even harder to believe. There must have been some time that you saw something, something you believed was magical, but it was explained away. It happened when you were a child, I'd wager."

"Why as a child?"

"Children are open to magic." He took one end of the rope and began to tie it in a simple square knot. "They're newer to this world; their minds aren't shut and demanding logic like adults."

A gleam of recollection flickered through her mind. "Wait . . . I think . . ." She tried to grasp it.

He stopped his busywork. "A memory?"

"Perhaps," she said slowly. "I think that when I was a child, I thought a pixie used to visit me at night." Speaking of it sharpened the remembrance. She spoke more eagerly. "It had dragonfly wings, and its skin was the color of opals. It wore a tiny cap decorated with a hummingbird feather."

"Did it have a name?"

London searched the caverns of her memory. "I believe . . . it called itself Bryn."

His sudden laughter made her start. "Bryn! That old gnat!"

"You know it? The pixie?" She stared at him.

"Know him? Bryn Enfys has been keeping an eye on the Heirs for centuries." Day shook his head, chuckling. "He'd deliver reports to the Blades' headquarters in Southampton, and always demanded a thimble of whiskey for his trouble."

"An odd coincidence," she murmured. "Him coming to visit me."

"Not so coincidental," he said, more seriously, "if you're the daughter of an Heir."

She darkened. "He urged me to run away. He said there was something evil in my home and that I had to flee from it."

"Bryn knew," he said, quiet. "He knew you were better than your family and the Heirs."

"I wonder, though. What might have become of me, if I had heeded his advice?" She looked up at him. "I wouldn't be here, now." But whether that was a good thing or something to make her sad, she could not determine.

Day slipped the coil of rope over one shoulder, then took her hands in his own, keeping her reddened, chafed palms turned up. He looked at her, and she could not turn away, because she saw that here on the water, his eyes were the exact crystalline color of the sea, liquid, yes, but deeper and hotter than the sea, and he had a way of looking at her as if she, and only she, existed and it was enough for him.

"Bryn tried," he said, his voice warm brandy and just as intoxicating. "He tried to liberate you. For years, you've been lied to, deceived, but now your eyes are open. It's up to you alone how to live, what choices you make. You can choose anything, do anything. You're free."

Then, he carefully lowered her hands and walked away. She stared at the space where he had been and began to truly feel, for the first time, that the sea was not so much empty as it was without limits.

Chapter 7

Natural Wonders

London squeezed herself into one of the two small cabins below deck. She had the unenviable task of trying to undress and dress herself in a space no bigger than a closet. She kept banging her elbows into the bulkheads. The cabin held a berth wide enough for a single man, a tiny table, and no mirror. Clearly, pride in appearance wasn't high on a seaman's list of priorities.

"And how does it fit?" Athena's voice said outside the door.

"Depends," London said, emerging into the narrow passageway, "on whether I want to look like I am shrinking. If that is my goal, then I would say we succeeded admirably."

Athena covered her mouth, but her laugh escaped anyway. "It is a trifle . . . loose."

"Loose!" London plucked at the sagging bodice of the gown borrowed from Athena. "I've room enough to smuggle puppies."

"A whole litter," Athena agreed. "I am sorry."

"Don't apologize. It is not your fault that my bosom is deficient."

Athena scoffed. "Not deficient! You are slim, like a beautiful river reed. While I," she continued, glancing down at herself, "am built like one of those Cretan snake goddesses, all breasts and hips. So vulgar."

"Womanly, not vulgar," London disputed. She added, with a sly, female smile, "And it seems that our captain approves."

"Bah!" Athena threw up her hands in dismissal. "Of course he likes the large breasts—he is a coarse boor who would rut like an animal if given the chance." The witch's gaze suddenly went far off, considering this very prospect. Her dusky cheeks flushed before she shook her head as if to clear it of a particularly robust image.

London smothered a smile and busied herself with adjusting the bodice of the gown. It was a simple but exquisitely made day gown of blue and white striped cotton with a charming bow at the waist. On Athena it would be lovely, but London was several inches shorter than the witch, and considerably less curvaceous.

"If you've a needle and thread, I might be able to make a few temporary adjustments," London offered.

"No need for such tedious work," Athena said with a dismissive wave. "Let me see." She peered closer at the sleeves. "Too long here." Her fingers brushed over the cuff.

London started when the cuff shrank back to the perfect length. "Good God! Is that magic?"

The witch laughed. "Arachne's Art, something the Galanos women have practiced for generations. Excuse me, I am not trying to get fresh." Her hands lightly trailed over London's bosom, and the bodice shifted until it fit London's more modest figure.

"Seems quite convenient."

"It is. It allows us a considerable amount more freedom than other women." She knelt and took the hem of the dress between her fingers. "We are not tied to our needlework. Or any man."

"How wonderful that must be," London said earnestly.

Athena glanced up, her eyes grave. "Galanos women value our independence. We make our own paths in this world. If there is something we want, we take it, and do not apologize. Especially not to a man."

London said, rueful, "Most women aren't lucky enough to be born into the Galanos family."

"That is true. The majority are yoked from birth. However," Athena added, giving the hem a tug, "*you* are now free to choose your path and do as you like. You have the gift of ultimate freedom."

London watched the hem of the dress raise until it was the exact height she needed. If the seamstresses of Paris ever found out about Arachne's Art, anarchy would follow. The fashion houses of France would fall just as the Bastille did.

"I am not certain it's a gift," she admitted.

Athena rose to face London. "It is," she said fiercely. "You are finally the only person in control of your life. That does not mean it will be easy, but whatever mistakes you make, the injuries you suffer, and your victories are *yours* to own."

The witch's vehemence surprised London. It had seemed that little could disturb her calm. But London's doubt had. "Including the affairs of my heart?"

"Especially those." More placid, Athena brushed the hair back from London's forehead, much as an older sister might. "Bennett can be reckless and infuriating," she said quietly. "But his heart is good."

London's own heart contracted just to hear his name spoken. "You know him well."

"Over ten years have we been friends. And not once have I ever seen him behave the way he does around you. It is more than desire."

"What else can it be, if not just desire?" London asked.

Athena shook her head. "You will have to discover that on your own."

London understood. "And what about you? Even an independent woman has her needs."

Athena's smile was just a little melancholy, almost wistful. "I do. But it is almost impossible for me to find a man who can abide by my terms. I require absolute freedom. I leave before he makes demands, before the heat of our animal desires cools into mere toleration. So I go, and he goes, and everyone is satisfied."

"Typical," snorted a man's voice.

Athena and London watched Nikos Kallas descend the companion ladder leading from the quarterdeck house to below decks. He stalked up to Athena and glowered at her, filling the narrow space of the passageway with his presence.

"How like a high-born woman." He scoffed. "Cold, like the northern seas."

"I am *not* cold," Athena challenged, drawing herself up. "I am sensible."

"Sex isn't sensible. It isn't a polite business arrangement. For you, sex is shaking hands and agreeing on the price of fish." Mocking, he stuck out his hand as if offering it to seal a bargain.

London looked on, fascinated, as Greek man and woman stood toe-to-toe, glaring at each other. They seemed to have forgotten that London was even there, observing everything.

"Would you prefer if I shrieked and pulled at my hair when it is time to part?" Athena shot back. "Demanded vows of love when there are none to give? I would rather keep my pride."

Kallas pointed at her with the stem of his pipe. "This isn't about pride. It's about the beast of desire. I tell you this, Lady Witch, once I get a woman in my bunk, she won't want to leave."

With that parting salvo, the captain stormed past Athena,

down the passageway to the cargo hold. London watched him go, then she turned back to Athena. The witch stared at the spot where Kallas had stood, her lips pressed tightly together, breath coming fast. She was furious.

Or fiercely attracted. London was beginning to realize that it was almost impossible, sometimes, to tell the difference.

With London and Bennett Day, however, things were much more complicated than navigating the twin poles of anger and desire. It was up to London to find her way.

Four men hunched over a map in the steamer ship's wheelhouse. Overhead, a lantern swayed with the rocking of the ship, casting its sulfurous light in arcs, back and forth. Shadows swung like weighted pendulums, almost as dark as the night outside. The men did not speak, but watched the map, one on each side of the table on which it spread.

Across the surface of the printed sea, moving east by northeast, rolled a single drop of blood. A dark garnet, moving not with the roll of the ship, but under its own power, deliberate and steady. The blood sought something, some place.

"Where are they headed?" Edgeworth demanded of the steamer's captain. "They're moving away from the Cyclades."

The Greek captain shrugged. "There are many islands in the Aegean. Thousands. Some never make it on to a map."

"Lost, do you think?" asked Fraser.

Edgeworth gnawed on the end of his cigar. "No, they are too direct. They know where they're going. I just wish we did, too."

"Rest easy." Chernock smiled down at the map. "The

Bloodseeker Spell will lead us to your daughter. And if she knows where to find Greek Fire, then we shall know, too."

"My ship is faster than any caique," the captain said. "We lost some time at the beginning, but I assure you, we'll overtake them. Tomorrow morning, no later."

"I'm holding you to that," Edgeworth snapped. He stalked from the wheelhouse, with Fraser close at his heels. Both men stood on deck, staring out at the darkness. The glowing end of Edgeworth's cigar made red, angry trails as it journeyed to and from his mouth. Fraser clasped his hands behind his back and pretended to study the stars, while his mind chugged along like the steamship.

Fraser considered himself a brave man. He'd faced storms, riots, murderous natives, disease. God knew how many damned Blades he'd had to tangle with over the years, with the scars to prove it. He prided himself on never backing down from a mission, stepping over or on anyone who got in his way. He feared almost nothing. Except Joseph Edgeworth.

The Edgeworths stood as the backbone of the Heirs of Albion. Some ungodly number of generations ago, an Edgeworth forefather helped establish the group's headquarters in central London. And ever since then, an Edgeworth sat in the inner circle, wielding influence and power the likes of which a monarch could only dream about. Joseph Edgeworth could make an Heir's life hell, if that Heir fell out of favor. Either death, or the wish for death. There was no part of the world free from Edgeworth's influence. Should he take a disliking to someone, they'd find themselves with a bullet in the eye or a knife in the belly. Not by Edgeworth's hand, of course, but his intent would be there, just the same.

Yet, if a man wanted to make a name for himself in the Heirs, he could do no better than ingratiating himself with the Edgeworth family. Wealth. Influence. Respect. Bestowed and granted in abundance.

That's exactly what Fraser had intended when he planned on courting London Harcourt. There'd be no sweeter role for an Heir to play than Edgeworth's son-in-law. Lawrence Harcourt's death was a blessing for Fraser and any other able-bodied young Heir. It didn't hurt that London Harcourt was damned pretty, but Fraser would've fucked a sow if it meant gaining Edgeworth's approbation.

Damned bitch, Fraser fumed. He could have been in the catbird seat, if not for her whorish ways. Best to take a philosophical approach, though. He wouldn't have wanted a cuckolding trollop for a wife.

Still, he could ally himself with Edgeworth now, slut daughter or no.

"What will you do, sir, when we catch up with them?" Fraser asked.

Edgeworth took a long draw off his cigar and exhaled the smoke. "Kill Day," he said simply. "And that other Blade, the Galanos bitch. Chernock recognized her on Delos. He might like to toy with her for a bit, though, before we kill her. She's a born witch, and bound to know some new magic."

Fraser took a breath, and risked, "And . . . and London?"

The older man answered at once, "Once she sees how she'd been beguiled by that seducer," Edgeworth said, "she'll come back to me like a good girl. She's my daughter, after all. A female can easily be controlled by any man, but her father will always hold sway."

"Of course," Fraser said quickly.

"Then she will lead us to the Source, and gladly. That's what we're here for." Each puff on his cigar made the ash glow, a small inferno. "When the Heirs can claim the secret of Greek Fire, we'll finally have the necessary tools to crush the Blades once and for all. The Primal Source will ensure that."

"Exactly," Fraser seconded. He couldn't wait for such a moment. What he wouldn't give to see Bennett Day and

Catullus Graves and the rest of them lying at his feet, dead as winter. Or, it might be even more pleasant to hear them beg and snivel, *then* send them to hell.

"Don't worry, Fraser," Edgeworth said, indulgent. "Once we rescue London and take the Source, I'll see you properly rewarded. How does an upper-level position within the Heirs sound to you?"

"Capital, sir," Fraser said, his chest constricting with excitement at the prospect.

"And perhaps I may give you London, too," Edgeworth added. "As your bride. That is, *if* you do your duty."

And take Bennett Day's leavings? Fraser felt sick at the thought. Even though Edgeworth refused to believe it, his daughter was a calculating whore who knew exactly what she was doing. But Fraser couldn't refuse Edgeworth's offer. He'd marry the slut, if it helped his cause. Then he could enjoy her a little while meting out her punishment for her treachery. Fraser preferred to take his women hard, especially if they were delicately made. There was something quite wonderful about bruising soft, tender skin.

"Rely on me, sir," Fraser said eagerly. "I won't fail you."

Edgeworth scowled then. "Yes—my own daughter's will wasn't strong enough, and I'll not tolerate anyone else's failure. Now I'm going to bed. No one's to wake me unless the Blades have been spotted."

"I'll pass the word on, sir."

Edgeworth stared at his cigar with disgust, then threw it overboard. Without another word, he stalked from the deck, leaving Fraser alone with his plans for the future. A future with Britain as leader of a global empire, the Heirs heaped with honors and riches in gratitude, especially him. And every last member of the Blades of the Rose nothing but rotting meat.

Cheered with these thoughts, Fraser went back into the wheelhouse, where Chernock kept watch over the blood-dotted map. Not even the dolorous sorcerer's glowering could dampen Fraser's mood. Tomorrow they would catch up with London Harcourt and the Blades. And, oh, the things Fraser planned on doing to Bennett Day. That bitch London would have to watch while Fraser carved up her lover. Yes, tomorrow was going to be a wonderful day.

Bennett dozed lightly in the cabin. He and Kallas were taking turns at the wheel, spelling each other in three-hour increments. They hadn't the time to find a beach, drop anchor, and sleep through the night. The Heirs would follow, that much was certain, so it was a matter of staying ahead of them as much as possible. One day, there would come a reckoning, but Bennett would rather it to be some time in the future, preferably with London safely out of the way.

Across the passageway, she and Athena shared a bunk. Both women had protested when Kallas and Bennett agreed to split the time at the helm, leaving them out. Yes, there were women Blades, capable women, but the idea of leaving London and Athena alone on deck in the middle of the night was untenable. So, grumbling and complaining, the women went below to a cabin to pass the night rebuilding their strength. All the spellcasting had taken a toll on Athena, and London had been through hell over the last few days.

Bennett shifted on the narrow bunk, trying to sleep. He punched the wafer that passed for a pillow, but it didn't help. He grumbled in frustration. He'd need his wits about him tomorrow and the days that followed. Falling asleep was never a problem. He could catch a handful of sleep on a bed of broken glass, and find himself refreshed.

Of course, he'd never had London Harcourt asleep across the passageway before. He'd already seen her asleep, and just picturing her soft and warm and lithe made him hard. Even the rocking of the bloody boat called to mind the rhythm of two bodies moving together. A damned good thing that Athena shared her cabin, playing Argus.

In times like this, he'd normally take matters into his own hand. But this was Kallas's cabin, and Bennett would be damned if he had a wank in some man's bed. A gentleman had his honor. Other measures were needed. He tried to lull himself into sleep by reciting Latin names for plants. Somewhere around *campanula persicifolia*, a slight noise at the cabin door sprung him into alertness. Kallas knew enough to announce himself.

"Don't skewer me!" squeaked a female voice.

He lowered the throwing knife. "Hell, London," he muttered, stuffing the knife back under his pillow. "A little warning, if you please." He propped himself up on his elbows to look at her.

"I didn't expect knives." She shut the cabin door behind her and leaned against it. The single porthole let in only more night, so the cabin was a small, black velvet-lined box. He smelled her, her warm female scent, close about him. His head spun. "Next time," she said, "I'll come in banging the kettle."

He rubbed at his face. "You should be asleep. Just a moment. I'll light the lantern."

"No, don't," she said. "What I have to say . . . I need the darkness."

He tensed. This could be when she told him to stay the hell away from her, that she loathed the sight of him, she despised his touch. A swift, sharp pain lanced through him. He didn't think he could stand it, if she hated him.

At last, her voice came from the darkness. "When they told me Lawrence was dead," she began, "it was awful."

God, how could he lie here and listen to this? It was like having his heart slowly torn out of his body.

"London—"

"Let me finish." She ran her hands down her skirt, smoothing the fabric, but it was a gesture of momentary deferment. She drew air into her lungs. "It was awful because I had to hide from them how I truly felt. I had to pretend. For two years I had to mourn Lawrence, keep myself shut away, and playact that I was a grieving widow." She was silent for a moment. "I didn't want him *dead*, but . . . I was . . . glad." She sucked in a breath at her own admission, but seemed to gain strength from it. "Glad I was free of him. He hated it whenever I asserted myself. I had to keep my study of languages a secret from him, because he would have burned all my books if he had known." Her voice turned corrosive. "He wanted only a pretty ornament for his home, and I could never be that."

Emotion clogged her throat, and she paused to collect herself. He wanted to go to her, hold her, but kept himself on the bed, knowing it was too soon. There was more.

She continued, "I wasn't supposed to be relieved that he'd died, yet I couldn't help myself, and then I would just feel even worse. That makes me a terrible person."

It took some time for what she said to penetrate Bennett's brain. He wasn't a religious man, but any part of him that held an iota of spiritual feeling sent thankful benisons to the gods. She didn't blame him. She didn't miss her rotten bastard of a husband. He wanted to climb the mainsail and shout his relief.

"I think," she continued, "that when I was so angry with you earlier, it was because I was angry with myself for how I felt. And I turned it on to you. It was easier. Not right, but easier."

"London," he said, and his voice in the dark of the cabin was a beast pulling at its chains, "when I found out who you were, it scared the bloody life out of me. Especially after I kissed you. Because I wanted you so goddamned much, and I thought you'd hate me."

"I don't hate you—"

"Now you let *me* finish."

She fell silent.

"Then I came to know you, who you were—not Edgeworth's daughter or Harcourt's widow, but *you*, London. And what you just said . . . for the first time, I'm glad I'd killed someone. I'm sodding *happy* that Harcourt's dead, and that I'm the one who'd ended his miserable life. Because of what he'd done to you. Because you're free now." He felt his heart slamming in his chest, the caged animal trying to free itself.

"Free," she repeated. "That is what Athena said. That I'm free to do what I like, to please only myself."

"That's right. Only you."

He could almost hear her thinking, the complex machine of her mind turning and processing. It was difficult to remember, sometimes, that women were held to different standards than men, that they were almost never in control of their own lives. Yet, here was London, liberated at last. What would she do, now that she had freed herself?

"If that is true," she began, "then what would please me is . . . you."

Exaltation and desire roared through him. Only ruthless control kept him from leaping toward her. He edged closer to the bulkhead, making room for her. "Come here." He held out his hand.

She took a step, putting her hand into his, then froze. Her uncertainty vibrated in the tiny room. "I don't . . . this is very new," she said.

"I'm an excellent guide. London." Just saying her name sent hot need shooting through him. He sat up and put his hands on her elbows, drawing her nearer. Her breath hitched.

So did his. "I want you so much." It frightened him a little. He couldn't remember needing a woman as he needed her.

He slid his hands up her arms, feeling her shiver at his touch, then over her shoulders, until he cupped her head. His heart threatened to beat right out of his chest, her hair rough silk, the creamy skin of her jaw. He drowned in a thousand details—the rustle of her dress, its fabric brushing against his legs, the slight shift of her weight from foot to foot in time with the boat's motion.

Their last kiss was rushed, a bare glimpse of what could be. He would take his time. But he couldn't seem to make himself take a leisurely pace.

Only the slightest urging, and her mouth met his in a kiss. Such a mouth she had, sweet and soft and meant for languid, thorough kisses. Slow, slow, he ordered himself. He needed that, for both of them. Yet the first soft brushes of their lips together burned away the control he desperately sought. He pulled her closer so she stood between his legs as he sat. He kissed her deeply, and her shyness melted across his tongue, turned to something altogether bold. She threaded her fingers into his hair, holding him as tightly as he held her.

He tore his mouth away long enough to breathe, "Your hands."

"Athena," she panted. "Made a poultice. Things from the galley."

"Thought I smelled honey." But it was she who carried the fragrance of woman and sea air and desire, so he consumed her, devoured her with his demanding mouth. Perhaps she had been uncertain moments earlier, but there was nothing uncertain in her now as she sighed and made soft noises of pleasure, pressing herself against him. He felt her loosening, freeing herself from the cage of society and decorum. She was so damned responsive it nearly made him burst into flames.

Bennett ran his hands down her, learning her. He traced the lines of her collarbone through the fabric of her dress, then went lower, stroking her breasts. Small and full, they just fit his hands, the tips hardening as he brushed his thumbs over them. She moaned, or maybe he did, or both of them. It didn't matter because he was touching her, kissing her and that's all he knew or cared to know.

One of his hands moved down to the curve of her waist—she still wore her corset, so some veneer of society clung to her, he'd have to do something about that— then circled to cup her bottom. Sweet, she was sweet all over, everywhere meant for his touch, and she knew this, too, the way she met him at every caress.

His jacket and waistcoat were gone, somewhere, and her hands left his hair to smooth their way along his shoulders. She shoved at his braces. He shrugged them down, reluctant to break contact with her for a moment; then she felt him everywhere with the small masterpieces of her hands. She discovered him, mapped him, the width of his shoulders, the tight muscles of his arms, the planes of his chest that heaved like the deck of a storm-tossed ship under her touch.

When her hand slid lower to caress him through his trousers, an animal growl clawed from his throat. She pulled away a little, suddenly unsure, but he pressed her back with his own hand. Together, they stroked him. His hips rose from where he sat on the bed as she explored. His cock pounded, ached, under her exquisite torture.

"Stop, stop," he groaned, stilling her hand.

"Does it hurt?"

"No—too good. I'll spend in my trousers like a boy."

A warm puff of air tickled his face as she laughed. "Ah, too bad."

"You like torturing me." He brought their mouths together.

"Yes, but no," she said between open, greedy kisses. "Do I torture you?"

"Painfully."

"Good." He felt her smile against his mouth. "You're mine to torment."

"I am."

"Mm, what a wonderful feeling. So powerful." A shy but proud admission.

"A witch." He chuckled. "But a woman, all the same." To prove his point, he gathered up her skirts until his hands met the satiny flesh of her legs. He nearly exploded. She wasn't wearing stockings. He traveled up farther, past her knees, the fabric of her skirt falling around his arms. His fingertips brushed the delicate hem of her drawers, the cotton so light as to be almost nonexistent. Her legs trembled under his touch as he went yet higher, finding the delicious crease between her buttocks and thighs. He found the opening of her drawers. He let his fingers lightly brush her there, felt her radiating heat. His fingers slipped inside the opening of the fabric to touch her, her outer folds. She trembled. Then, only then, he let himself dip into her. Ah, God. She was slick and eager. She whimpered into his mouth.

"So beautiful," he growled. He pressed in closer, tracing her inner lips. His fingers dripped. "Here."

She dropped her head to his shoulder, then he grinned with feral satisfaction when he felt a hard pinch just behind his clavicle. She'd bitten him.

He wanted to plunge into her, his fingers, his cock, his entire being, but he was ruthless with himself, holding so fast to his control that he shook. Instead, he stroked her, touched her, softly at first, but then she began to move, rocking into him, meeting his hand with growing desperation, and he let slip his control by a fraction. His fingers claimed her, touching deeper, delving inside where she was molten and tight. The heel of his hand rubbed at her clit, and it seemed she would climb onto him, wrap her legs around him so he might take everything.

"Bennett," she gasped. "I'm—" Then her teeth clamped down on his shoulder as she stiffened and cried out, sending a glistening, golden thread of pain through him, straight to his cock. He'd never come without being touched, but he was so close, his breath burned in his throat and chest and his body was tight everywhere.

Barely had her tremors begun to subside before she was tugging at his shirt, fumbling with the fastenings of his trousers. He was all too happy to assist. If he wasn't inside of her, *now*, he'd burn the boat down around them.

The cabin door opened.

"Your shift, Day," said Kallas, then, "Hell!" The captain quickly shut the door. From outside, Kallas said, "I need you on deck."

"Now?" Bennett would kill him.

"Now. The wind's shifted. I need you to run the rigging." Then his footsteps, retreating.

The cabin filled with the sound of Bennett and London panting, each of them motionless. Jesus, he hadn't even heard Kallas approaching, and his hearing was excellent. He'd been lost, lost in her, lost in his own desire that still clung to him like a fiery web.

Bennett gently moved London away from him. Even in the darkness, he saw the glaze of passion in her eyes, in the fullness of her mouth. They stared at each other for some time.

As much as he hated to, Bennett stood and began to adjust her skirts before righting his own clothing. He seldom had a valet and knew how to dress himself, but suddenly all clothes were alien and he couldn't remember how to button his shirt. "I have to go." He didn't recognize his voice. He sounded like a bear about to slip his tether and maul his trainer.

Having conquered the mystery of his shirt, Bennett pulled up his braces, then began to hunt for his boots.

"But you didn't—"

"I'll live," he growled, though he doubted at that moment if he would. Could a man die from sexual frustration? Very likely. All blood gone from one head and into the other. He found his boots, pulled them on, then shrugged into his jacket. It felt abominably tight, a vise.

Dressed, he wrapped his arms around her and kissed her savagely. She clung to him, her mouth hungry and bold, and he knew that if he didn't leave the cabin in the next minute, he would throw her onto the bunk, toss up her skirts, and plow into her with all the finesse of a sailor on leave. But Kallas was waiting and the boat needed tending.

"Get some sleep." He opened the door. "Tomorrow is going to be very . . . full."

Then he left her, and he'd never felt a pain like it in his life. Not just in his cock, which begged for release, but everywhere. His hands shook as he climbed the stairs to the top deck. The faint fragrance of her lingered on his fingertips. He licked them clean.

"Give a man some warning." Kallas laughed as Bennett joined him at the wheel. "Go sweat up the halyard."

Bennett considered ripping Kallas apart and feeding him to the gulls. The ship needed its captain, though.

"Next time," he said darkly, before heading off to perform his task, "I'll hang an anchor from the doorknob." There would be a next time. If he could trade having a single, entire night with London Harcourt in his bed for a lifetime of celibacy, he'd choose her, and never regret his choice.

Chapter 8

Natives, Both Friendly and Hostile

London awoke from fevered dreams of Bennett's mouth and hands to hear Kallas shouting orders above deck, boots moving over the wooden planks. Sitting up, she stretched, her back a mass of knots after sharing a one-man bunk.

The small porthole showed the approach of a rocky coastline, but it was difficult to see much through the narrow window.

She glanced over at Athena, busy rubbing sleep from her eyes.

"If I was more conventional," Athena said, "I would say you must marry me now." When London blinked in confusion, the witch explained, "While you slept, you attempted liberties with my person. You called me 'Bennett,' and commanded that I make love to you."

"Oh, dear God!" London gasped, mortified. "I'm so sorry!"

Then Athena laughed. "A joke." She sat up and swung her legs around. Even just waking, the witch's aristocratic beauty shone. London had a feeling that she herself did not look nearly as regal upon rising from bed. "You did groan a little and say his name, though. Your encounter with him last night must not have been altogether satisfying."

London's face flamed. Both Athena and Kallas were quite aware of what was transpiring between her and Bennett. Even when married, London never discussed what went on in the bedchamber, though she had longed to ask someone, anyone, if carnal relations were often so uncomfortably formal. Now she and Bennett had crossed over into physical intimacy, and on the tiny planet of the caique, this was global news.

"It was satisfying," she said, intent on smoothing out her wrinkled skirts. "But, ah, incomplete. We were . . . interrupted."

"That explains it." Athena nodded sagely. "The restless sleep, it is the body demanding more."

It wasn't only London's body that wanted more. Having shared such intimacy with Bennett, it felt wrong and painful to separate. She thought of all the ancient love poetry she had read. Those antique words had planted needs within her. Those needs were never met by Lawrence, and she had shut them away into a locked cabinet within her, believing she was to endure a lifetime of cold solitude. But now, with Bennett, those needs broke the cabinet door and, in the wreckage, demanded to be satisfied. She wanted to sleep beside him, wake up in his arms and have him look warmly down at her with drowsy eyes while they spoke softly to one another about trifles. Yet, she did not even know if he was willing to do such things.

Rather than answer Athena or face the uncertainty of her feelings for Bennett, London got to her feet. "We should join the men on deck." She went to the cabin door and added, without turning around, "You might want to consider what your own body demands, rather than mine. I recall you mumbling 'Nikos' a time or two last night." As Athena sputtered a denial, London went out into the passageway, hiding her smile.

On deck, the day glowed. Light poured over the world, an exultation of clarity and brilliance. London's eyes adjusted to the crystalline perfection. The sky, the blue of dreams, held not a cloud, and the sea lapped at the hull, content and irreproachable. The water shifted from cobalt to aquamarine and then to pale blue so clear, the gold of rocky sea floor shimmered underneath.

The approaching island was white rock and green pine, its narrow sand beaches weaving down to the sea in small arced bays that gathered the waves. From their approach, it was difficult to see whether the island resembled a dolphin, but she trusted Kallas's assessment. The sharp smell of pine threaded through the saline breeze. London stood at the rail, inhaling deeply and feeling the caress of sunlight on her face.

But she could not idly enjoy the pleasures of an Aegean morning. She turned to help bring the caique in. She lost her breath watching Bennett move with masculine grace and confidence around the boat. The lean muscles of his arms flexed as he trimmed the mainsail, his shoulders bunching and moving beneath the fine linen of his shirt. Bracing himself on the deck, his legs were long and powerful, the work of a master sculptor celebrating the male form. The sea wind ruffled his dark hair, and he smiled with the joy of movement.

Aware of her presence, he stared at her as she approached, his bright blue gaze hot and hungry. She pressed a hand to her belly, feeling the pull and demand of that gaze within her innermost self. And this man, this beautiful man, shared a bed with her last night?

Not entirely. There was still the matter of actually making love, having him inside her, beyond those skilled, blunt-tipped fingers. She desperately wanted that. Not once had she experienced a climax as potent or intoxicating as the one Bennett had given her through touch alone. Yet rather than feeling sated, as she thought she might, her release only triggered the need for more. More of Bennett.

He was Bennett to her now, not Day, after all they'd done and shared.

"I hope you slept well," she said, coming closer so that only a foot separated them. An inane thing to say, but how did one greet a lover the morning after an abortive tryst?

"Terrible," he said.

"Perhaps tonight you'll sleep better."

"I hope not." Searing heat from his gaze burned her, and she felt a leap of excitement and need.

"Then the night cannot come too soon." To hear her speak! The proper and decorous London Harcourt of English society would never dare to say such things. But she was far away from English society, and might never return.

The ice of reality cooled the heat of desire. She considered the island, then asked, "Is this the dolphin-shaped island?"

He noted her shift in mood, adjusted his own. "So Kallas says."

"It is almost as small as Delos," Kallas said. He nodded toward the island. "A mile across, four miles long. We are approaching the curve of its tail."

"That is still a considerable amount of ground to cover," Athena said, coming up on deck. "The stream could be anywhere, and time is scarce." London could have sworn she saw a blush in the witch's dusky cheek when she looked at the captain.

A muscle twitched in his jaw. "And that is why, Lady Witch," he answered, "I will put in near the village. The villagers will tell us."

"*If* they are willing to talk, and *if* they speak truthfully."

The captain scowled, which seemed to be his perpetual expression whenever Athena Galanos was nearby. "We islanders are honest, forthright people. Unlike mainlanders."

"Shall I be forthright with you now?" Athena asked sweetly.

"Now's a good time for a lesson on bringing in a boat, Captain," Bennett interjected.

It was enough of a distraction. Kallas issued orders to all of them, even Athena. London's hands were much healed, thanks to Athena's poultice, so she was able to help adjust the sails without pain. She looked down at her hands. They were already quite different than they had been only a few days ago—stronger, more resilient.

At the wheel, Kallas called out commands while he guided the boat into the shallows of a bay. Satisfied with their position, he gave Bennett the helm and dropped anchor. The caique was too large to attempt a beach landing, yet it was small enough that they didn't need to row into shore. The sails were lowered.

"Where is the village?" Bennett asked.

"Just beyond those rocks." Kallas pointed to an outcropping bristling with pines. "I warn you, 'village' is too grand a word for that place. But you should find people willing to help."

"I'm not worried," Bennett assured him. "I've a way with people."

London didn't doubt that. If the village or hamlet or collection of shacks housed even one woman, there would be no shortage of assistance. Perhaps Dionysian offerings of wine or olives would be made. Bennett went to the bow, where the boat was shallowest, then climbed over the rail and jumped down into the surf. The water licked at his hips.

London went to the bow, as well, and stepped over the rail, preparing to also jump into the water, but Bennett held out his arms to her. "Ferry service," he said.

She smiled down at him. "What's the charge?"

"Three kisses. Except you, Kallas."

"Four kisses?" asked the captain.

Athena smothered a laugh.

"How about this?" offered Bennett. "I pay *you* in bottles

of ouzo to stay on the boat. And let's you and I never speak of kissing again."

"Deal."

"And am I offered the same rate to come to shore?" Athena asked.

Bennett shook his head. "You stay with the boat." The witch started to object, but Bennett cut her off. "If the Heirs come, we'll need you ready."

She acquiesced, not looking particularly pleased with the idea of being alone again with Nikos Kallas.

"I'll teach you my favorite shanty about the sea nymph and the fisherman," Kallas said.

Deciding it was an opportune time to get off the boat, London lowered herself into Bennett's waiting arms, wrapping her own around his neck. His hold was strong and sure, his body solidly muscled. The stance brought their faces close together. She was mesmerized by the black fringe of his eyelashes, the planes of his face shaded with a few days' worth of stubble, the sensual perfection of his mouth.

"Will you claim your fee now?" she murmured.

"Later." He tore his gaze from her own mouth. "I start collecting now, the whole day's lost."

"Please go," Athena grumbled. "Or I will surrender my nonexistent breakfast."

Bennett strode through the shallow water, carrying London. Fish the size of hairpins darted around his boots, and she smiled at them. The world was a jewelbox she had just opened.

"This would be a lovely place to swim," she said.

He stopped walking and closed his eyes.

"What's wrong?" she asked.

"Just enjoying the mental image. You. Wet." A wicked smile curved his mouth.

London swatted his shoulder, even though she wanted to

put her lips to that wicked smile. "Mr. Ferryman, this is not the time to entertain salacious imaginings."

He opened his eyes, sultry pools of azure. "It's always the time for salacious imaginings. Even better for salacious doings." But he continued on through the water until they reached the beach, where he set her lightly on her feet.

To reach the village, they had to climb a small rocky hill. While Bennett took the hill easily in long, limber strides, London struggled. Even though the hem of the dress had been shortened, she scrambled for footing. She felt herself a long way from the tame seaside at Brighton, hunting for shells or strolling on the West Pier. Bennett slowed his ascent to give her a supportive hand, helping guide her up the hill. Even in the heat of the morning, the feel of his large hand enfolding hers made her shiver with awareness.

A rough collection of low white buildings clustered together at the top of the hill, surrounding a single well. They resembled a child's blocks left behind by a forgetful titan. A tiny blue-domed church met the village's spiritual needs, and in its shade lounged a sleepy orange cat, unconcerned with godly matters. The cat paid no mind to the goats ambling through the cluster of buildings, nor did it bother to look up when Bennett and London walked past. In a doorway sat an old woman watching them as she shelled beans. A child's laugh twinkled behind her.

"You came on the caique," said a man's voice.

London turned to see a craggy-faced man emerge from a doorway, dressed in a mix of modern and traditional clothing. He regarded them impassively.

"We're seeking fresh water," Bennett said. "For our voyage."

The man eyed the revolver on Bennett's belt. "Dangerous voyage."

"They always are."

The man tilted his head toward the well. "That's been dry for years, otherwise you would be welcome to it."

A goat meandered over and began nibbling on London's skirt. She tried to tug the fabric from its mouth, but it was a tenacious beast.

"I have heard tell that there is a stream on this island," Bennett said, "its water of surpassing sweetness."

With a proud nod, the man said, "It is our blessing. Without it, we would have dried up and blown away like dead leaves. No matter how little rain we get, the stream always runs, always sings for us."

London and Bennett shared a quick glance. So the singing stream was here! She made herself appear calm, when inside, her heart pounded with excitement. The ruins were leading them to the Source.

"It would be an honor to see this stream," said Bennett, "perhaps even drink from it."

"We have money," London said, then realized too late that she had not a single drachma or even shilling. Everything had been left behind at the encampment at Delos. And even if she did still have money, she would never spend it, knowing that it came from the Heirs' work.

Fortunately, the man waved off her offer. "There's no need for money here. What would we buy?" He pointed behind the church. "If you follow this hill seventy paces, you will find a grove of olive trees. Go through there, head east, and then you will be in a valley. At the bottom of the valley is the stream. Here." He handed two earthenware jugs to Bennett. "You cannot carry water in your cupped hands."

"Many thanks," said Bennett. "It's true, what's said about the generosity of islanders."

"Just the same," said the man with a wink, "I wouldn't mind going to the mainland every now and then. These accursed goats have eaten every blanket I own."

The goat at London's skirt bleated in protest. She took advantage of the moment to snatch her skirt free from its relentless teeth. She sighed in frustration. Athena would get her dress back with several goat-chewed holes in it.

Wishing them well, the man turned and went back into his playing die of a house.

Following the villager's instructions, London and Bennett passed the church and continued on through a field of scrub and pink wildflowers. On land, the sun bounced off the ground, baking the air. A trickle of perspiration ran between London's breasts and filmed her back. A swim did sound lovely, but she knew they hadn't the time to indulge. Always at the back of her mind was her father, the look of shock and disbelief as she sailed away. He would come for her—whether as a self-perceived rescuer or an agent of vengeance, she did not know, but she had observed him over the course of her whole life and knew that his determination was singular, unbending. No man clung more tenaciously to his ideals and goals than Joseph Edgeworth.

London tripped over a rock, but Bennett caught her while juggling the clay pitchers. "Blast," she muttered. "I can't move in a skirt."

Bennett righted her on her feet. "I'll carry you."

She shook her head. "And the pitchers? All the way to the stream? No. I have to walk on my own. But," she added, moving forward, "I can see why the reformers advocate trousers for women. It's impossible to do anything with a dress tangling in one's legs."

"You're becoming positively radical."

"It's the dissipated company I keep."

"Not dissipated. Liberated."

The villager had spoken true. Bennett and London soon found themselves within a grove of olive trees. Some of the trees were young and slim, but others twisted with generations of growth, their gnarled branches reaching up to the sky in an ancient dance. Silver leaves cast patches of shadow upon the rolling earth and rustled in the breeze.

London trailed her hand along the pitted bark of an older tree, almost a honeycomb of holes. She pulled back in surprise when a small owl hooted irritably from its burrow.

"Athena's keeping an eye on us." Bennett drew her onward.

"The Blades of the Rose allow women in their ranks," London said. "The Heirs do not."

He nodded. "We're unchivalrous cads who throw our women in front of cannon fire."

"Is it wrong to protect women?"

"No man wants to see a woman hurt. But if a woman wants to fight for a cause, that's her choice."

Choice. London mulled over the word as she and Bennett walked through the natural cathedral of olive trees. She'd never had choice in her life before. Everyone made decisions for her. As a child, she was subject to the rule of her parents, nurse, and governess. When she came of age, her mother supervised all aspects of her entrance into society— the gowns she wore, which parties she attended, the young ladies London was to befriend. London's suitors, too, were all carefully selected. She was told when Lawrence approached her father, requesting permission to make an offer, told that she was to accept him. London did as she was bid and married the man of her parents' choosing. Then Lawrence held dominion over her, and she kept house according to his wishes. Even when he died, London's mother directed her on the proper means of mourning. Only where linguistics were concerned did London have agency, and that was done in secret, so it held little weight.

Now London had choice in abundance, and her head spun with possibility. She could do anything, go anywhere. If, somehow, she and the Blades managed to find and protect the Greek Fire Source, then she would find herself completely at liberty. She had no idea what to do.

London glanced over at Bennett striding behind her. He

was alternately gilded in sunlight and dusted with violet shade as they moved under the trees' canopy. He swung the pitchers easily, keeping in time with his steps. A beautiful man. Who desired her. Who offered her choice. It would be foolish, very foolish, to lose her heart to him, to lean on him. Easy to do this, but unwise.

She was only just learning how to stand on her own, so she must keep herself whole. She had tried to love Lawrence. That had proved to be a failure. Given choice, she must now act wisely, especially when faced with such a temptation as Bennett Day. Her entire life, men controlled her. Her father. Lawrence. Her father, again. She wondered if she could let Bennett into her life and maintain command over herself. Now that she had it, she would not let it go. Yet she also wanted him.

Twigs snapped, snaring her attention. She brought herself up short when a group of five young men emerged from the shade of the trees, blocking the path. They had sullen faces and greedy eyes, raking over London with predatory interest and looking at Bennett with undisguised aggression.

London glanced over at Bennett. He stood almost casually, light and easy on his feet, arms loose at his sides. She gulped, trying to hide her own apprehension. But she was no Blade of the Rose, had not a lifetime of experience facing danger, and could not quite suppress a shiver of fear.

"Mainlanders," one of the youths said in Greek, his lip curled in derision.

Another took in Bennett's well-tailored, English clothing, and sneered, "Foreigners."

The first young man swaggered forward, pushing his cap back on his head. The leader. He ambled toward Bennett, his chest puffed. "What do you want here, outsider?"

"Water." Bennett wore a pleasant half smile, as if discussing horse racing.

"Plenty of water in the sea," the leader said, and his companions sniggered at his wit.

Bennett still smiled. "To drink." He gestured east, still holding the pitcher. "We were told there's a good stream nearby. A man in the village said we were welcome to it."

"Kostas." The leader spat upon the ground. "Foolish old man. Letting English outsiders stomp all over our home, taking what they want."

"Islanders are known for their hospitality," Bennett said mildly.

The youths barked their laughter, harsh and scornful. They were young, barely out of their teens, hardly able to shave, but brawny, full of undirected energy in their small island home. London tried to calculate if she could outrun them. Not likely.

She did her best to remain motionless, praying for invisibility. She knew what happened to women.

"Islanders aren't stupid," a third young man jeered. "We don't give things away for free."

The leader nodded. "There's always a price." He abruptly wheeled from Bennett to London. She tried not to edge backward, but it was difficult to keep her feet rooted. "This pretty songbird will do nicely." He reached for her, leering.

"You don't want to do that." Bennett's voice was icy steel.

The leader's hand dropped, and he shuffled back, then tried to cover his move with bravado. "Too scrawny for my tastes," he smirked. He turned to Bennett. "But you'll pay us a toll. We'll take whatever you've got. Drachmae, pounds, marks."

Bennett said, "No payment for something that costs you nothing."

The leader's jaw tightened. "Where's your respect, outsider?"

"Saved for those who deserve it," Bennett said pleasantly. "Not bored little boys."

The leader made to lunge at Bennett, but one of the

youths, gangly and only just on the other side of childhood, yelped, "He's got a gun, Vasilis."

"This?" Bennett set one of the pitchers down and unholstered his revolver. The gang scuttled back. "Men don't need guns." He opened the cylinder, shook out the bullets, put them in his jacket pocket, then reholstered his weapon. He picked up the pitcher. Neither of his hands were free to either make a fist or load his revolver.

London gaped at him. "What are you doing?" she hissed in English.

He had the temerity to wink at her. She decided to kill him later, if they survived this encounter.

"Showing off for your woman?" the leader scoffed.

Bennett said, "She knows me better than that. I've nothing to prove."

"Only that you bleed like everyone else." The leader charged at Bennett. His companions cheered.

She barely saw it. Bennett's left arm swung out, practiced, smooth. The pitcher he held slammed into the leader's head, sending the youth reeling sideways from the blow.

Bennett glanced at the pitcher. "Didn't break," he murmured. "Good craftsmanship."

The cheering died, but two of the young men, seeing their leader stagger, surged forward. Animal rage, long pent up, finally released, and they had fists ready.

Bennett stepped forward as if to meet them in a dance. He jabbed the bottom of a pitcher into one attacker's stomach. The youth doubled over, gasping, retching. At nearly the same moment, Bennett trapped the ankle of the other attacker between his own shins and gave a little twist. Down went the youth, sprawling in the dust.

The fourth young man immediately leapt onto Bennett, wrapping tough arms around him in a parody of an embrace as the fifth youth grabbed Bennett's knees and pulled. Everyone toppled back together. London winced at the sound of them hitting the ground. The pitchers rolled out of Bennett's hands as his back met a large rock half-buried in the dirt.

Seeing their opportunity, the others collected themselves enough to pile onto Bennett like massing jackals. All London could see were limbs flailing, punching.

She had to do something. London whirled around, searching, and her eyes fell on a thick fallen branch. It was heavy in her arms, but she hefted it as fast as she was able. She staggered over and brought it down with a slam onto the shoulders of one youth. He howled in pain. Then turned and wrested the branch from her. The rough bark scraped her hands as it flew from her grip.

She had no weapon.

So she started kicking him.

He tried to shield himself, but she wouldn't allow him any protection. Anything undefended, she kicked, wishing she had stouter boots and not ones of dainty kidskin. When he grabbed at her leg, she aimed with her heel and brought it square into his face. A gruesome, satisfying crunch and spatter of red upon his upper lip. He rolled over, cradling his nose and moaning.

London spared him no thought as she moved to help Bennett. And saw that her help was not needed.

He shoved one knee into the chest of an attacker, and drove his elbow into the youth's chin as he fell backward. The youth sprawled on his back, staring up at the sky with dazed, glassy eyes.

London did not even see Bennett get to his feet, but suddenly, there he was, standing loose and tall. He landed a series of quick punches into the jaws and chests of the attackers, each in turn. A right uppercut hook, delivered with neatness and precision. The assailant crumpled with a whimper. Another was sent flying into the trunk of a nearby tree, sending a rustling cascade of leaves down upon him as he momentarily lost the ability to breathe.

Leaving only the leader. The youth, panting, glanced around at his fallen comrades, all nursing injuries, two quietly praying for divine intervention or at least the solace of their mothers. He looked at Bennett.

Bennett smiled. He wasn't even breathing hard. Deliberate and calm, he picked a few leaves off his jacket, then gave the garment a final tug to right it.

The leader backed up, stepping on one of his prone friends. A yelp of protest and pain.

Picking up the pitchers, Bennett said, affable as a publican, "The stream is toward the east, correct?"

All the leader could do was nod mutely and point in the proper direction.

"Excellent." Bennett gestured London forward. "Let's go, my love. Sorry I can't offer you my arm, but my hands are a bit full."

"Think nothing of it," said London.

"Was ever a man blessed with such an agreeable traveling companion?" Bennett asked the heavens. Then he began to walk.

The youths on the ground scurried out of his way, while the leader of the group darted behind the twisted trunk of an olive tree, seeking shelter. As London and Bennett walked onward, no one spoke.

After strolling twenty yards on, London heard a frantic scuffling. She braced herself for another attack. When none came, she chanced a look over her shoulder. The gang, supporting each other, stumbled off toward the village, not even daring to glance back. London almost felt sorry for them, the little worms. But her hands still shook with commingled fear and unleashed violence— she'd never caused someone to shed blood before—and she wasn't sorry at all.

When they were gone, she turned to Bennett. "What the devil were you thinking?" she demanded hotly. "Why did you remove the bullets from your gun?"

He gave a negligent shrug. "They were just boys. Besides, with the gun loaded, they'd just try to take it from me, then wind up shooting themselves."

"I don't see what's so bad about that," muttered London.

A smile tugged at his mouth. "Already you're demanding blood sacrifices. But Blades minimize casualties where they can."

Unlike her father and his associates. The thought slowed her heartbeat with a shiver of sorrow.

"You *were* ferocious back there," he added, and she basked in the admiration warming his voice. Strange, she never thought to be praised for kicking a man in the face.

"An Amazon," she said, recalling his words on Delos.

"Stronger than Heracles."

She valued his good opinion. It held a weight that few things in life carried. But it was not a sweetmeat handed out by an indulgent adult to a covetous child. Rather, it passed from one equal to another.

The ground sloped downward into a valley shaded by bay laurel trees, the air scented by the fragrant, glossy leaves. Bennett tucked one pitcher under his arm and kept a careful hand on her elbow as they edged with sideways steps into the valley.

"Listen," Bennett said, stopping for a moment and holding up his hand.

London cocked her head to the side, searching. Then she heard it. A liquid tumble of water over rocks. "The stream."

Moving more quickly, they hastened into the sun-mottled valley. Sparse grasses and fallen leaves crackled under their feet. Sunlight glinted at the bottom of the valley. There, they stopped.

Carving out a path for itself at the base of the valley, the stream flowed over pebbles on its banks and large rocks and boulders in the center. Though the stream was barely ten feet across, a test by Bennett with a fallen tree branch revealed its depth. The water could come over London's head, if she stood on the floor of the stream. Dense grasses fringed the banks, ribbons of green fluttering alongside the clear water.

Bennett dipped one of the pitchers into the water, then brought it to her. He held the pitcher as she drank from it. The water was cold and sweet. When she had taken her fill, she stared, fascinated, as he placed his mouth where hers had been and drank deeply, the strong column of his throat moving as he swallowed.

"What are we doing here?" she asked, dazed, when he finished and set the pitchers aside.

He rubbed his thumb across her lower lip where a few droplets of water clung. "The hell if I remember."

She blinked, trying to collect herself. "The stream. The Source."

That broke the small spell around them. He shook his head as if to clear it. "Right."

For a few moments, he and London stood on the bank, listening. "I do not hear any singing," London said after some minutes. "It sounds like water in a stream, but nothing more."

Bennett frowned in concentration. "Move around a bit. Let's try hearing it from different points."

She obliged, walking up and down along the bank, straining to hear something beyond the soothing, but quotidian, sound of running water. Bennett did the same, then, without a word, backed up and started running for the stream. London barely gulped her warning before he sprang across the stream with an athletic leap. He landed in an easy crouch, then smoothly came to standing.

"You must have driven your poor mother mad," London gulped.

"Still do." He was like a boy. But no boy moved as Bennett did, potently virile, effortlessly confident.

Rather than spend the day watching him, London made herself continue to patrol the bank of the stream, careful to listen for any change in the sound of the water. Bennett did the same on the opposite bank, attentive and alert.

Then, a shift. She halted immediately, adjusted her position. "I think I have found it." London strained, then nodded. "Come and hear."

Bennett again jumped across the stream, then joined London where she stood. He pressed close to her, his front to her back, his hands on her shoulders. She was aware of every inch of him and his solidly muscled body, his breath warm in her hair, the strength of his hands. *Concentrate, London,* she scolded herself.

"Do you hear it?" she asked.

"A voice," he confirmed.

"A singing voice." Together, they listened. Astonishing. The melody was simple, a single refrain in a voice that was neither male nor female, but elemental and of the earth. Plaintive, verging on melancholy. It repeated the same phrase over and over, rising up from the stream and glimmering in the sunshine.

"I don't understand what it's saying," said Bennett.

"A very old dialect." London tilted her head to hear it better. "A mixture of Samalian and Thracian." She closed her eyes, focusing, though it was difficult with Bennett so near. *"Come into my arms. Come into my arms."*

"Later, love," Bennett said.

She turned so he could see her scowl. "Not me, the stream. That is what it is singing. *Come into my arms.*" She put a small breadth of distance between herself and Bennett.

"A charming sentiment, but what does it mean? Whose arms? Where?"

Bennett paced for a moment, rubbing absently at his jaw. Then, with a gleam in his eyes, he shucked off his jacket. He unbuckled his belt and set it and his revolver carefully on the ground. After pulling down his braces, he removed his waistcoat and began to unbutton his shirt.

"I said it was the stream, not me!" London yelped. She stared as his fingers made quick work of his shirt buttons, revealing the sculpted lines of his chest, the ridges of his abdomen. Dark hair lightly dusted his chest, then trailed in a line down to the waistband of his trousers. In a moment, he tossed his shirt to the ground. London had only seen a handful of men shirtless, knew she was inexperienced in this realm, but Bennett's body, she realized, was utterly perfect. He surpassed any sculpture or painting she had ever seen because he was real and flesh and very much alive.

His perfection was not marred by the small collection of scars marking his body. Rather, they revealed he was a man who lived by deed as well as word.

He saw her eyes moving over him, taking in the scars. "Lawrence Harcourt gave me this," he rumbled, pointing to a line of scar tissue crossing the hard plane of his stomach.

She gasped in horror. "It looks like he wanted to gut you."

"He tried."

The idea appalled her. "Bennett—"

But he didn't need or want any apology or explanation, dismissing the past, burning her now with the heat of his eyes. "I prefer this mark to any other." He glanced down to his shoulder.

London followed his gaze and saw the red crescent upon his skin. She realized it was the imprint of her teeth from the night before. Deep within her, in her most intimate and warm places, she felt a contraction of pure lust.

He tugged off his boots.

"We cannot do this now!" London said, though her pulse raced like a deer in flight.

"Oh, we are. Now." He held her gaze as he began to unfasten his trousers. He said, his voice a wicked tease, "Strip."

Chapter 9

The Glimmer in the Water

She stared at him, aghast and also more than a little intrigued. Bennett hadn't missed the way she had watched him while he undressed. The clear desire and admiration in her gaze made him tight as a bow, ready to be loosed. A man could grow needful of such a gaze, knowing he had the power to entice this woman. Yet she enticed him, too, more than he could comprehend. Last night proved that. She'd freed her passion and he the lucky bastard she had picked to share it with.

At this moment, she hesitated.

"Come into my arms," he sang. Then, when she still wavered, he said, "We're supposed to swim in the stream. That's what the song means."

She looked relieved and a bit disappointed. God, he couldn't wait to get her alone for several hours or maybe days. The things he wanted to do to her, with her.

"Will we find something about the Source that way?"

"Seems likely."

With a nod, she began to unfasten the gown, then hesitated. She turned a delicious pink. "Please . . . turn around."

"Still shy? After last night?"

"That was in the dark." She flushed deeper.

"Surely you've been naked in the daylight before."

"Yes, but *alone*. Or with a maid, helping me dress."

"Just a maid?"

"No man has ever seen me undressed in the day."

"Not even your husband?"

"*Especially* not him." She glanced away. "Soon after we were married, I thought I'd surprise him one afternoon. He'd been out, and I waited for him in his bedroom. Naked."

Bennett stifled a groan. He could just imagine what a delicious picture she made, pink and nude in the afternoon light, standing on a Persian rug, or, even better, sprawled across a bed, her hair loose about her shoulders, the ends curling around her breasts. His already tight body grew even more taut.

"Then he came in, talking about some dinner we were supposed to go to that night. And saw me. He was horrified. Covered his eyes and threw me a robe. Lawrence said it wasn't proper for us to see each other like that."

Bennett scowled. "He was a fool." And worse, to keep a luscious creature like London in darkness. Bennett wasn't one to enjoy killing. Even though it was sometimes necessary, he hated to do it. Still, at that moment, he was glad not only that was Harcourt dead, but also that Bennett had been the one to send him on to Hades.

Bennett would do everything in his power to rid London of the shame and trepidation that had cloaked her for years. He wanted to see what sort of phoenix she would become. *Burn me up.* Now, however, wasn't the time. There was still the tiny matter of the Heirs that surely were in pursuit.

"I'll undress," London said, "but I can't let you watch me."

"Yet," he added.

She made an impatient gesture demanding he turn around.

Obliging, he did so. He continued to unbutton his trousers. His fingers stumbled when he heard the soft whisper of fabric being pulled down from London's body, the gown as she shucked it. Then the rustle of petticoats. As he stepped out of his trousers, he was confronted with the spectacle of his cock, hard and demanding. *Naked woman nearby. Want.*

Bennett wondered if the sight of him, huge and stiff, might disturb her. God knows he was a little disturbed—he was so hard, it bordered on penance. But she may as well look. She had to know how she affected him. The sooner she saw the strength of his desire, the sooner they could revel in it.

"You can turn around now." Her voice was husky, breathless.

He did so. And thought he very well might go up in flames. "Oh, Christ," he murmured.

She wasn't naked, but nearly, clad only in a sheer, sleeveless chemise that brushed the tops of her knees. Her drawers and corset lay with the rest of her clothing and boots. Slim ivory arms, long legs equally slender. Through the gauzy fabric, her breasts were high, rosy-tipped, perfect handfuls. The curves of her waist and hips tantalized, barely hidden by the chemise. The triangle of gold between her legs could only just be seen through the cotton—she was fair all over.

Red burned in her cheeks, but she did not try to hide herself from his perusal. And when she caught sight of his eager cock, her eyes widened, but he almost groaned when she unconsciously licked her lips.

"No drawers?" she whispered.

He shook his head. "Damned things are too restricting. That water better be bloody cold," he growled.

She made a choked laugh. "For both of our sakes." She waved toward the stream. "Let's swim."

Bennett went first, wading into the stream. The water shivered and bit with tiny, icy teeth. Its chill raced up his legs, but only slightly tempered the heat of his arousal. He moved deeper into the stream so that it reached his hips, then turned to help London.

"Careful," he warned, taking her hand. "The shelf of the bank is steep."

She stepped in, then yelped. "So cold!"

"Cold enough?"

She pressed her lips together in a playful pout. "Not quite. For you, either, I see." She glanced down at him, at his erection bobbing in the water, and raised a brow.

"Come on, Naiad," he rumbled, drawing her forward. "Swim."

With a show of obedience, she walked forward, deeper into the stream. Her mouth flattened into a hard line as the frigid water rose up to her calves, her knees, and then higher, but she made not another word of complaint. Her chemise billowed up in the current, drifting like a lily. As the fabric swirled, he glimpsed the dark honey of curling hair between her legs. The goddamned cold water wasn't helping at all.

They both moved farther into the water, him leading, guiding her. The water rose to his chest. Suddenly, she gasped and slipped on the slick pebbles lining the stream bed. She plunged forward. He dove to catch her. Then they were pressed together, her arms wrapped around his neck, his clasping her waist. He felt every silky inch of her. His cock surged against her soft, curved stomach. There wasn't enough cold water in all the world's oceans to bring down his fever.

She looked up at him through her lashes.

"You did that on purpose," he said.

"If I did, then I'm just tormenting the both of us."

"No pain. Pleasure's much better." *There's a mission, in case you've forgotten, randy idiot.* He made sure she had stable footing before reluctantly disentangling, holding only her hand. "Ready?"

At her nod, they both took deep breaths, then sank underneath the water. The stream ran gently, so it wasn't difficult to swim against its current, though navigating around the large rocks in the middle proved a small challenge. He took his time, keeping his eyes open so he could scan the stream bed for something, anything that might be a clue. Pebbles and rocks of every hue lined the bed of the stream, and grasses rippled in the current. Distraction also came in the form of London swimming, as lovely as a river spirit, her hair darker in the water in a rippling banner, chemise clinging to her lithe body. Undulating, she smiled at him.

Something in the center of his chest constricted, sharp. He wouldn't look away, reveled in it.

After a few minutes, they both rose up to the surface for more air.

"What are we looking for?" she asked.

"Hell if I know. Keep going."

Back down again. Several times they did this. The initial burst of warmth he got from swimming leeched away in the frigid water. London, too, grew awkward in her movements.

"Wait for me on the bank," he said when they surfaced. "Your lips are blue."

"I'm f-fine."

"London," he warned.

"I'm done with having a m-man tell me what to d-do."

He could carry her out, force her to wait, but she was determined to test herself, see what she was capable of, and he had to give her that room. The problem with London was that she wasn't just beautiful and clever. She kept impressing him with her courage. At this rate, he'd be entirely infatuated by sundown. And in a week . . . well, he wouldn't dwell on the future. The Heirs were out there.

Without another word, he dipped back under the water. If she followed him, it would be her choice. When she truly endangered herself, though, he would make a unilateral decision to get her out of the water.

They each skimmed over the bottom of the stream, looking for anything, growing more desperate. This whole exercise could prove futile, a ruse to throw any who sought the Source off the path. It had happened before. He'd spent one extremely bitter winter in Lapland chasing the Heirs who, it eventually turned out, had been sent on a wild goose chase by a set of runes. All either of them received for their troubles were frozen beards and near cases of frostbite.

Bennett hated to think that London endangered herself for some will-o'-the-wisp.

There. A flash and gleam, small and brief, just at the edge of one of the largest rocks. He almost missed it. But he swam back, dove lower, and shoved away handfuls of pebbles. A burst of tadpoles wriggled away, disturbed from their hiding. Yes. The glint of metal, the edge of something, but what, he couldn't tell. Most of it was buried underneath the rock.

London appeared next to him. He pointed at the metal. They shared an excited smile, cold water forgotten. The thrill of discovery never went away, no matter how long he'd been with the Blades.

One final surfacing for air, and down to the stream floor. Bennett pushed at the rock, but it didn't move. He swam around to the other side and set his shoulder to the rock, pushing it downstream. It jostled slightly, yet not enough. He shoved again, and again, digging his heels into the rocks and pebbles on the floor. A few cut his feet. He waved off her concern when threads of red stained the water. Silt clouded up. His lungs burned, but he didn't want to stop. Not when it felt so close. One more push . . .

The rock heaved forward, uncovering more of the metal. London darted forward and grabbed it, just before the rock rolled back into its original place.

London and Bennett shot up to the surface, gulping in air, then raced for the bank. Bennett reached the shore first, and pulled London out. He nearly fell over backward, thunderstruck, to see her.

Women in all states of undress were not uncommon to him. He ventured to guess that he'd seen more nude women than most men had seen clothed. He loved all the shapes women took—slim, lush, spare, abundant. In dishabille or fully bare. They all held their charms. And now, London. The wet chemise clung to her, entirely transparent, and he saw everything. Breasts, belly, thighs. The perfect oval of her navel. Her woman's mound.

None of those other women ever stopped his heart as did London Edgeworth in her sopping chemise.

"Please don't look at me that way," she gulped. "Or I'll forget why we are here in the first place."

"Good," he growled. But he knew she was right.

Several small, brown birds scattered from the branches of nearby laurel trees, reminding him of his duty.

Together, they knelt in the grass, the warm sun drying their skin, as they examined their find.

A bronze mirror, round, with no handle. Instead, a hole at the top indicated where it would hang on a wall. A pattern of rays, like those from the sun, encircled the reflective surface. Bennett felt the faint hum of power he'd come to recognize when handling magical objects, through his fingertips and to the very ends of his hair.

"There's writing here," London said, peering closely. "In the same Samalian-Thracian dialect as the song. Which would date this as being at least two thousand years old. But," she added, wonder tingeing her voice, "there is not a bit of corrosion anywhere. Even if it had been at the bottom of the stream for a few years, it would be tarnished."

Bennett and London's faces stared back at them from the perfectly reflective surface of the mirror.

"Sources and some magical objects are like that." He studied the mirror. "Time and the elements don't affect them. Can you translate it?"

"Yes."

"We'll take it to the boat, and you'll translate it there."

She glanced at the water with concern. "Is it all right to remove it from the stream?"

"If we leave the mirror, the Heirs will find it. And I'd rather have it in our hands than theirs."

Seeing the lesser of the two evils, London acquiesced.

He rose to his feet, and almost sank back down as London's eyes moved over his body. Her damp chemise still clung to her. "We need to get back," he said, more for himself than for her. She nodded, but with reluctance. Damn and hell. The passion in her was going to kill him, and he'd die happy.

They made their way back to their clothes and dressed quickly, but not before he had to endure the torment turning away so she could remove her chemise to wring it out, then put it back on again. Bennett did not don his jacket, instead swaddled the mirror in it. Before they left the stream, Bennett filled the pottery jugs with water. "This'll still serve us well," he said. The water, cold as it was, had been delicious, just as the villager promised.

London carried the wrapped mirror back up the valley, with Bennett toting the water. She fared better on the return journey, tripping less and maintaining her footing. As they passed through the olive grove, Bennett indicated the tree that held the disgruntled owl. The bird was still there, eyeing them sulkily. "Hold the mirror up to the bird. Don't bother to unwrap it."

Frowning in puzzlement, London did so. The owl began to hoot loudly, dancing from side to side until it finally took flight, shrieking. London ducked out of its way, but was careful to protect the mirror.

"Birds are sensitive to magic," Bennett explained. "A good test when looking for Sources. That's why the birds scattered from the trees when we got out of the stream."

"I wondered why my father always kept a parrot," London murmured, "even though it was a horrible, mean-tempered beast. Pulled my hair and tried to peck out my eyes every time I walked past him. Wellington." She shuddered at the memory.

"You'll roast him and serve him with chestnut dressing." He drew her forward.

She made a face. "Welly would be too tough to eat. Maybe just shot and stuffed for my mantel."

"I'll bring the brandy. A nice fireside rendezvous at home."

The idea pleased her, until, "I don't have a home any-more." Her gaze went far off, searching for purchase amidst instability.

It struck him anew, how much she'd given up and lost in the span of only a few days. Even *he* didn't know what would become of her, after the mission had been achieved. *If* it was achieved. *If* they survived.

Two things Bennett vowed to himself, watching her as she strode with straight shoulders through the silver-green shade of the olive grove: He would succeed in this mission for the Blades. And he would protect London Harcourt. At the cost of his own life, if necessary. She was brave and intelligent, but a mission for the Blades always held danger, the kind of danger she had no experience facing. He, on the other hand, was a seasoned soldier on the frontlines of the battle for the world's magic. And he'd use his knowledge to keep her safe.

They passed through the tiny village, but the man who had directed them was nowhere to be seen. The orange cat now lay on its other side, the only evidence that the feline had moved at all. When a goat trotted close to London, she glared at it until it backed down with a bleat.

"What a fierce creature you've become," he said.

"The daring foe of parrots and goats everywhere."

"And island thugs." He nodded toward the shadow of one house. The five youths who had attacked them in the olive grove skulked there, watching Bennett and London with sullen, bruised faces. They scattered like sheep, bleating, when Bennett smiled at them.

"You've attracted your share of admirers, too," London remarked. She looked pointedly at the window of another house, where three girls, freshly arrived in early womanhood, stared and giggled. It was safe to assume they weren't interested in London.

He glanced at London and saw pinched disapproval in her expression, which made him absurdly pleased. He couldn't understand why. Usually, he avoided jealousy, both in himself and his women. He demanded and gave complete freedom. Yet seeing London's possessiveness, he exulted.

"To those girls, anyone who isn't a goat seems like a fairy tale prince," he said.

"Between those oafs from the olive grove, the goats, and you," she said dryly, "the choice seems obvious." But she didn't say which she would pick.

He laughed, then the laugh died in his throat. "Bloody hell," he swore.

London followed his gaze. Her "Good Lord!" was slightly more decorous than his curse.

Approaching the island, less than half a mile away,

chugged the Heirs' steamship, its smoke a black smear against the azure sky. At that rate, the ship would reach the island within minutes.

Bennett dropped the water jugs, and they shattered on the rocky ground. "Can you run?"

"I believe so."

"Then we run."

"Thank the Chaste Warrior," Athena called when she saw London and Bennett speeding down the hill to the beach. "We did not know where you were."

London's heart slammed in her chest, knowing that her father and the Heirs approached.

At the water's edge, Bennett stopped and held out his arms to carry London to the caique, but she brushed the offer aside.

"As my lady wishes," he said in response.

Then he was speeding through the shallow water to where the boat was anchored. London followed, finding the task of slogging quickly through water to be a bit more difficult than she had imagined. Her skirt dragged, heavy, through the surf. Still, she reached the boat soon enough, and Bennett lifted her while Kallas pulled, until she found herself back on the caique's deck, clutching the bundled mirror. Bennett swung himself over the railing.

"How fast can we get out of here?" he asked Kallas.

"Not soon enough," came the grim answer. "We need a distraction."

"I can provide one," Athena said, stepping forward. She cast a quick glance at the sodden, dirty hem of London's borrowed gown, but did not seem to mind the poor garment's defacement. Thank goodness for that. London had no way to repay her for its loss.

"What will you do?" asked London.

"A spell," answered the witch. "Rather big, but I think I can do it."

Bennett, already assisting Kallas with the mainsail, asked, "Have you tried the spell before?"

Athena shook her head, but appeared calm. "Not yet, but I have read about it. Do not be concerned."

As Bennett pondered this, London marveled again at Athena's presence and confidence. The witch spoke with utter conviction, not only that she could accomplish the spell, but that her word had weight and significance. Athena had no doubt that Bennett would listen to her and give her opinion the same consideration as a man's opinion. Because he was Bennett, who listened, and she was Athena, who had faith in herself. London wanted that for her own self. Confidence could be hers, now. She had only to command it.

"Do it," Bennett said after a brief pause.

"I need some nails," Athena said to Kallas.

"Please, don't hurt my father." London placed a hand on Athena's sleeve. "I know he's done terrible things, but I can't let you hurt him."

"Do not worry," Athena assured her. "He will not be harmed." She turned back to Kallas. "The nails."

He frowned, but did not, for once, question her. "Down below, in the cargo hold."

Without another word, Athena hurried below.

"London, we'll need you to help getting us out of here."

"Of course." London set down the mirror inside the quarterdeck house, then hurried to her position by the foresail, ready to spring into action.

The caique became a frenzied hive of activity, directed by its captain, as London, Bennett, and Kallas made sail. Both Bennett and London remembered much of what Kallas had told them the other day, so the process went much faster, each of them raising their sails at the proper moment, keeping enough slack in the sails to keep them luffing in the wind. The boom swung to the breeze, giving Kallas a better feel for the wind. With main and foresails hoisted, London raised the jib while Bennett brought up the anchor. The boat began to drift backward, Kallas at the helm, shouting commands to Bennett and London. She kept casting nervous glances out to sea, where the Heirs' ship plowed steadily toward them. The small, dark shapes of men began to form on the steamer's deck. One of them was her father. She didn't know which, but he was there.

In the middle of this organized chaos, Athena came back on deck with a small crate, then removed its lid to reveal neat stacks of nails. She stood with her eyes closed, chanting softly but steadily, holding the crate. London kept to her post, trimming the foresail when Kallas directed, but she watched Athena, wondering what kind of magic the witch conjured.

There came a metallic clicking. The nails rose up from the crate. They hovered around Athena in a cloud. London almost lost her hold on the jibsheet. Each instance of magic astonished her. Perhaps it would always be that way, as though continually finding a hidden door in the same ordinary room and opening it into another world.

Athena continued to chant. Then, moving like a swarm of bees, the nails darted off, narrowly missing Bennett, Kallas, and the sails. London watched as the nails shot across the water, toward the Heirs' ship.

"Now what?" London asked Bennett.

He trimmed the mainsail as Kallas steered them out of the bay and into open water. "We keep running like hell and hope her distraction works."

London fervently prayed that it did. She would have to face her father eventually, but she hoped it would not be today.

* * *

"Christ, can't this ship go any faster?"

The steamship captain, already sweating behind the wheel, could only shrug at Joseph Edgeworth. "My men are stoking the fires as quick as they can," he said.

"We'll lose them!"

"But they're under sail, and we have steam."

Still, Edgeworth wasn't satisfied. He slammed out of the wheelhouse to stand at the rail. They were so damned close! A brass spyglass showed the tiny form of London moving about the deck of the caique. Edgeworth nearly dropped the spyglass in shock to see her actually helping to hoist the sails. No genteel lady ever performed such manual labor—he'd made sure London knew that. It had to be a measure of how beguiled she was by Bennett Day that not only was she helping the Blades to escape, but she was doing physical work. Unless she was wearing gloves, her hands had to be mangled pieces of flesh.

He had to get her away from Day. The longer she spent with him, the more tainted she became. As her father, he'd set her back on the right path.

Edgeworth let out a breath of relief and lowered the spyglass as the steamship closed the distance. It wouldn't be long now.

Fraser stomped up beside him, just as eager to catch the Blades. "What the hell is that noise?"

"The engines," Edgeworth snapped.

"Steam engines don't buzz," Fraser shot back, then, remembering to whom he spoke, added deferentially, "sir."

The crewmen on deck began shouting and pointing in the direction of the caique. At first, Edgeworth thought they indicated the boat, but then a strange dark haze caught his eye. He raised the spyglass again. It was headed straight for them.

"Hell," he spat. He shouted over his shoulder, "Chernock!" When the sorcerer came out on deck, Edgeworth said, also pointing at the thick, moving haze, "What the devil is that?"

"Whatever it is," Fraser gulped, "here it comes!"

The men all fell to the deck as a cloud of sharp, pointed objects darted overhead. They flew around the deck with a harsh whir. Crewmen threw themselves to the ground, shielding themselves from the objects. They moved too quickly for anyone to see what, exactly, they were, but those too slow to protect themselves wound up with angry, bleeding scrapes across their faces and hands.

"The Golden Wasps?" Edgeworth yelled to Chernock. The tiny, deadly assassins had been used with great success by Heirs in the past. Except for that time in Southampton, when Gabriel Huntley miraculously survived an encounter with the Wasps. But he was the rare—and troublesome—exception.

"Not nearly as elegant," the sorcerer answered. "A crude enchantment."

"Crude or not," Fraser shouted, "it's heading below decks!"

"Well, stop it, whatever it is!" Edgeworth said to Chernock.

The sorcerer rose up in a crouch and lifted his hands to begin a spell. But it was already too late. Men's screams and shouts rose up from below, and within a moment, sooty-faced crewmen came running up on deck in a panic. Red burns dotted their skin.

"The boiler," one yelled. "These . . . flying things . . . shot right into the boiler and tore it apart! Damned thing almost exploded!"

The paddle wheels began to slow, then they stopped entirely. An awful silence fell over the ship.

Edgeworth hauled to his feet. "Raise the bloody sails," he snarled at the captain.

The captain gave the order, but it wouldn't matter. By the time the sails were hoisted and the ship fully under the power of the wind, the caique would be long gone. Edgeworth could only stand at the railing and watch, fuming and helpless, as his daughter disappeared over the horizon.

Through his spyglass, Bennett saw the steamship lumber to a dead stop. He grinned.

"Hell of a job, Athena," he said. "What did you do?"

No answer.

"Bennett!" London cried.

He turned around and saw London on the ground, cradling a pale and motionless Athena. Immediately, he was on his knees beside them, snatching up Athena's limp hand. The witch breathed, but shallowly. Kallas, stuck at the wheel, looked on with a concerned scowl.

"Perhaps Chernock has cursed her," Bennett said.

London frowned in confusion. "Chernock? That awful crow?"

"He's a sorcerer," said Bennett. "Uses dark magic for the Heirs."

London paled briefly in horrified surprise. "I didn't know." She stroked Athena's brow, smoothing back the strands of dark hair that clung to her damp forehead.

The witch did not stir.

"There's brandy in the quarterdeck house," Kallas said.

Bennett fetched the drink, then put it to Athena's lips. He carefully dribbled in a few drops of the brandy, but they slid from her mouth.

"What's wrong with her?" London asked. "Dark magic?"

"Don't know," Bennett said, grim. "I don't think she's ever cast such a directed spell before."

London rocked Athena gently, as if she were a baby that needed soothing. "It must have taken something out of her."

"It took a hell of a lot out of the Heirs," Bennett said. "Whatever she did, it stopped them."

"Get to the sails, Day," Kallas growled. He began to turn the wheel, redirecting the boat.

Getting immediately to his feet, Bennett trimmed the mainsail. "Where are you taking us?"

Stone-faced, the captain revealed nothing of himself, only that he gnawed on the stem of his pipe as if he would snap it in half. "Kallas men always have friends somewhere on the sea. We go to them."

Once their course was secure, Bennett carried Athena below decks, with London close on his heels. He lay the witch down upon her bunk, and pain shot through him when she did not move even an eyelash.

London bent over Athena and stroked her dark hair, her own brow creased with worry.

"Blades know we risk our lives every day for our cause," Bennett said, his voice a low rumble, "but that doesn't make it easier when a comrade falls."

"We *have* to make her well again." London turned imploring eyes to him, as if he held the witch's fate in his hands.

"We will," Bennett said with a conviction he didn't feel. "I've known Athena many years. She's not just as brilliant as her namesake goddess. She's a fierce fighter, too."

Looking back at the terribly still form of the witch, London's eyes shimmered. "I would give her all of my strength, if I could."

Impulsively, Bennett took hold of London's hand and pressed a kiss to it. "You've the strength of armies. If Athena taps even a fraction of that, she'll be annoying our captain in no time."

London's chuckle was brief and watery, but her eyes were warm as she regarded him. "You overestimate me."

"You underestimate yourself."

Silent and waxen, the witch lay on the bunk. Jesus, how

could Bennett tell her mother if something happened to Athena? The love of one Galanos woman for another was stronger than their legendary pride.

"For Athena's sake," London said, "let us hope your faith is well placed."

Chapter 10

The Sleeping Witch

What had been a fairly pleasant wardroom used for the officers' mess now resembled the aftermath of a riot. Chairs were piled in broken heaps upon the decking, the table lay on its side like a wounded animal, and the books had been ripped down from their shelves and torn apart, scraps of their pages in drifts about the room. The captain observed balefully from the doorway. Someone would have to pay for the damage, but now wasn't the best time to mention that. Joseph Edgeworth was in another frenzy.

The respected gentleman of society and pillar of English values rampaged, and nothing was safe, not even the glass shades on the lamps mounted to the bulkheads. He smashed them with his fists, ignoring the cuts to his knuckles. He flung a ceramic ashtray across the room. It just missed Fraser.

"You do not tell me 'no,'" Edgeworth thundered. "Do you understand that? I won't hear it. No one says that to me. No one."

"Yes, sir," Fraser said. "Only—"

Edgeworth kicked the spittoon with a clang. "Only what?"

Fraser gulped down a breath. Damn Chernock and the

ship's captain for making him their sodding mouthpiece. He hated having to tell Edgeworth bad news, and this news was the worst. "Only, we've got to have a new boiler. We can't catch them under sail."

"What the bloody hell is wrong with the boiler we've already got?" Edgeworth demanded.

"It's full of holes, sir. From the nails the Galanos witch sent."

"Then patch them!"

Fraser tugged on his collar. "There are too many. The boiler would just explode. We'd be lucky if only half the ship caught on fire."

The words that spewed out of Edgeworth's mouth shocked even Fraser. He knew Edgeworth had a temper, just as Jonas Edgeworth did, but this was downright terrifying of the trouser-soiling variety. Fraser cursed Bennett Day for turning what should have been an easy mission into a big sodding mess. A plum position within the Heirs, a new wife, the honor and respect of his colleagues and nation. All of this would have been Fraser's, if Bennett Day had just kept his cock to himself. But no, the son of a bitch had to go seduce Edgeworth's daughter, and Fraser had to clean up the mess.

"Why doesn't Chernock do something?" Edgeworth snapped. "Cast some bloody spell to fix the boiler or make the ship fly or some other goddamned thing."

Chernock, the coward, peered around the safety of the doorway, his long, thin nose like a carrion-eater's beak. "There are limits to magic, Edgeworth," he intoned. "It's not some tinker's shop you can use to patch boilers. And a steamship flying over the Aegean is not only nearly impossible, but downright conspicuous."

More ranting from Edgeworth. What hadn't been broken before was now demolished. Until, at last, he panted, "So get another boiler."

"We must go to Mykanos," the captain ventured. "It is the nearest island that will have what we need." But it meant the loss of several days. Everyone knew it.

"Make sail for Mykanos, then," said Edgeworth. The captain bowed and hurried away. "And once we do get that new boiler," Edgeworth said, pointing at Chernock, "you'd better have a way of catching up with the Blades, or I'll chop off your fingers and feed them to you. Every moment London is with the Blades, her mind is being poisoned. If I don't get her back soon enough, she'll be lost to me."

God, what would it take to break Edgeworth of this delusion? Fraser hadn't an idea, but it would take bollocks of iron to even suggest to Edgeworth that his whore of a daughter was acting of her own volition. At least Chernock, the funereal bastard, was smart enough to say, "Yes, sir."

"Does the Bloodseeker still track them?" asked Edgeworth.

"It does."

"Good. I'm looking forward to giving Day a nice, slow death. And, Chernock, if you do your job properly, I'll let you have the Galanos witch, so long as you kill her when you're done with her. Something painful."

Chernock approximated a smile and faded into the shadows.

Fraser and Edgeworth were alone now in the ruin of the wardroom. Fraser shifted from foot to foot, uncertain what he should do, and he was made even more uncomfortable when Edgeworth turned haunted eyes to him. Fraser hated to see vulnerability in anyone, especially someone as powerful as Edgeworth. It made him despise the older man.

"I cannot lose my only daughter," Edgeworth rasped.

He had to ask the question that preyed upon his usually dormant mind. "What if she's too far gone, sir?"

Vulnerability fell away, and a cold mask took its place.

"Then, for her own good, I'll have to kill her. It's the honorable thing to do."

In deepening waves, dusk fell. A sky of saffron, the sea a golden, inky reflection burnished by the setting sun. Clouds, the blue of robins' eggs and softest pink, spread in waves, the remains of a god's dream.

London hadn't anything within her to see such beauty. Not when Athena lay below decks in impenetrable slumber. No one spoke of their darkest fears—that Athena would not wake again. No one spoke at all.

London dribbled wine and water between the witch's lips, did whatever could be done to make Athena comfortable. The silence was unbearable, tight and strained, yet London could not break it. Even Bennett, who always had something light to say, kept his counsel. Kallas seemed to hold the same opinion, for he was also mute, trusting London and Bennett to know what the sails needed as he guided the boat toward an unknown destination.

Every few minutes, London hurried below to check on Athena. Whenever she came back above, Kallas looked at her with a plea, and she shook her head. The sturdy captain's shoulders fell. No change. Whatever the spell had done to Athena, neither London nor Bennett nor Kallas knew its remedy. Their best hope, the witch, suffered for it.

Adjusting the jib halyard, London saw a necklace of small islands appear, their forms dark, craggy gems spread over the surface of the water. The islands were much too tiny for even a single village. The islands hadn't even beaches, just sank straight into the sea and the reefs that surrounded them.

"Where are you taking us?" London asked Kallas.

"To someone who can help our witch."

The triangular sails of another, smaller caique came into

view as they rounded one of the islands. This boat was anchored, dancing slow and somnolent upon the water. Fishing nets dried upon its decks. Two men sat upon upended crates, mending nets with fast, deft hands. They glanced up as Kallas steered closer. In the growing dusk, London could not make out their faces, whether they nodded in welcome or stared back with hard eyes.

Kallas waved his arm overhead, once. One of the fishermen repeated the gesture. He shouted something indistinct over his shoulder. Someone came above deck, wiping his hands on a rough cloth.

"We're coming alongside," Kallas called. "You, stay with the sails," he said to Bennett. He turned to London. "Prepare to anchor."

They sailed in slowly as she worked the jib and Bennett the main. Kallas brought them several boat lengths upwind from the other caique, and signaled to adjust the sails until they stopped moving. London began to lower the anchor. She felt the bump along the line as the anchor hit bottom, then paid out the line as the caique drifted backward. More leaps along the line as the anchor bounced along the sea floor, then the anchor dug in and the line tightened.

The caique now bobbed beside the fishing boat. Three men stood at its rail, watching.

"Set the anchor," Kallas said, but London already knew. She had been taught well. As soon as she did this, lines were thrown from one boat to the other. Kallas and Bennett secured them, then the men pulled until the hulls of the boats bumped gently against each other. A flotilla.

Kallas turned to her. "You make a good sailor." His face was stone, but the praise was genuine.

Too tired and frayed to blush, London ducked her head in thanks. The captain's unadorned praise gave her more profound gratification than a finely crafted sonnet ever could. "I had a good teacher."

"What about me?" asked Bennett. "I'm a good sailor, too."

"And a whore for compliments," Kallas grunted, but he gave an echo of a smile.

"These aren't your usual waters, Kallas," said the eldest of the men on the fishing boat, his hair snowy and wind-blown, his hands gnarled. His accent marked him as a man who seldom left this corner of the sea. He turned jet eyes to London and Bennett, but addressed Kallas. "They your cargo?"

"My friends."

The three fishermen stared at Kallas's passengers, and London was well aware of Bennett's proprietary hand at her waist, him drawing her close so that her hip touched his. She glanced at him from the corner of her eye. Even though he smiled, it was a smile of warning. *Mine. You look or touch, you lose your bollocks.*

What primitive creatures were men. But perhaps that was why women kept them around, to remind themselves of their humble, animal beginnings.

And she wasn't Bennett's. She was no one's. Belonged to nobody. Only to herself, to give as she saw fit.

The older man answered to the name of Stathis Psaltou. "And my sons," he said, waving to the two men next to him. "Konstantinos," a thickset but agile fisherman with his father's face, "and Odysseas," the younger of the brothers, lankier yet still sturdy. The brothers both nodded, holding their caps in their hands. Their gazes would linger on London, then paddle away like sea turtles whenever Bennett glared at them.

"We've need of you, Stathis," Kallas said. "To undo a spell."

The old fisherman nodded. "Permission to come aboard?"

he asked. He looked at Bennett. "Or will your English wolf bite my hand off?"

"I'll keep him chained," said Kallas.

"For now," added Bennett, smiling.

Stathis seemed to respect this. He nimbly jumped from one caique to the other. Impossible to know his age, only that he seemed as old as Poseidon and hale as a tempest.

"Below deck." Kallas waved Stathis toward the quarter-deck house.

As the old fisherman ambled away, London gripped Kallas's arm. "Can we trust him? And his sons?" The Heirs had much wealth and power at their disposal. It would not be difficult to find and turn men—if not to the Heirs' cause, then at least to provide might or information. London was certain it happened many, many times. Who knew what poison was concealed by a friendly smile, even here in the midst of the Aegean?

"We hold together, the brotherhood of seafarers," answered Kallas. "All of us have the same mother."

"But brothers can turn against one another."

"Don't fear, Lady Oracle." Kallas glanced at Stathis, who waited for them by the companionway. "I've saved that goat's life dozens of times, and he's saved mine. I drank wine with him when his sons first grew beards."

"Those two look like they started shaving minutes after birth," muttered Bennett, glancing at the brothers.

"Not minutes. Months. So, yes, Stathis is trustworthy."

"Here," said the captain, once they were all below in the passageway. He opened a cabin door, revealing with a lantern Athena on her bunk. Again, London's heart squeezed within her chest to see Athena completely still, like a flame shrinking before extinguishing completely.

Stathis went to Athena, pressing his ear to her chest. His thick, knotty fingers lightly touched the witch's face before he picked up her hand and turned it over so he could examine her palm. He grunted, then gently set Athena's hand back down beside her. Kallas, frowning with worry, searched the old fisherman's face for some expression, some indication of anxiety or relief, but Stathis kept himself removed.

From around his neck, Stathis pulled out a small charm that hung on a cord. A medallion of St. Nicholas oscillated slowly in the lamplight. Stathis stilled the medallion's movement, then held it over Athena's prone body. It twirled, then spun in helixes. Stathis gave another grunt, then replaced the cord around his neck.

"What does it mean?" London whispered.

The fisherman's lined face looked as ancient as centuries. "It means that you came to me just in time."

Laid out, Athena reminded London horribly of the funeral effigies she had seen in Westminster Abbey, a queen posed as though eternally slumbering, while her actual, physical remains moldered beneath layers of marble. The effect was only heightened by the scattering of small oil lamps around the deck of the ship, casting flickering, somber light over Athena's face. She almost expected the witch's skin would be cold. London had to touch Athena to assure herself her friend was warm and alive.

Kallas had carried Athena above deck, where London spread out several coarse woolen blankets. Now, with Bennett at her side, she knelt next to Athena, Kallas facing them. Konstantinos and Odysseas kept to the shadows as their father walked to the rail of the boat with a wooden bucket, then lowered the bucket on a rope to the water, softly chanting.

Stathis spoke too lowly for London to hear the words tumbling from his mouth, but she heeded only Athena, the shallow rise and fall of the witch's chest, and feeling

Bennett's hand engulfing her own. She drew steady assurance from his touch, but, even so, there were some things he could not command or control—including the enchanted slumber that imprisoned Athena.

With easy, practiced movements, Stathis brought the filled bucket up. He set it onto the deck. Konstantinos hurried forward and handed his father a small, battered tin cup that looked as though it had quenched the thirsts of generations of seafaring men. Stathis whispered into the cup, again too quiet for London to hear specific words, yet she felt in them the swells of tides, the eternal rise and fall of oceans and the silent kingdom beneath the surface of the sea. The water within the cup blazed azure, spreading blue light across the old fisherman's face.

He strode across the deck and stood at Athena's head. He and Kallas shared a look, before Stathis drizzled some of the seawater onto Athena's brow.

For a moment, there was nothing. No movement. No sound. Only the waves surrounding the boats, splashing against the rocks of the nearby islands. Athena did not stir.

London's throat seized. Had the spell not worked? She tried to rise, but Bennett held her in place.

Then—Athena inhaled deeply. Her eyes opened. A flash of panic, followed by calm. London sagged against Bennett, felt his lean, muscled arm wrap in support around her shoulder. He was solid and true.

The witch turned her head, saw Kallas kneeling beside her.

"Why will you not rid yourself of me?" Athena asked Kallas, her voice a rasp.

London saw relief in the captain's fierce frown, relief he would deny if accused of it. "Too easy for you," he said.

She looked away from him. "Now I've proof how foolish you are." But she reached for his hand and, when it was given, gave it a gentle squeeze before letting go. The witch turned to London and Bennett. "Did my spell work?"

"The Heirs' ship was crippled," Bennett said, and the witch smiled at this. "They're far behind us."

Athena sighed, her smile fading. "You lost time because of me."

"We're *Blades*, Athena," said Bennett. "This is what we do. It's why we're different from them."

Athena was silent for a moment. She nodded slightly. "Thank you, and," she said, gazing at Stathis, who had come around to stand at her feet, "blessings of the Virgin Warrior to you, sea mage."

The old fisherman's face broke into a weathered smile, lines fanning across it like a chart mapping the sea. "I'll take no thanks, land witch. The waters take life and give it with the same hands."

With a soft groan, Athena struggled to raise herself. She gave another slight nod of gratitude when London helped her rise to sitting.

"This is why I do not perform such powerful spells," the witch grumbled. "It is awful to lose control of oneself."

"What can I get you?" London asked, dabbing at her friend's damp forehead.

Athena's patrician brow creased with a small frown, as if finding something strange within her own mind. "I have a powerful craving for . . . quince spoon sweets."

"Then you'll have some," said Stathis. He turned to his sons, but Odysseas and Konstantinos were already jumping from one caique to the other. He beamed. "Good boys."

Brimming with irrepressible joy, London glanced at Bennett. Their eyes held, sharing in the moment. He took London's free hand, his own large and warm and exactly what she needed. She felt her heart soar up toward the top of the mainsail mast. Nothing could stop her ascent into the silken night.

* * *

Night was held back by lanterns and bottles of wine, dark as the sea, and apricots like little suns, passed from hand to hand. Everyone sat in a circle upon the deck of Kallas's caique, joined in an unadorned feast. There were bowls of steaming, fragrant fish stew, handed out by Stathis, the magnanimous emperor. Cubes of salty feta. Tiny fried anchovies. No bread, but none was needed. And, as Athena had hoped, a thick glass jar of syrupy preserved quince, *glyko kythoni*, presented by one of the shy brothers. A small, dented spoon stuck into the rose-hued preserves, and everyone in turn ate a spoonful before handing it off to their neighbor. Ancient, timeless hospitality. The world united, if only for a moment, with a shared sweet.

Athena sat propped against the quarterdeck house, wrapped in a blanket, her natural coloring gradually returning. When she stuck a spoon of preserves into her mouth, she closed her eyes and sighed with pleasure. Bennett nudged London sitting beside him. He directed her gaze to Kallas, at the brief longing that passed over the captain's face before busying himself with packing tobacco into the bowl of his pipe.

London saw and shared a small, secret smile with Bennett. Meeting the warmth of her eyes, he felt a kick of lust, pure and uncomplicated. Since Athena's awakening, life returned to the caique, to everyone, and London especially.

As Konstantinos and Odysseas, at their father's urging, produced stringed bouzouki and played the wild, spinning music of the islands, everyone clapping along accompaniment, Bennett watched London. In the soft evening breeze, her unbound hair became dark gold satin, the strands already lightening from the sun. Her ladylike pallor, too, was disappearing. Throughout her skin and gleaming in her eyes, vitality bloomed.

Who the hell would shut her away, lock her in a cabinet like a waxwork figure kept from the sunlight? *This* is where she belonged, sitting on the deck of a Greek cargo caique, singing along to songs about dashing pirates and dark-eyed girls.

Bennett didn't try to hide his grin. Why should he? Athena was well. The Heirs' ship was debilitated. It was night on the Aegean, his belly was full, and a beautiful woman sat beside him, lifting her voice in song. A beautiful woman who would soon share his bed. He wanted her. Badly. He could wait. He liked the waiting. It was part of the dance, and he loved to dance.

Metaphorically, anyway. Stathis pulled Kallas to his feet, and the two sailors stood side by side, resting their arms on each other's shoulders. They waved to Bennett as the music turned almost manic.

"The *pentozali*," Kallas said. "The dance of men." He puffed out his chest, knocking a fist into it.

"Don't know the steps," said Bennett.

"We'll show you."

He glanced over at London. Wreathed in a smile, she motioned him forward with a wave of her fingertips. "Show me your manly dancing."

With a cheerful shrug, Bennett got to his feet and joined Kallas and the old fisherman. Kallas clapped a hand on Bennett's shoulder, and he did the same, so they formed a line. Several minutes were spent trying to decode the hieroglyphics of their feet, intricate steps in beats of five. He was clumsy at first, but laughed and, after several more gulps of wine, felt himself move into the dance. It was lusty and muscular, leaps and footwork, and soon Bennett had thrown off his jacket and waistcoat, a healthy and wonderful mist of perspiration covering him. Kallas and Stathis tried to outdo each other, jumping like stags. No wonder it was the dance of men.

Only someone as reckless, or ridiculous, as a man would attempt it.

London and Athena clapped when the *pentozali* was done. Bennett took his bow, grabbed a bottle of wine, then drifted toward the rail at the boat's stern to watch the evening sea and cool off a little. He'd barely been able to stop himself from hauling London up, savaging her mouth with his, then dragging her below deck and fucking them both senseless, waiting be damned. His blood was high. He'd skirted danger today, found a clue to a Source, seen London deliciously wet and eyeing him with desire. All inducements to a good, strong shag. But, even though she had separated herself from the world of English society, she was a lady, and deserved better.

For now, anyway, he thought to himself with a smile. If she wanted to treat *him* like a trollop, well, he had no complaints with that.

Even with the sounds of music and talk at his back, he heard London approaching. Or rather, he *felt* it, felt her nearing, a subtle shift within his body that was aware of her at all times.

She leaned against the railing beside him, bracing her elbows upon it and staring out at the liquid ebony water. The sky was a lighter indigo, scattered with stars.

He rested his hip against the rail and faced her. She held his interest a hell of a lot more than the view. He drew a swallow of wine from the bottle, then pressed it into her hand when she reached for it.

There was something profoundly wonderful about watching a genteel young woman take a lusty swig of wine directly from the bottle, putting her mouth exactly where his had been. A princess in the vineyards, the hem of her silk gown stained with grapes and mud. He liked to watch her draw from the bottle, her lips at the opening, the movements of her slim throat as she swallowed.

In companionable, but charged, silence, they shared the wine. It tasted of the blood of titans, rich with earth, heating and cooling at the same time. He let it roll over his tongue as he stared at London's lips, full and red.

He continued to watch those delectable lips as she said, "Wonderful dancing."

"My Greek ancestors are stomping their feet with approval," he murmured.

She raised her brow in surprise. "And here I thought you were English through and through."

"One-eighth Greek, on my mother's side."

"Ah." She nodded sagely. "That explains it. I believe there are women in England who would pay fortunes to see you dance."

"Only England?"

"The Continent, too. Including Greece. Oh, probably the Americas, as well."

"But not Asia or Africa."

"We can't let them know about you. Otherwise there would be global anarchy. Nations of screaming, rampaging women."

He reached for her, needing her mouth, but she edged back.

She shook her head. "No—I'm a little drunk. I want my mind clear when I kiss you." He saw that she swayed a bit more than the rocking of the boat.

Bennett took the bottle from her. "Start sobering up. Quickly."

London stared out at the undulating water, the reflection of the waxing moon, drawing evening air into her lungs in a slow, sensual inhalation. "If we were alone, I'd say we should throw off our clothes and go for a night swim."

"Chemise?"

"No chemise."

"Jesus." His cock felt like a hungry beast, heavy and

insistent as it pulsed against the front of his trousers.
"Don't say things like that then tell me not to kiss you or
touch you. Bloody unfair."

"Sorry," she said, not sounding the least bit apologetic.
The little witch.

He tried to distract himself. "How'd you learn to swim?
Most well-bred young ladies don't know how. Indecorous."

"Oh, yes. Too much improper motion." She reached up
and pushed her hair back from her face, the movement
causing her breasts to rise and press against the bodice of
her dress.

He gripped the neck of the bottle tightly. Was she driv-
ing him mad on purpose? "So—how?" he gritted.

"My family has a country home in Somerset. Spent my
summers there. There was a pond. Jonas could bathe there,
but I wasn't allowed. One day, I must have been about ten,
my governess fell asleep under a tree and I snuck off and
taught myself how to swim."

"Taught yourself," he repeated, trying to understand. His
father taught Bennett and his brother during trips to the
Cornish coast. As he recalled, there had been a lot of swallowed seawater and near disasters before the skill was
learned.

"I'd read about it," she said, with a wave of her hand.
"Some Latin treatise on swimming."

"Sounds dangerous."

"Not a bit." She shrugged. "It wasn't a deep pond. But my
governess caught me and threatened to go to my parents."

"So, no more swimming."

A slow smile spread across her face. "There was swimming. I threatened her right back. Said if she told my parents, I'd tell them that she fell asleep reading French novels
when she was supposed to be watching me. After that, I
could swim whenever I wanted."

A startled laugh from Bennett. Damned impressive, that will of hers, the early seeds of defiance. "A child Machiavelli."

"Ruthless," she agreed, then turned somber. "Must run in the family."

Her pain echoed in him. He didn't know what to do, how to help her.

"I wonder how they found us," she murmured. "At the dolphin island."

"That needs pondering," he said. "I haven't seen any birds following us, so that's one thing to cross off an endless list."

London turned and leaned against the rail. "Does this sort of thing happen to you often? Being chased by Heirs? Running for your life?"

"All the time." He smiled.

Her laugh was part exasperation, part respect. He was glad to hear it after the darkness that had overtaken her. "You Blades are mad. And you, Bennett, are the Hatter at the tea party, presiding over the madness."

"And you're Alice," he answered, "struggling to make sense of it all here in Wonderland. Don't try."

"Nothing makes sense anymore." Her look clouded once more, and her hand drifted up to rub absently on her chest, which sent a peculiar pain through his own.

"Admit it," he said, trying to draw her back from the shadows within her, "some part of you liked that." He nodded back toward where they had sailed from, the dolphin-shaped island. "The search. The thrill of discovery. Even the chase."

"Not what happened to Athena. I didn't like that. But everything else . . ." A tiny smile curved her lips, but she didn't deny what he said. "I suppose that makes me mad, too."

"As much as the March Hare."

Though her smile was small, it didn't fade. Such

surprises she held, a continual unfolding mystery that he wasn't sure he could ever weary of. Even the other female Blades he knew—including Athena, Thalia Huntley, and Astrid Bramfield—didn't quite have the hunger for experience as London did, perhaps because they had known about the world and Sources for so much longer, yet he wasn't entirely certain that was the only reason. There was something in London, an inner fire, that kept drawing him toward her, like a moth to light. The question was whether or not he'd burn up in this woman's flame. For the first time in his life, he truly believed it might be so.

Chapter 11

The New World

Though it had its moments of darkness, the day had unfolded in a series of small pleasures. She'd swam in a stream. Heard a genuine example of the Samalian-Thracian dialect. Felt the sun on her bare skin. Shared a meal with fishermen as their boats swayed at anchor, sung with them their songs. Watched Bennett dance, movements so potently masculine she was surprised she hadn't simply climaxed on the spot from merely observing him.

She had wanted to experience the world, and here she was, deeply enmeshed in life. It wasn't all joy. Her father was out there, searching for her. The Heirs chased the Source, wanting to claim it for their own ruthless agenda. She still had no idea, if she should survive this mission, what would become of her afterward. Without a man controlling her life, away from the rules and structure of society, London was entirely free. Which meant there was nothing between her and the sheer drop into disaster. Nothing but herself.

She alone guided her toward whatever she wanted. And what she wanted was Bennett.

London pressed a hand to her chest as if her heart

threatened to spring forth. It might. Beside her, Athena slept, still recovering. After the meal and music, the witch's energy flagged, and London had taken her below to rest, then stayed with her to ensure her friend's comfort. Athena quickly fell into a hard but honest sleep, but London, full of the day, could not find her slumber.

London heard Bennett, Kallas, and the fishermen above deck, their voices low and masculine, as they boasted and told jokes that women shouldn't hear. She heard their laughter, Bennett's especially, and at the sound of him, slick heat gathered between her legs.

She bit down on her lip, stifling commingled excitement and trepidation. London hadn't even made love with Bennett yet, but she would. Even this agonizing anticipation filled her entire being with acute sensitivity, a reckless, giddy joy. London Edgeworth Harcourt, ornament of polite society, was no longer. A new woman was taking her place, one who chose her own path and took men of her own selecting.

After she and Bennett had rejoined the company, there had been more music and stories and camaraderie, but there was anything but simple platonic friendship between her and Bennett. No one said anything about it. Yet, despite the tact shown by all, there was no denying the atmosphere of sensual possibility that turned the air thick and tangible. Bennett did not help matters. He stared at her all through the evening as if she were the dessert he planned to savor. London sported a continual blush, knowing she was flushed everywhere, even beneath her clothing.

There was no room for fear or embarrassment, only a ready willingness to embrace sensation and experience. She would touch Bennett and he would touch her, and she would enter a new world.

A brief consultation with Athena before that voyage. The witch had given London a foul-tasting tonic, the Galanos women's secret to preventing conception. London was to drink it daily. She did so, and gladly, despite its noxious taste, for her world was too uncertain to risk bringing a child into it.

She probably would not need the drink for some time, but London wanted to be certain, ready for any possibility. She needed to rest. The day, wonderful as it had been, was also long and draining. Sleep was what she needed, not fevered imaginings of what she wanted to do with, and to, Bennett.

Sleep. How could she? She was tingling with life and felt ready to single-handedly row the caique to Spain and back.

The sound of Bennett's boots in the companionway nearly made London leap out of her bunk. She forced herself to lie still as she listened to his steps in the passageway, then he entered his cabin, closing the door behind him. Instead of jumping up and rushing to him immediately, as she wanted, London made herself wait a little longer. Perhaps he had things he needed to attend to, personal things. Maybe he would like a few minutes of solitude. And she wanted to prove to herself that she could wait, that she was strong enough to bide her time and think of other matters. For example, if she returned to Athens, she would make time to visit the antiquarian booksellers to see if she could find rare and arcane volumes on linguistics. Why, there could be books in and about languages she hardly knew, such as Phrygian, Volscian, Marrucinian, Illyrian, and—

Oh, the hell with it.

In a moment, London was up, across the passageway, into Bennett's cabin and in his arms.

"You took your time," Bennett said, after surfacing from a long, deep kiss.

London grabbed the back of his head and brought it

down to her again. "I'll have you know," she said, breaking away for a moment, "that I waited, I believe, an agonizing five minutes before coming over here."

"Four minutes and fifty-nine seconds too long." He enfolded her, kissing her with a burning need, his mouth hot, demanding, but she also had demands, and so they gave and took in a liquid fever. His hands were in her hair, along her sides, cupping her breasts, her waist, her bottom. Only that day she had seen the glory of his unclothed body, the sculpture and power of his muscles, and so what she felt beneath her own hands now had images, pictures of him branded into her mind.

"What about Kallas?" she gasped between kisses.

"He's still up there with Stathis. They'll be gossiping for hours."

"He won't come down?"

"Not for a long time. He knows."

She couldn't even feel embarrassment that the captain knew exactly what was going to happen in his cabin. "Good."

"Still a little drunk?"

"Not from wine." London tugged at Bennett's jacket, pulled at the buttons of his waistcoat and shirt, even fumbled with the fastenings of his trousers. She had to feel his skin. She had to have him inside her.

"There's no rush, sweetheart." He chuckled, low. He took hold of her hands, capturing them with his own. He kissed her fingertips.

"I shall explode."

"When I let you."

London raised a brow. "Let me? So my pleasure is *yours* to bestow when *you* feel like it?"

His grin flashed in the darkness. "Ah, there's that fire I love."

"I shall see to my *own* pleasure, thank you," she said. "Starting now. Take off your jacket and shirt."

His satin and smoke laugh. "A woman who takes charge. How delectable."

"Stop talking. Start stripping."

Still laughing, but with delight and not mockery, Bennett did as she bade him. Yet he had control here, too. With a leisurely pace, he slipped his arms from the sleeves of his jacket and tossed it onto a narrow chest of drawers. His waistcoat followed. Then, holding her gaze with his own, he began to unbutton his shirt. Slowly. London stared as his long, square-tipped fingers pushed each button through its buttonhole with the precision of a gem cutter. As each button slipped free, his chest was bared to her, inch by inch. Lord, but he was beautifully made. Nothing extraneous or too bulky, but sleek as a wolf, all strength and movement. She reached out to touch him, but he batted her hand away.

"Let me finish, woman. You'll distract me."

She let him be, for now, as he tugged his shirt free from his trousers and finished unbuttoning the garment. He pulled the shirt off and set it atop his jacket, breaking eye contact for only a moment.

"Why is it so blasted dark in here?" London demanded. "I want to see you."

"See with these." He took her hands and put them on his skin, his shoulders. As soon as her fingers contacted his flesh, he sucked in a breath.

Though she felt her head spin with the wonder of him, she managed to say, "Now I have permission to touch you?"

"Yes, minx," he rumbled. "Now."

She stopped wasting time with idle insolence and let her hands roam where they willed. He was tight silk, a feast for touching. Solid, capable arms, wide shoulders in exact proportion to his narrow waist. The planes of his chest, the ridges of his stomach, the chevron of muscle that ran from each hip to disappear beneath the waistband of his trousers.

Experimentally, London leaned closer and ran her tongue from just below his pectorals down to his navel. He made a sound, an animal growl.

"You taste very nice," she said. "Warm, masculine."

He gripped the back of her head and kissed her, hard and savage. "You've the sweetness of oranges and the spice of cinnamon in you." He picked her up by her waist and sat her on the low dresser, unconcerned that she crushed his jacket, waistcoat, and shirt beneath her. "But there are other places I want to taste."

She gulped. "You mean—"

"I mean. And I do."

They came together in another kiss, he standing between her legs. He pressed against the heated, aching juncture of her thighs, and she moaned into his mouth. She felt her skirts being gathered up, her drawers being pulled down, until it was his hands on her bare skin, stroking her thighs. He touched her intimately. She jumped.

"Shh. Easy, love," he crooned. "You're so ready for me. So wet. What a beautiful pussy you've got here."

No one had ever said things like that to her before. She and Lawrence never spoke when they'd made love, so it became an exchange between two civil strangers. To hear Bennett speak with such earthy candor, impolite words that were crass and wonderful, London felt her climax already begin to build.

"No, no," he said, lightening his touch so that he only just brushed her. "Not so fast. I want you begging for it."

London panted, "A gentleman . . . would never . . . make a lady beg."

He nipped at her mouth. "I'm no gentleman."

"Thank God for that."

"In fact," he said, gripping her skirts in handfuls, "no

one but the worst scoundrel would ever do something like this." Then he lowered his mouth to between her legs.

London clapped her hands over her mouth to keep from screaming. She bowed up from the dresser. If there had been any thoughts of coherence in her mind, they melted or else incinerated, leaving her sensation only, and that became everything. He sucked and stroked with long, velvet licks, down to the molten core of her, revealing parts of herself she never knew existed and now that he'd found them, she wanted his claim.

She writhed under his hands, and if he didn't grip her tightly, she would have flung herself off the dresser. And when the tip of his tongue teased at her sensitive nub, she nearly slammed her head against the bulkhead. Again, her orgasm beckoned, a fiery point that grew and expanded and nearly engulfed her, until . . . it retreated. London gulped, surfacing. He'd stopped his wonderful torture.

"Now, please, now," she nearly sobbed.

Even in the darkness of the cabin, she saw the gleam on his face where her juices covered him. And that smile of his, wicked and tormenting. "Not yet. Tell me what you want."

"I want to . . ." She tried to force the unfamiliar words out. "I want . . . to come."

"Anything you desire, but that. Remember? Only when I say you can come, will I let you."

She could kill him. She wanted him. She forgot herself entirely and was only hunger, lust, demand.

She would make him suffer as she did. She thought about leaving, going back to her cabin, and letting him stew in frustration. That idea she discarded almost at once. She very much did not want to leave.

What else could she do?

An idea came to her, sinful and superb. But did she have the courage to do it?

In the darkness, his eyes were ink, but warm, so warm. He desired her, yes, as she did him. But she felt him pushing her toward something, toward a greater understanding of herself. She could find comfort in a quick release, and hide in that. This way, this suspension and play, brought her out, challenged her. And she would meet that challenge.

London pushed him back lightly, so he stepped away. His erection jutted up, pulling the fabric of his trousers tight. London curled her hands into themselves to keep from stroking him. She wriggled her way off the top of the dresser until she stood before him.

"Sit on the bed," she said.

Though he raised a brow at her imperious tone, he complied, wide-legged, leaning back on his elbows like an indulged pasha.

"Is it bright enough?" she asked. "Can you see me?"

"I can."

"Now," she said with all the hauteur she could muster, "watch me."

London set her mind free, as one might a bird from a cage. She felt herself take flight. *I can be anything, do anything.*

With a deliberate languor, she began to unfasten her dress. A series of small hooks ran down the front of the bodice—the sort of dress a woman might wear when traveling alone or far from a maid to assist her—and she started at the top, at the collar. Yet she did not proceed immediately down the bodice. London undid four or five hooks at a time, pulling the fabric open, then reaching in and lightly, very lightly, caressing herself. Her throat and chest were most responsive, since no corset guarded her skin there, and she made herself shiver. He watched her do this. Unhook, pause, caress. Again. And again. She reached such sensitivity, that, even when she did reach her corset cover, she still trembled at her own touch.

His eyes were hungry and bright. His breathing grew labored. Impossibly, he seemed to grow even bigger, his erection lengthening and thickening, as he watched her undo the fastenings on the side of the dress and step out of it. Then she removed her corset cover, and finally, slowly, she unfastened her corset and put it aside. Now all she wore was her chemise.

Yet even this wisp of cotton was too much. London trailed her hands up and down her body, beginning at her neck, the hollow of her throat, then the very top of her chest. Then lower. Beneath the fine chemise, her breasts were full and needy. She'd never truly touched her own breasts before, not without some measure of awkwardness, but now she touched them as she wanted *him* to, gathering them in her hands, feeling their roundness, their softness, the hard nipples that rasped against her chemise and palms.

A small moan curled from her mouth. He reached for her. She slid away.

"No touching," she breathed. "Not until I say."

She thought she heard Bennett's teeth grind against each other. But he did not try to touch her again. Instead, he nearly set her aflame with his gaze as he panted like a man who'd run up a mountain. His hands gripped the woolen blanket, knuckles whitening.

Power, the likes of which London never knew, filled her. She felt mighty and female. Eve and Lilith and Isis and Aphrodite and Lakshmi. All her.

Confident that he would do as she commanded, London resumed her exploration of her body. Just under her breasts, her skin was tight and sensitive, and she felt the narrowing of her waist, then the flare of her hips. She had not Athena's abundant curves, but that didn't trouble her, because she was herself and she was enough. Her belly was soft and feminine, a woman's belly. And when she touched herself through the chemise, touched her pussy, as Bennett called it, ripples of pleasure cascaded through her, ever widening. She gasped.

"I can't—" he growled. "Have to—"

Instead of trying to touch her, Bennett ripped open his trousers. His erection was straight, full and gorgeous. He stroked himself, his large hand on his own flesh. For a few moments, their eyes were locked as they each touched themselves. Seeing how aroused he was, that *she* had done that, worn away at this man's control until he was forced to pleasure himself, made London lose the fragile hold on her own desire. She tugged off her chemise.

She stood before him, naked. The only man to ever see her thus.

"Touch me now," she gasped. "Touch me everywhere."

His trousers disappeared in moments. Now as nude as she, he swept her up in his arms and lay her down upon the bunk. He stretched out beside her, lean and hard, and they kissed with open mouths, breathing each other in, eating each other up. Against her thigh, she felt the rigid thickness of his penis, nudging her, leaving small slick trails of fluid on her skin. She'd touched him before through his clothing, but now she took him in her hand and reveled in the feel of him, the energy and life in him, and how, as she stroked him, he groaned into her mouth with the sounds of a man in ultimate rapture.

"You feel so good on my cock," he growled.

"Pussy, cock," she whispered with a laugh. "You will ruin my vocabulary."

"That's not all I'll ruin. Say it again."

"What?" she asked, feigning coyness. "Cock?" As she said this, she stroked him, hard, giving her hand a little twist. "Pussy?" She did it again. His hips surged.

"What a delightful strumpet you are," he said, though his words were guttural, hardly words at all.

"I learn from the master."

"Oh, no," he said with a wolfish grin. "This is all you, my love. So is this." His fingers dipped into her pussy, and she writhed. "Mm. Very small, very tight."

A frisson of worry. "Too tight?"

"No such thing." He moved over her, positioning himself between her legs, his cock at her entrance. He circled her, coating himself in her wetness, then, with her legs wrapped around his waist, her arms around his shoulders, her whole body vibrating with need, he sank into her.

She arched up with a cry. He stretched her, filled her, almost to bursting, but it felt so good.

"See?" he panted. "Perfect fit."

London couldn't have answered him if she tried. Words were gone. Self was gone. Everything was pleasure. And when he started to move, sliding in deeper, then pulling back with an exquisite drag, London felt her body dissolve, while at the same time she was all body, all sensation.

They moved together, learning angles and rhythm. She raised to meet his thrusts, pressing her heels into the small of his back, locking her ankles together so she clasped him to her, as if he might get up and leave. The only place he seemed to want to be was inside her, as far within her as possible.

Soon, they rocked together, hardly drawing apart. Even those seconds when he slid back for another thrust were too long to bear. His skin was sweat-slick, the cords of his neck tight, ecstasy carving his face into hollows. She loved to watch him feel his pleasure, for he gave himself to it utterly. As she did.

He shifted his position, so that, with each plunge into her, his hips rubbed her swollen, pulsing flesh. And all at once, she was lost. The orgasm hit her with the force of tempest. Everything contracted, then exploded with re-lease, and a sound came from her she'd never heard before, a primitive cry issuing from the depths of herself, low and throaty.

Then he was gone, stiffening, groaning. On and on. London, in the after haze of her own climax, could only dimly marvel at the duration of his orgasm. He, too, seemed surprised, for when it was finally over, he collapsed on top of her with a startled laugh.

"I was very naughty," she said when at last she could form words. "I broke the rules."

He raised a questioning brow.

"I didn't wait for you to say I could come," London said.

He laughed once more. It was something he did easily. "Then we'll just have to do it all over again, bad girl."

She kissed him, then said with a smile, "Oh, I like being bad."

Bennett spent most of his life avoiding expectations. They only led to disappointment, bitterness. Whenever he traveled, he kept his mind open to all possibilities, expecting nothing, glad for every and all eventuality. The same with people. He kept his expectations to a minimum, especially when it came to women. He made no demands on his lovers—other than what he exacted of them in bed, and they were eager to comply—and was happy to receive whatever was given. Everything was a gift.

But he was human, after all, and a man, so expectations were inevitable, despite his precautions. He did have certain preconceived ideas about certain paramours, and sometimes those ideas fell short while other times, he felt himself generously rewarded. A wonderful, unexpected treasure.

Yet, in his over sixteen years of sexual experience, he'd never, not once, had every single one of his expectations completely and utterly decimated as they had been this night with London Harcourt.

As they lay in the narrow bunk, twined together, suspended in the honey of afterglow, Bennett marveled. He'd had his suspicions, of course. He'd known, even in the marketplace at Monastiraki, that a passionate woman dwelt beneath the precise tailoring of her exterior. He'd seen the barely banked fires in her dark chocolate eyes. The kisses they had shared told him much the same. Here was a woman who, when given the chance, would burn down the world with the heat of herself. Taking her to bed would be an extraordinary privilege, a peerless, carnal delight.

Even that was nothing compared to the reality. Bennett was struck, awed by her. Her fearlessness. Her hunger. To see her grow and evolve before his very eyes into a woman who commanded the universe, itself.

This is what it's like to see a galaxy born, he thought. Stars and planets and life, life everywhere, filling the sky with brilliance. What could anyone do but marvel.

An unaccustomed humbleness settled over him, that he, of all men, should be witness to her evolution, that he may have even had a hand in it. Hell. If he'd known that a lifetime of dubious behavior would net him such honor, he would have started his transgressions a good deal sooner. Say, shortly after birth. He could have crawled to the neighbor's place and seduced their teenaged daughters, clad only in a nappy and a smile.

"What are you laughing about?" London asked drowsily.

"Childhood memory."

"Something scandalous, no doubt."

She snuggled closer, and he tightened his hold on her. She felt so damned good in his arms. Then he realized something.

"You didn't bite me," he said.

She laughed, and he felt the thrum of her laughter

throughout his body. "Last night, I was trying to be quiet. Tonight, I forgot to be quiet. I'm sure everyone heard me." Yet she didn't sound particularly upset by the idea.

"I like that I can make you forget yourself." Made him feel like a titan, actually.

"I am entirely forgotten." She leaned closer and nipped his shoulder. "There. That should satisfy you."

"Never satisfied."

He kissed her, first her mouth, then along her jaw and onto the tender column of her neck. Under his lips, her pulse throbbed like music.

She asked, "Have you ever been in love?"

His kisses stopped. "All the time."

She pulled back a little to look him in the eyes. "I mean *really* in love."

"The answer's still yes."

"What happened? Did things not work out between you two?"

"More than two, sweetheart," he said, smiling. When she frowned in puzzlement, he explained, "I love every woman I'm with. Some of them I don't even take to bed."

"But that isn't *real* love," she protested.

"Why not? There's no book that contains the one true definition of love, or, if there is, I sure as hell haven't read it." He started to kiss her again, both as a distraction and because he needed to.

Yet she was not readily distracted. "Can it be love if you feel that way for more than one woman? Love is for just one person, someone special. Or, at least," she said quickly, as if correcting herself, "that's what I have heard."

Resigned now to the conversation, he said, "Every woman is special." She snorted in disbelief, so he continued, "That's not some scoundrel's patter. It's true. There's something to love in each woman. So I do."

"You love me, too?" she said, dry.

"Oh, most definitely," he said readily, without hesitation. "I do love you, London."

She gave a faint, melancholy smile. "I thought that when I finally heard those words, it would mean something."

A hot rush of anger struck him, surprising him with its speed and intensity. "It *does* mean something, damn it. Or you think so low of me that you'd just toss away my words like tin trinkets."

She looked down, contrite. "I'm sorry, Bennett." She ran her hands across his shoulders, down his arms, to link their fingers together. "That is not what I meant. I do value what you say, what you feel. Yet, there's a part of me that still believes love can only exist between two people. Maybe three, if they are exceptionally broad-minded," she added with a smile.

His anger ebbed, but he still felt its effect, or, more specifically, his shock that her dismissal of him could cause such a quick and painful wound. To distract himself, he ran his lips back and forth across the silk of her hair. The scent of the ocean clung to her, fresh and cool.

"I've never been in love," London said on a sigh. "I thought I would grow to love Lawrence, but it never happened."

Bennett, who usually did not mind his lovers talking of past affairs, found himself knotted up with a strange emotion to hear London speak of her dead husband. A tight clenching throughout his body. More anger. It took a moment for him to recognize what it was. Jealousy.

Good Christ, what was happening to him?

"There are so many words for love," she said quietly. "*Liefde, amour, die Liebe.* Greek has so many words. *Agape, philia, eros.* They all mean something different. So perhaps there is no one definition of love. But I know what I want it to be for myself."

It was dangerous territory, the land of expectations that

Bennett so scrupulously avoided—if a man such as himself could possess scruples. Yet he needed to know, for reasons he couldn't figure, everything that was inside of her. "How'd you come by this concept?"

"I didn't learn it at home," she said. "Not between my parents. They were business partners, or rather, my father ran the company and my mother was a fairly valued employee, but nothing more than that. Certainly, there wasn't love between Lawrence and me. And what the girls I knew spoke of when they talked of sweethearts seemed to be childish infatuation. Not *real* love. In the world in which I lived, it didn't seem to exist."

"So you invented something, an idea."

"I suppose I did," she murmured, trailing her fingers up and down his chest. Her touch lit tiny fires, like a signal from one camp to another, passing along the message of desire. "Based it on all the ancient love poems and epic tales that I'd been reading ever since I was a child. I would read of heroes and goddesses, or even ordinary people, falling in love, how it was described, how they felt. And I wanted that."

She grew pensive, far off. "I thought, 'When I am with the man I love,'" she said, her voice thoughtful and low, "'everything else' will disappear. I'll see only him. He will be the person I want to share everything with. If I am walking alone and I see something beautiful, like a wildflower poking up from the pavement, or something ridiculous, like a monkey in a hat, I will rush to tell him these things. And in the dark of night, he alone is who I will want beside me, and I'll listen to him breathe in sleep and I shall put my hand upon him and hope he dreams of me, for I couldn't bear even a moment apart from him.'"

She turned sparkling eyes to Bennett. "Even now, after my marriage, after everything, I want these things. Foolish of me."

When he tried to speak, a hoarse rasp came out. He turned away to clear his throat. "I think," he said when he could trust himself not to croak like a bullfrog, "that nothing's foolish where the heart's concerned. You want what you want, and nobody can slight you for it. But, London," and here he tipped up her chin so their eyes met and there could be no mistaking what he was about to say, "I can't love you the way that you want."

"You don't know that," she said at once.

He kept his voice level. "I do know. I've known it my whole life. I can give affection, desire, pleasure. These things are, to me, love. But the kind of love you're asking for, it's not possible, not from me. I can't bind myself forever to one woman, and I don't want her binding herself to me." He placed a kiss, one after the other, upon her temples, the softest of touches of mouth to flesh. "And to think otherwise is only going to hurt us both."

"Should we stop this, then? This . . . whatever it is between us."

The idea caused a twist, low in his gut, as though a knife slid into him. They'd both crawled through fire to reach each other, to bring their bodies and hearts together. He felt as though he had died and been reborn many times just to experience the ecstasy of London as his lover. And now, he was to give her up? Impossible. "I won't stop." He couldn't.

"Me, either." She nestled close to him as he let go of the breath he'd been holding. "So, there will be no demands for something that cannot be given. I'd rather have now, in whatever form it takes."

He stroked her hair, feeling its softness between his fingers. "We'll have our now."

"Maybe, one day, it will happen for me with someone," London mused aloud. "I would like that. I want to experience my kind of love at least once before I die."

He thought about that man, the unnamed, faceless man

who would, someday, receive beautiful, passionate, and brave London's love and would be able to reciprocate it as she needed. Who would be everything in her eyes. Who would hear her stories of sidewalk wildflowers and monkeys in haberdashery. Who slept beside her and dreamt of her because she touched him to be near him always. Bennett hated that man.

Chapter 12

A Dangerous Strait

Tacitly, everyone agreed not to examine the mirror until the morning. Before dawn, Stathis and his sons had loosened the lines between the two caiques, then, with promises of a future reunion, sailed off to make their catch.

London heard Athena and Kallas arguing below deck. Something about her resting more, which the witch refused to do.

"It never seems to stop with them," London murmured, "the arguments."

"Surely that doesn't surprise you," said Bennett.

She rolled her eyes. "I *do* know how anger and lust fuel one another." When he raised a brow at her, she explained, "It was like that, sometimes, with Lawrence and me. We'd fight about something I did to the house or an aspect of my behavior that he disliked, and I would get angry that he'd make demands but was hardly around, so why should it matter if I went riding by myself or expanded the library." She waved away the memories of those rows.

"The best part of those arguments," she continued, "was what happened afterward. The lights were off, of course," she added with a blush, "but things became a good deal less . . . routine." That passion between them never lasted, though. Only in the heat of wrath did London and her late husband find any form of desire between them. And the pleasure they'd achieved had been selfish, each clawing toward gratification, using the other's body as a means of attaining climax. She never felt truly fulfilled after such encounters. Only more alone.

"So you understand what goes on between Kallas and Athena," Bennett said with a scowl. Interesting. He did not strike London as the sort of man who even comprehended jealousy, let alone felt it. Surely, London had to be mistaken in her interpretation.

"It seems that there is more to what is happening between our captain and our witch than mere desire," London said. "Affection, perhaps."

"Our witch has got a new fancy," Bennett allowed. He watched the wind in the sails, noting its direction. "But nothing lasts. She moves on."

"Like you," London said softly.

He gazed at her steadily. "Like me."

"There's freedom in that." She would not frustrate herself, grasping at what could not be. "To unloose the passions and let them run where they will with no fear of tomorrow."

"Think you did a rather good job of it last night—freeing your passions."

The heat of his voice made her tremble. "I did, didn't I?" She felt proud of herself, proud of what she and Bennett had done, how little she cared what anyone else thought.

At last, Athena and Kallas joined them on deck, the witch looking considerably improved, though a bit vexed with the captain, a sentiment he shared.

Bennett uncovered the mirror. It gleamed even more brightly than it had when it was first removed from the stream.

"Such brilliance in its surface," Athena marveled, then asked London, "Are you sure of its age?"

"Quite," said London, and felt certain of herself. Where language was concerned, she needed no other assurances besides her own. "The dialect died out millennia ago. Only a few fragments remain, but there are perhaps only a half dozen people familiar with it, maybe even less."

"Including you," added Bennett. His smile warmed her deeply.

"And me," she said, pride and modesty butting up against each other. She was used to comments about her appearance or her clothing or other inconsequential things, but Bennett was the first man, the first person, to value her skill with languages.

"And the writings?" Kallas asked, scattering her thoughts. "What do they say?"

London held the mirror, tilting it this way and that to better read the words encircling its rim. She cleared her throat, then began:

"My eye is golden and lost.
The rocks tumble, seven three nine, on the east;
Then the precarious narrow path that must be taken,
Else find yourself stranded, walk upon the water.
Onward, and reflect toward the dawn.
Find me then, if you can, to see
What I see."

Finished, she looked to Bennett to see what he could make of such a riddle. "I wish, sometimes, that these ancients spoke plainly."

"Then there'd be no fun in it." He stared at the mirror as if it could reflect back an answer. London watched the light bounce off the mirror's surface to bathe Bennett in a golden halo, but he was far more devil than angel. She had proof of that in the wonderful soreness throughout her body.

"You sure that's some magic something?" Kallas asked. "Because it sounds like a sailor giving directions."

Athena frowned, but did not scoff. "What do you mean?"

"There's a stretch of the sea to the northeast of here, a few days' sail," Kallas explained. "A chain of islands, more rocks in the sea than islands, in groups. The first of seven, then three, and then nine. Once past those, there are two islands that face each other with a narrow strait between them—maybe three times the width of this boat. A difficult sail. No one has ever dared it. Around the islands are wide shoals, too shallow to sail, but it's said a man could walk on them and the water would only come to his ankles. Then, *toward the dawn* would mean go east from there."

"Then this mirror is a map," said London.

"A map of words," the captain said. He drew on his pipe as punctuation, but could not quite hide some deserved masculine preening when Athena gaped in admiration and amazement.

"The men in your family must all be incredible sailors," said Bennett, approving.

"Always. It's said one of my ancestors taught Jason how to sail, and another sailed with Odysseus. Will they sing of me, the Muses?"

"Without a doubt," said London.

"You, too, will be in their song, Lady Oracle, who reads the words of the past."

"An extraordinary little boat we've got here," said Bennett. He rubbed his hands together. "Now, let's have ourselves some breakfast. I'm so hungry, I could eat a halyard."

London looked around the deck of the caique, at Kallas attending to the sails of his beloved boat, at Athena still shaking her head in wonderment, at Bennett heading off toward the galley below. He was the man whose bed she shared. For a few hours. For a few days. And then . . . and then she did not know, but she would not let herself dwell on uncertainties. For now, she was here, in the middle of the ocean, on this swift-sailing boat, with these people.

Sea captain. Noble witch. Life-loving scoundrel. And her. An odd group, but one in which she was discovering her most truthful self.

London adjusted the tension on the jib's halyard, keeping its leading edge straight as the wind shifted. She didn't need Kallas's guidance anymore. She knew what the boat needed.

Certain moments in one's life would always be returned to, even years, decades, later. Some of them were painful— heartbreak, mortification, loss—but there were others that held the clarity and perfection of cut gems, to sparkle against the velvet drape of memory. And, as the years progressed and unfolded in their relentless march, again and again would the mind revisit those moments. Eating a plum, the juices running down your hand, as you walked an esplanade along the shore. The day that the weather cleared and the ground was finally firm enough to be ridden upon, and the leap of your heart as your horse took the first fence. A new old book being delivered and unwrapped from its brown paper, sitting upon your desk, full of possibility, and the musty, rich smell of its pages as you opened it.

You returned to these moments, sometimes to ease a current suffering, and sometimes for the simple pleasure of revisiting a past joy, but they were there, and held and treasured in the cupped palms of your mind.

London knew that, no matter what the years brought her, or even the next few weeks, she would always cherish her days spent on the caique, as they sailed toward the mirror's destination. Though she hadn't much experience with the larger world, she understood enough to see these days as miniature miracles painted in azure, cobalt, turquoise. Perhaps they were all the more precious because they could not last.

Squinting in the sun, she checked the jibsheets, both port and starboard, feeling the power in the lines, taking their power into herself.

Knowing the transience of her happiness, she reveled in each and every heartbeat, each breath. Daytime was filled with light and sky and sea, the glitter of gold upon the waves, the snap of the sails as she learned the wind, passing other brightly painted boats in the timeless rhythm of seafaring life. She felt softness leave her arms, her body, in the joy of movement. Her hair smelled of saltwater and sun. She laughed often. Stories were told, many outrageous, some entirely fabricated. She drank dark wine and ate briny olives. She became a sailor.

And the nights. She felt like Psyche, visited each night by the embodiment of sensuality. In truth, it was *she* who visited *him*, since London and Athena shared a cabin, but the general idea was much the same. Though she prized her days, London could not wait for night, after dinner, when Kallas took the wheel for a few hours, leaving Bennett and her free to do unspeakably wonderful and wicked things to one another in dark, intimate seclusion.

She explored every inch of Bennett's magnificent body and, in so doing, came to know her own completely. How, when he bit the tender juncture of her neck and shoulder, she shuddered with pleasure. The insides of her arms, she discovered, were sensitive, and she ran them over his back, across his broad chest, feeling the textures of his skin, his hair. Her breath on the inside of his thigh caused him to growl. His tongue, lapping at the folds of her pussy, made her whimper and writhe. She loved to clutch at the tight muscles of his buttocks as he drove into her, pulling him closer until they were almost one creature.

He taught her things. She guided him. They tangled together.

The heat that now suffused her cheeks was not caused by the sun, but by exquisite memory of what she and Bennett had done the night before.

London was sure that every morning, she emerged on deck with the sleepy, satisfied look of a woman who had been thoroughly pleasured. God knew that Kallas and Athena had to hear her moans each night. She could not bring herself to care. Shameless. She was without shame. And it was wonderful.

It wasn't only the physical aspects of their lovemaking that had London smiling to herself. Once they had temporarily sated themselves with each other's bodies, she and Bennett would lay together in the narrow bunk and talk of everything—weighty matters, trifles. She learned about his life in England as the second son of a noted barrister, his restlessness at the idea of settling down, practicing law himself, and how, when he was recruited for the Blades, life finally made sense. He could at last make good use of his skill with codes, his ease in the darkness. A man like him, of excellent breeding and solid English values, clever of mind and strong of body, could have been an Heir. To her utter astonishment, she learned that he had, in fact, been approached by an agent of the Heirs of Albion while in his second year at Cambridge. Bennett rejected their advances, their appeals to his vanity, his cupidity. Soon after that, a man by the name of Catullus Graves sent him a letter, inviting him to Southampton to decode some ancient Scandinavian ciphers. That's when he learned about the Blades, and that's when he vowed to make their cause his own.

At his prompting, she told him about her own life, but it was far less interesting, in her opinion, than his. Unlike him, she'd never been to Lapland, Tangiers, Bucharest. She hadn't scrambled up the sides of snow-covered mountains, seeking shelter before a blizzard hit. She never shared a Berber's hookah while watching kohl-eyed, veiled dancers in firelight. But, oh, she wanted to, and he described his adventures with such vivid detail that she felt as if she'd lived a whole other life, one outside of books. He asked about the numerous languages she studied, her joy in them, and took his pleasure in hers. She had never spoken to anyone about her linguistic scholarship, always afraid of their response. Bennett was different. She knew she could trust him; he wouldn't turn on her or decry what was so important to her.

She thought about them following the mirror's direction. It would be a difficult voyage—the mirror guarded its secrets well. London hoped Kallas had the skill of generations to navigate treacherous waters.

Satisfied that the jib's rigging was in order, London drifted from the bow of the boat toward the quarterdeck. There, she found Athena and Kallas passionately arguing about whether Jason should have abandoned Medea. Naturally, the witch defended the sorceress. Kallas insisted that Jason rightly found a new woman, as Medea was of a less-than-sane disposition.

"But she killed her own brother to help him escape Colchis," Athena protested.

"Exactly," said Kallas. "She was several sails short of a clipper."

Athena made a noise of outrage.

London smothered her laugh, then asked, "Where is Bennett?"

With the stem of his pipe, Kallas pointed toward the stern of the boat.

Leaving the witch and the sailor locked in their dispute, London picked her way toward the back of the caique. As she neared, she glanced around with a frown. Bennett wasn't there.

But he was. London got closer and saw him. Sprawled on his back along the decking, his head propped on a coil of rope, Bennett lay across the stern. His chest rose and fell in gentle swells. He was asleep.

For a few moments, she watched him. He'd had the opportunity to watch her sleep back on Delos, and she seized her chance for reversal.

His long legs stretched out, the fabric of his trousers outlining the clean shapes of his muscles. An athlete at rest, the subject for sculpture. His fingers interlaced over the breadth of his chest—she shivered, remembering how, last night, those deft fingers felt as they trailed along her spine, over the curve of her behind, and down her legs in a whisper caress. In sleep, his face was as beautiful as a night full of stars over the sea. Long, dark eyelashes that trembled slightly with dreams. His mouth, delectable, full, turned in a half smile, for even asleep there was lightness in his heart. A surge of tenderness swept through her.

London realized that they never actually slept together. She always had to return to her cabin, so that, when Kallas's shift at the helm was over, he had a bed to himself. She and Bennett might doze, briefly, but then it was time for her to struggle into her clothing and stagger across the passageway, and for him to go above. To wake beside him in the glow of morning, both of them warm and naked, talking of half-remembered dreams as they surfaced into wakefulness, it was a pleasure she might never experience.

A pain tightened within her, but she struggled to banish it. *No demands*, she reminded herself. *Nothing but now.*

She could watch him all day. Yet she didn't want to wake him. Perhaps she would join Kallas and Athena's disputation, even though she felt as though her presence was not necessary. The two Greeks always had some variety of argument brewing.

London turned to go back, but at the faint sound of her skirts, Bennett opened his eyes. He saw her and smiled, stretching like a cat.

"Don't go," he rumbled.

"I didn't mean to disturb you," she said.

"I'm already disturbed." He reached out a hand toward her. "Sit with me."

She came forward and took his hand, reveling in the feel of his skin against hers. When he drew her down, she readily acquiesced, sitting cross-legged and cradling his head in her lap.

"Mm," he murmured, nuzzling her thigh. "Much better."

Even this turned her blood tropic. Her hands ran through his dark hair. Here was another of those moments, she realized, that she would return to many times over in the course of her life. "Poor beast," she said, soft, "have I been wearing you out these past few nights?"

"Worn down to the bone." He took one of her hands and rubbed it against his cheek. Slight bristles prickled against her palm, and she adored the masculinity of it, of him.

"Perhaps I should let you sleep at night instead of demanding ravishment."

His bright aqua eyes held hers, sharp and intense. "I'm not giving you up. Not even for a night. Either you come to my cabin or I go to yours."

"Athena might not appreciate that," she said placidly, yet inside, she rioted, knowing that he needed her as much as she needed him.

"She's a grown woman," he said with a shrug. "God knows she's seen me doing worse."

London raised a brow. "So, you and she *were* lovers." Try as she did, it was impossible to keep the edge from her voice.

"A long time ago. Briefly." He gripped London's hand tighter. "But that means nothing. We're friends now. Only friends."

London said, "I'm not quite as . . . sophisticated as you. I wonder how you'd feel if one of my former amours was on this boat. Not that I had any, but if I did."

"I'd tie raw steaks to him and throw him overboard. But not before beating him into a paste."

"Very bloodthirsty."

He flashed a vicious grin. "Love, where you're concerned, you have no idea."

She bent forward and kissed him, mouths upside down. Then, for some time, they were quiet. She continued to stroke his hair, and he closed his eyes, leaning into her touch, almost purring.

"What kind of name is London?" he asked suddenly. "I've never met anybody with that name before."

Who knew what directions his clever mind would take? "My full name is Victoria Regina Gloriana London Edgeworth Harcourt."

"Great God, how cumbersome to embroider."

London chuckled. "Yes, well, my father is possessed of a rather overdeveloped patriotic fervor. When I was very small, everyone called me Victoria, but as soon as I learned to read—"

"At the age of two."

"Four, Clever Britches," she said, tugging hard on his hair. He grimaced comically. "When I was four," she continued, loosening her hold, "I saw that everywhere we went in the city, my middle name kept popping up. On everything. Signs. Newspapers. Painted on the sides of wagons. And I thought that, if my name was everywhere, then everything belonged to me."

"A greedy little imp."

"Not greedy," she defended. "I thought that our Queen could rule the country, and I would rule the city."

"Power mad," he said sagely. "I knew it. Not so meek and mild, after all."

She shook her head at him, torn between amusement and exasperation. "So I insisted on being called 'London.' Miraculously, even my father agreed. And that is what I have gone by ever since." Even speaking of her father cast a pall over what had been a lovely afternoon. She tried to turn the conversation to more pleasant topics. "And what about you? I've never met anyone named Bennett."

"My mother was, is, a great admirer of the novels of Miss Austen. *Pride and Prejudice* is one of her favorites."

"Lucky that you weren't named Fitzwilliam."

"Tell that to my brother."

"No!"

"Yes. Fitzwilliam Darcy Day. Couldn't even take refuge in his middle name. I believe it shaped him into the venal man he is today." He sighed mournfully. "A barrister."

"My condolences," she murmured, but a smile curved her mouth.

They were smiling together in the Aegean sunlight when Kallas's shout had them both leaping to their feet and running to the helm, hand in hand.

"What's wrong?" Bennett demanded, awake and alert.

"Nothing's wrong," Kallas answered. "But I thought you should know, we have been guided properly by your mirror. And me. Look."

He pointed off the portside bow, and London squeezed Bennett's hand tightly. There, lined up in groups of seven, then three, and then nine, were tiny islands, more like the jagged peaks of a dragon's teeth above water than true islands, but they were there just the same, as the mirror had directed. Her heart pounded. They were getting closer to the Source.

London thought she saw something else. She darted into the quarterdeck house and returned with the spyglass, which she trained closer to the horizon. She observed dim, low shapes of two more islands, a narrow strait between them. It was precisely what Kallas and the mirror said they would find.

"Are we going to have to sail through that?" London asked, pointing at the strait. The spyglass was passed around, each of them taking a turn to peer through it. "It seems hardly wide enough to fit a stout man, let alone a boat."

Everyone fell silent, considering this.

"Now is the time for worrying," Athena said.

The caucus was brief and didn't soothe anybody's nerves. Bennett paced as they debated their options. As they neared the strait, it showed itself to be lined with spiked rocks, a tight squeeze for even the most adept seaman. Surely Scylla presented less of a threat.

"What about sailing around it?" asked London.

"Can't," Kallas answered. "The shoals are wide and treacherous. If we skirt them, the wind catches us and throws us far off course. We'd be halfway to Constantinople before we got our direction back."

"How are we supposed to sail through the shoals to get to the strait?" Athena asked.

"Day, take the helm," Kallas said. Bennett, knowing it was best to trust the knowledgeable captain, did as instructed, even though the strait approached quickly.

Kallas ran to the bow of the boat and peered closely at the nearing shoals. He returned and took the wheel from Bennett.

"There's a narrow dip in the sands of the shoals. It's deep enough to sail through." His tone left no doubt that the captain, who had saltwater running through his veins, could do just that. Bennett was damned grateful that the captain hadn't called upon him to perform the nigh-impossible task.

The wind gathered in strength as the caique reached the edge of the shoals, as though pushing them toward it, toward the possibility of running aground. And beyond that, there loomed the dangerous rocks of the strait, and the likelihood of being smashed against them.

Ordinarily, such prospects gave him a thrill, another chance for him to flirt with and escape from death. But there were other people to consider besides himself.

"Either we sail through or turn back," said Athena. "Those are our choices."

"I cannot turn back," London answered.

"Nor I," Bennett seconded. "And you?" he asked both Kallas and Athena.

Athena drew herself up, proud. "Galanos women never shy from danger."

"I'm going to forget you asked me that," the captain growled to Bennett.

Bennett nodded, satisfied, but couldn't entirely smash a niggling fear that poked and jabbed at his heart. He realized it wasn't his own skin he worried about. He glanced at London, watching, grave and courageous. The fear spiked. Bennett swore softly, and it didn't help a damn. So he strode to her and took her mouth in a brief, demanding kiss. Her hands barely had time to cup his jaw before he moved away.

Action removed doubt. They were at the shoals.

"Man your stations," Kallas barked, and Bennett was again all too glad to obey the order. He took the mainsail, with London at the jib and Athena at the foresail. They would all have to work quickly—the wind rammed them onward, giving no quarter or possibility of a sane, calm navigation. Both London and Athena struggled against their long hair blowing in their faces, and skirts tangling in their legs. Even Bennett felt the invisible, pitiless hands of the wind shoving at him, forcing him to anchor his legs to the deck to keep from being blown about like so much flotsam. Everyone crouched low, shielding themselves. They fought the wind, battling it.

Kallas stood at the helm, his pipe stem held tight between his teeth as he threaded the caique through the tight confines of the shoals' passage. But the captain grinned, his eyes burning bright. Bennett chuckled to himself. Kallas was breaching the shoals' maidenhead, and felt a proprietary, feral pleasure in taking its innocence. He caught Bennett's chuckle and laughed, as well. Athena and London stared at them in confusion. Bennett wasn't about to tell the women why he and Kallas exulted. Only men knew the pleasure of breaching a narrow opening, sliding through the wet to find home.

There wasn't time for triumph. No sooner had the caique navigated the shoals than they were at the mouth of the strait, its red rock walls stretching steep and ominous against the perfect blue of the sky.

Nowhere to go but onward. The end of the strait wasn't far, but to Bennett's eyes, it seemed leagues away.

"We take the middle," Kallas shouted above the wind. "Keep the sails close-hauled. London, don't pull the jib flat. Keep a slot between the jib and the main. Day, trim the main. No one make them fast—we need them at hand." He wrestled with the wheel as the steep, pitted faces of rock towered over them on both sides.

They raced forward. Bennett kept his station, following Kallas's yelled commands, as did Athena and London. Both women squinted in the harsh wind but stayed rooted to their posts. The sheer faces of rock crowded the boat on both sides, looming, close. It would take nerves of steel, and close cooperation between everyone on board, to make it through without tearing the hull to matchsticks.

Beneath the wind, Bennett felt it. A rumble. Growing in depth and strength.

He looked up.

"Bollocks," he muttered to himself, then shouted, "Watch your heads!"

Everyone gazed upward, eyes wide.

Kallas said something in Greek that Bennett couldn't translate, but no doubt it was a filthy curse. London didn't mind. She said the exact same thing a heartbeat later.

A boulder came plummeting down the face of the cliff, bouncing off rocks. It skipped off an outcropping and headed for the bow of the boat. Exactly where London stood.

Bennett ran and threw himself at London, sending them both slamming to the deck as the boulder shot across the bow. It shattered on the other cliff, spraying them with gravel.

Seeing her close call, London turned shocked and grateful eyes to Bennett.

"Stay at your posts!" bellowed Kallas. "There's more!"

Rocks of every size rained down on them. The smaller ones struck the hull and deck of the caique, splintering wood, and peppering everyone on board with bruises. Despite Kallas's command, Bennett continued to shield London with his body.

"Kallas needs you on the mainsail," she said, her voice muffled. "Go. I'll be fine."

A rock clipped his right shoulder. Bennett swore. It would have hit London if he hadn't been covering her.

When he didn't move, she shoved at him. "I'm not made of porcelain. And the boat needs you. Needs *us*," she added, glancing up at the unattended jib, clattering in the wind.

He reluctantly peeled himself away, knowing she was right. He took up the mainsail and saw London return to manning the jib. Small rocks pelted her. She winced from the impact but didn't leave her post, holding the jib tight. Bennett cursed, hating to think of her hurt.

Kallas grappled with the wheel as heavy boulders crashed into the waters just off the starboard bow. Water splashed up, soaking London and Bennett.

More boulders tumbled into the water along the starboard side of the boat. Even in the chaos, Bennett wondered why the rocks were coming down only on one side, and not both. The ancients always protected their Sources well. They were leaving too much of an opening on the port side.

"I'm taking her port!" Kallas yelled. He began to turn the wheel to make the adjustment.

No, something wasn't quite right.

"Hold, Kallas!" Bennett shouted back. "Keep us starboard!"

"We'll be flattened," the captain growled, still turning the wheel.

Bennett dove from his post by the mainsail to wrestle the wheel back. The two men grappled while London and Athena could only look on in horrified confusion.

"Give me back my damned wheel," Kallas snarled. He punched Bennett in the ribs, not hard enough to break anything, but enough to hurt like hell. A punch like that would have finished most men, but Bennett held on.

He gritted, "No—Kallas, you ass—that's what they *want*." Bennett dug his heels into the deck and held fast. Kallas was as strong as men nearly twice the captain's size. He had to be part minotaur.

"Who?" demanded Kallas.

"Just . . . trust me," Bennett said, panting with effort. "I know how . . . these things . . . work." He gripped the wheel, keeping them to the right.

Just as the last rocks and boulders tumbled down, the boat rocked, listing starboard. An ungodly roar. From the sea floor, giant stone pillars three feet wide and tall as trees, shot up on the left.

Kallas's curse and Athena's prayers split the air. London hunkered beneath the jibsheets as displaced seawater washed over the bow. The hull of the boat just grazed the pillars as Bennett and Kallas both steered the caique away from them.

If they had sailed away from the rocks, they and the boat would have been mercilessly shattered on the pillars. This was plainly written on everyone's faces, including a pale but steady London, who looked at Bennett with wide eyes.

"How did you know?" the captain asked. "About the rocks and those pillars?"

"Counterbalance mechanism. Boulders tip the weight, pillars come up."

There wasn't time to discuss matters further. The pillars lined the port side of the rest of the strait, cutting their maneuvering room in half. Bennett strode back to the mainsail as Kallas issued more orders for the boat to tack.

The hull of the caique scraped against the spikes, gouging the wooden planks. Kallas guided the boat away from them. On the starboard side, the rocky cliffs grated the hull before their course was corrected. Everyone shuddered at the sounds, knowing that it could have been much, much worse.

And then it did get worse.

Cannon fire thundered over the wind. The boat shook with the percussion as pebbles clattered down, rattled loose from the cliffs. Bennett glanced back.

"Set another place at the table!" he shouted.

Everyone followed his gaze.

"Oh, hell," said London.

The Heirs' ship was just entering the strait. Their sails were down, instead using steam to power their way. Which meant they weren't at the mercy of the wind, like the caique.

"Maybe the fallen boulders will stop them," said Athena.

Bennett shook his head. "Not so easy to lose those bastards. Look where their guns are aimed."

The steamship's cannons pointed at the boulders piled up along the starboard side. Then, with a tremendous boom, the guns fired.

Boulders exploded into gravel. One moment, giant rocks blocked the strait, and then, with a roar, they turned to dust. Kallas had guided the caique carefully around the boulders, but the Heirs took their usual subtle approach by blowing the huge rocks straight to Hades.

"Goat-fucking bastards," growled Kallas.

Having conquered the first obstacle, the hulking iron monster of the steamship plowed on, straight toward the caique, threading through the narrow passage.

"The stone pillars," Athena said hopefully.

Bennett heard the sounds of the cannons being repositioned, orders shouted to men. "Cover yourselves," he commanded. No sooner had those words left his mouth than the cannons fired again, tearing chunks of stone from the pillars. The caique listed from side to side with the force of the impact.

Bennett wasn't worried. He let out a breath as the caique neared the end of the strait. The wind gentled like a broken horse, ready to be ridden. While the Heirs attempted to pulverize the stone pillars, making way for their cumbersome iron ship, the caique could navigate the shoals and make their escape. Simple.

Except—

"Captain, you need to see this," London called back from her position in the bow.

Without speaking, Bennett took the wheel from Kallas as the captain dashed forward. Curses that Bennett was sure hadn't been invented yet streamed from the captain's mouth, and, once Bennett saw what so angered Kallas, he decided to add his contribution to the swearing lexicon.

Instead of a narrow, but straight, path through the shoals on the other side of the island, this path twisted and turned, a labyrinth. The boat could run aground a million times over on the sandy banks of the shoals. Oh, it might be traversable, but only with a hell of a lot of guts and even more time.

Time was something they didn't have. The Heirs' cannons were working to make mince of the stone pillars.

And then the gun turret turned in the direction of the caique.

Bennett's blood chilled. The sailboat would be shredded by gunfire before they cleared the shoals. Like a shooting gallery target.

Just as Bennett thought this, the first round of gunfire whizzed overhead, narrowly missing the mainsail mast. Hell. The Heirs weren't planning on bringing down the boat. They'd take out its sails, leaving the Blades as juicy little plums ready to be plucked once the Heirs' ship made it through the strait. Jesus, what would Edgeworth do to London once he got his hands on her?

The boat glided from the strait and into the shoals. It was Kallas's boat, but Bennett had to seize command.

"Kallas, take the helm," he ordered. "London, stay in the bow, keep your eyes on the path through the shoals. You'll guide Kallas. Athena, you've got the sails."

Everyone hurried to obey, even the captain, who took no offense in Bennett's assumption of leadership. Not in such treacherous times.

"What about you?" asked London.

Without a word, Bennett dashed below to the cargo hold, grabbed a few things, then sprinted back on deck. London saw what he held and shook her head.

"No." Her voice was hard and sure.

But there was only one thing he could do. He checked the rifle. It was loaded, and he had slung a cartridge belt over his shoulder. He tugged off his boots and threw them to the deck. "Yes," he said. "A diversion." Then he kissed her, fast and hard.

Before she could argue, he vaulted over the side of the boat.

Chapter 13

The Sorcerer's Plan

London ran to the rail. She thought she would see Bennett swimming, if not sinking to the bottom of the sea. But he was running. Across the water.

Not on the water's surface. It rose to his calves. It seemed some minor miracle, or form of magic, then she remembered. The shoals. Bennett ran over the sandy surface, water churning around him. It couldn't be easy, running on wet sand, yet he did so with fluid grace, holding the rifle confidently. Straight toward the Heirs' ship, and her father. Men with guns massed on the steamer's deck just as the gun in the turret fired again, tearing a hole in the foresail.

"I need you guiding me at the bow," Kallas shouted.

Casting a searching, apprehensive look over her shoulder, London moved to her position. She prayed her last glimpse of Bennett wouldn't be him racing off across the face of the sea to his death, chased by his reflection.

He wasn't going to have much cover. Damn. Yet he'd rather take the chance out here, without protection, than let his friends, let London, be taken by the Heirs. He spared a quick glance back to see the caique begin its chancy navigation of the shoals. He couldn't see London, but maybe that was for the best. His mind had to be clear, no distractions, and she definitely commanded his attention.

At least he wasn't wearing his boots. They were already waterlogged disasters, but he could move faster without them.

The sandy bank of the shoals ran right up against the island. Bennett took up position behind the rocks at the opening to the strait. It wasn't ideal, but better than nothing.

A bang as the gun turret fired again. Thank Ares that the caique was moving in a serpentine direction, otherwise the mainsail mast would have been nothing but kindling. But it had a distance to go before it cleared the shoals.

Time to provide that diversion.

He took aim, steadied his breath. Squeezed the trigger. Hardly felt the rifle's recoil as it fired.

Men on the steamer's deck scattered as his bullet dented the wall of the gun turret. A grim little smile curved Bennett's mouth. Panic was his ally.

He fired again. Another dent in the turret. He'd never be able to take the weapon out with just a rifle. But, as much as he wanted to cut back or eliminate the Heirs' firepower, his main goal right now was distraction.

And he got that distraction as the gun turret aimed in his direction. He ducked when it fired, shattering rock over his head. The Heirs' mercenaries added their rifle fire to the assault. Bennett wheeled away, flattening his back against the rocks of the cliff. More chips of gravel as bullets whined and slammed into the cliffs, barely a foot above his head.

He watched the caique slowly moving through the shoals. Halfway there. London was almost safe. But not yet.

He turned back to the strait and the Heirs' ship. Kneeling, he braced himself on one knee, and shot.

A man went down. Bennett never liked to kill, but he

couldn't afford to be naïve. If he had a chance to take out a threat—especially to London—he'd take it, and face the consequences of his conscience later.

None of the fallen man's comrades paid him any heed. They kicked the body aside as they sent a volley of bullets Bennett's way. The gun in the turret added its contribution.

More rocks tumbled down on him, blasted free from the cliff. He glanced up. Not only was the aim of the Heirs' mercenaries improving as their ship neared, but he'd be flattened by rocks as his cover crumbled.

He ducked back as several boulders crashed down. His mouth curved in a tight smile. The Heirs just provided him with more cover.

He repositioned himself behind the boulders before resuming his sniping. Bullets slammed into the boulders as he fired—the men on deck had already arrayed themselves to get a better angle on him. The gun turret wasn't as speedy as it swung around.

The cannons had almost completely decimated the stone pillars, which meant the Heirs could be even closer, could take better aim at the boat. He chanced a look back at the caique. Nearly there. London was nearly safe.

Something stung his cheek. He touched a hand to his face and it came away red. So much for his pretty face. But he really didn't give a damn.

He took out three more men, but, hell, none of them were Heirs. Doubtless Edgeworth had himself safely secreted away in the bowels of the ship, content to let others kill and die for him. Even Fraser and that vulture Chernock were nowhere to be found.

Just as he was reloading his rifle, London's voice carried across the water as she called his name. Even the sound of her sent his pulse speeding faster than it had been moments earlier, exchanging gunfire with his enemies.

"Come back, Bennett!" she called. "We're almost clear!"

He fired off one more salvo before starting his sprint for the caique. It was a full-out run, racing not only the Heirs' guns, but the caique. In a moment, the sailboat would make open water. He'd rather be stranded than have them turn back for him, or he could swim for it, but he hoped he wouldn't have to pick between those options.

Another sting at his shoulder. Hell. He couldn't let himself be wounded. There wasn't bloody time for it.

He ran, legs churning in the water. The caique was half a mile off, but it felt farther out as he skirted the twisted opening in the shoals and dodged bullets.

Finally, lifetimes later, lungs and legs burning, he came alongside the caique. When London's face appeared over the rail, his heart gave a leap. Jesus, was he glad to see her. She and Athena reached down and, with groans of strain from everyone, hauled him up, just before the boat cleared the shoals.

The three of them fell onto the deck of the caique in a heap. For a mere moment, Bennett allowed himself the pleasure of feeling London beside him, her limbs tangled with his, her breath against his face.

She raised herself up on an elbow, and her eyes widened as she looked at him. "You're hurt!"

"Kitten scratch."

Her scowl was fierce and beautiful. Before she could scold him, Kallas's command sent them all hurrying to their positions. They adjusted the sails to let the wind carry them as fast as possible from the shoals and the island. And the Heirs, still negotiating the strait, continued to fire on them.

Kallas proved himself again, harnessing the wind and currents to speed them away. Bennett didn't allow himself a sigh of relief until the boat was well out of the cannons' range. Even when the Heirs' ship breached the strait, there was still the matter of the serpentine shoals. Not only was their vessel much bigger than Kallas's caique, they also didn't have his uncanny seafaring knowledge to see them through the dangerous sand banks.

"I think, for now, we have bested them," Athena said. She strode to the captain and seemed to debate for a moment whether she should throw her arms around him. Instead, the witch settled for a congratulatory handshake. "Nicely handled, Captain," she said.

Kallas accepted it with a wry smile. "And to you, Lady Witch."

Athena released the captain's hand and went to Bennett. She tsked when examining his wounds, but said, "These will heal quickly with a poultice."

"Later," said Bennett.

He watched as London carefully tied off the jib and then lowered herself to sit on the deck, hands pressed to the center of her chest.

Alive. She'd made it through alive. And only slightly bruised instead of crushed under a boulder or smashed to pieces by a giant stone pillar or shot by cannons. Or captured by the Heirs. Jesus. Bennett needed a drink.

"You'll need to repaint your boat," Athena said to Kallas.

Bennett adjusted the mainsail, tied it off, then went to London. He needed to touch her, to hold her.

"I'm fine," she said as he approached.

"I'm not." He gathered her up in his arms and held her tightly, his heart beating against hers.

When he felt her shuddering, his heart wrenched. She wasn't a Blade, with danger an old, familiar friend. What the hell was he thinking, dragging her into jeopardy? London was a woman bred to the salons of the gentry— cultured, erudite, not a gallivanting fool like him.

"Please, love, don't cry," he murmured into her hair.

Then she looked up at him. And his heart stuttered then pulsed back to life.

She was laughing.

"That was exciting," she said. Her whole body shook with laughter, her dark eyes sparkling.

Something melted inside Bennett. "Exciting?" he demanded. Then, "It was, wasn't it?"

His fear was gone, replaced by unbound happiness—not merely from cheating death again, but from London's joy, her limitless hunger for experience. His head spun with it; he felt his blood throughout his whole body, thundering to life.

At once, he hardened. He needed inside of her. Now.

She caught the instant need in his eyes. Her laughter quieted and was replaced by her own immediate desire. Her hips pushed against his so he felt the warmth of her cradling his pulsing cock. Their kiss was a hot explosion, deep and desperate. She clung to him as he pulled her close, as close as possible. The wet heat of her mouth, her searching hands. Holy God, she was a hell of a woman.

Without speaking, he broke the kiss, took her hand in his, and strode with her toward the quarterdeck house. They would go to his cabin. Or hers. He didn't care.

"Aphrodite and Adonis," Kallas said, dry, "before you run off into the woods, we've a few more matters to address."

Growling, Bennett rounded on the captain. Damn it, Kallas was right. But tell that to his body, his body that wanted London so badly Bennett felt he could power dozens of steam engines with the heat of his desire.

"We sail east now," London said. The husky undercurrent in her voice nearly undid Bennett.

"Toward what?" asked Athena.

Bennett glanced at the mirror, lying on a table in the quarterdeck house. Its surface cast a reflective circle of light onto the roof of the small structure. "Toward wherever the Source wants us to go."

* * *

London, holding the mirror in her hands, stared down at it. Her own face looked back at her with searching eyes. If she had been back in England, in some acquaintance's drawing room, her appearance would have qualified as an utter disaster. Hair in wind-tossed snarls, face dusted with freckles, gown stained with seawater.

She wasn't in England any longer. And she loved how she looked. Like a woman experiencing the world. A woman feeling herself grow and change. Surrounded by people, by a special man, who encouraged that growth, that change. A gift. She had been given a gift, and would not squander it.

Which meant she must find the Source.

She felt as though her fingertips just grazed the edge of an answer, but the more she reached for it, the more she pushed it away. And it was difficult to concentrate, knowing that her father and the Heirs of Albion were so close behind them. She hadn't seen her father on the ship back at the strait, but knew he was there, felt his presence. What would he do, if he caught up with her? Would he punish her? How? But even that mattered not at all. She knew with certainty that her father would kill Bennett, kill Athena and Kallas. She couldn't care about her own fate when faced with the surety of her friends' deaths.

She refused to let that happen. She would surrender to ensure the lives of her friends, if that's what it took.

Yet she hoped it would not come to that.

Athena tended to Bennett's wounds, reminding London how very close he had come to either serious injury or being killed. She fought a shudder.

"The mirror told us to head toward the rising sun," she said, pushing aside her dark thoughts, "which means east. But the sun isn't rising now. It's just afternoon."

"There are old tales," said Kallas, "sailor's lore of an uninhabited island on the other side of the strait. Some believe the tale began with Odysseus when he came home from Troy. It's said there is great treasure on the island, but no one's ever been. Crossing the strait's too dangerous."

"We're on the other side of the strait now," said Bennett with a grin.

"Then I'll find it," Kallas said. "We can anchor there for the night. Give us time to mend the sails and get some fresh water."

"Is it safe from the Heirs?" asked London.

The captain grinned. "It's said that only Atlantis is better hidden."

With a yelp like a startled dog, the gunner fell, knocked back by the fist of Joseph Edgeworth. He yelped again when Edgeworth lunged forward across the wheelhouse, grabbing the gunner's neck, and slammed his head into the bulkhead. The gunner's eyes glazed over as blood dampened his hair and smeared onto the metal behind him.

"Why didn't you keep shooting at the boat?" Edgeworth snarled. "You were supposed to take out its masts."

"The sniper . . ." The gunner's words slurred as unconsciousness beckoned. He choked when Edgeworth's grip tightened on his throat. His fingers struggled to pry away Edgeworth's hand, but the older man's hold could not be broken.

"Was a bloody *distraction*. One you fell for."

The gunner couldn't answer, on the verge of passing out.

"Mr. Edgeworth," Fraser said in English behind him, "sir. It might not be good policy to throttle a member of the crew to death."

"Why the hell not?" Edgeworth didn't turn around, but

watched with satisfaction as the gunner's face purpled. "Teach them a lesson for disobeying orders."

"Punish the man, yes." Fraser stepped closer, his tone conciliatory. "Make an example of him. But killing him won't put the right fear into the rest of the crew. Suspicious and frightened men aren't as easy to control."

Cursing aloud, Edgeworth realized that Fraser's assessment was correct. He needed the steamship crew to obey his every command without thought, without question. Money and a bit of intimidation worked well, made them compliant. But if they felt their employers might turn on them, the crewmen could rally against the outnumbered Heirs. Murder Edgeworth and Fraser and Chernock as they slept, if not worse. Better to keep the crewmen's lives than receive the rest of their payment. Self-preservation trumped even greed.

Edgeworth released the gunner, then, as the man struggled to regain his senses, hurled a fist directly into his face. The gunner crumpled to the deck, utterly insensible. For good measure, Edgeworth kicked the man's chest and belly, but the gunner was too far gone to even groan, so it wasn't particularly gratifying.

"You've a brig, right?" Edgeworth barked to the captain standing nearby. When the man nodded, Edgeworth said, "Take him there. No medical attention. No food or water for three days."

The captain nodded again, his eyes flat and expressionless. Crew were scum, disposable, but harder to replace far from port. He signaled to two sailors, and they stepped forward to drag off the unconscious gunner. Each took an arm and hauled the gunner away, suspended between them like a cut marionette, his legs dragging behind him.

Once the gunner was gone, Edgeworth wheeled on the captain. "That's twice now we've lost the Blades."

"You can't blame me for the boiler," protested the captain. "It was that witch."

Edgeworth didn't care about excuses. "But your men cost me the Blades at the strait. By the time we got through those damned shoals, they'd slipped away." With London. Hell, she'd been so bloody close. He'd watched her from the safety of the wheelhouse, using a spyglass, and saw her not only helping the Blades but—and this made his gut twist and sicken—*kissing* Bennett Day just before Day leapt off the caique to the shoals. It hadn't been a little peck, either. Edgeworth's revulsion was two-pronged. No father liked considering his daughter as a woman. Even worse was knowing, seeing, that London was taking not just any man to her bed, but none other than Edgeworth's most despised enemy.

Yet that gave him some comfort. It was simple seduction, not deliberate betrayal. Day used his skill as a seducer to manipulate London. Women didn't have men's capacity for logical thought. They let their wombs think for them. Right now, London was too much in Day's sensual thrall to understand what she was doing was wrong.

As her father, Edgeworth must correct her, discipline her. It was his duty. And once she'd been properly punished, he'd welcome her back into the fold, as his position within the Heirs demanded. Wedded, of course. She had to have a husband to control her.

"But we'll catch them again, sir," said Fraser, interrupting his thoughts. "The Bloodseeker takes us straight to the Blades."

Edgeworth cut his eyes to Fraser. Smart enough, but not too smart. Thomas Fraser could keep London well contained, but be easily manipulated by Edgeworth.

"Would you like to kill Day?" Edgeworth asked him.

Fraser's face lit up like a boy offered an orange on Boxing Day. "Yes, sir!"

"When you get a chance to kill him," said Edgeworth, "do it. Do it, and London is yours."

"Thank you, sir!" Fraser practically skipped away, heading to his cabin to presumably sharpen his favorite knife. Fraser liked using knives.

When Chernock emerged from the shadows in his silent, unctuous way, Edgeworth contained his urge to shudder. It was damned handy keeping a sorcerer, but sometimes using magic rather than outright force gave Edgeworth an oily, unclean feeling that slithered through him like pools of grease floating on the Thames. Chernock stirred that feeling often.

"What the hell are the Heirs paying you for?" Edgeworth snapped to hide his unease.

"Neville Gibbs and Albert Staunton are working on the Primal Source as we speak," said Chernock. "Only fitting, since they were the ones who retrieved it from Africa." And managed to kill a Blade, Michael Bramfield, in the process, an additional benefit.

"But what about here and now? Every time we get close to the Blades, they find a way to slide away."

The sorcerer never blinked and barely ate, more uncanny than human. If Edgeworth didn't have a file on Chernock, detailing his undistinguished birth in Norwich, his educational career at Oxford with frequent dabblings in dark magic and alchemy, and his subsequent recruitment to the Heirs, Edgeworth would have hardly believed Chernock was an ordinary man.

"We *will* catch up to them," intoned Chernock. "And when we do," he gave his *memento mori* smile, "I have something particularly special planned. Something I believe you will greatly enjoy."

"What is it?"

So Chernock showed him. Edgeworth emerged from the wheelhouse, his face pale but his mouth curved in triumph.

The Heirs were lucky to have a sorcerer like Chernock on
their side. He could produce and harness monstrosities
from which even the gods would hide.

Kallas's promise held true. Here, in an obscure corner
of the Aegean, sat a little pearl of an island, barely two
hundred acres, white rocky shores sloping down to white
beaches and aquamarine water. Small, tenacious phrygana
scrub clung, dusty and green, to the rocks, and purple wildflowers nodded sleepily in the afternoon breeze. Further
back, pines formed pockets of shade and seclusion.

The seclusion, London understood, was brief and illu-
sory. No matter the distance she put between herself and
her father, he kept finding her. The danger he presented
never vanished. But she would allow herself a literal island
of calm for just this night, knowing that she and her friends
had a moment only to catch their breaths before the chase
began anew in the morning.

They had made anchor and waded onto the beach, even
Kallas, lured away from his beloved boat by the miniature
pleasures of the island. For the first time in nearly a week,
London stood on dry land, her bare feet curling into the
warm sand, Bennett tall and comfortable beside her. A rifle
was slung over his broad shoulder. While her eye was
drawn to the island, she could not stop watching him as he
strode, long-legged and masculine, through the tall grasses
that sprouted over the sand and rocks.

He had never been pale, but life on the sea turned his
skin golden, so in the contrast, his eyes were as clear and
blue and warm as the waves that lapped at the beach. It was
easy to see his Greek blood now in his gilded skin and dark
hair curling and ruffled in the wind. She watched as he
scaled a small, rocky hill, his body sleek, never showy in
its motion, but possessing both economy and art. Only

today, she had seen the beauty of him, the efficiency of his strength, running like a myth across the surface of the water, and his skill with a rifle—never bloodthirsty, but precise and sure.

Now she watched the firm muscles of his legs as he climbed, and every so often, a fortuitous breeze came along and lifted the tails of his jacket so she was treated to a view of his edible backside. She had, during their night-time trysts, felt those muscles tighten under her hands as he plunged into her hungry body, and their slickness as sweat covered both London and Bennett in their frenzy. The vivid memory sent a fast stab of need blazing through her. Last night felt very long ago.

When he reached the top of the hill, he looked back, and, at London's wave, smiled and waved before striding off to scout the island.

"You look at him as if he is the last bottle of wine left in the world," Athena said dryly, standing beside her.

London barely blushed. She was now very familiar with her desire for Bennett. "I am a woman of exceptional thirst."

"And will it be quenched, that thirst?"

London glanced over at her friend, considering. Her body still hummed with unallayed need for Bennett. It knew him now, and wanted him always. He'd been the match to her tinder. She could not douse the fire he had lit. How long would it last, this flame of need? She almost prayed it was soon, so, when the time came for their in-evitable parting, the pain would not be too great. But she knew, deep within herself, that this hope was futile.

Athena saw her answer in London's face, and sympathy softened the witch's expression. "Perhaps you are sorry."

"Not at all," London said immediately. "I'm glad I was given this chance and I took it, no matter what happens after." She looked over at Kallas, who had made himself comfortable on a large rock farther down the beach and was smoking his pipe in the afternoon sun, his eyes closed. He was a handsome man, rough like the coast, but possessing his own craggy charms.

Athena followed London's gaze, then frowned. "That man," she said darkly. "I should push him overboard."

"I'm sure he can swim."

"But I cannot."

"If you want to get wet," London said, with a smile, "take the plunge."

A glimmer of humor sparkled in the witch's dark eyes, then rare uncertainty creased her brow. "And if I drown?"

London understood that uncertainty. "Galanos women won't drown. They always learn to swim."

Before Athena could respond, Bennett reappeared at the crest of the hill, his teeth white as he grinned with excitement. "Come and see," he called down to them. "Kallas, you, too. Stop sunning yourself like a lizard."

The captain grumbled, but soon everyone climbed the hill and was following Bennett through the shaded forest carpeting the island. Sharp and clean, pine needles scented the air. Even though Bennett had only just scouted the terrain, he held the lead as if born to do so, assured in his stride, never once hesitating or stumbling.

"A little treat for us weary travelers," he said, coming to a stop in a clearing. He waved toward a small, bubbling pool. The water was so clear, London could number each and every pebble lining the pond.

Bennett smoothly knelt on one knee beside the pool and dipped a hand into it. He drank the water cupped in his palm, droplets escaping between his fingers to sparkle in the light. He resembled some forest god, a creature of darkness and sunshine.

"Sweet and cold," he said with a laugh.

London had not realized how thirsty she was until she saw shimmering drops of water cling to Bennett's neck and slide beneath the open collar of his shirt. She came forward, then sank to her knees to also drink from the pool. Just as Bennett had said, the water's icy sweetness rolled down her throat, sending bright clarity into her belly. She scooped up handfuls of water and drank deeply, also letting the water run along her neck as some spilled from her hands.

Her hands stopped in midair as she caught Bennett's hot, hungry gaze on her.

"Woodland nymph," he rumbled for her ears alone.

She only smiled at him, but it was a smile of wicked invitation. Even though it had been many hours since the danger at the strait, her still body held a shuddering hunger for release, release that only Bennett could provide.

But that release would have to be delayed, for a little while longer. London made herself look away, at the pool, the trees, anything but Bennett, otherwise she'd launch herself at him right here and now, in front of Kallas and Athena. She felt much more free, that was true, but not so free that she wanted to make love with Bennett with an audience watching.

After Kallas and Athena had also drank their fill from the pool, Bennett rose gracefully. London did notice, however, him slightly adjusting his trousers, and she bit down her smile. At least she wasn't alone in this enormous, unshakable desire. "There's more to see," he said, and disappeared into the woods.

When she, Kallas, and Athena caught up with him, they all stood and marveled. Set in another clearing, ruins glowed like ivory in the pine-shaded enclave. Several Doric columns lined up in varying states of erosion, forming the supports of what had been the roof. Lichen and years wore at the marble columns' fluting. But the ruins' isolation had been its boon, for one of the pediments still stood, supported by the columns, though the figures carved into it were barely visible.

Stones set into the ground formed the ruins' floor, and resting heavily upon it was a large marble block, waist-high, and wide around as a dining table. Some grasses sprouted between cracks in the block. Nearby, the remains of a statue of a woman lay half buried.

"What is this place?" London breathed.

"A temple," said Athena. She examined the pediment. "Dedicated to the pool. A sacred spring."

"Like Bath in England," Bennett murmured.

Athena waved a hand. "That is Roman," she said, dismissive of the entire empire. "This is Greek, and much older. For the goddess Demeter."

"Perhaps we shouldn't disturb it," ventured Kallas. He seemed slightly less in command on land than on the sea, glancing around with caution.

"The goddess wants people to make use of her temple and her spring," said Athena. "It pleases her."

"Then, by all means," said Bennett, his eyes blue fire as he gazed at London, "let's please the goddess."

Many things sharpened one's appetite. Obviously, going without food was one of them. But there was also the after-math of danger which could hone one's hunger until sharp and keen. Bennett, in his work for the Blades, often found this to be the case. Most missions would have him face death, and he always emerged from those battles famished in more ways than one. That time near Tripoli, after he and Catullus Graves had gone up against a sand djinn under the Heirs' control, Bennett had eaten platters of chicken stewed with dates, piles of fragrant couscous, and mountains of sweet almond biscuits, all washed down with many glasses of mint tea. After that substantial meal, Bennett had spent the rest of his evening disporting himself in a house of pleasure, exhausting several highly appreciative dancing girls before he finally succumbed to satiety.

A sybarite, Catullus had called him, but not without a little admiration. Poor Catullus, a man of abstemious inclinations save where his inventions and his wardrobe were concerned. Food and women did not much capture Graves's interest, not when there were so many ideas for diabolical devices rattling around in his brain, and so few truly fascinating women who could genuinely capture his interest long enough to look up from his workbench. And the man was addicted to waistcoats.

Bennett was most definitely not Catullus. His needs were not complicated. He was a cryptographer for the Blades, but found his greatest pleasures not in papyri or codices but in the flesh. Action. Movement. Food. Sex.

Today, he'd sailed through a strait riddled with traps, then played sniper at an advancing Heirs' gunboat. Even if London hadn't been nearby, his body would have been demanding gratification. But having her beside him, seeing how close *she* had come to danger, turned him into a beast he could hardly control. His need for her went far beyond his usual inclinations. If he'd had to, back in Tripoli, Bennett would have been able to suffice with a small meal and going straight to a solitary bed.

Watching London sit, bare feet dangling over the deck of the caique as Kallas taught her to fish, Bennett knew that if he didn't make love to her that night, if not sooner, he would lose his mind. He'd been hard and hot as newly forged iron since they'd left the strait, a condition that had not diminished one iota in the intervening hours. And it was because of her. Lovely, courageous, fiendishly clever, and open to the world's experiences.

He needed inside of her. Physically. Mentally. However he could. Right now, he would be satisfied only by everything.

Dinner on the beach at sunset. Roast fish caught by

Kallas and London. Wild greens picked by Athena. The meal could not go fast enough. Bennett wolfed down his food like a man breaking a fast. He hardly tasted anything. His mouth wanted only her flavors. He could barely speak during the evening conversation, reduced to monosyllabic replies. In the light of dusk, her hair golden, her eyes dark, laughing and talking, London could not be more beautiful, more desirable.

And when her gaze caught his, the responding fire he saw there, Bennett felt sure he'd go up in flames and burn the island around him.

Finally, finally, when the meal was done and the last drops of wine drunk, London rose from their gathering. Bennett leapt to his feet, not caring if Athena laughed at him or Kallas scowled at how readily he showed his need for London.

He held out a hand to her as they moved away from Kallas and Athena. "Let's walk." His voice was no more than a growl, sounding from somewhere low in his chest.

"A walk sounds perfect," she said. "I want to explore the island some more."

"Don't want to *explore*," he rumbled. "Not the island, anyway."

With a small, timeless woman's smile, she danced up the beach, toward the hill that led into the interior of the island. "But *I* do. There's still that treasure to find."

"It'll be there in the morning."

"This can't wait." She climbed up the hill quickly, far faster than she would have a week earlier, but he wasn't much in the mood to appreciate her growing physical strength.

Bennett muttered, "Neither can I," yet he followed her, just the same.

She truly was a nymph, and he a satyr, as she skipped ahead of him, flitting between the trees, humming bits of an old sea tune Stathis the fisherman had sung. Bennett stalked after her, intent, drawn forward by invisible hands. He caught glimpses of her dress, a gleam of her hair, as she darted around the pines, letting her rich, soft voice torment him.

Had he wanted to, he could have caught her. Yet, even though he desperately wanted to touch her, he enjoyed this game, the playfulness of it, of her, and so, as she continued her dance, he followed, unhurried, steady.

The sound of water bubbling reached him, and he stepped into the clearing that held the sacred spring. But London was already on the other side of the clearing, and she smiled at him as she slipped back into the forest. He paused for a few moments, helping himself to a cooling handful of water, then continued his steady pursuit.

"Holy God," he growled when he arrived at the ruined temple.

London stood in the middle of the temple, next to the remains of the altar. She had already stripped off her clothing so she was quite, quite naked.

"No," she corrected him with a devilish smile. "Holy goddess."

Chapter 14

The White Temple

Bennett had been accused of being many things before: scoundrel, rogue, charmer, cheat, libertine—one of his favorites—and bastard. Most of those allegations were true. But no one ever accused him of being stupid.

As soon as he saw London standing without a scrap of clothing in the middle of the temple ruins, her body a soft glow in the twilight, he immediately began to shuck his own clothes. Jacket first, thrown onto the ground. Then he started working on his waistcoat. The bloody buttons felt tiny under his shaking hands.

"Slow a little," said London, walking toward him. His hands stilled, and he stared, utterly mesmerized by the sight.

Even though she was completely nude, she walked with absolute feminine confidence, the curves of her hips swaying with each step she took. His eyes roamed everywhere—the full roundness of her breasts, tipped with pale coral, the narrowing of her waist, the smooth satin of her arms and legs, the golden down between her thighs. In this sacred place, she was the embodiment of Woman, lush and alluring and so very, very powerful. He loved to see it in her, how much she had changed from the tethered lady he'd met in Monastiraki.

Now she stood in front of him, in this hidden, sacred place, her own eyes raking him up and down. She saw plainly his chest rising and falling, his hands curled as if already touching her, the aching length of his cock pressing tight against his trousers. And she smiled.

"The goddess demands a sacrifice," she murmured.

"I hope like hell it's me," Bennett growled.

"Let us prepare you for the ritual." She took one of his hands in both of her own and drew him slowly forward, until they both stood within the confines of what had been the temple. In the dusk, the stones gleamed white and marmoreal, but nothing compared to the radiance of London as she led him toward the large slab of stone at the temple's center.

"I don't know this ritual," he rasped.

"You will learn it well. And I shall guide you." She stepped close to him, her breasts brushing the front of his waistcoat. Hell. He wanted her skin touching his, not the barrier of fabric. When his hands came up immediately to try again at unbuttoning his waistcoat, she brushed them aside. "I will ready you for the sacrifice," she whispered. "Place your hands upon the altar behind you, and do not move them until I say you may."

He knew better than to disobey. Seeing her in complete command, heady with her own power, resounded deep within him even as she drove him to madness with desire. So, his back to the altar, as she called it, he slapped his heated palms down onto the cool stone.

"Very good. First, we begin with a kiss." She tilted her face up to his.

He leaned forward, bringing their mouths together. Since he could not touch her with anything but his mouth, he unleashed a kiss of impossible heat and irreproachable tenderness. He stroked the inside of her mouth, her warm heat. Their tongues met, tangled, lapping at each other. It felt like sex, like lovemaking, from only their mouths. Her fingers threaded into his hair. From the back of her throat, she made a sound that could only be described as a whimper. Just as she began to press her body against his, she seemed to catch herself and move back a few inches. He ground his teeth together, sure he'd break his jawbone by the time this was over.

With an agonizing slowness, she undid the buttons on his waistcoat. He obediently lifted one hand, then the other, as she removed the garment. He shrugged from his braces. Next came his shirt. Each button carefully slid through its hole, her fingers dipping in to stroke his bare skin. He was shaking like a sail in a monsoon by the time she pulled the shirt off of him.

"Your body pleases the goddess," she breathed, trailing her hands over the planes of his chest, down the ridges of his twitching abdomen. She found the raised flesh of his scars and the newer injuries, the scratches from bullets, bruises, and traced them softly, her eyes brimming with compassion. "Such wounds you've borne in service to your cause."

He didn't care about that. He didn't care about anything but her, the heat and heart in her gaze.

When she bent to tug off his boots, he broke her rule and pulled them off himself. She was no lackey, to dirty her hands on his battered boots. But as soon as he was barefoot upon the stone floor, he replaced his hands upon the altar.

She nodded regally at his obedience, but something of her usual self slipped through when she smiled quickly, like a playful girl. He smiled back. Then she resumed her role and the queenly demeanor of a goddess.

She brushed her breasts against him, the hardened points of her nipples a delicious rasp over his chest, and she closed her eyes at the pleasure. His skin was tight as a drum, and he felt even this small touch everywhere, especially between his legs, where he twitched with each press of her flesh to his.

Her hands went to the front of his trousers, stroking his straining cock through the fabric. He hissed, his eyes squeezing shut, as his hips thrust forward of their own volition. "It seems the goddess pleases your body, as well," she murmured.

"She has no . . . damned idea . . . how much," he said between his teeth.

"I think she may have a damned idea how much."

She left off stroking him, but he wasn't sorry, because she was unfastening his trousers. As soon as the placket was open, she pushed the trousers down his hips, where his cock leapt free, released at last. Past his hard thighs she slid his trousers, past his calves, and then he stepped out of the trousers. They were now both naked. And panting.

She took him in her hand again, and her fingers against his bare skin were excruciating, wonderful. Her thumb rubbed lightly back and forth over the crown of his cock, spreading the drop of moisture there over his flesh. She moved her hand lower, enclosing his shaft with her hand, sliding up and down.

"So beautifully hard," she whispered. "You are almost ready for the sacrifice."

"Almost?" he repeated, hoarse. If he was any more ready, he'd spend all over her hand.

"There is another rite to perform." She released him, then grabbed the heap of her discarded dress and bunched it together. She set the bundle of fabric on the ground, in front of Bennett. He knew at once what she meant to do and felt dizzy.

She knelt upon the fabric and looked up at him through the fringe of her lashes. His nod was clipped, barely a movement of his head, he trusted himself so little but trusted her entirely.

Her fingers silken torments, she wrapped them around his cock, and took him into her mouth. His fingers dug into the stone as she ran her tongue over him, along the shaft, over the swollen head. Pulling, sucking, lapping at him. Her mouth was wet and hot and perfect.

How to decide? Watch her sucking him—her lips wrapped around his flesh, the bob of her head as she sank down onto him, her fingers stroking. But if he watched her, his climax would be a matter of seconds. Yet to close his eyes and focus only on the sensations was itself an agony.

She eyed him with stern disapproval when one of his hands came up from the stone and tangled in her hair, but she did not stop or tell him to release her. Instead, her own eyes fluttered closed with pleasure as he gently pushed her down, guiding her to take him deeper into her mouth. His hips moved, forward and back, and his body was tight and straining everywhere with tension. It was so goddamned good.

He pulled her back, almost roughly, so that his cock sprang from her mouth. Even in the fading light, he saw the flush covering her luscious body, the stain of arousal high on her cheeks, and her thighs rubbing together. He drew her up, so she stood, and they met in a fiery kiss. One hand he kept cupping the back of her head, the other gripped her hip, bringing her flush to his body. His wet, pounding cock pressed into the curve of her belly. She moved, angling herself, so that, when she writhed against him, her slick pussy slid along his shaft. He caressed her breast, one then the other, plucking at her nipples so that she moaned.

He broke away just long enough to grab his waistcoat, shirt, and trousers. She watched him with glazed curiosity as he made a pillow from the shirt, then two more pads with the other clothing, and set them all upon the altar.

Everything became clear when he climbed onto the altar and lay back, his head cushioned on his jacket, and the other pads on either sides of his hips. He beckoned her forward.

She needed no encouragement. She also climbed onto the altar, then, with his hands upon her hips, straddled him. The pads protected her knees. In the violet light of dusk, surrounded by the white temple and green shadowed woods, he'd never seen anything as beautiful as she.

"It's time for the sacrifice," she said with a husky breath.

"Thank God for that," he rumbled.

"Thank *goddess*," she corrected, and sank down onto him.

An animal groan tore from him. He became all sensation. The tight clench of her pussy surrounding him. The drip of her juices as she slid up and down, his hands on her waist, her, bracing herself above him. The muscles of her legs, grown stronger and leaner in the past week. The sway of her flushed breasts with her movements. Her gasps as she rode him, her head tipped back with her hair streaming around her shoulders, grinding her hips against his so they were as tightly fitted against one another as anyone could ever hope to be, two interlocking pieces meant only for each other.

She drenched him. She had no mercy, for him or herself. Her need was feverish. She impaled herself, again and again, until she stretched herself taut and cried out, clenching around him.

No sooner had she reached her climax, then Bennett moved with an inhuman speed and strength, fueled by colossal desire. He positioned them so that she stood on the ground, facing the altar, her hands braced upon it, and his hands on her hips as he stood behind her. He pressed her down so that her febrile body contacted the cool stone, the sensation making her cry out again, then he thrust into her.

Low, guttural sounds clawed up from him as he took her, worshipped her, his mind shut down entirely. She pushed herself back into his thrusts, the softness of her buttocks under his hands. And when one of her hands slid from the altar to rub at her clit, first with trepidation and then with growing confidence, her fingers also brushing his cock, whatever tenuous threads of control he might have still possessed snapped. He came with a shout, heat pouring through him as he gave himself up utterly to her, to how she made him feel. Her own orgasm followed quickly.

His legs shook as he held her tightly, chest pressed to her damp back. Their breathing came in labored gasps. He nuzzled her hair, licked the sweet curve of her neck, inhaled her scent. He reached up and turned her head to the side, then he kissed her, mouth open, and she kissed him back in kind. Everything was open to each other, nothing held back. She overwhelmed and humbled and delighted him.

He gasped, between kisses, "I love you."

London's heart leapt to hear his words. Then she remembered. Bennett's definition of love and her own were very different. When he said, "I love you," to her, it meant, "I like you very, very much." Gratifying, but not entirely the same effect on a person's soul.

Yet it was more than she had ever received from anyone, from any man, and she accepted Bennett's declaration for what it truly was, without regret. She would receive his love, in whatever form it took, for as long as it was offered.

As for her own heart . . . she had to protect it. At some point, she and Bennett would part. She had to be ready for that day, make sure it did not devastate her. But she was growing stronger every day. Surely she could withstand it when the passion cooled between her and Bennett and they separated, perhaps to meet again only as friends.

"Is the goddess appeased?" She felt the vibrations of his voice through her body as he curved around her. "Or does she demand more?" He pressed his hips against her bottom, and she could already feel him firming, despite his intense climax moments earlier. Incredible.

"It seems the supplicant is not satisfied," she murmured, wriggling against him.

"I'm a deeply holy man. However many times I need to perform the ritual, I'll gladly do it." He punctuated this statement with a light thrust against her. He was almost fully hard.

Immediately, she wanted him again. But she knew it wasn't to be. She sighed. "Much as I wish to stay here and worship all night, we need to get back to the beach. We have to be up at dawn to watch the sunrise."

"I didn't do a proper job," he mumbled against her neck, "if you're thinking so coherently."

She didn't feel coherent. She felt unmoored, floating, cast adrift on the desire and need between them.

Still, they disentangled from one another, he helping her up from where she sprawled against the altar. Slowly, languorously, they dressed, pausing every now and then to kiss and caress and murmur meaningless words of sated appreciation. He deftly performed the task of ladies' maid admirably, hooking her back into her dress with agile fingers in the growing darkness.

Once they were both dressed and shod, Bennett gathering his jacket from where he'd thrown it, he drew her back into his arms and kissed her sweetly. His smile was warm honey that covered and filled her. "Such a bold creature you've become. A demanding goddess."

"I never thought to rise to the heights of a deity."

"But you have. You are. Divine. London, lusty goddess of the consecrated spring."

She tilted her head back, closing her eyes. "Mm, that has a pleasant sound to it."

"Not as pleasant as your moans of pleasure."

Opening her eyes, she smiled. "You're very good at performing the sacred rituals."

"I live to serve my goddess."

She looked at Bennett, his sculpted face of pristine masculine beauty, his eyes heavy lidded with repletion, gazing down at her as if she was something both precious and powerful. Only with him could she have dared to act as brazenly as she had, revealing her most private self, trusting him not to laugh or be shocked or judge. An extraordinary man.

She felt herself sliding toward danger. But she let herself go, fall into it, because it was better than shutting herself away in a protective cage as she had for so much of her life.

"Your devotion will see you handsomely rewarded," she said, then stifled a yawn. "And now the goddess is so sleepy, she can barely walk."

"Easily remedied."

He swung her up in his arms as if she weighed no more than a bird. She felt as though she ought to protest that she was perfectly capable of walking on her own, which she was, but a heavy, delightful lassitude had woven itself throughout her limbs. So she looped her arms around his neck and rested her head on his shoulder as he strode back through the forest. He felt solid with muscle, utterly capable, and smelled of wind and sea and man.

"Wake up, love," Bennett murmured, rubbing his mouth over the crown of her head.

London stirred, her eyes drifting open. They were at the beach. The shapes of Kallas and Athena moved about on the deck of the caique, anchored a small distance out.

Lights from the boat cast shining reflections in the gentle surf. Night had fallen.

"Wasn't asleep," she mumbled.

He laughed. "I won't contradict a goddess."

Moments later, they were back aboard the caique, with London standing on her own feet. She had awakened enough to observe Athena and Kallas arguing—this time about whether olives were better grown on the mainland or the islands—but she was able to see a more contemplative look cross the witch's face whenever Kallas had turned away.

"I think relations may be thawing," she softly noted to Bennett, when Kallas and Athena were out of earshot.

He paused in his task of bringing up several blankets and pillows from below, glancing back and forth between the captain and Athena. A smile quirked Bennett's lips. "Thank God for that," he answered quietly. "I think our esteemed captain is on the verge of tearing down the masts with his bare hands."

Yet the captain was not going to have a reprieve any time within the next few hours. Athena took notice of the pallet Bennett was preparing on deck, a pallet large enough to accommodate two.

"Am I to have the bunk all to myself tonight?" she asked.

Despite everything she and Bennett had done together, including wildly make love in a ruined temple, a small blush crept into London's cheeks as she nodded. Spend the whole night with Bennett! True, they would be on deck, entirely exposed, but to have him beside her for the entire night, even if they only slept, was a treat she readily anticipated.

He seemed to be looking forward to it, as well, judging by the grin he didn't bother hiding, the scoundrel.

London snuck a quick peek at Kallas, and saw the brief look of hope that flashed over the captain's weathered face. Then Athena bade them all good night and went down to her cabin. The sound of her locking the cabin door was faint, but it reverberated throughout the boat.

Without speaking, Kallas extinguished the lamps around the ship, stomped down to his cabin and slammed the door.

London turned to Bennett with a grimace. "Perhaps I spoke too quickly."

"The steps to Athena's dance are deuced complicated, but I think she's chosen her partner." Bennett shrugged. "For this set, anyway."

London could only shake her head at the continual mystery of men and women. Yet thoughts of the witch and the captain fled as Bennett finished preparing their bed and waved a welcoming hand toward it.

"Will this please the goddess?"

With a drowsy laugh, London said, "The goddess is so tired, she could sleep in a cast-iron bathing tub."

"I think you'll find this more comfortable. And the company better than a sponge."

He stripped down to only his trousers and she her chemise. He lay down, propping himself up on an elbow, and held the covers open for her with an enticing smile, as if she needed further enticement.

London slid under the covers, stretching out fully beside him. Even though the deck was hard beneath her back, it didn't bother her at all. She had wanted this for a very long time. The blanket enclosed them, capturing the warmth of their intertwined bodies. He wrapped her in his arms, and together they stared up at the night sky. Stars spread in profusion, a sorceress's embroidered gown, and the moon her diadem.

In his deep, rich voice, he told London stories about the constellations, some true and others entirely fabricated by his whimsy. There were Virgo and Leo and Leo Minor and Boötes, but there were also the Hot Water Bottle and Richard, the Articled Clerk, and the unholy union of a blancmange and a trebuchet, which fired projectiles of pudding at poor Richard across the sky.

She fell asleep laughing.

Many hours later, she had no idea of the time, she was awakened by his hands and mouth on her, the already frantic need of her body for his. Though she had led their lovemaking in the temple ruin, here he took command, wordlessly, confidently shifting her this way and that, caressing, stroking, trailing hot kisses everywhere. He drove her to madness. When she felt sure she would truly lose her grip on sanity from his sensual torture, he pinned her hands above her head, moving her thighs apart with his own, and drove into her. She arched up with a cry, filled everywhere by him.

On the deck of the boat as it swayed at anchor, in the depths of night, hidden somewhere in the Aegean, they moved together. Slowly, at first, gradual, delicious slides of flesh. Then with building speed and hunger. He was strong and able and alive, and he claimed her with his body, his mouth and hands. She felt his brand upon her skin, felt him within her.

Consciousness almost ebbed away as she climaxed, a fierce contraction of muscle and pleasure. His own release came seconds later. He was taut as a bow, hard everywhere, his head thrown back as he poured into her, with the stars overhead and stars within her body.

And when he said, again, "I love you," she felt her heart seize. Because she wanted desperately to say those words back to him, because she knew then that, despite all her intellectual understanding and self-protection, knowing full well that there would come a time that they would separate, she loved him. Not *his* version of love, but her own.

The pleasure of sleeping beside London all night was much too brief. Kallas woke Bennett and London an hour before sunrise—the captain looked as though he could easily strangle a bear in his current foul mood—and, once they were all dressed, the blankets and pillows stowed, everyone drank bracing, small cups of coffee, speaking lowly in the predawn darkness.

As he sipped the revivifying coffee, Bennett watched London nurse her own cup, blinking and yawning in the cool of morning. He sometimes spent entire nights with women, but not often. It wasn't that he disliked sharing a bed, or the routines of morning, for in those quotidian moments he found a muted gratification that felt much like a worn and comfortable jersey. But no matter how much a lover insisted she had no claims on his heart, most believed that, if he slept next to them, shared a bed for an entire night, things changed. Demands and expectations that he could not meet. So, to save himself and his lover distress, he usually retired to his own bed after making love. Much better for everyone.

This was the first time that Bennett wanted more.

More sleeping with his arms around London. More silly, drowsy conversations with her about made-up constellations. More middle-of-the-night lovemaking. More seeing her face the moment he woke up. More of *her*. Anything. Everything.

He bolted down the rest of his coffee, wincing when he burnt his mouth, but it was a distraction from the turn of his thoughts. Something was happening to him. Something he didn't understand and wasn't completely certain he wanted to confront.

Further distraction came when Kallas barked at everyone to make sail. Grumbling but dutiful, Bennett, London, and Athena all performed their tasks, and soon the tiny island shrank to a smudge as they sailed away. Bennett decided to take Kallas aside later and find out the exact location of the island, just in case he wanted to go back to it later. The spring, the temple. They were part of his prized memories now. Memories he would share with no one but himself. He wondered if he ever would return, and the thought that he might not or, worse, that he might return alone, felt like lead collecting in his belly.

They put the island behind them just as the sky whitened with the dawn. He watched the horizon, waiting for the sun.

Then it came, delineating the boundary between sea and sky, a crimson curve that bathed the sails of the boat, the faces of the people upon it, with aureate light. London, gilded, stood at the railing, a vision of arresting beauty as she, too, watched the sun as it rose.

"This is lovely." Her voice was hushed and low, the way one might speak in a holy place. "But I do not see anything that will guide us to the Source."

"Consult the mirror, perhaps?" suggested Athena.

Bennett quickly retrieved the mirror and studied it, crouching near the mainsail. The sun continued to rise, turning from a curve into a disc. Soon, it would be above the horizon. They were running out of time. But for what, he didn't know.

"Onward, and reflect toward the dawn," he recited aloud. At once, it made sense to him. He stood, then turned his back to the sun.

London must have seen his purpose, because she was at his side immediately. "You think . . . ?"

"Look."

He held up the mirror, so that it reflected the sun cresting the skyline. Both he and London peered into the mirror.

"On the horizon." She gasped.

Kallas and Athena crowded closer, so they all looked into the mirror's reflective surface.

"A giant." Kallas scowled in disbelief.

Bennett said, "Colossus."

In the mirror, they saw it. Reflected light gleamed on the horizon, coalescing into a massive, glimmering shape.

Whatever, whoever it was, it took the form of a towering man, but how tall, Bennett couldn't determine. The sea destroyed all sense of proportion. Even if the figure was only a hundred feet away, it was huge. A man, or titan, standing upon the surface of the sea. Upon its mammoth head, a spiked crown, and he was nude, save for a cloak draped from one arm.

Bennett glanced over his shoulder, back to the horizon, and saw nothing. But when observing the same location through the mirror, the giant stood, plainly visible, gleaming as he stood upon the water. Everyone followed his example, turning their eyes back and forth between the reflection and the actual skyline.

"Can you plot our course using the mirror?" Bennett asked Kallas.

"Done." Kallas needed no compass or quadrant—the sea was his birthright. He knew it as he knew the tendons of his own muscles.

And just in time. The sun climbed higher, and the vision of the giant disappeared from the mirror. Now it was only morning. Bennett lowered the mirror and saw London watching him, an extraordinary brilliance in her eyes. She glowed, not with the rays of the sun, or with anything supernatural. What shone from her, in her face, her eyes, was a respect and affection Bennett had never seen before— never directed by any woman toward *him*, anyway. But London looked at him as though he was truly admirable, as though he was something more than a wayward reprobate with a mad case of wanderlust.

He didn't know if he was that man, the one she saw when she looked at him, but he sure as hell wanted to be.

* * *

The clarity of Aegean air confused. Distances flattened into nothing. What was in truth far away seemed close enough to brush with the tips of one's fingers. London felt as though she could lean over the rail of the caique and gather armfuls of tiny islands like a shell collector. She wanted to set them in jars upon a window ledge, to catch the sun, or to prevent fading, into a shaded cabinet, then perhaps label the jars. *Eastern Aegean Islands, May 1875*.

Should she collect and label Bennett as well? *The First Man I Loved, Late Spring,1875*. No. He was not the sort of man to be trapped and categorized. She loved him for his freedom, and would not take it from him. So she kept silent on her new discovery, but the wise eyes of Athena Galanos saw much.

"Please don't say anything," London said quietly when she and the witch had a moment alone in the quarterdeck house.

"He should know."

"I'll tell him. But not yet." She glanced at Bennett who, at Kallas's request, was entertaining the captain with stories of his travels. Most Englishmen prided themselves on their reserve, the impenetrability of their façade. Not Bennett. He smiled and laughed often. He had the masculine beauty of a classical statue, but he was irrepressibly full of life, responsive to everything around him. Nothing cold or remote about him. As he spun a tale for the captain, he wove images in the air with his long hands, hands that could fire a rifle with deadly accuracy or caress her into erotic delirium. How many women had fallen in love with him? Likely thousands, and no wonder. He could not be resisted. Her own resistance had been, at best, token.

"When?" Athena pressed.

London looked away. "I don't know. This is new for me, too."

The witch pressed a kiss to London's forehead, her

own expression faintly melancholy. "Go, then. I shall keep silent."

Midday came with the sharpness of an armory. Yet as they sailed steadily onward, the giant failed to materialize. The only thing on the horizon was another island.

"No disrespect, Captain," London said, "but are you sure of our bearing? We *were* looking through a mirror, after all."

"I'm sure," Kallas said. "That island is exactly where we are headed. Shall I change direction?"

"Stay the course," said Bennett.

As they neared where the giant had appeared, the shape and size of the island were gradually revealed. London tested her own sight and the spyglass, but what she saw she could not truly understand. Not until the boat was less than half a mile away, did things become clearer.

"Great Lord," London breathed. She had a very bad feeling about what was going to happen soon.

The island rose sharply up from the water in a sheer cliff face, without even a beach. Instead, the surface of the cliff plunged directly into the sea, which crashed in booming, churning waves along the jagged rocks. Kallas brought them in close, so that the caique lurched and heaved, but he kept it well contained so the caique did not slam into the rocks. Athena looked green. But it was entirely possible that the motion of the boat was not to blame. Instead, a sight that made even Bennett whistle low loomed over them.

The cliff shot straight up, stretching toward the sky, harsh and white in the sun. Over a hundred feet high. Imposing and terrible. Nothing grew along its face, not even weeds in the crevices and cracks. London tilted her head back to see the top, where the tiny forms of seabirds wheeled. She couldn't make out the top of the cliff, and grew dizzy from contemplating it. Alarm prickled her like a million insect stings.

Bennett said with a smile, "Time to start climbing."

Chapter 15

Colossus

"Do you seriously mean to climb that?" London glanced up again at the towering cliff, her eyes round with apprehension.

Bennett shucked off his jacket. He slipped his arms through the straps of a rucksack, hefting its weight. He'd already checked the contents of the pack and knew that everything he would need was there. He still wore his revolver at his waist, and tucked a cartridge belt into the pack. A flex of his hands, testing their strength. Soon, they would be all on which he could rely.

"No other way to go but up," he answered. There was no fear in him, only the familiar thrum of excitement that seized him whenever he faced something decidedly dangerous.

They had sailed the entire circumference of the island and found it to be sheer cliff all around, like a column on a Brobdingnagian scale. Bennett had never seen anything like the island, and itched to explore it.

"Yes, but—" She glanced up again, trepidation clearly written across her face. "I only wish there was something I could do to help."

He stepped to her and cupped her face in his hands. He looked into her eyes, the color of darkest chocolate, but infinitely more sweet. She put her hands over his, her thumbs brushing his wrists, as if to feel the beat of his pulse. When he bent to kiss her, she rose up on her toes to meet him halfway. He tasted her, cinnamon and oranges.

"This is as close as I can get," Kallas called from the wheel of the boat.

Bennett broke the kiss, reluctantly, to see that the captain had maneuvered the boat nearer to the cliff. With Kallas's usual skill, he had managed to bring the caique within several feet of the jutting rock face without slamming the boat against the rocks.

"It'll do." Bennett gave London's hands a squeeze of farewell before striding to the rail. He needed to keep his mind focused on the task at hand—easier done when he hadn't a care for anyone but himself. With every step he took, he felt her, felt the tie between them grow taut but not break.

The boat heaved on the swells, but he balanced himself in a crouch on the rail, breathing slow and deep. He scanned the surface of the cliff, finding its niches, learning its hidden secrets. Then—he leapt.

He scrabbled, gripped the cliff, his boots finding purchase as his knees banged into the rocks. Good thing prizes weren't handed out for jumping from caique to cliff. He wouldn't have won any trophies for that display. But it got the job done. Now came the fun part. The climb. He'd never scaled a cliff this size before. And there'd be no rope to catch him if he fell. Either he'd plunge into the crashing sea or smash through the deck of the caique.

He couldn't move with undue haste. He didn't want to tax himself too quickly. Over a hundred feet to go, and if he tried for speed, he'd be spent midway. So, deliberate and steady, not too quickly, not too slowly, he found small crevices in the cliff face, and wedged his fingers into them.

He stayed on the balls of his feet, testing and then using outcrops for footholds.

No looking far down. No anxiously measuring his distance to the top. It must be the continual search for footholds and handholds, nothing else. Not London, below him.

He unmoored his mind and became only the motion and clarity of climbing.

The pull of muscle, the heft of his body, legs pushing, arms pulling. The feel of the rock under his fingers. Sun on his shoulders, reflecting off the surface of the cliff. He tried to keep his arms loose, his hands giving position and balance. Search for an opening or outcropping, test it, then hold fast. Again. Again.

His thoughts wandered. The view from the top would be something. A shame London wouldn't get a chance to see it. But better to have her safe on the caique and miss the view. And no matter how much stronger she'd become in the past weeks and days, she wouldn't have the ability to scale the cliff.

He felt the weight of his body pulling on his arms, tried to keep his center of gravity over his feet. Time lost meaning, dissolving into rock. Sweat stung his eyes, and he tried to wipe them on his sleeve, but with little success. He couldn't chance relying on just one hand to support him as he dried his face. Winds picked up, tugging hard, blowing grit into his eyes and mouth. He held tighter as the wind shoved at him, trying to throw him from the cliff.

A step up, and the foothold crumbled under him. His boot slid along the rocks, searching for purchase, his hands wedged into small fissures in the cliff face. Far below, the rock struck the deck of the caique, and it took a damned long time to get there.

Moving quickly, he gripped a new handhold and hauled himself higher, until he found new outcrops for his feet.

The first true burn in his muscles, an ache in his lungs. But he pushed on.

A clattering above. He flattened himself against the cliff as rocks and pebbles tumbled down, pelting him with a multitude of bites. A larger rock hit his right hand. Bennett swore to himself as he fought the pain, refusing to lose his grip.

The next handholds stretched high overhead. No choice but to swing and grab for them. He breathed in, then pushed upward, the momentary sensation of air all around him. His fingers found the holds. Yes.

"Hell!" The rock he gripped turned to dust under his fingers. His feet scraped for support under him and found none. He was flung backward. Only his left hand, holding fast to an outcropping, kept him alive.

Muscles in his arm screamed, and his fingers locked in stiffened agony as they bore the full brunt of his weight. He looked down and swore again, dangling seventy feet in the air. Blue water churned against the base of the cliff. The caique was a child's toy beneath him, and London, Athena, and Kallas merely dolls looking up at him, helpless to do anything but watch. They would watch as his fingers lost strength and he plummeted down to them, another Icarus dashed to pieces. London would see him impaled on the caique's masts or else his neck broken from hitting the water.

No. He'd make himself survive. With a groan, he flung his other hand up, searching the face of the cliff for even the tiniest crack in its surface. There. Barely able to fit the fingers of his right hand, but he wedged in tight. Now both arms burned, but the pain was slightly lessened, giving him the opportunity to find new footholds.

He found them, and took a moment to gather his breath, his lungs aflame. But he couldn't linger. Already, his hands were sweat-slick, ready to lose purchase if he dallied.

Noises of animal force shoved from his chest as he pushed himself hard and fast. Higher he climbed, the wind picking up speed and strength, clawing at him. He refused to think of failure, of falling, of tiny London, so far below. There was only up.

Now he tilted his head back to see how much farther. Ten feet. Every part of him shouted with strain, but he forced himself on. Nine feet. Eight. He dodged another rock coming loose from the face of the cliff. Seven. Nearly there. He wouldn't give in to the greedy maw of the wind. Six feet. Five.

Then he stretched out. His fingers brushed against horizontal rock and grasses. The top. Another push from his legs. Another. There. There.

He hauled himself over, and splayed out, face up, eyes closed, lying atop the rucksack. His chest heaved as he let his arms and legs rest for the first time in . . . God, how long? He couldn't make himself consult his pocketwatch. An eternity. A minute. Didn't matter. He'd reached the top. He felt like a god. A breathless laugh rasped from his throat, then grew in strength until he shook with laughter.

Bloody hell, but he loved his job.

After a few minutes, when he felt his limbs wouldn't collapse under him like soggy towels, he rolled onto his stomach and crawled on hands and knees to the edge of the cliff. It was, indeed, a gorgeous view. The sea stretched out in endless azure brilliance, sunlight sequined upon its surface, and the sky glowing with midday radiance, barely dusted with clouds. Far below, the caique danced on the water like a leaf, the forms of London, the witch, and the captain barely visible from Bennett's height.

From a pocket on the front of his pack, he took the Compass. He turned it so light gleamed across the glass, signaling everyone below. A moment later, an answering signal from Athena. He'd made it, and they knew.

Back into the pack went the Compass. He stood, his

taxed legs momentarily wobbly, but that lasted hardly a second before he gained his strength back. He took a drink from a canteen and splashed his face. Feeling revived, he drew another inhalation as he stowed the canteen. Now it was time to do what he came here for. What that might be, he didn't know, but he had a fair share of brains. He'd figure something out.

Bennett turned. And just barely caught himself from stepping back, over the edge of the cliff.

He'd seen plenty of strange and wondrous things as a Blade. But this was a first.

Facing him was a massive golden human head, the shoulders and neck rising up from the ground as if its enormous body was buried within the cliff. The head had to be at least fifteen feet high, possibly higher. Upon its brow, it wore a huge, spiked crown. One eye was missing, a dark chasm. The other stared at Bennett. Scowled, actually.

The Colossus didn't seem very pleased to see him.

How did one approach a giant? Bennett glanced at its frowning mouth, wide enough to gulp him down like a minnow. He hoped the Colossus wasn't a maneater.

Cautiously, he stepped closer, but not close enough to be within biting distance.

"You have come alone." The Colossus's voice, speaking in classical Greek, rang low, the sound of dozens of huge bronze bells ringing the hour. Under Bennett's feet the ground rumbled and shook.

Bennett steadied himself, keeping his head respectfully lowered. Always best to approach from a position of deference.

The giant waited for an answer.

"I've come far to be in your presence," Bennett said, also

in classical Greek. "From the singing stream, through the crushing strait, always with enemies at my back."

This seemed to intrigue the Colossus, massive creases like bundled blankets appearing between its brows, but it did not speak again, so Bennett continued. "They seek to enslave the Greek Fire, so they may enslave their fellow men. Yet I and my friends wish only to protect the mystery of the Fire. I humbly ask that you counsel me, that I might find this Source and keep it safe."

Bennett bowed his head, a hand pressed to his chest, where he felt his heart knocking into his ribs. The giant kept silent. Bennett's mind raced. Would the Colossus require a sacrifice or offering? He hadn't brought anything with him, not even wine. Greek deities and immortals didn't require human sacrifices, did they? Damn, maybe they did. If so, the Colossus would be disappointed. The Blades would find another way to find the Source. How, he hadn't any idea, not yet, anyway. What if—

"Solver of Secrets," boomed the Colossus, shattering Bennett's whirling thoughts. "I will not speak to you alone. Bring forth the Oracle's Daughter. One man is a liar. But a man and woman together cannot hide their hearts. Only to you both shall I then reveal what I know." With that, the giant's mouth shut with finality.

Oracle's Daughter? Who the hell was that? Again, Bennett's thoughts scrambled for footing. Then, understanding. And with it came a knife of fear. He didn't want to do it. He had no choice. Good thing for the Colossus that the giant was both huge and magical, otherwise Bennett would have punched its enormous face.

London checked the urge to look into a mirror. She was certain her hair was now streaked with white. It hadn't been so bad, watching Bennett scale the cliff. Rather arousing, in truth, seeing the bunch and movement of his muscles, his masculine surety as he climbed, never hesitating. Potent and nakedly virile. She actually felt herself heat with desire as she watched, one hand pressed low to her belly. It wasn't a particularly intellectual response, but she wasn't mind alone. Her body had its own demands.

Her desire dried to dust when his footing gave way, and her fear grew even worse when a rocky outcropping he held crumbled, leaving him swinging from one hand over a deadly drop. And there wasn't a damned thing she could do about it, just watch in terror through the spyglass, trying to keep her hands from shaking right off her wrists. Even Kallas swore a streak leagues wide.

"Can you do something?" London asked Athena.

"I have not the ability to create a shield around him," the witch answered, frustrated.

London wished she had wings to fly, but such wishes were futile as the man she loved struggled to right himself stories above her. Awful, powerless.

Saints and gods were praised when Bennett found another handhold and, after a pause, continued upward. London clutched the spyglass like salvation as her gaze followed Bennett up the rest of the cliff. When he finally reached the top, disappearing over the edge, she barely had the strength in her numb fingers to shut the spyglass and put it aside, rather than let it drop from her hand.

A light gleamed at the top of the cliff. Athena, holding her Compass, flashed a signal back, then smiled.

"He has done it," she said. "He is safe."

London blew out a shaky breath, so Athena came over and placed a comforting hand on her back.

"And now?" London asked.

"Now we wait," said the witch.

Several minutes went by, slow minutes that left her with little to do but pace. What had Bennett found up there? Her pacing stopped when deep noises, more rumbles than actual sound, shook the air. London looked to Athena for guidance, but the witch could only shrug. At least London wasn't alone in her mystification, yet that was not especially comforting.

"He's signaling again," said Kallas.

Everyone squinted, looking up. More flashes of light at the top of the cliff, in a specific series.

Athena translated the code: "L-O-N-D-O-N."

Both the captain and the witch turned to London. She stared back at them.

Finally, London said with a calm that surprised her, "It appears I'm following him up."

But not bare-handed and not without some assistance.

Everyone crouched on the boat's deck, splicing rope. The captain's tough hands moved faster than London and Athena's, but Kallas had a lifetime of learning ropes and the women were latecomers to the art.

Once there was enough rope, Athena went below to the cargo hold. Minutes later, the witch returned, carrying a wooden box, then set it upon the deck.

Athena reached under the high collar of her gown and produced a key, dangling from a thin chain. After releasing the clasp on the necklace, she unlocked the box using the key. Polished brass and steel gleamed as the lid to the box was opened. She reached into the box and pulled a device from its snug velvet lining.

A hollow cylinder had a notch running along its top, and was mounted onto several gears. Cranks extended from both sides of the gears, attached to a spring.

"Another of Catullus Graves's infernal mechanisms," Athena said to a curious Kallas and London. "It is built along similar principles as a mortar. We place the knotted end of a rope into the cylinder, with the long end threaded through the notch. Two people must crank the device to build up enough momentum in the compression spring, so that, when the release is pulled, the knot is hurled up to the top of the cliff."

Though the design astounded London, she was compelled to ask, "Why didn't we shoot the rope up there before Bennett scaled the cliff? Then he would have had something to hold on to besides the rock."

"Someone still needs to secure the rope to the top of the cliff. In this case, it will be Bennett."

"Secure it with what?" asked Kallas.

"This." Athena reached back into the wooden box and produced a small metal instrument. With several quick motions, she unfolded it and locked it into place. "A spike, secured with gunpowder so that it cannot be dislodged. At least, not without considerable work." She refolded the spike so that it measured only a few inches long. "This goes into the knot we shoot up the cliff. Bennett will know what to do when it lands."

Both London and Kallas could only gape. The captain eventually muttered, "This Catullus Graves is a second Daedalus, to make such impossible things possible."

"He and his family are among the Blades' greatest assets," Athena said with pride.

"Time to put his work to the test," London said. "Bennett needs me up there." For what, she had no idea, but she didn't care. Bennett would not have asked for her unless he felt it necessary, and she would not disappoint him.

Athena handed the job of knot-tying to the captain, who produced a monkey's fist knot wide enough to accommodate the spike, but able to fit into the mortar. He spliced the knot onto the long coil of rope everyone had fashioned. As soon as that task had been accomplished, the knot was loaded into the cylinder. Kallas took one of the hand cranks, while London and Athena took shifts on the other. The gears eventually grew so tight, London and Athena had to hold the crank together, fighting to turn it.

Finally, when it could be wound no more, Athena pulled the release.

A whoosh as the knot shot upward at incredible speed, the rope speeding after it like a comet's tail. The coil of rope unwound quickly, a hissing snake. Then the knot vanished over the top of the cliff. London could not believe it. Catullus Graves's machine had worked.

Moments later, there came three sharp tugs on the rope. Bennett had secured it.

"I've spare trousers in my cabin," Kallas said to London. "You'll need to change into them."

"And take one of my shirtwaists," added Athena.

London hurried below and shucked off her gown, then dressed in the trousers and shirtwaist. As an example of fashion, it was ludicrous, and somewhat revealing, but it made up in practicality and freedom what it lacked in modishness and modesty. Fortunately, neither Kallas nor Athena were of a mind to judge her appearance when London joined them back on deck. Athena made several quick alterations to the garments using Arachne's Art so that, while not entirely *à la mode*, the fit was substantially better.

With the tail end of the rope, Kallas fashioned a harness, then fastened it around London's legs and waist. "Don't tell Day I did this," the captain warned as he looped the rope around her thighs, his hands brushing against her as impersonally as possible. "Otherwise he'll use my bollocks for playing marbles."

"I'm sure he won't mind," said London.

"He minds when the *wind* touches you," Kallas said darkly. He checked his efforts with businesslike precision. "All in? Secure?"

London tested the feel of the ropes around her thighs and at her waist, and nodded. She had no doubt the captain's handiwork was excellent, but that didn't stop her pulse from beating like crows at a dark window.

"Ready?" asked Athena.

London's mouth dried, so she could only nod again. Then she tugged on the rope, three times, as Bennett had done.

A jolt, and then her feet lifted from the deck of the caique. She was drawn upward, pulled, presumably, by Bennett. Such a strange sensation, as though slowly, slowly flying. More and more distance separated her from the boat, and Athena and Kallas began to shrink beneath her as she rose.

Bennett was a strong man, and she wasn't precisely corpulent, but London wouldn't allow him to bear her weight alone. As soon as she drew up close to the cliff, she searched for foot- and handholds, trying to pull and push herself upward. Even with the support of the harness, it was tough work, straining her every muscle. Thank heavens she had been laboring on the boat these past days, developing her strength, else she would have merely dangled on the end of the rope like a puppet.

She chanced a look down, then cursed herself. Even though she knew falling was not a possibility, her head spun with the height. Still, she found a gratification in her elevation, the harsh wind and sun raking her, as though completely exposed before the eye of God. When she banged her knees into the rock, or scraped her face and hands, she allowed herself some prime swearing, but kept her resolve for as long as she was able. Better this, to scrabble up the side of a cliff, with the sea below and the sky stretched overhead, than be shut away in a plush prison, safe from danger, entirely numb.

Her fingers felt like tender, uncooked sausages and her legs shook by the time she neared the top of the cliff. If

Bennett hadn't been there, pulling her up, she wouldn't have made it. Or, at the least, it would have taken her a day to make the climb.

When Bennett's dark head appeared over the edge of the cliff, smiling, of course, liquid joy poured through her. Filled with new energy, London pushed herself hard to scale the rest of the way. After everything she'd seen and done today, she burned with the need to touch him.

She clambered over the cliff's edge just as he gave one final pull on the rope. She stumbled forward, knocking him back. They sprawled together, gasping, her lying on top of him. He wrapped his arms around her, holding her tightly. Beneath her, she felt the heat and solidity of his body, the body she knew so intimately, and she pressed her face into the crook of his neck, inhaling him. She could hardly move. Not merely because her limbs were exhausted, but because he felt exactly right, touching her.

She brought herself up just enough to kiss him, eating him up like a savage woman. He kissed her back with the same hunger, slipping the harness off of her, then pulled away slightly.

"There's someone I want you to meet," he said, when she frowned in confusion. He sat up, taking her with him. That's when she saw it. And forgot how to breathe.

"London Harcourt, Oracle's Daughter," Bennett said in classical Greek, "allow me to introduce you to the Colossus of Rhodes."

A giant, buried to his shoulders in the rock, nodded regally.

"Um, charmed," said London.

What London had learned about the Colossus of Rhodes came from piles of dusty tomes, scholarly and ancient accounts about one of the Seven Wonders of the World. It had been constructed in the fourth century B.C., a bronze monument to the sun god Helios to celebrate victory after a long and painful battle. London had seen many different renderings of the massive statue, some depicting the god astride the Rhodian harbor, others showing a more classical pose. London had always been impressed by the spectacle, wondering what such a gigantic statue might be like in person. Awe-inspiring, she imagined. Spectacular, in the truest sense of the word.

Nothing, neither her books nor her imagination, truly prepared her for standing in front of what was very much *not* a statue, yet not truly alive, an enormous creature somewhere between metal and flesh. It only had one eye, but the eye it did possess was easily two feet across, gleaming like fire in the afternoon light.

And looking right at her.

"Am I the Oracle's Daughter?" she whispered in English to Bennett, standing beside her. She held his hand tightly, and felt some grounding from the familiar and wonderful texture of his skin against hers.

Lowly, Bennett said, "He insisted he would only speak with me, the Solver of Secrets, if the Oracle's Daughter was here, as well. It's been your language skills that have brought us to this point, communicating the words of the ancients to us now. I remembered that Kallas called you Lady Oracle, and it made sense."

"Are you sure I'm not some variety of virgin sacrifice?"

Bennett's glance at her was both droll and reproving. Of course he wouldn't bring her up to the Colossus if the giant meant to eat her like a kipper. And, as for virgin, those days were quite, quite behind her. She had the blushes and bite marks to prove it.

"What does he want?" she whispered.

"Only one way to find out." He took a step forward. Addressing the Colossus in classical Greek, he said, "I've

brought to you the Oracle's Daughter, as you requested."
Bennett tugged on London's hand so she also stepped forward, though with a bit more reluctance.

The giant stared at her, its gaze as weighty as time. Despite everything she had done over the past weeks, all she had seen, to be in the presence of a magical being, particularly one so enormous as the Colossus, left her more than a little lost.

"How do you do?" she said, also in classical Greek, then winced at her gaucheness. This wasn't a blasted tea salon! She pictured herself lifting a teacup the size of a birdbath up to the mouth of the giant, and fought down a hysterical giggle.

"Are you truly the Oracle's Daughter?" the Colossus thundered in the Samalian-Thracian dialect.

London barely managed to keep herself from covering her ears from the tremendous boom of the giant's voice. Such a gesture would read as disrespectful, and she most assuredly did *not* want to offend this huge creature.

And she could *not* let him see any signs of fear or hesitation. "I am she," she answered in the same dialect.

The Colossus inclined his head in approval, appearing to London as if a mountain were tipping onto its side.

"The Oracle's Daughter and Solver of Secrets seek the terrible waterborne gift, the fire that burns upon water," the Colossus said in classical Greek, its voice resounding throughout the soft tissues of London's body.

"For the protection of the gift, not for our own use," Bennett answered, his own voice remarkably level for a man addressing a giant.

The Colossus's gaze moved over them both, so penetrating she felt as though her every secret had been laid bare. She prayed the giant did not see the time she stole a penny from her governess to buy a piece of boiled sweets.

After moments of this examination, the Colossus rumbled, "I read your hearts as I had desired, and find them true."

London allowed herself an exhalation of relief. Bolstering her courage, she asked, "What must we do to find this gift?"

"I see far," the Colossus intoned. "I see the spans of generations as though they were mayflies, decades and centuries no more than glints upon the surface of the rocks. I see the millennia fall away. I see my destruction. The monument honoring me fell, torn asunder by my brother Poseidon's earth shakings." The Colossus's mouth twisted bitterly. "Jealousy. Yet I expect no better from him, the waterlogged fool."

London exchanged glances with Bennett. It seemed even gods had difficulties with their families.

"For hundreds of years, my monument lay in pieces," continued the giant. "Until, piece by piece, it was taken away upon the backs of nine hundred camels and melted down, lost to time. Everything gone, except my Eye, the Eye which held the terrible gift."

"And if we find the Eye, we will have control over the waterborne fire," said Bennett.

"It has been used before for such a purpose."

Even though speaking with a partially buried giant was not precisely ordinary, London's pulse sped up even further at the mention of the Source. It was precisely what the Blades sought to protect from the Heirs. "Where is the Eye?" she asked.

The Colossus's sigh would have tipped London onto her backside had Bennett not been holding her. "I cannot show you where it is," the giant said, mournful. "I have but one Eye to see it."

London's heart sank. Even this incarnation of the sun god could not help them in their quest.

"We shall be your eyes," said Bennett. "We will find what you have lost. But without more information, our sight is just as hindered as yours. Tell us the first steps of our journey."

The Colossus's scowl was a terrible thing, yet Bennett didn't seem to mind it overmuch. Oh, dear. Sometimes bravado wasn't the best tactic to employ. Perhaps that was why the Blades included women in their ranks.

"If we find your Eye," London said quickly, "then we can restore it to you. Will that not make it secure and keep it from the hands of wicked men?"

This appeared to mollify the Colossus. "You speak as a sage, Oracle's Daughter. I shall tell you what I can, but, in turn, you must swear solemnly to return my Eye to me."

"That was the plan all along," muttered Bennett in English.

"You might've said so," London hissed back. "We will swear," she said louder in Greek, "as our hearts attest."

The giant seemed appeased. "You will find the Eye in the Black Temple," he said. "I know not where to find this Temple, alas. But you shall find it there. The Oracle's Daughter and the Solver of Secrets must navigate the Temple together. The future of the earth is in both your hands."

"And once we do all this?" London prompted. "Do we bring the Eye back to you?"

"No, this image you see before you is naught but an illusion. I belong to the sea, the sun, and the sky. To restore to me my Eye, the Solver of Secrets and the Oracle's Daughter must take the light of the sun to a place on the sea floor that has never seen sunlight, and there, let the Eye rest. Only then shall my sight be restored."

"Many thanks to you," said Bennett, bowing.

"My thanks shall be yours if you succeed in this," the Colossus thundered in reply. "But if you liberate the Eye and do not restore it to me, the consequences will be most dire. Mankind will have in its possession the means of destroying itself. And so it shall."

With those booming words, the Colossus faded into air. All London saw before her now was the top of the cliff, dotted with grass swaying in the breeze. It seemed hard to believe that moments earlier, she had been speaking with an almost completely interred Colossus. Yet the vibrations in her body from the giant's voice still resounded.

"That went well," said Bennett. "All we have to do is find this Black Temple, get the Eye of the Colossus, and put it on the bottom of the sea."

"It sounds very simple," London said. "It sounds incredibly difficult."

"A typical day for a Blade." He smiled, and bent to kiss her. "By the way, I didn't tell you how damn impressed I was by you coming up the side of the cliff. Like a Valkyrie soaring to heaven."

She smiled against his mouth. "I had some help."

"Don't be modest. These trousers surely aren't." He ran his hands down her hips and cupped her bottom. "I could get used to this."

"Kallas might want his trousers back."

"To hell with him," Bennett growled playfully.

They pressed close. London hoped Kallas and Athena could wait a little while longer.

A horrific shriek rent the air, as if the fabric between Heaven and Hell had been torn apart. London and Bennett were thrown to the ground, stealing their breath. His arms tightened on her to shield her from whatever had battered into them. Something clawed at his shoulder, and he grunted in pain.

More shrieks, chilling her to her marrow. London looked up from the shelter of Bennett's embrace and shuddered. Maybe she had died, and now found herself in the underworld, for that was the only way she could explain what she saw.

A beast of impossible hideousness, it would be branded

upon London's mind for all eternity. Over eight feet tall, the creature vaguely resembled a human, but its skin glistened a jaundiced yellow, its eyes two glowing embers, fangs protruding from its slavering mouth. The beast had two legs and six arms, each hand and foot tipped with shredding talons. It beat the air with scaled wings, bathing London and Bennett with the smell of sulphur and carrion. The stench nearly made London gag.

Thomas Fraser stood, gloating, not ten feet from London and Bennett, with the creature hovering behind him. He brandished a wicked knife in one hand, its blade jagged and curved, a pistol in the other. Two brutish mercenaries flanked him, the barrels of their rifles pointed in her and Bennett's direction.

Fraser smirked. "London, you've made your father very cross."

Chapter 16

Depths and Heights

London's mind spun frantically as she and Bennett rose to their feet. Even if the way to the rope wasn't blocked by Fraser and that awful, hovering *thing*, she and Bennett would not be able to climb down from the cliff fast enough. The winged beast would be on them in moments, shredding them to pieces with its fangs and claws. And Fraser and his mercenaries had guns—Bennett had one revolver. Ten feet separated London and Bennett from Fraser and his men. Too far to grab their guns, too near to evade their bullets.

Quickly, she glanced around the top of the cliff to see what other options they might have. Nothing. The top of the cliff was a barren expanse of weeds, barely thirty feet across. It offered no cover anywhere.

But *she* was cover.

London stepped in front of Bennett, shielding him from the barrel of Fraser's revolver. Fraser's eyes widened, and Bennett swore.

"Get the hell out of the way," Bennett growled. He moved to shove her aside, but the mercenaries raised their rifles higher in threat, pinning him in place.

"My father wants me alive," London said to Fraser. "You have to go through me."

Fraser scowled. "Stupid whore," he spat. He leapt to the side, attempting to go around her so he could put a bullet in Bennett. London shuffled to block him, but, when Fraser suddenly cursed in shock and frustration, she glanced behind her and started.

Bennett was gone.

For a moment, everyone standing atop the cliff stared in frozen amazement. It was as if Bennett simply disappeared into nothingness. London's pulse hammered. Had he fallen off the other side of the cliff? Not caring about the guns trained on her, she ran to the cliff's edge and looked down. All she saw was more sheer rock plummeting into the sea. Where was he?

She turned around, just in time to see Bennett, revolver in hand, rucksack still on his back, spring up over the rim of the cliff close to where Fraser and the mercenaries stood. She realized he had been hanging from the edge on his fingertips, moving to flank Fraser without being seen by anyone, herself included. Her heart ricocheted in mingled relief and fear as he landed in a crouch. Before the other men could react, Bennett shot, hitting the mercenary standing farthest from him. The man cried out as he fell, a circle of red widening in the center of his chest. As the mercenary crumpled, his finger instinctively tightened on the trigger of his rifle and fired a round. Straight at the winged beast.

With a roar, the creature reared away. One of its wings slapped Fraser, knocking him down so that he rolled almost over the edge. The knife dropped from his hand as he scrabbled in the dirt. London tried to grab the knife, but the beast's flapping wings kept her at bay.

Over the shrieks of the beast and the buffeting wind, London heard the sounds of men grunting in pain and exertion. She saw Bennett grappling with the remaining mercenary, both gripping the rifle, digging their heels into the ground as they fought. The mercenary shoved at the butt of the rifle, trying to plow it into Bennett's ribs. Bennett shoved back, landing an elbow right in the thug's face. Dazed, the man's grip on the rifle loosened slightly. Bennett grabbed the rifle and slammed the side of the barrel into the mercenary's head.

The mercenary stumbled, then pitched over the edge of the cliff. London winced, hearing his prolonged scream as he plummeted over a hundred feet to his death. But it was better that he should fall than Bennett.

London tried to run to Bennett. The creature, hovering above, its wings beating, dove at her, talons outstretched. London darted away.

"Don't kill her, idiot," snarled Fraser as he struggled to his feet.

The beast pulled back with a snarl. Whatever control Fraser had over the creature, it chafed at its restraints.

"Contain her!" Fraser barked.

It lunged at her, trying to herd her, and she dodged from side to side, protecting herself with her arms flung overhead. Waves of stench poured off of the creature, causing London's eyes to tear and her throat to close. Whatever unholy beast the Heirs had summoned, she could not imagine anything more foul. She felt its claws clutch at her, tearing the back of her shirtwaist, gouging into her skin. Her flesh burned.

From the corner of her eye, she saw Fraser face off against Bennett. Both men had their revolvers drawn, pointed at each other. A stalemate. She didn't doubt Bennett was an excellent shot. She'd seen the proof. But she could not let Fraser have even an opportunity to test his own marksmanship. Not against Bennett.

As the winged creature reared up, trying to corral her, London darted toward Fraser. His focus solely on Bennett, he didn't see her run at him. Summoning every remaining ounce of strength, she kicked Fraser's hand, knocking it high. He kept his grip on his revolver, but, when he squeezed the trigger in reaction, the shot went wide.

"Bitch!" he yelped.

And then London was flying. Over the side of the cliff.

Bennett's arms wrapped around her like steel cables as they fell together through the air. Her stomach pitched up into her throat, her eyes filled with the pitiless blue sky as she watched the edge of the cliff grow smaller over Bennett's shoulder. A thought flashed through her mind—was Bennett so determined to keep them from the Heirs that he'd prefer suicide to capture?

"Hold tight to me!" Bennett shouted above the rushing wind.

She clutched at him like a lifeline. He fumbled for a moment at the side of the pack, then tugged hard on a dangling strap. The back panel of the pack flew off, and, with a metallic jangle, lengths of connected brass pipes unfolded then snapped into outstretched position. Silk fabric was strung between the pipes. As the fabric caught the air, it tautened with a snap.

Their freefall descent immediately slowed. London, clinging to Bennett like a vine, glanced around as they glided down in wide circles. She saw the caique far below them, and, close by, the Heirs' ship, belching smoke. Gunfire popped faintly as rounds volleyed between the caique and the steamship.

Wings. Bennett had fixed wings strapped to his back like an improvised angel. They caught the wind and held like a gliding hawk. The sensation of flight swirled through her as she held fast to Bennett's lean, powerful body. She felt as though Eros himself whisked her away to his lair, borne aloft on silken wings, sea and sky a spinning kaleidoscope.

"Catullus Graves?" she asked, astonished beyond imagining.

A corner of Bennett's mouth turned up as he nodded. His smile died when the shrieks of the winged creature pierced the air.

The beast swooped close, claws outstretched. Bennett held London with one arm and used the other to fire his revolver at the creature. It snarled, flapping backwards out of the path of the bullet, then dove at them again. Bennett shot again, this time clipping the tip of the monster's wing. Black blood splattered into the sky as the creature bellowed in wounded outrage.

"What the hell is that?" London shouted.

"Rakshasa," Bennett said, grim. "Hindu demon. Chernock's controlling him. Hang on."

She and Bennett swooped lower and flew over the deck of the Heirs' steamship. Men scattered on all sides, throwing themselves to the deck as they shouted in alarm. One man tried to grab London's ankle as she and Bennett sailed overhead, but she kicked the man's hands away. Bennett nodded in approval. She was getting quite good with her kicks.

No time for self-congratulations. The demon sped after them, close at their heels. Bennett tugged on the straps at his shoulders, altering their path. London's breath stopped when she saw that he guided them into a collision course with one of the steamship's sidewheels.

Just before they slammed into the sidewheel, Bennett pulled on the straps again and they climbed up, over the metal wheel. The demon hadn't a moment to realize what happened before it bashed into the sidewheel. Its screams and the sounds of crumpling wood and metal filled the air.

Bennett piloted them to the caique, skimming them over the waves like a gull, the Heirs' ship at their backs. He landed in a run. He slid the wings' straps from his shoulders as London continued to cleave to him. Her feet touched the deck of the caique for the first time in what felt like days.

"All right?" asked Bennett, wrapping his arms around her. His gaze on her face was fierce and protective.

She couldn't stop her giddy laugh. "I'd like to do that again, under better circumstances."

He started, grinned, then buried his face in her hair. She couldn't tell if the shaking came from him or her, but they couldn't part from each other, not even when Kallas and Athena came running up, both holding rifles and chattering with excitement.

"Graves truly *is* another Daedalus," Kallas exclaimed.

"We had no way to warn you." Athena, slightly less exultant, was all information. "The Heirs concealed their ship until it was already on us. Kallas and I held them off as best we could. And then Chernock summoned that *rakshasa*." She glanced over with a sneer at the steamship, where the demon still lay in the twisted wreckage of the sidewheel. Men ran about the deck of the ship with buckets and equipment as a trickle of smoke leaked from the smokestacks on the disabled ship. "Did you get what you needed?"

"Think so," panted Bennett, who still held London. She wasn't eager to let him go, either.

"Then let's hoist anchor," said Kallas.

"Release my daughter," a very familiar voice said, icy cold. "Or I'll put a bullet in the witch."

Everyone's heads turned to see London's father standing on the deck of the caique, a revolver pointed at Athena. London had never seen her father as he was now, darkest fury twisting his distinguished features into a grotesque mask. It was like witnessing a demonic possession. London fought the urge to cower in Bennett's arms.

"Do it!" her father barked, when Bennett continued to hold London. Her father pulled back the revolver's hammer. Athena blanched while Kallas swore.

Bennett, seeing no other choice, slowly let his arms fall away from London, but he continued to stand behind her, his body pressed to hers.

"Come with me, London. I have a rowboat." Her father tipped his head starboard. "I'll take you away from these people, get you safe again."

Swallowing hard, London stepped away from Bennett. She heard his sharp intake of breath, like a man cut.

London would not let herself look back. She held her father's gaze as she walked closer to him. "I'm staying, Father."

She thought she heard a breath of relief from Bennett, but the sound was too low for her to know for certain.

London waited for her father to shout or rage, but he merely looked grimly determined, as though he expected her answer. "No, you are not. It's all right, London," he said, placating. "I understand. You aren't thinking clearly. Your emotions have led you astray. You are even wearing *trousers*." He grimaced. "The London I raised would never wear such indecent clothing."

"I haven't—"

But her father plowed on, unheeding. "It's not your fault. You're only a woman. Easily beguiled by your sensitive nature. That's why we men need women like you. To ensure we have hearts as well as minds. Day knew this. He preyed upon you, seduced you." Her father sent Bennett a vicious glare before returning his gaze to her. "You couldn't help yourself."

Frustration began to replace fear. Her father wasn't listening.

"Father, no," she said. "Bennett didn't seduce or beguile me. He told me the truth. He was the first man to ever tell me the truth."

"Filled your head with nonsense!"

"It wasn't nonsense," she returned, determined to keep

her voice level. Any sign of passion or emotion would only be read as female hysteria. "I learned about you, about the Heirs. And the more I heard, the more I realized that what you are doing is wrong. One country should not determine the fate of the entire world. One race of people is not superior to all others. And to enslave magic for your cause is immoral."

When her father had no answer, she stepped closer. Confusion swam in his eyes. He seemed much older, all of a sudden. It was strange that here, now, on the deck of the caique, in a far stretch of sea thousands of miles from home, London saw him now not as her father, but as a man. Fallible, vulnerable. Human. She wished, suddenly, fervently, that she might convince her father of the Blades' cause, that he might leave the Heirs so that she and he could repair the tatters of their familial bond.

"I made a *choice*, Father," London said, gentling her voice. "A deliberate choice. One I thought about for a good long while. I cannot let the Heirs subjugate the world for England's gain. It is wrong. And I think, I hope, that deep down, you know what I say to be true. Please, Father," she whispered, feeling her eyes grow hot. She stood not five feet from him, saw his chest rise and fall as he gulped air, almost panting. "It isn't too late. Not for you or for us."

She waited, her pulse a speeding river, everything she ever was and would be in her eyes for her father to see. A memory leapt into London's mind, of her father taking her as a very small girl to the Zoological Gardens in Regent's Park and buying her a toy lion. He had wanted to give her something more suitable for a girl, a pretty toy zebra or even a giraffe, but she would have nothing but the lion, and he had bought it for her, a fond smile upon his face as he gave her the toy, and he said she would have to feed it often or else it might get hungry and eat one of the housemaids. She had promised to feed the lion, sneaking it bits of biscuits after tea, during nap time, until her nurse scolded her for bringing food into her bed, and then she got older and forgot all about the toy. Where was it now? In some dusty corner of the nursery? Given away?

"Oh, London," her father said sadly. He heaved a great sigh, as if crumbling from the inside, and his shoulders sagged. He lowered the revolver. "I see now. I see what I must do."

Her chest tightened with hope. He understood! They could both be saved. And Mother, too. Jonas . . . would take time. But surely if she could convince her father to abandon the Heirs, it could be done for Jonas, too. And then—

"Father!" London yelped as her father raised the revolver again. And pointed it at her heart.

"This is a mercy," her father said. "To save our family's honor, and yours."

She stared at him. He was glacial, impenetrable, a frozen edifice where, moments earlier, he had been a man, a parent. In his eyes, there was no recognition, only cold determination to eliminate an adversary.

London knew she should flee or duck or do *something*, but she was rooted to the spot, unable to fully comprehend what was happening. Her father would kill her. Her *father*.

Then there was a blur and a grunt, and London hardly knew what was happening until she saw Bennett throw his shoulder into her father's chest. The older man, startled, hadn't time to defend himself, and he dropped his gun as he toppled backward, over the rail. She heard a splash and a shout.

Bennett leaned far over the rail, but halted his momentum enough to keep from joining her father in the water. He turned and didn't spare her father a glance. "Get us the hell out of here," he commanded Kallas.

London could only stand as Athena and Bennett helped

with the sails, Kallas raising anchor and steering the caique away from the damaged steamship. Dimly, she heard men in another rowboat coming to her father's aid, pulling him from the water.

She was vaguely aware of the caique's motion, sailing swiftly away from the island of the Colossus. Wind and sun, the pitch of the boat. She felt these things from a great distance. It wasn't until the island was far behind them, and the Heirs, and her father, that London was finally able to move. She took several leaden steps toward the quarterdeck house, not sure where she was going, feeling entirely entombed in ice.

Bennett strode to her, and his arms came up around her, pulling her against him. He was warm, so warm, that she began to thaw. He rocked her, softly.

"Don't cry, love," he crooned.

Her hand came up to touch her cheek and came away wet. "I never truly believed. Not until now. Some part of me prayed things could be set to rights." Fire lined her throat. It hurt to speak, yet she could not stop herself. "He wants to kill me, Bennett. My own father will murder me, if given the chance."

Profound sorrow gleamed in Bennett's eyes as he gazed down at her, brushing her hair from her face. "I'm sorry. I'm so bloody sorry."

She buried her face against his chest, solid and broad, allowing herself this moment to fully lean on him, take some of the strength he readily offered. "I don't regret my choice," she said, her voice muffled as she pressed herself tight. "If I had to, I'd make the exact same decisions. But it hurts so damned much."

"Give me your pain, love," he said, holding her against the steady beat of his heart. "Let me take it for you."

She shook her head. "No, the pain is mine to bear. I need it." She took a ragged breath. "To make me stronger."

* * *

As concisely as possible, London and Bennett told Athena and Kallas what the Colossus had said to them. They gathered around the wheel to conference, and even this helped give a slight ease to the ache around London's heart. She needed to keep moving forward, to find the Source and give meaning to herself when truly everything she had ever known of her old life was gone.

"The Black Temple," mused Kallas. "Even with my sailor's lore, I've never heard of such a place."

"We will have to find a means of locating it," said Athena.

"Yes," London agreed, "but what worries me is how the Heirs keep finding us." Her father was an Heir now, no longer her father. She must learn to think of him that way.

"I haven't seen any birds following," said Bennett, leaning against the rail with his arms crossed. "But it must be magic of some kind. We're the only ones who've been able to find and follow the clues."

"There may be a way to learn what magic they use," mused Athena. She went below and returned moments later with a red silk pouch. Holding out her hand, she poured the contents of the pouch into her palm. "This is sand I collected from the island with Demeter's spring," she explained. "It is imbued with the goddess's sacred essence."

The witch waved her other hand over the sand, chanting softly. "Harvest Mother, guide us. Reveal to us the cunning tricks of our enemies, the enslavers of magic, that we may shield from greedy eyes your gifts of enchantment."

With a sound of whispers, the sand began to swirl in a tiny whirlwind, contained within Athena's palm. The small vortex grew in size and speed, rising up from the witch's hand until it spun away from her. Soughing, it scudded over the wooden deck in widening concentric circles. It seemed to move steadily, without purpose, passing Bennett and Kallas, but when the whirlwind neared London, it lingered.

London moved aside, thinking she blocked the vortex's path. Yet, stepping away, the vortex followed her, almost like a dog sniffing at her to determine if she was friend or foe. She looked at Bennett, slightly alarmed. She had no wish to be bitten.

"Do not be afraid," Athena said. "It cannot harm you. Stay where you are."

Easy for the witch to say, without a magical sand whirlwind trailing her. Still, London rooted her feet, even when the vortex grew even larger. It shifted, moving over her, encompassing her in its swirling walls. She squinted and shielded her face from the scouring sands. From within the whirlwind, she saw the vague outline of Bennett striding toward her.

"Not yet," Athena's voice clipped. "I must read the sands."

"Hurry the hell up," Bennett growled. "I don't like it."

"A moment more . . . yes . . . I release you!" With the witch's clap, the sand fell to the deck, scattering. As soon as the vortex died, Bennett was beside London, threading his fingers with hers, pulling her close so their shoulders brushed.

"What did the sands say?" London asked. Seeing Athena's somber face did not help the frisson of fear winding its way up London's spine.

"It is the Bloodseeker Spell." The witch's mouth flattened into an unhappy line. "A drop of a kinsman's blood is used to track a blood relation. It is strongest when the ties are close."

"Like a father and daughter." Bennett tightened his grip on London's hand when Athena nodded.

Even though London was not truly responsible for the spell, guilt clutched at her. All this time, her own blood betrayed her and the Blades. "How do we break the spell?"

Athena glanced at Bennett, apprehensive, as if she feared his reprisal more than anything else.

"How?" Bennett demanded.

"What they say about killing the messenger," Athena said, "please remember that."

"Athena," Bennett warned.

The witch saw that she had no choice but to reveal what she knew. "Blood. It is broken through blood."

Athena had been right to be frightened. When Bennett learned what had to be done to break the Bloodseeker Spell, he swore so long and foul that even Kallas was impressed.

Bennett hated it. He hated everything about it.

"There's got to be another way," he insisted.

"I am afraid not." Athena looked apologetic. "Only through the shedding of the shared blood can the spell be undone."

London, who had been following this exchange silently, gave Bennett's hand a squeeze. Her voice was low but steady. "It's all right. I will do it." She gave him an encouraging smile, as if *he* was the one that needed comforting, then turned to Athena. "Do we need a special knife?"

"One with a black blade. I keep such a knife with my magic implements."

"Please get it," said London. "I'll make myself ready."

When Athena went below, Bennett stepped even closer to London, needing the feel of her. London had already weathered so much today, so much over the past days and weeks, and strain tightened in the corners of her eyes and mouth. His life—dodging from one close call to the next— thrilled him. He had no regrets, no desire to pursue a quiet and safe life, and he knew it was the same with the other Blades. They believed in their cause, and they were also, truthfully, slightly insane, part of the small breed of people who courted danger. That breed was kept small by natural selection. Some of them lived, others didn't. It was a fact, and he and the other Blades knew it. So when they fought side by side, they did watch out for one another, never seeking death or harm, but they were ready when such things happened.

London wasn't a Blade. She might be ready to embrace danger, could take hits when they came. God knew she'd received her share only today. But Bennett hadn't grown the armor to protect himself when she hurt. She could tear him apart with her courage.

"I wish you didn't have to do this," he said, low.

Absolute conviction shone in her dark eyes. "Me, too. But I do. The sooner, the better." She leaned up, on the tips of her toes, brushing her mouth against his. "It will be fast. Hardly anything."

Again her impulse to console *him* was almost more than he could stand. Before he could speak, she slipped from him, gliding toward the rail of the ship and rolling up her sleeve.

"I see you have prepared yourself," said Athena, emerging from below with the knife. The black blade absorbed light rather than reflected it, and silver branches wove around the hilt. Bennett wanted to knock it from Athena's hand so that it disappeared into the sea, but he held himself ruthlessly in check.

Athena presented the knife to London, hilt first. "The symbol looks like this." She traced upon her own forearm the outline of a bird in flight. "It signifies freedom, and must be deep enough to draw blood."

"I understand." London took the knife, and her hand looked small and fragile wrapped around the hilt. She drew a deep breath, extending her exposed arm out so that it was suspended over the water. Even in the bright light of day, her face looked pale. Pale but determined.

Bennett wondered if he should close his eyes. He'd seen more than his share of field surgery, having either performed it on others or himself. The sight of blood wasn't one he welcomed, but it didn't bother him, either. A part of his life, and the world of the Blades. Seeing *London* shed blood, on the other hand, made him want to rip up forests and punch mountains.

He kept his eyes open. But his fists curled so tightly that they turned to rock, aching worse than when climbing. He didn't feel it. He felt only London's pain when, after drawing another, steadying breath, she took the knife to the flesh of her forearm and began to carve into it. Stroke by stroke, the symbol of the bird emerged in bright crimson upon her pale skin.

The knife never wavered. She did not stop, and made one soft, hardly audible hiss as blood flowed from her arm. Red and rich, her blood rolled from her flesh to drip into the sea.

"That better be enough," growled Bennett to Athena.

The witch scooped up some of the sand that spread across the deck, then sprinkled it into the air. She watched the form it took as wind scattered the grains. "It is. The Bloodseeker Spell is broken."

As soon as those words left Athena's mouth, Bennett swept London up in his arms and carried her below. He didn't break stride, not even when grabbing a roll of muslin stored in the quarterdeck house.

"I'm ruining your shirt," London said, looking at the ruby stains she left on his clothes.

"Don't care." He kicked open the door to his cabin, set her on the bunk, and immediately took a wad of muslin and dabbed it on her wound. He didn't trust himself to speak. Cupping her arm in his hand, pressing the muslin there to staunch the bleeding, he felt the slimness of her, but also her toughness. Once satisfied that the flow of her blood slowed, he took fresh strips of muslin and wrapped them around the wound, as careful as if binding a bird's wing.

"What happened to your hands?" London asked.

He glanced down to see the red, angry indentations his fingers had left in his palms. "I didn't like that."

A small smile tilted her mouth. "I didn't, either. But it's done now." Her smile faded, leaving behind quiet determination and acceptance. "The link has been severed."

Bennett tipped her chin up. His eyes were brilliant gems, shifting from aquamarine to darkest sapphire, as he took her in, caressing her face with his gaze. The clean angles of his jaw, brow, and nose, the sensuous perfection of his mouth, now uncharacteristically serious. Lord, he was a beautiful man. All the more so because he was bruised and bloody, a warrior as much as a scoundrel.

She had seen him climb and fight and defend her, almost to the death. He flew, literally flew. And now he looked at her with such heat and soul, she felt the last slivers of ice around her heart turn to mist.

"I love you," he said, solemn.

She was so battered inside, she couldn't hide her wince. She hadn't the strength right now to protect her heart. "I know."

He shook his head, looking fierce and intent. *"I love you."*

"I know," she repeated. "You've said so." She might truly cry now, to think of what she felt for him, how it could not be reciprocated. Must she eventually lose everything?

Bennett squeezed his eyes shut for a moment, as if frustrated. "Damn, this is what I get for talking too much." He opened his eyes. "Monkeys in hats," he said.

She blinked at him, uncomprehending. "Did you hit your head?"

"Monkeys in hats," he said again, with growing heat. "That's what I mean when I say, 'I love you.' I mean that you're the woman I need beside me, all day, every day. I mean that I can't imagine my life without you. I mean that when you hurt, it feels like a knife in me, cutting me from the inside out." He paced in the tiny cabin, ricocheting back and forth like a bullet. "I mean that I hate the idea of anyone but me touching you. Just the thought makes me want to kill. I mean that I hate the idea of me touching anyone but you. I mean that when I see a goddamn monkey wearing a goddamn hat, I want to tell *you* about it. *You* and no one else."

She remembered what she had said to him the first night they had made love. Her palms grew damp, her mouth dry, the pain of her cut arm forgotten.

"You mean," she breathed, "you're *in love* with me?"

"I don't care what words anyone uses," he growled, stopping his pacing to stand in front of her. "Use the words of all the languages you know. Or make some up. Doesn't matter. What matters is that I want to be with you forever. Only you. And I hope to God," he said, his voice rough as he stroked her hair, her face, "that you only want me." There was no glib charm now, only the raw truth of his heart, laid bare before her.

He *was* shaking. She felt that as he touched her. And she trembled, too. Surely he felt that.

She was long past being safe or smart or protective, yet she felt compelled to ask, "Are you certain? You might grow tired of me, you know, long before forever comes."

"I've lived with myself for thirty-two years," he rumbled. "I know what the hell I'm talking about. *I love you*, damn it."

He was breathing hard now, his cheeks flushed, jaw tight. She'd never seen him so impassioned, so serious. He was still a scoundrel, but he was so much more, now.

When she at last found her voice, she said, "I monkeys in hats you, too."

Chapter 17

The Daughters of the Sea

At the very least, the stars should shift in the sky, the poles reverse or maybe something as minor as tigers learning to fly. Bennett, who had never once believed himself capable of giving his heart and body utterly and without regret to one woman, truly thought any of these miracles should have transpired the minute he confessed his love to London. Perhaps a second sun should burst to life in the sky when London, incredibly, admitted her own love for him.

Or, if none of those natural phenomena were to happen, then time itself should stop, completely suspended, leaving Bennett and London to spend days, weeks, months, and years exploring each other, discovering everything about each other, bodies and minds. Nothing else but that, an enchanted bubble surrounding them.

But the world, he learned, didn't stop because his life had been completely and wonderfully upended. He loved London, she loved him, and the damned Heirs were still out there. Those bastards' greedy claws sought dangerous magic. They would rip down or kill anyone who stood in their way. Not only that, but while Joseph Edgeworth was still alive, London's own life was in danger.

No rest, then. No enchanted bubble of lovemaking and revelations. Not yet.

There would be, by God. As Bennett and London gathered with Kallas and Athena on deck, Bennett swore to himself that he'd see this mission through to the end. He would ensure London's safety, carve a secret place out of glaciers or granite mountains for himself and her. He always took his duty to the Blades seriously. Now, his motivations were multiplied a hundredfold. Find the Source. Protect London. Love her. These demands were branded onto his heart, now and forevermore.

Late afternoon and the sky was aflame with blue, the sea burnished copper. The quartet of colleagues and friends massed around the wheel. Bennett had always liked being at sail, but now this caique had become a home to him, the people on it bound together with their own kinship. The Heirs wouldn't harm them. He refused to let that happen. The alternative—no, he wouldn't even consider it.

"We've got to find the Black Temple the Colossus spoke about," he said.

"But not even the Colossus knew where to find it," London noted, standing beside him. She was unaware that she played with his fingers, unconsciously stroking and fondling each with her own slender fingers, and consequently, a goodly portion of Bennett's thinking capacity settled warmly in his groin. But her touch felt too damned good to make her stop.

"If there ever was a written record of such a place," said Athena, "it is either lost or buried beneath centuries."

"Sailor lore holds nothing," muttered Kallas. "And I've heard everything. It could take a lifetime to find the damn place."

Bennett growled. "We don't have a lifetime." Even with

the Bloodseeker Spell broken, the Heirs would find some way to track them. The faster the Eye of the Colossus was found and secured, the better for everyone.

London frowned in thought. "If not a sailor, who then knows the sea?"

"Someone who makes it their home," Athena answered.

"Fish," Bennett said, only half in jest.

Grinning with sudden understanding, Kallas whipped off his cap and slapped it on his thigh. "Yes."

Athena raised her brow. "You cannot mean to ask the fish about the Black Temple."

"Fish?" Kallas scoffed. "No, that'd be ridiculous—no offense, Day," he added.

Bennett shrugged, affable. "No man has ever called me ridiculous. Son of a bitch, sometimes. Bastard, usually. But not ridiculous."

London bumped her shoulder against his arm. "And what do women call you?"

"I can't remember anyone before you."

The witch hadn't the patience to listen to Bennett and London's affectionate banter, perhaps because she always argued with the object of her own grudging interest. "Not the fish," she muttered. "Who, then?"

"You're a mainlander," Kallas said, smiling with white, straight teeth around the stem of his pipe. "But now it's time for you to learn respect for the sea."

The sails were lowered as the captain gathered an assemblage of things from the quarterdeck house and cargo hold. A bottle of wine. A jar of honey. Another jar, this one filled with olives.

"All gifts from the earth," Kallas said, setting them by the rail. "They want these delicacies, having nothing like them of their own."

"Who is 'they'?" Athena demanded.

The captain only gave the witch an enigmatic look, making her throw up her hands in frustration. Bennett hid his smile, but London saw, her own lips twitching in response. If Kallas and Athena ever made it over the hurdle of their pride and into bed, there wouldn't be enough water in the world to douse the resultant flames.

"Don't think you're the only one who knows a bit of magic," Kallas chided. "When sailors find themselves in trouble, they have an ally. Fifty, actually," he amended. "But they might not all show. Depends on their whims."

Athena, determined not to give Kallas any further response, merely folded her arms over her chest, clamping her mouth shut sullenly. Bennett bit the inside of his cheek. She was a far different creature than she had been when setting off from Piraeus weeks ago. Even her immaculate coiffures were long gone, and now her hair streamed wild about her shoulders. Bennett wondered if Athena the Greater would either congratulate Bennett for the changes wrought in her daughter, or daily send an eagle to tear out his liver, another Prometheus.

While Kallas finished setting up his collection of food-stuffs, Bennett's gaze was drawn to London, as it often did. He couldn't help it. She captured his every thought, ensnared him without effort, and he didn't mind in the least. Every time he saw her, that radiant happiness unfurled inside him like a standard, snapping and bright in the sunshine. This was so far beyond what he'd ever felt for any other woman, he at last understood what London meant in the difference between his old definitions of love and this one.

As Kallas made one more trip down to the cargo, London finished dousing the sails and glided toward Bennett. She had changed into one of Athena's skirts, and the fabric molded itself to her slim legs as the wind blew over the deck. Bennett couldn't decide if he liked her better in trousers or skirts. Each held their own appeal. She saw the admiration in his gaze, and her own heated in response. Combustible.

"Now, we are ready," said Kallas, appearing with a handful of grape leaves. He stood at the rail, holding his bounty of land-grown treasure.

"Do we need to do anything?" London asked.

"Only to keep your respect of the sea," the captain answered.

Everyone nodded in agreement, even Athena. Satisfied, Kallas turned to the water and began to sing.

It was a plain tune, the kind sung by sailors over countless generations as they mended nets or kept themselves company on long voyages. Simple, but not crude, only pared down to the sounds of a man's voice over the waves. Bennett didn't recognize the dialect, however, and could only listen to the rise and fall of Kallas's song as it moved in undulations like the sea.

As he sang, Kallas methodically emptied the bottle of wine into the water, the dark liquid spraying over the waves. The image reminded Bennett a bit too much of London shedding her blood, and he forced his breath to calm. Next, Kallas poured golden threads of honey into the water, followed by handfuls of olives. He then tossed the grape leaves across the water, the strong breeze catching them and sending them wheeling over the waves like green birds.

Then, faint at first and then with growing strength, the song was returned. Sweet female voices answered, and Bennett could have sworn they came from *underneath* the water. The voices were liquid, resonant with the sounds of coral reefs and hidden palaces. His body hummed with the presence of nearby magic.

"There!" London exclaimed, pointing to the water.

Kallas cursed faintly in surprise. "I didn't think it would work."

Dorsal fins broke the surface, carving the cobalt water clean and silver. They skimmed alongside the caique. Bennett heard a chirp, followed by another, and another. An inhuman laughter. Dolphins. Massing in playful pods, their backs slick and gray, they danced around the boat.

Peering closer, Bennett thought at first his sight was faulty. Hands grasped the dolphins' dorsal fins. Women's hands.

The dolphins, circling, rose higher in the water. Waves parted around them. The pale arms of women emerged from the sea, then their heads and shoulders. Long hair, adorned with coral beads and polished shells, flowed behind them. The women's eyes were a fathomless green, the color of deepest grottoes. None of them wore a scrap of clothing, except ropes of pearls loosely draped over their luminous bodies. The maidens sang in their liquid voices as the dolphins whistled in chorus. Bennett caught his breath to hear it.

The presence of immortal beauty stirred anyone, men especially. But Bennett did not feel his blood heat with desire to see the perfect bodies and lovely faces of the sea maidens, only the wonderment that such perfection could exist in an imperfect world.

London stared at the maidens, almost as enraptured as Bennett, joy at their presence flushing her cheeks. He forgot to mention to her that magical beings were not always monstrous, like the *rakshasa* demon. Now she had proof that magic had many faces, and he was glad to share it with her.

When the song faded, one of the nymphs called to Kallas in classical Greek, "My sisters and I are pleased by your offerings, sailor. You show proper reverence for us and our home."

"Your home is mine," Kallas answered, also in classical Greek. "My father and his father and all the men of my line owe our lives to you, Nereids. No tribute is ever enough."

Bennett had never heard the captain speak so formally or with such eloquence. It seemed Kallas could draw upon the art when pressed. Bennett snuck a glance at Athena and saw her regarding the captain with a newfound appreciation.

All of the maidens smiled at the captain's deferential words. "We shall grant you a boon, in kind," another trilled. "Ask it of us."

"Your munificence humbles me." Kallas bowed, one hand pressed to his chest. "If I may make a request, your guidance would be a great bounty. We seek a place that cannot be found. Yet we know that, of all the beings in the sea, the daughters of Nereus, truthful, compassionate, and gentle sea-god, possess a knowledge of the waters that surpasses all others."

This gratified the Nereids. Regally, but with a bit of preening, the first one said, "This is true. There is nothing in these waters that we do not know. What place do you seek?"

"The Black Temple."

The jeweled eyes of the Nereids widened. They chattered to each other in an unknown tongue.

One of the maidens said, regret dampening the bell of her voice, "That is a secret we keep for ourselves."

"But it is *very* important that we find it," London said, stepping forward.

The Nereids regarded London coolly. "Which does not concern us," one replied, haughty.

Seeking to add her persuasive voice to the discussion, Athena coaxed, "The fate of the world's magic rests in the balance."

This impressed the Nereids even less than London's plea.

The sea maidens grew noticeably more aloof, pursing their shell-pink lips in disapproval. What could make them so unresponsive, when moments earlier, they smiled indulgently at Kallas.

At Kallas, not London or Athena.

Bennett leaned down and whispered into London's ear. "Sorry."

"For what?" she asked, a small frown appearing between her brows.

He pressed a quick kiss to the side of her neck. "This." Bennett went to stand beside Kallas. "Afternoon, ladies," he said to the Nereids. He gave the sea maidens what Catullus Graves called Bennett's "damp-drawers smile." The Nereids weren't wearing drawers, but he hoped the effect was much the same.

"You are not a sailor," a Nereid with earrings of branched coral said, but her voice was more breathless.

"Alas, no," Bennett answered. "But I've been taught well the ways of the sea by my friend, Nikos Kallas." He clapped a brotherly hand on Kallas's shoulder. "Truly, if my work did not take me far on to land, I'd never leave the sea's breast."

Almost all the Nereids blushed to hear Bennett say the word "breast," regardless of the fact that none of them wore a stitch and their own bosoms were entirely bare.

"It would be a pity to lose you to the land," said the first Nereid. "The sea always needs good men."

"Surely you've no shortage of able-bodied seamen," Bennett answered.

Some of the sea maidens giggled, the sound like chimes. Bennett cast a quick look over his shoulder, and saw London scowling. Athena, too, appeared irritated. He shrugged, man's ancient sign of, "What can you do?" London made a shooing gesture with one hand, telling him to just get on with it.

"I am sorry that you cannot help us," Bennett said, turning back to the Nereids. "As my friends have pointed out, it's rather urgent we find the Black Temple."

"Such a place is kept hidden from the eyes of man," a Nereid with a diadem of shells said. "It is for the good of everyone."

"Very true," replied Bennett. "Most men are greedy and thoughtless children."

"Are *you*?" asked the Nereid with the coral earrings.

"Never a child, madam, always a man," he answered with a flirtatious smile. It was a role he played, a role he'd inhabited most of his life, and with pleasure, but now he wanted to smile in such fashion at London alone. He would only fulfill the promise of his smile with her. Still, the Nereids didn't know that. He hoped London did.

Urging her dolphin to swim a little closer to the caique, the diadem-wearing sea nymph stared up at Bennett with heavy-lidded eyes. "How do we know your intentions at the Black Temple are honorable?"

"You've but my word. And I don't give it lightly."

"Is there anything you *do* give lightly?" asked the Nereid. "A kiss, perhaps?"

Bennett thought he heard London's growl. A tigress. Oh, he had such plans for her later. For now, though, he had to concern himself with these rather trying nymphs. He used to like the game of seduction. Now, he was impatient, wanting to be finished so they could go about their business, so he could be alone with London.

"My kisses are given to only one woman," Bennett said, and he was glad of it.

"A pity," sighed the Nereid with the earrings. "What of your handsome friend? He sings well." She looked at Kallas.

The captain flushed, then cast a glance at Athena. The witch turned away, feigning interest in the grain of the wooden deck. Kallas seemed to wait for an objection from her, but she said nothing.

"Kallas men leave women sighing in ports across the sea," the captain said, turning back to the Nereid.

At once, the Nereids began to chatter amongst themselves, some kind of heated debate. It reached a crescendo, then the sea nymph in the diadem silenced her sisters with a wave of her hand. Her sisters looked supremely irritated.

"It is decided," she said, addressing Bennett and Kallas. "I shall tell you how to find the Black Temple. But there is a price."

"And that price is?" Bennett asked.

"A kiss for me, from each of you men."

Shocked noises of outrage from both London and Athena as Bennett inwardly grimaced. Why must magical women have such a taste for mortal flesh?

The Nereid's green aquatic eyes moved over both Kallas and Bennett, a suggestive perusal. "My sisters and I have met so few mortals that intrigue us, hardly any since Odysseus and Jason crossed these waters."

"My heart belongs to another," Bennett said.

The nymph dismissed this objection with a toss of her head. "I ask not for your heart. Only your kiss." She guided her dolphin closer to the caique, so that she was a foot away, and tilted up her face with regal expectation.

Before Bennett could respond, London muttered in English, "It's all right. Kiss the bloody sea strumpet."

With an inward sigh, knowing he hadn't a choice in the matter, Bennett leaned over the rail to place a quick, fraternal kiss on the Nereid's mouth. Her lips were cool, beaded with seawater. He tried to pull back, but the nymph's arms came up and locked behind his neck, almost tugging him overboard. Her kiss became more insistent, her tongue pushing at the seam of his lips to force them open. It felt a little like kissing an amorous octopus.

Bennett managed to disentangle himself from the Nereid's arms and leaned back. He barely resisted the impulse to wipe his mouth on his sleeve as she pouted.

"Now, you," the sea nymph commanded Kallas.

The captain did as he was ordered, but, with no word of protest from Athena, his participation was a hell of a lot more enthusiastic than Bennett's. The Nereid clutched at Kallas as they kissed deeply, and a flush crept over her body while her sisters sighed with envy.

While Kallas was so occupied, he didn't see Athena's fierce scowl. It looked as though she was on the verge of either planting a foot in the captain's behind or committing nymphicide. Bennett suspected it was extreme force of will, and dedication to the mission, that kept the witch from unleashing her fury.

Finally, the Nereid released Kallas. The captain moved back, completely dazed.

"Delicious," the nymph said. "While *your* kiss," she said to Bennett, "left much to be desired, they both revealed your inner truths regarding your intent for the Black Temple. I may disclose to you its location without fear."

"Many thanks." Bennett spoke because Kallas seemed incapable of rational thought. Kissing immortal maidens had that effect on most men.

"A day's sail north. Three islands shall you pass, each a fortress. The fourth is what you seek. The Black Temple is beneath the Black Temple. You must bring the Oracle's Daughter, else the secret shall burn you."

Ah, another riddle. But it was one he and London would solve together.

From her sheltered spot at the bow, hidden by a large crate, London sat and watched the evening descend like a silken cloak. She had her knees curled up, her chin propped on her knees, her arms around her legs. Wind blew across her face with the scent of saltwater and possibility. Athena had wrapped an herbal poultice around the wound on London's arm, so that its pain was hardly felt, the healing already commencing. There might be a faint scar, however.

Even if the symbol she had carved into her arm faded completely, she would never lose the mark upon her heart. How did one go on, knowing that her parent sought her death? She thought of Abraham and Isaac, the venerable patriarch willing to slay his son for the sake of his faith. Somehow, London's father had convinced himself that he must sacrifice her for the betterment of England, if not merely himself and his reputation. What if Isaac leapt up from the altar to snatch the knife from his father's hand? How would the world be different?

She was orphaned, never to see her mother again, and to her father she was dead. She could have nothing further to do with him. Or he must die. The thought made her shudder, even as she acknowledged the truth. Even though she had broken the Bloodseeker Spell, she was not free of her father, not free of the Heirs. Not until either she or her father were dead.

Which meant it had to be him. She had found love where none was expected. Her life now was far too precious to surrender without a fight.

London waited for Bennett to finish his shift at the helm, unable to sit below. Tomorrow they would reach the Black Temple. Tomorrow might see their journey end, and how it was to end, she had no idea. Any number of possibilities ran through her mind, some wonderful, some terrible. It was not a night for confined spaces. She needed the sea and the sky around her, almost as much as she needed Bennett. While she could not have one this very moment, she could have the others.

"Kallas, a word."

London stiffened when she heard Athena's voice on the other side of the crate.

"What is it, witch?" The captain's voice was unusually restrained. Perhaps an aftereffect of kissing a Nereid.

For a moment, Athena was silent, and London could feel her friend's tension in that weighted silence. London debated as to whether or not to announce her presence, but the atmosphere between Kallas and Athena thickened with intimacy. If London let them know she was nearby, it might ruin the fragile moment. So London said nothing.

Finally, Athena asked, "Do you have many memories of your childhood?"

If the question surprised the captain, he did not say so. "Mostly of my father and his boat. Laughing. He laughed a lot. Showing me how to weigh anchor. The anchor was almost as big as I was, I nearly went over the side with it."

"I have few memories of my youth." Athena's voice was soft, ruminative. "I was always in such a hurry to grow up. My mother and grandmother were good to me, but I wanted to be an adult as soon as I could and join them in the world of decision-makers. They warned me, Yaya and Mama, that I should enjoy the pleasures of childhood freedom. I never listened. In that way, I was like all Galanos women. Stubborn."

"Headstrong," Kallas corrected gently.

Athena's chuckle was rueful. "I do have a particular recollection. A name day celebration at some friend's home. A boy my own age. There were sweets to eat, and I remember these two pieces of baklava, golden with honey and fragrant with walnuts and cinnamon. I stared at them for a long time, trying to decide which one I wanted. One of the pieces had more walnuts, the other, more honey. I just stared and stared, thinking, considering, unable to make up my mind."

"Why not take them both?"

"That would have been greedy."

"You were a child. Children are allowed to be greedy. I used to stuff myself sick on *loukoumades* when we'd get to port, and my father let me. A treat and a lesson."

"Even if my mother said it would have been all right, I wouldn't let myself."

"So, which piece of baklava did you take?"

"Neither. I spent so much time deliberating and thinking, some girl ran up and grabbed both pieces for herself. I wound up with nothing."

"I'll bring you as much baklava as you want when we get back to Piraeus."

"Many thanks, but no. I did not tell you that story because I had a craving for baklava."

"What *do* you have a craving for?"

Even London, on the other side of the crate, heard the sensual promise of the captain's softly spoken words.

"I do not give in to cravings," Athena answered, but her voice was throaty. "I never have. I always thought they were signs the body was trying to overtake the mind, and I would not let that happen."

"High time for you to start listening to your body."

"And my heart." The witch drew in a breath. "I do not want to waste an opportunity because I am thinking too much, trying to decide what is best or right."

"Athena—"

"Will you come to my bunk tonight, Nikos? When your shift at the helm is over?" She didn't wait for an answer, talking quickly as if to avoid hearing the captain's response. "I shall ask London to sleep in the other cabin. She will accept. She's grown tired of crawling back and forth between cabins, and I know it can be disruptive, so—"

Athena's nervous prattling stopped. London wondered why, until she heard the unmistakable sounds of kissing.

Leave it to the captain to let actions speak more eloquently than words.

Though determined to keep her silence, inwardly London rejoiced. The kiss between the captain and the witch had been a long time in the making, and, now that London had discovered love, she wanted to share it with everyone, especially her friends.

Some time later, Kallas murmured, "What's the word? Ensorcelled? I think you've ensorcelled me, Lady Witch."

"No more than you have netted me, Captain. I did not enjoy seeing you kiss that Nereid."

"It didn't look like you minded."

"I minded."

"Would it help if I said I was thinking of you the whole time?"

Athena chuckled, then said, softly, "Tonight, then."

"Tonight."

The taps of Athena's footfalls faded as she went below. Kallas let out a slow growl, then followed the sound with a litany of exaltation to hosts of saints and gods. London speculated that she would not get much sleep that night, kept awake by the sounds of lovemaking. But it was only fair. Lord knew that she and Bennett had probably cost everyone their sleep, with all their carnal carryings-on.

Later she heard Bennett and Kallas trade places at the helm, then the strong, sure sound of Bennett's boots on the deck coming toward her. Night had fallen, so she felt more than saw him when he stood close by. Her heart and body vibrated with barely contained energy, matching his.

Bennett easily lowered down to the deck, sliding behind her so that she sat between his legs as he cradled her in his arms. Warm, solid, and athletic, he surrounded her without entirely engulfing her. London leaned against him, her back to his chest, and she felt the strange double joys of serenity and excitement. She was safe here with him, but not stiflingly sheltered. He brushed his lips against her hair.

Neither spoke. It felt too good to sit in the prow of the boat in the darkness, the waves breaking across the bow, wind in the sails, the heat of his body blanketing her.

"Are you sure you wouldn't rather be with that Nereid?" London asked. "She seemed to fancy you quite a bit."

He gave a snort. "I don't fancy fish. Maybe for supper, but not for kissing."

"Prefer human women, do you?"

"Just one." He turned her head gently and demonstrated exactly what he meant.

Some moments later, when they had to pause to breathe, he asked, "What have you been doing up here?"

She worked to bring her mind into focus after the heady pleasures of Bennett's mouth. "Enjoying the night. Thinking."

"Alone?"

She thought of the exchange between Kallas and Athena, and, though she trusted Bennett completely, felt Athena might take umbrage if London discussed her private romantic affairs.

"Yes," London said, hating that she had to lie to him. "All alone."

"Did I ever mention that I've excellent hearing?" he asked, his voice low, a delightful rumble.

She should have known. "You heard them, too?"

"Oh, yes. And about bloody time, too."

His soft chuckle sent tremors rippling through her. She was very aware of him pressed into her backside, even through the layers of her skirt and petticoat. Thank heavens she'd long ago abandoned a bustle. Feeling him intimately snug against her was a wicked pleasure for which she would gladly forsake fashion. In fact, there was something to be said for being absolutely naked whenever Bennett was near.

"I'm glad for them," said London. "Glad they were willing to take the chance. I didn't think they would ever risk themselves."

He brushed her hair to one side, uncovering her neck. His warm mouth trailed just beneath her ear. Then he traced the curve of her neck with small, gentle bites, just hard enough to send bright currents of awareness through her, centering at the tips of her breasts and between her thighs. He soothed the bites with velvet licks of his tongue. "Not everyone's as brave as you," he said between ministrations.

"Not so brave," she gasped. "Just know what I want." Coherent thought, and the ability to talk sensibly, vanished under his touch.

His long hands slid up over her waist and ribs to cup her breasts. She arched her back, the better to feel his caresses. Yet neither of them were satisfied, not until he unfastened the buttons of her shirtwaist and pulled the garment open, baring the skin of her chest. She had taken off her corset before scaling the cliff, and beneath the shirtwaist she wore only a chemise. He stroked her through the fine cotton, teasing her breasts to hard points so that she writhed with pleasure. Then even the thin chemise was too much of a barrier, and he pulled it roughly up and out of her skirt's waistband. At once, his hands went underneath the fabric to caress her bare skin, and she gasped aloud.

"Tell me what you want," he growled.

"You, only you." She pushed back into him, feeling the thickness of his firm cock rubbing against her.

When he took his hands from her breasts, she almost wept with loss, but then he was gathering up her skirt, his hands stroking up her outstretched legs. Up her calves, past her knees, the lengths of her thighs. Then higher. She sucked in a breath when his fingers found her wet and desperate for him.

"Tell me why," he demanded, guttural. "Tell me why you want me." He traced her, touched her, while the other hand went back to attend to her breast.

Her mind slipped further from her grasp so that she became merely a vessel for a desperate need.

"Because—" She gasped.

"Yes."

"Because—" She reached behind awkwardly, fumbling with the buttons on his trousers. Yet she was determined, and soon had him unfastened and then, yes, he was in her hand, burning hot and thick. He hissed as she stroked him.

Then he lifted her, raising her up just above him, and moved his legs between hers. The very crown of his cock kissed her opening. She was giddy, spinning, and so desperate for him.

"Say it," he urged. He brought her down, and they both cried out as he filled her.

"Because I love you," she moaned.

If either of them had possessed any control before, her words broke that control. He plunged into her with fierce, sure strokes. She met each of his thrusts, frenzied, lost to everything but the feeling of his hands at her waist, his mouth on her neck, him deep inside her, stretching her, suffusing her with his heat and desire.

She struggled to keep her eyes open to see the prow cut the waves. Wind stroked her heated face as they raced into the night, and it felt, with Bennett thrusting into her, as though they were flying, carried aloft by their lovemaking. The pitch of the deck as it rode the waves pushed him even deeper within her. They were elemental, creatures of water and wind.

"I love you, London," he groaned. One hand glided from

her waist to stroke her where she was most sensitive. "No words to say . . ."

At once, climax seized her. She flung herself into it, into the pleasure and joy he gave her. She felt herself destroyed and reborn. A heartbeat later and his release followed hers.

They sank back together, panting, boneless, bound together in body and heart. And all around them was the sea, wine-dark and eternal.

Chapter 18

The Black Temple

A wail rose up and hovered over the deck of the steamship—mournful, enraged, helpless. The sound curled like acrid smoke, thick and terrible. Had anyone with compassion heard the cry, they would have fallen to their knees and wept. But no one aboard the steamship, from the captain to the men shoveling coal into the furnace, possessed an ounce of empathy. Such men had made the misery of others their occupation. To them, the sound of lamentation was ordinary and tedious, hardly worth a moment's reflection.

There were others, though, who found the cry to be stimulating.

Joseph Edgeworth and Thomas Fraser watched, one man disinterested, the other titillated as John Chernock crouched over the Nereid. The black blade in his hand gleamed with the nymph's blood. Long cuts ran down the lengths of her arms and legs, and her hair lay in clumps around the deck, bits of coral and pearl still woven into it. The Nereid, pinned under the weight of the restraining spell, could only sob and writhe, calling to her sisters massing around the hull of the steamship, but even they could do nothing but listen to the suffering of their sister. Chernock's spell sheltered the steamship, protecting it from the Nereids' retribution.

"Have you told me everything?" Chernock asked the imprisoned sea nymph. He sounded detached, like a dentist inquiring about his patient's holiday plans.

"Yes," the Nereid whimpered. "You know where the Black Temple is now. Release me."

"You had better not be lying to me," Chernock warned, still quite impersonal. He ran the blade down her neck, between her breasts, with the promise of more pain.

From the aft of the ship came a howl, the sound of the *rakshasa* demon scenting blood and pain. It longed to feed. But the enchanted chains that bound the demon held it fast. Only a word from Chernock could free it.

"Our kind is incapable of falsehood," the Nereid answered, flinching.

"Perhaps I can test that."

"Enough, Chernock," snapped Edgeworth. "We have all we need from the trollop. The captain's plotted our course. We haven't time for your little games."

The sorcerer's icy calm frayed with annoyance as he glanced over his shoulder. "But I want to see how much suffering an immortal body can withstand."

"Perform your experiments later." Edgeworth pulled a pocketwatch from his waistcoat pocket and frowned at the hour. "The delay with the ship's wheel already cost us time."

"Let me keep her, then."

"And have those damned sea bitches trailing after us?" Edgeworth tipped his head to the side, indicating the Nereids helplessly gathered around the steamship. "No. Throw her back."

"Must he, sir?" asked Fraser, disappointed.

Edgeworth shot him a disapproving glare. "Just do it. I'm going below to send a letter through the Transportive

Fire. When I come back, that thing better be gone." He strode away.

With an irritated sigh, Chernock rose to his feet. What a missed opportunity! Edgeworth hadn't a proper sense of proportion. All he cared about were missions. Especially now that the truth about his traitorous daughter had at last come to light, bursting his illusions like a blister. Edgeworth was mortified by the failure of his daughter, and pushed harder now to seize the Greek Fire Source as if to atone or prove himself. He chased it with a determination that bordered on obsession. But there was so much more to being an Heir—such as chances to study and broaden knowledge that few other men would ever experience.

When the Blookseeker Spell had been broken, the Heirs were adrift, without direction. It had been Chernock's idea to summon the Nereids—those saltwater trollops knew this sea better than any being—and it was a wonderful stroke of luck that he could ascertain more, not only as to where the Blades were heading, but also about the nymphs' pain tolerances. Or lack of tolerance, as it turned out. Yet so much more could be learned!

Perhaps Fraser could be an ally. Chernock dismissed that idea quickly. Even though Fraser would welcome any occasion to cause something pain, the fool was even more concerned with currying favor and toadying, particularly now that the possibility of Fraser marrying Edgeworth's whore daughter was no longer an option.

Still, the younger man looked visibly sorry when Chernock released the restraining spell with a wave of his hand. The Nereid rolled over and crawled to the railing, trails of blood smearing on the metal deck. With the heel of his shoe, Chernock shoved the Nereid into the water. Immediately, the other nymphs gathered around their wounded sister.

One of the sea maidens, her brow topped by a shell-encrusted diadem, looked up at Chernock. "We curse you, sorcerer!" she hissed. "The daughter of daughters shall cleave you before the eyes of the sea."

Chernock did not bother answering. Nereids were nothing, merely some sea god's over-numerous offspring. They held no real power.

He turned away with a dismissive shrug, then grabbed the arm of a passing crewman. "Clean that up," he said, pointing to the Nereid's spilled blood. "But don't touch it. The ichor makes it poisonous to mortals."

The crewman nodded, then went to fetch a mop and bucket.

"Tough luck, Chernock," said Fraser, his tone somewhere between regretful and pleased. There wasn't a drop of camaraderie between him and Chernock, especially where internal politics were concerned. Fraser was only sorry that his viewing entertainment had been cut short.

"No matter," the sorcerer sighed. "We'll catch the Blades tomorrow. I'm sure, once we have Day, the witch, and the slut, even Edgeworth will not object to a little magical experimentation."

Fraser grinned openly at the thought. "I hope not."

Athena, lying snug in Kallas's arms, shot upright with a gasp.

"What is it, *magesa*?" the captain asked sleepily. He stroked her bare leg.

"The bastard," Athena choked. "I shall tear him apart!"

Fully awake now, Kallas sat up and took her hands in his. "Who?"

Athena shook with rage and horror. "Chernock. The Heirs' sorcerer. He has tortured a Nereid. I can feel the sorrow of the nymphs calling out for vengeance."

Now the rage was echoed in Kallas. "*I'm* responsible. I was the one who summoned the Nereids."

"No, not you. The burden isn't yours but *his*. I will make him pay," Athena vowed.

"Not if I don't kill him first."

For some time, the witch and the captain sat in joined silence, both silently swearing revenge, both determined to protect the other from having blood on their hands. When at last their hearts stopped pounding, and sleep tugged at them, they lay down together, fitted as snug as two halves of a shell. But the peace they shared earlier had been shattered.

London never knew the Aegean could possess so many mysteries. Before setting off on her voyage to Greece, she had extensively studied maps, read accounts, in Greek and other languages. The sea itself was not so large. It surrounded where civilizations had been born, where learning and thought had reached their apotheosis. Sailors such as Kallas had navigated the deep azure waters for millennia. Everything there was to be known about the Aegean had been set down in writing and song. The human mind encompassed all.

She should have realized by now that the human mind, the constructs of man, barely brushed at the edges of worlds and ideas epic and limitless in scope. Even something as traversed as a merchant-crossed sea could hold secrets.

On no map and in no written account had London seen reference to what the Nereids and Colossus called the Black Temple. And yet, there it was, an island just off the portside bow. It grew larger as the caique approached, larger and undeniable.

"Have you ever seen such a place?" she asked Bennett, standing beside her at the rail.

"Never," he answered. "And I've seen a lot."

It took a sail once around the circumference of the island to determine its shape and size. It formed a parenthesis in the water, with a shallow bay, and a high craggy peak on its westernmost point. Huge, ancient plane trees and bits of scrub dotted the curved hills. The geography itself was not especially remarkable, but what the island contained just inland, beyond its eastern bay, made London's breath catch in wonderment.

The ruins of an amphitheater, carved from darkest stone. Seats had been hewn from the hillside, rising up above and around a semicircular area that had, at one point, contained dancers and a chorus. The remains of the stage sat directly behind the orchestra, so that the audience, when watching a performance, would have the beach and sea as backdrop.

In Athens, London had seen the ruins of the Theater of Dionysus and been suitably impressed by its age and consequence—even if most of the theater was lost to time. It had been the theater of the capital, the birthplace of drama, a white marble edifice that glowed in the noon-time sun, yet one would have to draw heavily upon the powers of imagination to fully envision the scene.

Somehow, on this tiny island in an obscure pocket of the Aegean, a theater of black stone stood in almost pristine condition, barely touched by the destructive influence of time. Almost as strange, no other buildings or signs of previous life marked the island, as though only the theater needed sustaining and everything else, even shelter, was unnecessary.

This strange place was known to few, or the long dead. Now she and her friends and the man she loved were added to that company. Would the knowledge of the Black Temple die with them, as well? And, if so, how soon?

She would not think of death now, or the Heirs at their back. *See this now*, she told herself. *Live this moment.*

They quickly anchored the boat off the beach. London, Bennett, and Athena waded to shore for reconnaissance.

Standing in the orchestra of the theater, London felt the powerful hum of something otherworldly resonating through her. What the origin of that intense sensation might be, she could not tell. As she scoured the amphitheater for writings she might need to translate, Bennett bounded up and down the tiers of seats with an alluring, muscular virility, searching for any other clues that might direct them.

"Why would this be called the Black Temple?" London asked Athena.

The witch turned from her examination of the stones lining the orchestra. "The first theaters were temples to the god Dionysus," she explained. "His worshippers performed songs and dances in his honor, and those evolved into dramatic performances. Yet I do not know why a theater such as this one, obviously not dedicated to Dionysus, exists all alone out here in the middle of nowhere."

Athena's words were precise, but her gaze was far and pensive. London initially ascribed her friend's uncharacteristic behavior to the exceptionally energetic night spent with the captain. But that morning, upon rising, Athena told London and Bennett about the lament of the Nereids that had pierced her sleep. The revelation had sickened everyone on the caique.

However, Athena had grown even more abstracted since the island of the Black Temple was sighted. And, now that they were on land, actually standing in the midst of the theater, London had never seen the witch so preoccupied.

"Are you all right?" London asked.

The witch's eyes were dark, darker than night, and glittering. "I can feel it. The magic of this place. The power. It would claim me, if I let it."

Of course Athena would feel magic more strongly than London. She had steadily been using her magical abilities with much more frequency than she ever had before. Now her senses were alive with it, turning her into a perfect conduit for a Source. Surely the Eye of the Colossus, the Source sought by everyone, had to be here.

Bennett joined them in the orchestra. "The Nereids said the Eye could be found in the temple beneath the temple. But I can't find anything that might lead us below. Not a doorway or crevice."

"Perhaps there's another way below," London said. "I saw a sea cave in the cliffs to the west of the beach."

A slow smile spread across Bennett's face as he followed the path her mind took. She saw in his face the same respect and consideration he gave to Athena, to anyone, man or woman. Though, she admitted, his expression when looking at London had a much more carnal undertone. It seemed, in truth, that one fed the other. And she had once despaired that any man could find her use of her mind to be at all enticing.

Oh, God, or gods, or goddesses, please let them make it through this mission. If anything happened to Bennett, she would find herself utterly destroyed.

"It's mostly submerged," London noted. "One couldn't wade or sail through it."

"Which would make sense," Athena said, "if one was trying to find a secure place for something powerful."

Bennett took London's hand, his eyes vivid and bright in the sun. "Looks like we're going to get wet again."

The cave peered up, a dark crescent, above the water. They had raised the caique's anchor and sailed as close to the entrance of the cave as possible. No way to know how far back the cave went or its height. From what Bennett could tell, there was just enough room for someone swimming through to bob up for air, but not much else. He wished he could scout the cave first before London went down there. The idea of sending her someplace unknown and uncertain maddened him. But time was short, and the Colossus had been clear in its instructions that both Bennett and London had to go to the Black Temple to find the Eye.

So it was with no small measure of trepidation that he and London readied the water-tight packs. The dry bags were of heavily waxed cotton, double-lined, and he packed his with a revolver, cartridges, the Compass, two of Catullus's illuminating cylinders, and a set of clothes, including his boots. A cumbersome load, but he was a strong swimmer. London packed her bag with trousers, a shirtwaist and her boots, a much smaller burden, but they hadn't tested her swimming ability in such arduous territory. Streams and ponds were not as challenging as the cave would likely be. She might not have the strength needed for the upcoming task.

He'd carry her on his back if he had to. Doubts about protecting her never entered his mind.

Athena came forward, her palms cupped. "These might be needed for your journey."

He and London peered into the bowl of her hands. Two fish scales gleamed there.

"You may find," the witch said, "in your swim through the cave, that air is scarce. I have placed an enchantment on these scales. One is for your journey out. The other for your return. To activate the spell, just cast a scale into the water."

Bennett picked up one of the scales. It seemed a perfectly ordinary fish scale, but he'd not question Athena's spell casting. Ever since the mission had begun, weeks ago, the witch's use of her powers increased dramatically, and with that usage, came growth in strength—even if she held back from the larger spells. As he examined the scale, Athena wrapped the other in a small parchment envelope and tucked it into his pack.

When he moved to cast the scale into the water, Athena cried, "Wait! The spell's life is brief. Do not put it in the sea until you are completely ready to swim, and swim speedily."

One way to assure that they would swim as fast as possible was to reduce drag, which meant swimming naked. Bennett, never shy, shucked his clothes quickly, but London, blushing, performed her task with a bit more slowness. Kallas politely averted his gaze. Bennett was tempted to watch and linger on the sight of her bare skin in the sunlight, but there would be time for that later. He hoped.

Only when London had slipped on the straps of her pack and slid into the water did Kallas turn back. Bennett also lowered himself into the water after donning his pack. At least the sea was warm and gentle, lapping in calm waves. They both tread water as Athena, standing at the rail, asked, "Are you set?"

"Almost," Bennett said. "Just be ready and be careful, both of you," he added, looking from Athena to Kallas and back again. "The Heirs are coming."

"That has not escaped me," Athena said gravely.

"Looking forward to pounding them against the rocks like octopi," Kallas said.

Good enough for Bennett. He glanced at London, treading water beside him. Her face, now impossibly beautiful to him, was set with determination and also—this is what he truly adored—illuminated with excitement at the prospect of an adventure. "Ready?" he asked her.

She smiled in response. He swam closer to her, then kissed her.

"I love you," he said.

"I know," she answered.

He grinned, then turned back to Athena. "Now."

Athena dropped the scale into the water. Almost at once, it grew, glowing, until it took the form of a fish. Bennett was an amateur angler, but he'd never seen a fish like this one before. It was the size of his hand, but emitted a bright golden radiance like a tiny, swimming sun.

"Through the cavern," Athena commanded the fish. It immediately darted toward the entrance of the cave. "Go! Hurry!" she shouted at Bennett and London. "You must stay with the fish or else you will not be able to breathe in the water."

Bennett and London swam in pursuit, he at the lead. They quickly breached the mouth of the cave. Inside, it was much darker and close, the roof of the cave sometimes only just missing Bennett's head when he rose up for breath. Damp, sea-carved rock loomed all around them. Light receded completely, so that the only illumination came from the incandescent fish. Then even the small headroom disappeared as the cave dipped lower, the passage entirely filled with water.

They paused just before the airway vanished, just able to tilt their heads to the side to draw breath.

"What do we do?" London asked.

"Go forward."

"But we don't know how far this goes, or if there's any air."

He wished he could tell her to turn back, but that choice wasn't available. "Stay with the fish. Athena said it would be all right."

There wasn't time to discuss it further. The fish, and its glow, headed away from them. They each took a final inhalation—maybe their last—before swimming in pursuit.

The cave stretched and twisted forward, its jagged walls lit only by the light radiating from the fish. Visibility was limited to a few feet. Everything else was utterly black. The water cooled as the cavern wound deeper into solid rock.

He felt as though he were swimming into the underworld, shadows thick on every side, nowhere to surface.

Bennett swam as quickly as he could, but always careful to stay with London. She wasn't far behind, her strength having grown over the weeks, and though the closeness of the cavern walls seemed to intimidate her a little, she never hesitated moving forward.

Soon, his lungs burned. He felt the roof of the cavern for even the smallest pocket of air. Nothing. London struggled. He fought, but it was undeniable. They could hold their breath no longer.

His mouth opened. Seawater flooded his mouth and down his throat. He choked, gagged, and then—

Breathed.

Incredible. Unbelievable. But true. He felt the water in him, even in his lungs, but breathed easy as if standing on the shore rather than swimming deep below the surface of the sea.

The same for London. Dawning awareness and amazement filled her face as she, too, discovered she could breathe underwater.

They shared smiles of commingled wonder and excitement. He never believed he could play the role of merman, and yet, here he was, and London, as well, both swimming, both breathing. And they had Athena's magic to thank for it.

But not for long. The glow of the fish dimmed as the creature swam ahead. They would have to keep pace, otherwise they'd both drown. And even if they stayed with the fish, Athena said the spell had a short duration. It might not last long enough to see them find air.

Onward they pressed. The cavern narrowed so that they could no longer swim side by side. His arms began to tire. Would they never see the end of this damned cave?

Then the cavern abruptly widened. An overhead surface

appeared, its flat expanse a blessed relief. The glow from
the fish illuminated what looked like a small rise.

Bennett broke the surface, London immediately after. He
found the bottom of the cavern and stood. Before either
he or London could look around, they both bent over,
retching up saltwater, until their bodies were empty.

"All right?" he gasped when he could speak.

"Don't feel *good*, exactly," she choked, "but I'll get by."

He rubbed her back as she coughed up a bit more water.
She soon straightened and glanced around, the space
weakly illuminated by the fish swimming in the waters of
the grotto.

"What is this place?" she asked, voice hushed and raw.

"The Black Temple."

The light from the fish winked out, thrusting them into
complete darkness.

London froze. She heard Bennett rustling through his
pack, then small metallic chiming. After what felt like
hours of blindness, he activated one of Catullus Graves's illuminating devices. Bennett took her hand, and together
they waded out of the water. Both dressed quickly in the
chill of the cavern. He strapped on his revolver while she
wrung out her hair. Each of them brandished the illuminating devices to assess their surroundings, moving slowly
deeper into the cave.

"Stay close," Bennett cautioned. His voice echoed hol-
lowly in the arches of the cavern. "Nothing the ancients
love more than booby traps."

She nodded, glancing around apprehensively.

In the greenish glow, the large cavern was numinous,
chthonian, dissolving into shadows. London half-believed
she and Bennett had swam to the very entrance of Hades.
A temple had been carved directly from the cave's black

rocks—a mixture of classical Greek columns and older, rawer shapes suggesting creatures emerging from the inky stone.

None of this unsettled her as much as the palpable power charging the air. Even though they were deep within the heart of the island, the atmosphere of the cavern danced with energy. It infused her body, the filaments of her mind, until she thought she might fly apart. Or grow to the size of a giant and conquer the globe. No wonder men killed for such magic. Untempered, the power could engulf and overwhelm, seduce the unwary.

"It's here," she said. "The Source." She shuddered.

"Makes my teeth feel like Roman candles."

She stopped walking. "Bennett—"

"I see it."

A pool, twenty feet across, had been carved from the rock. Set in regular intervals all around the pool's rim were eight bronze handles, wide enough to need two hands. What arrested London and Bennett's attention was not the work of man, but rather the object propped up on a mound in the center of the pool.

"The Eye of the Colossus," London breathed.

The Eye took the light of the illuminating devices, absorbing it, to cast the light out again with a potent radiance. Nearly two feet from corner to corner, almond-shaped, the Eye stared at them, unblinking, penetrative, as if seeing London and Bennett with the cutting wisdom of eternity. She felt herself diminish into almost nothing before its unyielding stare.

This was the object that men would kill to possess, men like her father and the Heirs. Empires could be forged and destroyed by harnessing its power. The knowledge sent icy fire flaring through her.

"Do you ever get used to this?" London asked, waving her hand toward the Eye.

"If I did, then I'd know I was dead."

After walking around the perimeter of the pool, she saw that the Eye was flat, hammered bronze with a slight curve, and leather straps and a bronze handle attached to its back.

"Someone could wield it like a shield," Bennett murmured.

London edged to the lip of the pool, holding her illumination aloft. What she saw cheered her. Perhaps this would not be so difficult, after all. "The water isn't deep. We could wade in and grab the Eye." She moved to do just that.

He darted forward and hauled her back, his grip an iron band on her arm.

"Remember," he said, voice tight, "the ancients are always crafty bastards."

Taking up a loose pebble, he dropped it into the pool. London jumped back with a gasp. The water roiled furiously around the pebble, a seething cauldron. Had she stepped into the pool, her flesh would have been scalded, falling away from her bones as she watched.

"It didn't look like it was boiling hot," she said weakly.

"The water's gone past that point." A thin smile cracked his somber face. "Too bad Catullus isn't here. He'd soil himself for a chance to study the phenomenon."

"Maybe it would be better if Graves *was* here." London, still skittish from her close call, stared balefully across the pool to the unreachable Source. "He could figure out a way to get to the Eye."

"The ancients already took care of that." He bent to examine one of the bronze handles at the perimeter of the pool. "These are water gates. Each handle is attached to a metal plate sunk into the ground." He pointed to the pool, where, London now saw, round holes were set into its walls. "Drains. Each gate is connected to a pipe, so that, when pulled up, the pool will drain. Clever buggers."

It stood to reason that the drained water would have to

come out somewhere. She glanced around the cavern, searching for an outlet. Best to be well out of the way, or else have super-heated water come pouring out on an un-suspecting victim. After searching the ground, she chanced to look up, and tugged on Bennett's sleeve.

At her wordless demand, he followed her gaze, and swore softly. "Clever *and* cruel."

Eight openings were cut high up the cavern walls, one above each water gate. Whomever opened a gate would re-ceive a scalding shower for their troubles—*if* each opening correlated to each gate. There was always the possibility, a very likely possibility, that there *was* no correlation, so that one gambled with one's life to drain the pool.

"How do we know which gate is the right one?" she asked.

He frowned in concentration, assessing the situation. "That's assuming there's only *one* gate. The Colossus said that both of us need to be in the Black Temple. Which means that it's a two-man operation."

"One of us is a woman," London noted dryly.

His grin was sudden and warming. "Believe me, love, I know."

She tried to push aside the fluttering low in her belly. It amazed her that even in this strange place, contemplating the prospect of being boiled alive, he could call forth her desire with hardly any effort. She was now so far changed from the woman she had been weeks earlier, London barely recognized herself, but the metamorphosis delighted her, as much as the man standing close by.

"The trick is figuring out which two gates to open," she said, attempting to focus.

"Our friend Colossus was clear that the Solver of Secrets—me—and the Oracle's Daughter—you—had to be in the Temple. So there should be something for you to translate." He walked with deliberate strides around the cavern, studying closely all the surfaces. London followed his example, trying to find even a fragment of written words that would give her some indication as to which two water gates were the right ones to open.

"Nothing," she said with a frustrated sigh some time later. "Not even a letter or pictogram. I don't know what the Colossus wants from me, from us."

Bennett dragged a hand through his damp hair as he thought. "It said that the future of the earth is in our hands. The answer's in that, somehow."

She scoured her memory. "It also said that we must navigate the Temple together."

Bennett's sudden laugh startled her. "Of course." He rummaged through his pack and produced the Compass. Flipping the lid open, he held the Compass up. After adjusting his position, he nodded. "True north is that way," he said, pointing to one side. "Each of the water gates corresponds to a direction on a compass. So, that is the northern gate, that is south," he pointed to the gate directly opposite, "and the others follow suit." He laughed again, caught up in the excitement of discovery. She saw the joy in him that came from untangling a puzzle and felt it in herself, too.

"The direction of the future is west," London said. "The sun rises in the east, but sets in the west."

He strode over to the gate that corresponded to the west, then swore darkly, glancing down at his feet.

"What is it?" London quickly went to stand beside him, yelping in horror when she saw what so discomforted him.

Bones. Human bones. Bleached—by scalding hot water, and arranged in a posture of agony next to the western gate, precisely as if the unlucky victim had selected the wrong gate to open. Which would be Bennett, if he followed the Colossus's instructions.

London swallowed hard, but grisly images still flooded her brain.

"But this poor sod was alone," Bennett said, grim. "The answer's got to be that two gates must be opened simultaneously. The fly in the custard is figuring out which is the second gate."

A small seed of an idea planted itself in her mind and suddenly flowered. She looked up at Bennett, her heart pounding. "In the Samalian-Thracian dialect, the words for 'earth' and 'south' are the same."

"And the Colossus said that the future of the earth was in our hands."

"Which means that I must open the southern gate," London deduced.

He kissed her, brief and fierce. "I never want to be apart from you," he growled.

Her pulse sped, but she said with an attempt at lightness, "Because I saved your bottom from a scalding?"

"Because you're *you*." His words were low and vehement. "We can talk about bottoms later," he added with a quick grin and a possessive caress of her own posterior. "For now, let's get ourselves a Source."

She kissed him, then moved into position at the southern water gate. Fear, excitement, and anticipation swirled as she bent down to grasp the bronze handle with suddenly damp hands. Would she and Bennett wind up like the cavern's other unfortunate occupant, nothing but brittle bones, a warning to all future trespassers? Would she have to watch in horror as scalding-hot water poured down on him, or would he have to hear her tortured screams?

"On my count," he said, his own voice steady and betraying none of her anxiety. "Three . . ." They both gripped the bronze handles. "Two . . ." They breathed deeply, adjusting their holds. "One. Now."

Setting her heels into the ground, London pulled. The gate's heaviness surprised her, but she tugged hard, groaning with effort. The metal groaned, as well, as it slid up from slots carved into the cavern's rock floor. No one had been foolish enough to attempt to drain the pool in a long, long while.

The gates locked into their raised position. Water quickly drained from the pool. At once, the sounds of gurgling, seething water rushed overhead, carried by unseen pipes throughout the cavern. London considered moving from her position, but nowhere guaranteed safety. Bennett held his hand up, a silent signal for patience, as they both stared up at the spouts above their heads. Nerves stretched taut. Was she calmly waiting for a terrible death?

With a whoosh, blistering water poured out of a spout. London jumped at the noise. Then her shoulders slumped with relief. The water gushed directly into the small bay from which they had emerged into the cave earlier.

She let out a shaky breath, exchanging exultant smiles with Bennett. Safe. They were safe. For now.

The pool now emptied, Bennett stepped into it and crossed the expanse to the Eye. For a moment, he simply looked at the Source, his chest rising and falling rapidly, his face alight with anticipation. Light from the illuminating devices bounced off the Eye's surface, bathing Bennett with a bright, phantasmal glow. His hands hovered over the Eye, then slowly, slowly reached forward.

"Could be another booby trap," he said over his shoulder. "Happens a lot in this situation."

London watched, clutching at the straps of her pack so that her knuckles whitened and fingers ached.

With excruciating slowness, Bennett gripped the Eye and carefully lifted it from its supporting small column of rock. He waited several moments, casting quick glances around for sign of another trap springing to life, head tilted to gather any suspicious sounds. But the cavern was entirely silent.

London did not loosen her death's hold on her pack, not

even when Bennett slid the straps of the Eye onto his arm and gripped the handle. He hefted it like a shield, the Eye glaring out at the cavern from where Bennett stood at the middle of the empty pool.

The earth jolted as a tremor shook the cave. Small rocks tumbled down the walls. Bennett braced himself on wide-planted legs, and London did the same. A spike of fear. From the roof of the cave, a pebble clattered to the ground. Then the shaking stopped.

A beam of daylight from above pierced the cavern, liberated by the fallen pebble. It hit directly in the center of the Eye. Bennett struggled to keep his footing as the light ricocheted off the Eye, tracing a hard beam along the wall of the cave. Arms up, London shielded herself from the hot intensity of the light that gleamed like a sword.

"Stop!" London cried. "I thought Blades couldn't use magic that wasn't theirs."

"I'm not doing anything," Bennett answered through gritted teeth. "It's the Source. Acting on its own. The power's tremendous."

The light sliced into the cavern wall. Like a blast of pure energy, it slammed into the stone. The wall crumbled beneath the light, rocks tumbling down. Then, in a chain reaction, more of the wall collapsed in a heap of rubble. Immediately, she felt Bennett surrounding her with his arms, shielding her with his body. London covered her mouth, ducking her head into his chest, but found herself choking on dust. As he held her, she felt it, too, the power emanating from the Source, engulfing them with vivid currents of elemental magic.

When the rockslide stopped, she cautiously peered out from the shelter of his body. She started. What had appeared to be a cavern wall of solid rock had been hiding a secret. A staircase of the same black stone, leading upward. Daylight poured into the cave through the stairwell. The outside beckoned at the top of the stairs. She could just make out a scrap of blue sky.

"This is a first," Bennett murmured. "Ancients usually aren't so accommodating." He kept the Eye on one arm, and with his other hand, he led London forward, sporting his devil's smile. "Let's join the others."

"Do you ever have ordinary days?" she asked as they ascended the stairs.

"Why would I want them?"

A good point. No day with Bennett was ever dull, which suited her very well indeed.

The stairs were quite steep, so they both carefully ascended, until they heard the distinctive boom of cannon fire. Without speaking, they sprinted up the rest of the stairs. They breached the stone to find themselves on a rocky hill.

The caique was to their left, at the entrance to the sea cave. Just below where Bennett and London stood was the Heirs' ship, cannons turned toward the caique. The sailboat had no chance against the steamship's firepower. What the cannons didn't accomplish, the *rakshasa* demon, loosed from the steamer and wheeling through the sky, would gladly finish. Men massed on the steamship's deck, rifles blasting.

There was no retreat. No escape. The time of reckoning was now.

Chapter 19

The Eye Unleashed

No one on the steamship had spotted Bennett and London, only fifty yards above. The Heirs' eyes, and cannon, were turned to the caique. The only firepower on the caique consisted of Kallas and Athena, armed with rifles. Unless Athena suddenly called forth some potent magic, she and Kallas would be shot to pieces along with the boat.

Bennett strained to see the activity on the caique's deck. What he saw was grim. Athena was too busy sniping and ducking for cover to summon magic. A distraction was needed. All Bennett had was his revolver. And the Eye of the Colossus, which he couldn't use.

"We have to help them," London said urgently.

"Got an idea."

It would give away their position, but then Athena could provide a counterattack. He'd have to take the chance the witch knew what to do.

He pulled his revolver, and steadied himself, taking aim. It would be a hell of a shot, if he made it. He had to make it.

Bennett sighted the aft cannon. Three men gathered around the heavy gun. One of the men had a shell in his arms, ready to load. Bennett only had a second, less than a second.

He drew in a breath, released it part way, held it again. Squeezed the revolver's trigger. The bullet whined, streaking through the air. Then it slammed into the cannon's shell.

With a roar, the shell exploded. The three men flew back from the force of the blast, their bodies already still by the time they fell onto the deck. The cannon became a heap of twisted metal, useless. Men on the steamship deck ran about in confusion as they shouted to each other.

"Incredible," London said, eyes wide.

"Come on." Bennett didn't wait for someone on the ship to figure out where the shot had come from. He waved London ahead of him, then followed as they started down the hill at a brisk jog.

Both he and London stopped their descent when a tremendous blast of wind pushed them back. A sudden storm? No, the sky was clear, a pitiless blue.

"Oh, my God," London gasped. "Athena . . ."

The witch rose above the caique, carried aloft by invisible currents of energy. Literally, she flew, hovering over the caique, her hair a wild tangle, her eyes ablaze with power and her face a hard mask of fury. Kallas stared up at her in reverential awe.

"She's like a goddess," London whispered.

"She's been pushed far enough," Bennett said. "She's not afraid of being overwhelmed by magic anymore."

"To protect Kallas."

One of Athena's hands stretched out to the caique. The boat rocketed backward, shoved away by the strength of the witch's power. The caique disappeared around the island's easternmost tip, safe from the cannons on the Heirs' ship. Truly, the goddess in her had emerged.

But Athena's triumph did not last long. The *rakshasa* demon hurtled toward her, all six sets of claws brandished and hungry for blood. Bennett aimed and fired. The beast screamed when the shot tore the membrane of a wing. It dipped in its flight, giving Athena enough time to call forth another blast of energy, tossing the demon backward like a spinning leaf.

Once it regained its balance, the demon wheeled and hurtled straight for Bennett and London. Hell.

"Take cover!" he shouted at her. "There." He waved toward an outcropping of rocks several yards away. London hurried off, then stopped.

"Bennett . . ."

He looked over and swore. Five of the Heirs' hired men charged up the hill, directly toward them, with rifles, Fraser at the tail of their line, also armed.

The Eye, strapped to Bennett's arm, vibrated with life. It wanted to be unleashed. He couldn't allow that. The code of the Blades was strict, even in such cases.

Bennett fired. The first man went down. His companions slowed to shoot at Bennett. He flattened himself to the ground, traded gunfire, and quickly reloaded. Hopefully, London had managed to get herself to cover. He glanced in her direction and swore again.

She had leapt forward to grab the fallen mercenary's rifle. Now she swung it at the other advancing men, coshing them on the sides of their heads or walloping their shoulders and knees. Damn, he admired the hell out of her. But she couldn't hold off the mercenaries by just swinging the rifle like a cricket bat. Fraser wouldn't be deterred.

A huge shadow fell over him. He rolled aside as the demon tried to tear him with its talons. Hot pain lanced across his chest as the beast's claws tore through his waistcoat, shirt, and flesh. He used the Eye as a shield, forcing the demon back, but it wheeled and dove at him, jaws snapping, trying to get around the Eye. How many bullets did he have left in the revolver's chamber? Not enough to finish this creature.

He shot at it anyway, trying to do as much damage as he could. A bullet shredded one of its wrists, another hit the demon's shoulder, but it wasn't close enough to an artery— assuming demons had arteries.

He didn't have time for this. London was facing off against four mercenaries *and* Fraser, alone.

The demon lunged at him again, then shrieked when Athena, eyes aglow, swooped close and pummeled it with another blast of power. She used electric clouds of energy to surround the *rakshasa*, then hurtle it into the rocky hillside, again and again, like a rotten plum being pulped. Bennett could hardly believe that sober, restrained Athena was capable of such wrath. The demon foundered, then collapsed—dead or unconscious, Bennett couldn't tell.

He used the reprieve to get to his feet and reload his revolver. He picked off a man trying to grab the butt of London's rifle. The others were still coming, though.

"Shoot the damn thing!" he bellowed at her.

"How?" She fumbled with the rifle.

"Pull the bolt counterclockwise, yes, now pull it back. Eject the shell. Good. Damn!" He dove aside as a mercenary's bullet nearly nicked his thigh, then returned fire. He gave London cover, shooting to keep the men back. "Grab some cartridges from the body. Just do it!" he yelled when she briefly hesitated to touch the dead man. Fortunately, her squeamishness lasted less than a second, because she raided the body's cartridge belt and came up with handfuls of bullets.

"Load it," Bennett shouted. She did. "Now push the bolt forward. Rotate the handle back down. Got it?"

"Yes!"

"Fire! And," he added, half a moment later when she stumbled back, "watch the recoil."

She'd almost tumbled over backwards as she fired, and her shot had gone wide. But it was enough of a deterrent so that the advancing mercenaries fell back.

When London loaded the rifle a second time, the process went much faster. She braced herself on the rocky hillside and fired again. A mercenary fell to the ground, clutching his wounded shoulder. That left two men, and Fraser, on the attack.

A hot wave of energy surged overhead. He glanced up to see Chernock, the tails of his black coat flapping like crows' wings, swoop down on to Athena. With an awful, fiendish grin, the sorcerer conjured a buzzing black cloud, dark as a swarm of locusts, which engulfed Athena. She tried to fight off the cloud, but it gripped her and sent her plummeting to the orchestra of the amphitheater. Chernock raced after her.

Bennett could do nothing for Athena as the witch picked herself up and squared off against Chernock. They faced each other across the expanse of the orchestra, a performance of epic proportions. Each summoned swirling eddies of magic—Athena's a kaleidoscope of gold and crimson light, Chernock's darker than black, an absence of color and life—and battered the other, until they were both panting and frenzied.

Bennett had never seen two magic users battle one another, but now was not the time for spectating. He wheeled and fired on the remaining mercenaries closing in on London, then charged. Sometimes, a fist could accomplish more than a bullet.

He swung the Eye, slamming the metal side into the face of one man reaching for London. Red spurted from a cut the Eye carved in the man's neck, and he shrieked, clutching at the wound. The remaining mercenary dove at Bennett. They grappled, grunting, swearing, throwing punches. The man was a brute, big and strong and stupid, precisely the sort the Heirs found all over the world. He might not have been smart, but he could sure land a punch. Bennett winced as he collected bruises, but gave back as hard as he got.

A woman's yelp of pain distracted him. He glanced over. And all rational thought vanished.

Everything had been going very nicely. Perhaps not nicely—she could not feel pleased to see men shot and killed, though wounding them was rather gratifying—but she'd actually loaded and fired a rifle, and the men charging up the hill toward her and Bennett were diminishing.

Then the rifle was torn from her grasp and a blinding pain clouded her head. London fell back, her shoulders slamming into the rocky ground. Her vision hadn't even cleared when her head was pulled back roughly by her hair, and a heavy weight settled on her chest, pinning her to the ground. Something cold and biting pressed into the center of her chest. A knife, just nicking her skin. A corset would have given her some protection, but she'd long abandoned the restrictive garment. Now, she thought better of her decision as a warm trickle dripped between her ribs.

"This was supposed to be *my* mission, damn it," snarled Fraser in her ear. "Simple. Get the Source. Get the woman. A seat in the inner circle. Everything I wanted. Mine. Then *you* had to send it all to hell." The fist gripping her hair shook her head. "Damned whore."

"I'd never . . . marry you. . . ." London gasped. She tried to kick him, but he held her down and her feet could only scrape on the ground. "You laugh . . . through your nose. Like a . . . braying donkey."

Fraser's face twisted into a sneer as he pushed his knife closer into her chest. The tip of the blade slid a quarter inch beneath her skin. "Looking forward to cutting you, bitch."

Before London could explain that he was *already* cutting her, Fraser suddenly disappeared. She struggled to sit, then saw Fraser and Bennett locked in vicious combat. The mercenary lay forgotten on the ground, his breath rattling and then stopping, while Bennett's attention turned to a new opponent. He and Fraser were savage, beating each other without cessation. Blood coated their fists. Someone, she couldn't tell who, lost a tooth. It glinted on the ground, next to Fraser's dropped knife.

She picked up her rifle, but it was impossible to shoot. Not without the very real probability that she might hit Bennett.

The men rolled together, punching and kicking, far removed from genteel fisticuffs. They wanted to kill each other. Nothing else would suffice. Awful to watch and yet London could not turn away. She looked for a way to help Bennett.

He growled as Fraser, straddling a prone Bennett, tried to pull the Eye of the Colossus off of his arm.

"It's mine," Fraser panted. "The Source is mine."

A dark smile curled one corner of Bennett's mouth. "Take it." With a grunt, Bennett shoved the Eye toward Fraser. The Source glowed, white hot. Fraser screamed as the metal burned him.

Bennett raised up onto one knee, his other foot braced hard on the ground, and pushed Fraser with the Eye. Fraser stumbled. He rolled backward down the hill, tumbling in an unstoppable freefall, feet over head, slamming into the unyielding rocky ground. It was a long fall, but it wasn't until Fraser reached the top of the amphitheater that he truly gained momentum. He bounced from tier to tier, cracking his head on the hard stone, limbs flailing until he was limp. When he landed at the base of the amphitheater, his body lay at an unnatural angle, his neck bent, eyes open. Dead.

Bennett was beside her in a moment, his fingers running tenderly over her face. She flinched when he lightly brushed the growing bruise from Fraser's slap, and Bennett swore. He cursed further to see the thin line of blood down the front of her shirt. "Maybe I'll go down the hill and kill him all over again. Slower."

Her own minor injuries didn't concern her. "Are you hurt badly?" Her hands hovered over the bleeding scrapes on his cheekbones, the drop of crimson in the corner of his mouth. He was covered in dust, clothes torn. But so beautiful, her paladin.

"Another day at the office." He grinned, then winced. "Ouch. No smiling."

London, at least, was relieved to see that the lost tooth didn't belong to him. Fraser wouldn't care about his damaged smile. Not anymore.

She thought she should feel sadness or horror at Fraser's death and was surprised to feel nothing at all.

"What did you do with the Eye?" she asked. "You made it burn him."

Bennett looked slightly abashed. "I tried not to."

"Why can't you use it?"

"Because it doesn't belong to me. It belongs to the Greek people."

"Bennett," she said, touching her fingertips to his chin, commanding his attention, "didn't you tell me you're part Greek?"

He went very still. "One eighth. On my mother's side."

They both glanced at the Eye, still strapped to his arm. She almost swore that it winked at them.

"Help Athena," London urged.

Below, in the amphitheater, the witch and the sorcerer hurled spells at one another, conjuring up clouds of magic that raked each other like storms. Athena swayed on her feet, unused to channeling such potent magic, but she remained standing, pushing back against Chernock with the power of generations of Galanos women. London thought she saw, in the swirling nebulae over the amphitheater, the forms of helmeted warrior women, Amazons and witches, battling against misshapen beasts. The air was thick with the sounds of combat.

Bennett rose and helped London up. He started down the hill, toward the amphitheater, but rocks exploded near his feet. He shoved her behind him, then pulled her toward an outcropping of rock. They both hunkered in the shelter, ducking down when more debris rained down on them. He peered around the rock, then whipped back, scowling.

"Damn, they've turned the cannons on us." Rocks exploded behind them. The Heirs were adjusting their aim. The next shot would likely be on target.

A little smile curved her mouth. "You can use the Eye against them."

He grinned in response, then winced again. "Ow. I can, can't I?"

Raising into a crouch, he angled toward the Heirs' ship. Then muttered, "Hell. Kallas, you heroic idiot."

The captain had sailed the caique around the island and was now barreling toward the steamship at top speed. The men on the deck of the steamship didn't see him. Yet.

"He's going to ram them," London whispered. "To provide a distraction."

"And sink himself in the process." Bennett surged to his feet, his expression set and determined.

A screech rent the air. London and Bennett whirled to see the demon, bloodied but alive, hurtling toward them, maddened savagery burning in its eyes like coals. Before Bennett could raise the Eye, the demon plunged straight at them.

She scampered aside, trying to draw it away from Bennett. One of its hands swiped at her, ripping a hank of hair from her head. Her scalp burned, but she wouldn't stop moving, dodging its grasping claws and snapping teeth.

London acted instinctively. She dove for a nearby rifle. The rifle's bolt flew in her hands as she ejected the spent shell and reloaded. Then, steeling herself, she aimed and fired.

Another scream as she hit the *rakshasa* square in its abdomen. The beast reared back, splattering black blood. Such a wound might kill or stop a man—but the demon was no man, and its directive was clear. Kill London. Kill Bennett. Do not stop until they were dead.

London flung an arm over her face as a blazing beam of light streamed from the Eye of the Colossus. Light poured from the Eye. London could barely look at it. The beam of light burned with a terrible radiance, spreading outward. It threatened to consume Bennett, and he groaned, pushing back, fighting the incandescent power.

She ran to Bennett. The Source would kill him. She moved to pull the Eye from his arm, the heat surrounding man and Source stronger than anything she had ever felt before.

"Get back," he gritted. "It'll burn you."

"Don't care," she shot back. "You'll be hurt."

"No."

The demon charged once more, and Bennett turned the light of the Eye on it. The beast's howl echoed, half-finished, as it turned to ash. Charred flakes caught on the wind and blew out to sea. The air smelled of burnt carrion. All that was left of the demon were its talons, glinting points stuck into the side of the hill.

The light from the Source disappeared, and London and Bennett stared at each other, panting.

They dove apart when a shot from the cannon slammed into the ground between them. She clung to her rifle, hoping she could use it to distract the cannons.

Bennett leapt to his feet. He aimed the Eye of the Colossus at the steamship, then sucked in a breath. He struggled, his eyes squeezed shut, all his concentration focused inward. "I see the trick. Don't try to master the Source. Give it room to exercise its own power." Then his face grew calm, his breath easy.

At once, the light receded around him, then coalesced into a beam shooting from the Eye. The light struck the water around the steamship. Fire sprung up on the surface of the water, giant flames reaching higher than the smoke-stacks. The fire raced up the hull of the steamship. Within moments, the ship was engulfed in flames, black smoke pouring up into the perfect blue sky. An explosion rocked the ship, sending waves of percussion in widening circles as the bodies of mercenaries were flung into the water.

Kallas quickly adjusted his course, pulling the caique away from the blazing steamship.

Getting to her feet, London said, her voice trembling only a little, "Be sure to thank your Greek great-grandparent, whoever he or she is."

Shaking his head and smiling, he reached for her. His hand stopped, hovering in midair, his attention fixed at something just beyond her shoulder. London spun around, and felt herself turn to ice.

Her father stood right behind her, the barrel of his re-volver pointed at her head.

For a moment, London thought she might be able to speak with him, reason with him, but the complete and utter lack of emotion in his eyes told her such efforts would be fruitless. She was nothing to him. A body in his way. There was no kinship, no blood between them. Tears sprang to her eyes. She blinked them back.

"This is for your own good," he said flatly, cocking his gun. "And the good of England."

Her rifle was empty, but that didn't mean she could not

use it. She leapt toward him, using the rifle barrel like a bayonet to jab at his chest. Clearly, he wasn't anticipating any sort of counterattack. The daughter he had raised would never think to do such a thing. But she was no longer Joseph Edgeworth's daughter. At the same time, Bennett also sprang toward her father, so that they both collided with him.

The blow was just enough to knock her father's aim slightly. The revolver went off. Her shoulder caught fire. London stumbled to her knees, pressing her hand to her shoulder and seeing red seep between her fingers. An irrational thought flitted through her mind—Athena's shirtwaist was ruined.

Then her father and Bennett rolled on the ground. If London had thought the combat between Bennett and Fraser had been fierce, it looked like puppies playing compared to this brutality. She scarcely believed there was at least a thirty-year difference separating the men. Each fought with an ageless savagery, eyes blazing, naked hatred singeing the air around them. Even when Bennett slammed his fist into her father's ribs, making them audibly crack, her father did not stop his own assault, ramming his elbow into Bennett's chin. Bennett's head snapped back, but he shook himself into consciousness before continuing his assault.

But her father possessed an advantage. Two advantages. Bennett had been fighting for some time this day, already taking down several mercenaries and Fraser *and* implementing the Eye of the Colossus. He was younger, stronger, but drained. And the Eye, still strapped to his arm, hampered his movements. He didn't have the freedom of motion her father did.

London tried to lurch to her feet, desperate to help, but the pain radiated out, numbing her limbs. She watched as the man she loved and her father locked in lethal battle.

Her father, growing even more frenzied, pulled a knife from a hidden sheath. Bennett grunted as the blade slashed at the arm bearing the Eye. It was as if her father meant to cut Bennett's very arm away to get to the Source. Bennett gripped the hand holding the knife, attempting to pry it from her father's fingers. They grappled for the knife, but Bennett couldn't quite stop a gash along his forearm. He bent her father's fingers back until they snapped. The older man howled, then punched at the wound on Bennett's forearm.

"No!" London shouted.

Bennett's fingers loosened just a fraction from the handle on the back of the Eye. It was enough of a window for her father. He leapt to his feet and kicked several times at Bennett's injured arm. When Bennett's hand spasmed involuntarily, her father grabbed the Source and wrenched it off Bennett's arm, then landed a few solid kicks into Bennett's side.

Slipping his own arm through the leather straps and grasping the handle, her father's face gleamed with demonic joy. So delirious with exultation was he, that he didn't notice London crawling toward Bennett.

She kept her weight off her wounded shoulder, cradling her arm against herself, but she had to reach him where he lay on the ground. His face was white as he fiercely fought against pain. London helped prop him up so that he leaned against her, and his expression was murderous when he saw the bloom of blood seeping from her shoulder. No doubt she looked the same way, taking in the bruises, scrapes, and gashes that marked him all over, especially his beautiful face and hands. She didn't care if he was scarred forever, but she hated seeing him hurt, in pain.

"Your shoulder," Bennett growled. He carefully turned her so he could examine her back, and his expression slightly eased. "The bullet went all the way through. That's good."

It didn't feel particularly good—in truth, the pain was unlike anything she'd experienced—but she nodded, lips pressed tight.

"Greek Fire," her father crowed. "I have it. The Source is mine. It belongs to England now, for the glory of England." He held the Eye aloft.

"You don't want it, Edgeworth," Bennett muttered. "Dangerous."

"Of course it's dangerous," her father snapped. "I saw what it did to my ship, to the demon. That's why it's the perfect weapon. An unstoppable fire."

Bennett shook his head. "Dangerous to the bearer. Put it down. Save yourself."

"Listen to him, Father," London said.

"Shut up, bitch," her father barked. "You cannot call me that anymore. You lost that privilege when you spread your legs for this bastard. Stupid woman."

His words were ugly, yet London didn't flinch from them. All she felt was a dull sadness. Her father didn't understand her at all. He never did. And she could not recognize the man she had known her whole life within this glassy-eyed beast.

Bennett growled and moved as if to lunge at her father, a gesture that made her father laugh.

"Give it up, Day. You failed. And," her father added, tipping his head to indicate the amphitheater behind him, "my sorcerer will soon make mince of your pathetic witch."

Indeed, even as he spoke, the battle between Chernock and Athena raged on. Athena seemed to be weakening, spells uncoiling from her hands at a slower rate. The creatures within the nebula were growing more numerous than the warrior women. If Athena did not rally, and soon, Chernock would overcome her.

"Now I'll truly claim the Source," her father sneered. He raised the Eye, directing it at London and Bennett.

"Cleanse the earth with fire. Erase all evidence of my mistakes."

"I'm warning you," Bennett said. "Last chance."

"Enough," her father roared. He narrowed his eyes in concentration, then gave a yelp of glee when a glow suffused from the surface of the Eye. It grew, widening, a furious burning, spreading outward. From where she knelt, several feet away, London felt the heat sizzling over her skin.

Her father groaned, squeezing his eyes shut as sweat poured down his face. He fought the Eye, grimacing.

"No," he gasped. "You're *mine*. Mine to command. You must obey."

But the harder he pushed against it, the larger the radiance grew. It rippled the air with its heat.

At Bennett's silent order, he and London edged back along the ground, putting distance between themselves and her father. Their hands brushed over something metal, and they both flicked their eyes down. A pistol.

The atmosphere around her father turned incandescent, white. His skin blistered. "Bend to my will," he snarled. "Do as I command you."

Bennett rose to face her father. Only she saw how Bennett swayed a little, fighting his injuries, and the pallor of his skin.

"Get down," London hissed, but Bennett's attention was fixed solely on her father. An expression entirely unlike Bennett settled across his face. He smirked, gloating and smug, the picture of a self-satisfied child.

"Looks like you're having a spot of trouble controlling the Source," Bennett sneered. "Just like you couldn't control your daughter. She leapt into my bed, practically begged me to ravish her. Did you know that? Just couldn't wait to have a Blade take her and spoil the pride of England. She was wild for it."

London gaped at him, at the hurtful words he said. Her father's face purpled with rage.

"Shut your fucking mouth!" her father shouted. The light from the Eye grew, its heat overpowering.

The pistol was heavy in her hands as she pointed it at her father. "Stop, Father. Put the Source down."

Seeing her turn a gun on him only enraged her father further. He grimaced as he struggled to control the Eye.

Bennett laughed, a hard, coarse sound. "Must feel bloody awful to see your only daughter turn on you like this. Betray you. Betray England. And for what? A tumble. In *my* bed."

Furious curses, unimaginably filthy and vile words, spewed from her father's mouth. Suddenly, the circle of fiery heat, shrank to a tiny dot. Her father laughed jubilantly. Then his laugh turned to a scream as the light exploded outward.

Bennett threw himself over London, covering her. Her father's screams turned to unearthly shrieks. London lifted her head and gasped in horror.

Her father was on fire. Flames coursed over him, turning his clothing to ash, roasting his flesh. He dropped the Eye, the light receded, but it was too late. The blaze swallowed him as he clawed at himself, burning hair a demonic halo about his head. He screamed, on and on.

Bennett took the pistol from London. He fired a shot directly between her father's eyes. A mercy shot. Her father died instantly.

His body fell like a meteor, tumbling down the hill, bits of charred skin and fabric flying behind him in a cascade of embers. By the time his body reached the floor of the amphitheater, it was nothing but black bone splinters, brittle as charcoal.

Bennett clasped her in his arms, holding her to his solid chest. London covered her face and sobbed. But they were dry sobs. She hadn't anything in her anymore. Was she happy? Relieved? Sad? Everything and nothing.

She raised her head, Bennett's face inches from her own. "Thank you," she whispered. "That was a kindness you did him."

"It was to spare you, not him."

She found her tears then, and they ran down her face. He kissed her, gently, and when she broke the kiss, she left streaks of moisture on his cheeks, cutting through the grime that coated them both.

"You knew," she said. "What the Source would do to him."

Bennett nodded grimly.

Chernock's cackle brought their attention down to the amphitheater. The sorcerer looked as though he'd been through a hurricane, his long black coat tattered and flapping behind him, but the blaze in Athena's eyes dimmed. She hadn't Chernock's experience wielding powerful magic, yet she continued to fight on.

"Athena needs our help," she said. "Can we use the Eye?"

Bennett shook his head. "She's too close to him. And with all those spells flying—no way to know what would happen. But we'll help how we can." He pitched to his feet, movements stiff and slow from his injuries, and gently pulled London up to stand beside him, careful to mind her shoulder.

"Or maybe she won't need us after all," Bennett murmured.

Kallas charged up the beach, an axe in one hand, revolver in another, headed straight for the amphitheater. He'd anchored the caique in the bay, unnoticed, after circumnavigating the burning wreck of the steamship.

Even from their position up the hill, she and Bennett heard the captain's bellow of rage, his war cry, as he stormed the sorcerer.

Distracted by Athena, Chernock did not shield himself

from the gunfire, and several bullets slammed into him. The sorcerer, snarled, moved as if to use magic to tear Kallas apart. Kallas moved faster. He swung the axe with all the strength of his powerful arms, hacking into Chernock's leg below the knee. The sorcerer screamed as blood poured from where his lower leg used to be. Now the limb, encased in black wool, lay like so much meat upon the black stone, the gleaming black shoe at the end of it a grisly taunt.

Chernock toppled to the ground, slipping in his own blood, and Kallas brought the axe down again and again upon the sorcerer with shouts of fury.

The appearance of her lover strengthened Athena. Her eyes glowed with renewed power. With a primitive yell, the sound of an Amazon at the height of battle frenzy, she summoned energy with her hands, calling forth razor-beaked owls, their eyes brilliant and merciless. Athena guided them, waving them on, and the birds descended upon the sorcerer. Kallas swayed back to give the owls room. The air filled with the sounds of beating wings, tearing flesh, and the tortured shrieks of Chernock. London turned her face into Bennett, unable to bear the sight.

Only when the screaming stopped did London look. There was nothing left of the sorcerer, save for a few scraps of black wool and spatters of gore. With a wave of Athena's hand, the owls gathered in a wheeling circle, then disappeared.

Gathering up the Eye, leaning on each other, London and Bennett slowly made their way down the hill and into the amphitheater. There were the remains of the Heirs—Fraser's broken body, the charred pile of her father's bones, the minuscule tatters of fabric and flesh that had once been a powerful sorcerer. The self-styled champions of England, brought to miserable death by their false ideals.

But also standing in the orchestra of the amphitheater, clasped in a fierce embrace, were Kallas and Athena. The

captain's bloody axe had been thrown aside, its work done.
They smiled at Bennett and London's approach, though the
smiles were strained from exhaustion and threaded with
concern. No doubt London and Bennett looked like hell,
since that is exactly what they'd just been through.

Bennett ripped off his jacket, then his waistcoat and
shirt. His bare torso shone with sweat and blood, a long
gash on his forearm dripping red, the essence of a warrior
embodied here, on this rocky island. He tore his shirt into
strips and, after unbuttoning her own shirtwaist, wrapped
the strips of fabric around London's wound, his ministrations tender but thorough. He'd performed field dressing
before and knew it well. London couldn't stop her gasp
from the pain, but his attentions helped.

"Better?"

"A little."

"Are you well?" asked Kallas.

London rested her head against Bennett's chest, feeling
his warmth, the steady beat of his heart that found its twin
in her own heartbeat. She felt the deep vibrations of his
words throughout her body, her soul, as he spoke.

"Never better."

Chapter 20

The Eye Restored

He found her in her favorite place, the bow of the ship. Though they were anchored just off the island, with the prow pointed toward the beach, she stared up, at the tops of the sails stretching to the sky. Her eyes were turned from the smoldering hulk of the steamship, most of it now lying underwater. He couldn't fault her for avoiding the sight. Even he found it a grisly reminder of what had happened a few hours earlier.

She had her knees drawn up, arms wrapped around them, head tilted back. His blood warmed to see her—worn and weary, beautiful beyond reckoning. They had only been apart a few minutes, but even that was too long to be without her. She'd become as necessary as his pulse.

"Your shoulder's feeling better."

She turned at his approach and smiled. His heart stopped at the sight, then pounded back to life.

"Athena's magic has grown considerably." She tested her shoulder, rolling her arm. "I can hardly feel the wound anymore. Just a little soreness. And the cut on my chest has vanished."

He bent to examine her shoulder, peeling back her fresh

shirtwaist to reveal the silky flesh beneath. Sure enough, a small, puckered scar, fresh and pink, was the only reminder that a bullet had torn through her only hours before. The thought of it brought a fresh surge of fury, but he made himself push past that anger. She was well. Her son of a bitch father was dead. Edgeworth would never threaten London again. That was enough.

"I won't be able to wear low-shouldered gowns any-more," she said with a rueful smile.

Bennett kissed her there, tenderly, upon that scar. "Wear them. Let the world see how brave you are." He didn't care if her beauty bore such marks. They made her all the love-lier to him.

She shivered under his touch, her eyes drifting shut as his kiss grew more heated. His tongue lapped at her collar-bone, the curve of her neck. He tasted salt on her skin and that indefinable essence of sweet and spicy uniquely hers.

"You seem to be . . . quite recovered," she said, breath-less. "More of Athena's magic?"

"Mm. We'll not talk of her, now." His lips moved to hers as he sank to his knees, facing her. "I want you."

"More of your post-adventure concupiscence?" she asked between kisses.

"It's *you*, love. *You* make me want you."

They tangled together, and he felt, in the heat of her kisses and press of her body to his, how she shoved away at this day's darkness, clinging to life and love and their promise of tomorrow. He would be there with her, every step of the way.

"I'll never get enough of you," she sighed into his mouth.

"Good," he growled. "Because I plan on never letting you go."

"Never?" She raised an eyebrow.

"Never." His voice was firm, immovable, as he stared into the gold-flecked sable of her eyes. The single word was weighted with everything he felt for her, more expressive in its tone than he could hope to achieve with a thousand honeyed words. Words had always come easily to him, but now he demanded more from them. She had to know his meaning, had to know what he offered, and he felt a stab of fear that she might reject that offer. The world was open to her. She could do exactly as she pleased. He wanted to please her. So much that he burned with it.

"Never, then." She smiled against his mouth.

The kind of wild joy he felt at the completion of a mission was only a dim flicker compared to the blaze of euphoria now consuming him. He pulled her tight against him, her soft, strong female body, her heart, her entire being, everything about her rare and entirely wondrous.

He started to lay her back onto the deck, when someone nearby cleared their throat.

"Perhaps the lovemaking can wait a little longer," Athena said dryly.

Bennett, grumbling, raised himself and London up to sitting, to see the witch and her captain standing close by, hand in hand. The surge of magic that had filled Athena earlier was now gone, and she seemed, aside from a bit windblown, her old self. Except, of course, for the palpable air of powerful magic that infused her with confidence. It wasn't the hauteur of her aristocratic breeding, but the sense that she was in complete command of herself and untapped founts of magic.

The presence of the fierce, devoted man beside her might have had something to do with Athena's poise, as well.

However, Bennett didn't really want to think of any of this right now. He wanted London, to think only of her and be a part of her for as long as possible. Maybe forever.

Still . . .

He was a Blade. And that meant making a sacrifice

every now and then. Including postponing making love with London.

"The Eye," he said. "We have to secure it. The Colossus said we must take sunlight to a place on the sea floor that's never seen the light of the sun."

"And let the Eye rest there," London added.

"You still have the second fish scale?" Athena asked.

"We didn't have a chance to use it," said London. "But how will we take sunlight to the dark sea floor?"

The witch and the captain shared a secret smile, the kind reserved only for those who know another's person as well as themselves. It made Bennett chuckle to himself. Patrician witch and lowborn sea captain, mates. Fitting, somehow. As fitting as Bennett finding love with his enemy's daughter, the widow of the man he killed. What a world was this, brutal and beautiful.

"Leave the sun to me," said Athena.

Naked, again.

"You always find a way to get me out of my clothes," London said to Bennett. They were treading water, waiting for Athena to finish her preparations. Bennett had used ropes to strap the Eye of the Colossus to his back for its trip to the sea floor. They had sailed just out of the bay of the island, where coral formations and undersea rocks were in abundance.

"You take them off readily enough," he answered. His grin was cheeky, naughty, and fraught with sensual promise.

A promise she fully intended to see he made good. Later. Other, more pressing concerns had to be addressed first.

Kallas stepped to the rail of the caique, careful to shield his eyes from London's state of undress. "If you head straight down, then off to the east, you'll find a place that should suit."

"How can you tell?" London asked.

The captain turned to give her a cocky smile, then turned away with a blush as Bennett growled a warning. "I can read the sea just as you read language."

"Everything is ready." Athena stood beside Kallas, and they unconsciously stepped closer to each other, brushing shoulders. In the witch's palm, London knew, was the last fish scale. "I will give you ten minutes, before I must do my part. Blessings of the goddess on you, both."

"And to you," Bennett said. "Now, let's finish this so London and I can get back to that lovemaking you interrupted."

Athena frowned, but her heart wasn't in it. With a shake of her head, she dropped the scale into the water. It glowed, expanding, and coalesced into a sleek fish. The creature immediately swam toward the bottom of the sea. A last squeeze of each other's hands, and then Bennett and London dove after it.

Difficult to say which delighted her more—the enchanted kingdom of turquoise water, coral reefs, and jewel-colored fish darting in the undersea currents, or Bennett swimming nude. Both were equally marvelous, feasts for the eye, but he drew her more. Not simply for his physical beauty, the breadth of his shoulders, his narrow waist, the sleek muscles of his backside and legs. But because, when he caught her watching him, she felt the undeniable heat and connection between them. They were bound together, in the best possible way.

Her breath strained, and she let seawater into her mouth. It still felt strange, to breathe through the water, yet she moved past her discomfort to focus on the task. Following Kallas's instructions, they swam straight down, past clouds of brilliant fish and two turtles, those wizened old men of the sea. Large formations of golden rock formed honeycombs and labyrinths on the sea floor. Hopefully, someday, the

twisted metal hull of the sunken steamship would house
coral and life, something beautiful from something terrible.

The glowing fish darted east, and they followed, snaking
through the rocks. It led them between narrow crevasses,
where soft marine plants swayed in the currents. Undersea
creatures that might never have seen a human before burst
from their lairs in flashes of silver and pink. When the
magic fish shot through a dark opening in one of the rocks,
London and Bennett had no choice but to follow.

They found themselves in a grotto, utterly dark save for
the illumination of the fish. It swam in circles around her
and Bennett, giving them the means to breathe. Stranger
creatures lived here, eyeless, wriggling, colorless, and shy.

Bennett unstrapped the Eye from his back and set it carefully on the sea floor. Small clouds of sand billowed up
from the disturbance, but otherwise, nothing happened.

Though they could not speak underwater, London gestured to Bennett, asking what they were supposed to do
next. He motioned that they should wait a moment longer.
It had been nearly ten minutes. Athena had her part to play.

And she did. Light pierced the grotto, slicing through the
dark water like knowledge piercing ignorance. The beam
was almost solid, concentrated sunlight, and it angled
straight to the Eye. The moment the light touched the
Source, it began to glow, filling the grotto with golden illumination. Then, a rumbling.

Bennett took London's arm as the sea floor began to
shake, but they were both pushed back against the grotto
walls by the sudden tremors. As she and Bennett watched
in amazement, the ground beneath the Eye split open. The
Eye tilted on the edge, then slid down into the abyss. Instinctively, London moved to grab it before it was lost, but
Bennett held her back. She understood. The earth reclaimed
its magic.

The ground continued to shake. It grew stronger, knocking

them about like playing jacks. Bennett pulled her toward
the entrance to the grotto, but the stone walls began col-
lapsing around them, sealing off their means of escape. At
the same moment, the light from the fish blinked out, and
with it, their ability to breathe underwater vanished.

To the surface. They had to get back to the surface immediately. Her lungs burned, water filled her nose and
mouth. There was no way out, and she was drowning.
Right beside Bennett. No. Not after surviving everything,
and finding him. She fumbled in the darkness, trying to
find a way out, a way to get them to safety, felt him doing
the same.

Part of the roof of the grotto tumbled down as the chasm
in the ground widened. There. She saw it the same time
Bennett did. The blue of the water, of the sky overhead. But
could they reach it in time? She already felt her consciousness begin to falter as her body demanded air.

Bennett grabbed her wrists and pulled her up, trying to
haul them both to the surface. She wondered if the last
things she would feel were his hands, long and skilled and
profoundly male, and this was some consolation, to feel
him in the moments before her death.

As the sea floor continued to split apart, giant bubbles
rose, swirling and buffeting her and Bennett as though they
were no more than flotsam. She felt herself borne aloft,
rising higher in an upward-spiraling cascade of froth. She
lost sense of direction, of self, spun about. Yet through it
all, she felt Bennett's grip, holding her tight. He would not
let her go.

They broke the surface together, gasping. Air, wonderful
air, filled her lungs. But the sight of the sky and the sensation of breathing were not half so extraordinary as the man
swimming beside her, laughing as he took in lungfuls of
air. He wrapped his arms around her waist, and, while they

hadn't the breath to kiss, they clung together, arms and legs intertwined as the sea continued to foam around them.

A loud roar. They turned to see the island of the Black Temple shatter into boulders before toppling into the sea. The sea churned as it swallowed the amphitheater, and the bodies of the Heirs. The visible edge of the steamship's carcass sunk down into the water. Within moments, nothing remained of the island but roiling water. Even this the earth reclaimed. Finally, the shaking stopped, the sea quieted.

Blankets were given to her and Bennett as they clambered back onto the deck of the caique. Athena and Kallas stood with bemused expressions as London and Bennett shook and shuddered and could not stop laughing, their arms clasped around each other.

"Thank you for the sunlight," London said to Athena when she could find enough breath to speak.

"Such magic is like this to her now," said Kallas, snapping his fingers and beaming with pride.

"Your mother will be beside herself with glee," Bennett said.

"She is very competitive, my mother," Athena replied. "She will see my powers, take one look at Nikos, and immediately set sail to claim such bounties of her own."

"Bringing him home to meet the Galanos women." Bennett whistled.

"I'm not afraid," Kallas said.

"That's a mistake."

London tugged on Bennett's hand. "I think you should see this." She glanced past the rail of the caique.

Everyone turned and fell mute, though London heard Kallas mutter several prayers.

The Colossus stood upon the surface of the water, ten stories high, gazing down upon them with both eyes.

"You have performed your service well," it thundered. "My sight is restored. The terrible, waterborne gift shall

never again fall into the hands of man. I shall keep watch."
The Colossus nodded its massive head.

And vanished.

They were silent for a long time afterward, staring at the space where the Colossus had stood. The world felt calm, profoundly peaceful.

"Is it done, then?" the captain asked in a hushed whisper.

"It's done," Bennett said, then, gathering London close, kissed the top of her head. "And just beginning."

Epilogue

Arrivals and Departures

Southampton, England. 1875.

Catullus Graves pushed back from his worktable and growled. His latest device was not coming along as quickly as he'd hoped. There was still the matter of making an internal combustion engine small enough to fit into a knapsack, and light enough to be carried without causing the bearer to crumple under the weight. He could discuss his design with his sister, Octavia, but he knew he could solve the problem on his own—if he could get his mind to clear.

He took off his spectacles and polished them with a handkerchief, a habitual gesture as deeply ingrained as respiration.

It was no use. He couldn't focus. Not now. He would be leaving soon, within the week, and his thoughts jumbled, preoccupied with details and logistics.

What he needed right now was a good, strong cup of tea. Tea always helped sharpen his brain. And while he was up in the kitchen, he could root around for some of Cook's cinnamon biscuits.

Catullus took the steps that led from his basement
workshop. There were brighter spaces available at the
Blades' headquarters, but the Graves family always worked
in the basement. The room was bigger, and the heavy
walls and lack of windows ensured discretion. It wouldn't
do to have their neighbors hearing the variety of explo-
sions and sounds of heavy welding equipment that em-
anated from the workshop at all hours. He never slept a
full night. The best he could do was a few hours here and
there, just enough to refresh him between sessions at the
workbench. But he was long acclimatized to his irregular
sleep patterns. Everyone in his family suffered the same
insomnia. The blessing and curse of the Graveses of Southampton.

Perhaps it was another reason why he was still single.

As Catullus entered the main house, heading toward the
kitchen, sounds of commotion in the main parlor arrested
him. Seeking out the noise's origin, he entered the parlor
and found a large group of people assembled there. Samuel
Ashcombe. Alex Hughes. Jane Fleetwood, returned only
last week from Ceylon. A host of familiar faces.

And, standing in the center of the group, Bennett Day.
Looking tan and relaxed, grinning from ear to ear like a
boy on his birthday as he shook hands of welcome. Even
Catullus, who had, over the years, seen Bennett looking
pretty damned pleased with himself, had never seen the old
scoundrel appear so happy.

"We haven't received a telegram of condemnation from
the Greek consulate," Catullus said, coming forward. "So
I assume the mission went well." He shook Bennett's hand,
and the bastard actually *winked* at him.

"Couldn't have gone better. London," Bennett said, turning to the woman standing beside him, "I'll do you the
insult of introducing you to Catullus Graves. Cat, you

sodding dandy, let me honor you by presenting London Day, expert linguist and my wife."

Catullus couldn't have heard that properly. "Wife?"

"I know," said the woman, extending her hand. She was, as fitting Bennett's usual tastes, exceptionally pretty, with honey-colored hair and sparkling dark eyes. Yet her eyes sparkled not with flirtation but a keen, perceptive intelligence. "We're all still waiting for the sun to go black and rivers to flow backward. Despite what my husband said, it's an honor to meet you at last, Mr. Graves."

Catullus shook the woman's hand. He still could not believe that Bennett Day, inveterate voluptuary, had actually gotten married. However, considering this woman's beauty and intellect, perhaps that wasn't such a surprise, after all.

"London," he said, musing. He frowned. "London Edgeworth Harcourt?" The assembled group of Blades all gaped in surprise.

The glimmer in her eyes dimmed slightly. "That had been my name, but no longer."

"You've heard of her?" Bennett demanded.

"Of course," said Catullus. "I make it a point to familiarize myself with the Heirs' families so that I'm never caught off guard by their sudden appearance. Don't you?"

Bennett scowled. "Too damn busy risking my neck to pour over Debrett's *Peerage*."

"Believe me, Mr. Graves," Mrs. Day said, sincerity shining in her face, "all connections with my family have been entirely severed. Bennett and I just came from the city, but my mother refused to see me. She took my father's death very hard. And I'm quite sure that if my brother ever spotted me on the street, he'd shoot me dead." She spoke these words flatly, as though inured to the idea. Catullus marveled at her strength.

"I'm very sorry, Mrs. Day," Catullus murmured.

"Please, don't be. I'm quite happy to trade one family

for another. And I would like it if you called me London. I've heard so much about you from Bennett, and benefited so much from your inventions, I feel as if we're already old friends."

Catullus bowed. "My pleasure. And call me Catullus, please."

"Only *I* call him Cat," Bennett said. "Just to annoy him."

"That is one of your strengths," Catullus answered.

More Blades ambled forward to meet Bennett's bride and offer their congratulations on the mission and his marriage. Catullus stood back and observed. London met each Blade with genuine warmth and courtesy, and she accepted their good-natured ribbing and questions with humor. None of this impressed Catullus so much as the way she and Bennett stood close to one another, constantly brushing their hands together, touching in small but weighted ways. It was clear that London loved Bennett, and the unmitigated adoration in Bennett's eyes whenever he looked at his wife made Catullus a little sad, that he himself had never experienced such a feeling and likely never would. Brilliant, intrepid young women like London didn't just fall from the sky.

Well, he had his work for the Blades, and that should be enough. Octavia ensured the continuation of the Graves line.

When all the felicitations and welcomes had been exhausted, the room emptied of Blades, leaving Catullus alone with his old friend and his friend's wife.

"I was headed to the kitchen for some tea," Catullus said. "I can ring and have it brought out here."

"Let's go to the kitchen together," London answered. She glanced around the large parlor, filled with maps and a ramshackle collection of furniture. Papers covered the available tabletops, and someone had abandoned a game of patience on top of an out-of-tune pianoforte. "This parlor is . . ."

"A disaster," sighed Catullus. Few of the Blades shared his love of order, and, truthfully, everyone was too busy chasing down Sources to concern themselves with maintaining elegant headquarters. The cleaning staff knew better than to try to keep order, lest they tempt madness.

"I was going to say, this parlor is not very cozy." London laughed. "I do want us to be informal and friendly with each other. To the kitchen?"

"Of course." Catullus bowed, liking London Day immensely. "What of Athena?" he asked as they headed down the hall together. He did not miss how Bennett kept a proprietary hand on her waist. "She hasn't written in some time."

"I'd say her time is rather filled at the moment," Bennett said dryly.

"Filled, in a good way?"

"A *very* good way," London answered, smiling.

"It's a fortunate thing you arrived in Southampton when you did," Catullus said. They reached the kitchen, where Cook and her assistants were busy preparing the evening meal for a dozen hungry Blades. Fortunately, Cook was well familiar with Catullus's odd eating habits, and she made no objection when he, Bennett, and London ensconced themselves in some settles installed for just such a purpose. Without prompting, one of the cook's assistants set a tea tray, complete with cinnamon biscuits, on a small table between the settles. Ah, the headquarters were a bachelor's dream.

"Why is that?" asked Bennett.

"I'm leaving for a mission next week."

Bennett sighed. "It's the way of the Blades. We're never in one place long enough to even leave a dent in the pillow."

"Where are you going?" London asked, nibbling on a biscuit.

"Canada."

Bennett started. "That's where . . ." His voice trailed off.

"Astrid lives." Catullus stirred his tea moodily. "I have to find her."

"Astrid?" repeated London. "She's the Blade whose husband—" She faltered, and they all knew what London could not bring herself to say. Astrid's husband Michael, also a Blade, had been killed in action when they were in Africa, five years prior. Her husband had literally died in her arms. In grief, Astrid shut herself away from the Blades, fleeing to the depths of the Canadian wilderness. No one had seen her in years, not since she exiled herself. There had been attempts to contact her, but those attempts had been often rebuffed. Now, there was no choice. Catullus had to find her and drag her out of her self-imposed banishment, whether she wanted to return or not.

"You know about the Primal Source," Catullus said, breaking the silence. "What it signifies."

Both Bennett and London nodded, somber.

"Our information has said that the Heirs have almost unlocked the Primal Source," Catullus continued. "Which means we will need Astrid. She and Michael spent one winter studying it in Africa. They knew the Primal Source better than anyone. And now she alone possesses knowledge about the nature of the Primal Source that is essential in our fight against the Heirs. So there's no choice but to find her and bring her back. She may hate the Blades, she may hate me, but none of us have the luxury of personal feelings or grief anymore."

Everyone around the small table lapsed into a grim silence, contemplating this.

Catullus shook himself. "This is what happens when you let an inventor out of his workshop," he said with a wry laugh. "You show up, full of good news, and I stomp all over it with my usual lack of tact."

"Lack of tact, indeed," Bennett snorted. "This from a man who owns a hundred waistcoats."

Catullus grinned, smoothing his hand over the bronze and forest green silk of the waistcoat he now wore. "We're all allowed a desire for variety."

"Not me," said Bennett. He picked up his wife's hand, stroking it between his own. "Once you find something exactly right, there's no need for anything else."

London laughed. "Are you comparing me to waistcoats?"

"No, love," said her husband. "For one thing, no waistcoat has your ear for language. The best one can hope for in a waistcoat is a smattering of French."

The lighter mood restored, they spent the next few hours talking of their mission in Greece and catching up on gossip and trifles. Everything Catullus heard amazed him, but he was especially gratified to learn of the success of his illumination devices and glider. Their teacups were refilled three times before Bennett stood and stretched, then helped his wife to her feet.

"We'll come back tomorrow," he said. "There's still much to discuss. And there's the matter of London's initiation."

"Aren't you going to stay here at headquarters?" Catullus asked. "I'm sure the staff could have your room ready in a trice."

Bennett shared a look of scorching intimacy with London. "We have lodgings elsewhere in town. No one would appreciate it if we slept here." His tone made it clear that sleeping would be fairly low on his and London's list of things they would do in a bedroom together. And London's carnal blush confirmed it.

Catullus was well acquainted with his friend's amorous pursuits, but not the love gleaming in Bennett's eyes. Once again, Catullus felt isolated, lonely. It was difficult enough for him to merely find a woman who understood his mania for his inventions. He was Negro, which meant that the color of his skin that forever marked him as a stranger in his own home country and, in fact, wherever he went. What woman could see him as a man first, and not a scientific anomaly?

Still, as Catullus walked Bennett and London to the door, he saw his friend's love for his wife, a love that was reciprocated wholeheartedly. If someone had told Catullus even the day before that Bennett Day would find one woman to whom he would be forever faithful, Catullus would have laughed at the impossibility. Now, it was not only possible, it was real. The scientist in him couldn't dispute the evidence.

If such marvels could happen for an unrepentant scoundrel as Bennett, then maybe Catullus might find his own miracle. After all, the world was full of magic.

Don't miss the rest of the
Blades of the Rose series!

In September, we met a WARRIOR in Mongolia . . .

To most people, the realm of magic is the
stuff of nursery rhymes and dusty libraries.
But for Capt. Gabriel Huntley, it's become
quite real and quite dangerous . . .

IN HOT PURSUIT

The vicious attack Capt. Gabriel Huntley witnesses in
a dark alley sparks a chain of events that will take him to
the ends of the Earth and beyond—where what is real and
what is imagined become terribly confused. And frankly,
Huntley couldn't be more pleased. Intrigue, danger,
and a beautiful woman in distress—just what he needs . . .

IN HOTTER WATER

Raised thousands of miles from England,
Thalia Burgess is no typical Victorian lady.
A good thing,
because a proper lady would have no hope of
recovering the priceless magical artifact Thalia is after.
Huntley's assistance might come in handy, though she
has to keep him in the dark. But this distractingly
handsome soldier isn't easy to deceive . . .

There was a knock at the wooden door to the tent. Her father called out, "Enter." The door began to swing open.

Thalia tucked the hand holding the revolver behind her back. She stood behind her father's chair and braced herself, wondering what kind of man would step across the threshold and if she would have to use a gun on another human being for the first time in her life.

The man ducked to make it through the door, then immediately removed his hat, uncovering a head of close-cropped, wheat-colored hair. He was not precisely handsome, but he possessed an air of command and confidence that shifted everything to his favor. His face was lean and rugged, his features bold and cleanly defined; there was nothing of the drawing room about him, nothing refined or elegant. He was clean-shaven, allowing the hard planes of his face to show clearly. He was not an aristocrat and looked as though he had fought for everything he ever had in his life, rather than expecting it to be given to him. Even in the filtered light inside the *ger*, Thalia could see the gleaming gold of his eyes, their sharp intelligence that missed nothing as they scanned the inside of the tent and finally fell on her and her father.

"Franklin Burgess?" he asked.

"Yes, sir," her father answered, guarded. "My daughter, Thalia."

She remembered enough to sketch a curtsey as she felt the heat of the stranger's gaze on her. An uncharacteristic flush rose in her cheeks.

"And you are . . . ?" her father prompted.

"Captain Gabriel Huntley," came the reply, and now it made sense that the man who had such sure bearing would be an officer. "Of the Thirty-third Regiment." Thalia was not certain she could relax just yet, since it was not unheard of for the Heirs to find members in the ranks of the military. She quickly took stock of the width of the captain's shoulders, how even standing still he seemed to radiate energy and the capacity for lethal movement. Captain Huntley would be a fine addition to the Heirs.

There was something magnetic about him, though, something that charged the very air inside the *ger*, and she felt herself acutely aware of him. His sculpted face, the brawn of his body, the way he carried his gear, all of it, felt overwhelmingly masculine. How ironic, how dreadful, it would be, if the only man to have attracted her attention in years turned out to be her enemy. Sergei, her old suitor, had wound up being her enemy, but in a very different way.

"You are out of uniform, Captain Huntley," her father pointed out.

For the first time since his entrance, the captain's steady concentration broke as he glanced down at his dusty civilian traveling clothes. "I'm here in an unofficial capacity." He had a gravelly voice with a hint of an accent Thalia could not place. It was different from the cultured tones of her father's friends, rougher, but with a low music that danced up the curves of her back.

"And what capacity is that?" she asked. Thalia realized
too late that a proper Englishwoman would not speak so
boldly, nor ask a question out of turn, but, hell, if Captain
Huntley *was* an Heir, niceties did not really matter.

His eyes flew back to her, and she met his look levelly,
even as a low tremor pulsed inside her. God, there it was
again, that strange *something* that he provoked in her, now
made a hundred times stronger when their gazes connected. She watched him assess her, refusing to back down
from the unconcealed measuring. She wondered if he felt
that peculiar awareness too, if their held look made his
stomach flutter. Thalia doubted it. She was no beauty—too
tall, her features too strong, and there was the added hand-
icap of this dreadful dress. Besides, he didn't quite seem
like the kind of man who fluttered anything.

Yet . . . maybe she was wrong. Even though he was on
the other side of the *ger*, Thalia could feel him looking at
her, taking her in, with an intensity that bordered on un-
nerving. And intriguing.

Regardless of her scanty knowledge of society, Thalia
did know that gentlemen did not look at ladies in such a
fashion. Strange. Officers usually came from the ranks of
the upper classes. He should know better. But then, so
should she.

"As a messenger," he answered, still holding Thalia's
gaze, "from Anthony Morris."

That name got her attention, as well as her father's.

"What about Morris?" he demanded. "If he has a message for me, he should be here, himself."

The captain broke away from looking intently at Thalia
as he regarded her father. He suddenly appeared a bit tired,
and also sad.

"Mr. Morris is dead, sir."

Thalia gasped, and her father cried out in shock and
horror. Tony Morris was one of her father's closest friends.

Thalia put her hand on her father's shoulder and gave him a supportive squeeze as he removed his glasses and covered his eyes. Tony was like a younger brother to her father, and Thalia considered him family. To know that he was dead— her hands shook. It couldn't be true, could it? He was so bright and good and . . . God, her throat burned from unshed tears for her friend. She swallowed hard and glanced up from her grief. Such scenes were to be conducted in private, away from the eyes of strangers.

The captain ducked his head respectfully as he studied his hands, which were gripped tightly on his hat. Through the fog of her sorrow, Thalia understood that the captain had done this before. Given bad news to the friends and families of those that had died. What a dreadful responsibility, one she wouldn't wish on anyone.

She tried to speak, but her words caught on shards of loss. She gulped and tried again. "How did it happen?"

The captain cleared his throat and looked at Franklin. He seemed to be deliberately avoiding looking at her. "This might not be suitable for . . . young ladies."

Even in her grief, Thalia had to suppress a snort. Clearly, this man knew nothing of her. Fortunately, her father, voice rough with emotion about Tony Morris's death, said, "Please speak candidly in front of Thalia. She has a remarkably strong constitution."

Captain Huntley's gaze flicked back at her for a brief moment, then stayed fixed on her father. She saw with amazement that this strapping military man was uncomfortable, and, stranger still, it was *her* that was making him uncomfortable. Perhaps it was because of the nature of his news, unsuitable as it was for young ladies. Or perhaps it was because he'd felt something between them, as well, something instant and potent. She did not want to consider it, not when she was reeling from the pain of Tony Morris's death.

After clearing his throat again, the captain said, "He was killed, sir. In Southampton."

"So close!" Franklin exclaimed. "On our very doorstep."

"I don't know 'bout doorsteps, sir, but he was attacked in an alley by a group of men." Captain Huntley paused as Thalia's father cursed. "They'd badly outnumbered him, but he fought bravely until the end."

"How do you know all this?" Thalia asked. If Tony's death had been reported in the papers, surely someone other than the captain would be standing in their *ger* right now, Bennett Day or Catullus Graves. How Thalia longed to see one of their numbers, to share her family's grief with them instead of this man who disquieted her with his very presence.

Captain Huntley again let his eyes rest on her briefly. She fought down her immediate physical response, trying to focus on what he was saying. "I was there, miss, when it happened. Passing by when I heard the sounds of Morris's being attacked, and joined in to help him." He grimaced. "But there were too many, and when my back was turned, he was stabbed by one of them—a blond man who talked like a nob, I mean, a gentleman."

"Henry Lamb?" Franklin asked, looking up at Thalia. She shrugged. Her father turned his attention back to the captain and his voice grew sharp, "You say you were merely 'passing by,' and heard the scuffle and just 'joined in to help.' Sounds damned suspicious to me." Thalia had to agree with her father. What sort of man passed by a fight and came to the aid of the victim, throwing himself into the fray for the sake of a stranger? Hardly anyone.

Captain Huntley tightened his jaw, angry. "Suspicious or not, sir, that's what happened. Morris even saved my life just before the end. So when he gave me the message to deliver to you, in person, I couldn't say no."

"You came all the way from Southampton to Urga to

fulfill a dying man's request, a man you had never met before," Thalia repeated, disbelief plain in her voice.

The captain did not even bother answering her. "It couldn't be written down, Morris said," he continued, addressing her father and infuriating Thalia in the process. She didn't care for being ignored. "I've had it in my head for nearly three months, and it makes no sense to me, so I'll pass it on to you. Perhaps you can understand it, sir, because, as much as I've tried, I can't."

"Please," her father said, holding his hand out and gesturing for Captain Huntley to proceed.

"The message is this: 'The sons are ascendant. Seek the woman who feeds the tortoise.'"

He glanced at both Thalia and her father to see their reactions, and could not contain his surprise when her father cursed again and Thalia gripped a nearby table for support. She felt dizzy. It was beginning. "You know what that means?" the captain asked.

Franklin nodded as his hands curled and uncurled into fists, while Thalia caught her lower lip between her teeth and gnawed pensively on it.

She knew it was bound to happen, but they had never known when. That time was now at hand.

In November, get lost
in the Canadian wilderness with REBEL . . .

*On the Canadian frontier in 1875, nature is a harsh
mistress. But the supernatural can really do you in . . .*

A LONE WOLF

Nathan Lesperance is used to being different.
He's the first Native attorney in Vancouver,
and welcome neither with white society
nor his sometime tribe.
Not to mention the powerful wildness he's always
felt inside him, too dangerous to set free.
Then he met Astrid Bramfield and saw his like
within her piercing eyes. Now, unless she helps him through
the harsh terrain and the harsher unknowns of his
true abilities, it could very well get him killed . . .

AND THE WOMAN WHO
LEFT THE PACK

Astrid has traveled this path before. Once she was
a Blade of the Rose protecting the world's magic from
unscrupulous men, with her husband by her side.
But she's loved and lost, and as a world-class
frontierswoman, she knows all about survival.
Nathan's searing gaze and long, lean muscles mean nothing
but trouble. Yet something has ignited a forgotten flame
inside her: a burning need for adventure, for life—
and perhaps even for love . . .

He had looked into her. Not merely seen her hunger for living, but felt it, too. She saw that at once. He recognized it in her. Two creatures, meeting by chance, staring at one another warily. And with reluctant longing.

Yet it wasn't only that immediate connection she had felt when meeting Lesperance. There was magic surrounding him.

Astrid wondered if Lesperance even knew how magic hovered over him, how it surrounded him like a lover, leaving patterns of nearly visible energy in his wake. She didn't think he was conscious of it. Nothing in his manner suggested anything of the sort. Nathan Lesperance, incredibly, was utterly unaware that he was a magical being. Not metaphorical magic, but *true* magic.

She knew, however. Astrid had spent more than ten years surrounded by magic of almost every form. Some of it benevolent, like the Healing Mists of Ho Hsien-Ku, some of it dark, such as the Javanese serpent king Naga Pahoda, though most magic was neither good nor evil. It simply was. And Astrid recognized it, particularly when sharing a very small space, as the Mounties' office had been.

If Nathan Lesperance's fierce attractiveness and unwanted understanding did not drive Astrid from the trading post, back to the shelter of her solitary homestead, then the magic enveloping him certainly would. She wanted nothing more to do with magic. It had cost her love once before, and she would not allow it to hurt her again.

But something had changed. She'd felt it, not so long ago. Magic existed like a shining web over the world, binding it together with filaments of energy. Being near magic for many years made her especially sensitive to it. When she returned from Africa, that sensitivity had grown even more acute. She tried to block it out, especially when she left England, but it never truly went away.

Only a few weeks earlier, Astrid had been out tending to her horse when a deep, rending sensation tore through her, sending her to her knees. She'd knelt in the dirt, choking, shaking, until she'd gained her strength again and tottered inside. Eventually, the pain subsided, but not the sense of looming catastrophe. Something had shaken and split the magical web. A force greater than anyone had ever known. And to release it meant doom.

What was it? The Blades had to know, how to avert the disaster. They would fight against it, as they always did. But without her.

A memory flitted through her mind. Months earlier, she'd had a dream and it had stayed with her vividly. She dreamt of her Compass, of the Blades, and heard someone calling her, calling her home. Astrid had dismissed the dream as a vestige of homesickness, which reared up now and again, especially after she'd been alone for so long.

The jingle of her horse's bridle snapped her attention back to the present. She cursed herself for drifting. A moment's distraction could easily lead to death out here. Stumbling between a bear sow and her cub. Crossing paths with vicious whiskey runners. A thousand ways to die. So when her awareness suddenly prickled once again, Astrid did not dismiss it.

A rustle, and movement behind her. Astrid swung her horse around, taking up her rifle, to confront who or whatever was there.

She blinked, hardly believing what she saw. A man walked through tall grasses lining the pass trail. He walked with steady but dazed steps, hardly aware of his surroundings. He was completely naked.

"Lesperance?"

Astrid turned her horse on the trail and urged it closer. Dear God, it *was* Lesperance. She decocked her rifle and slung it back over her shoulder.

He didn't seem to hear her, so she said again, coming nearer, "Mr. Lesperance?" She could see now, only ten feet away, that cuts, scrapes and bruises covered his body. His very nude, extremely well-formed body. She snapped her eyes to his face before they could trail lower than his navel. "What happened to you?"

His gaze, dark and blank, regarded her with a removed curiosity, as if she was a little bird perched on a windowsill. He stopped walking and stared at her.

Astrid dismounted at once, pulling a blanket from her pack. Within moments, she wrapped it around his waist, took his large hand in hers, and coaxed his fingers to hold the blanket closed. Then she pulled off her coat and draped it over his shoulders. Despite the fact that the coat was quite large on Astrid, it barely covered his shoulders, and the sleeves stuck out like wings. In other circumstances, he would have looked comical. But there was nothing faintly amusing about this situation.

Magic still buzzed around him, though somewhat dimmer than before.

"Where are your clothes? How did you get here? Are you badly hurt?"

None of her questions penetrated the fog enveloping him. She bent closer to examine his wounds. Some of the cuts were deep, as though made by knives, and rope abrasions circled his wrists. Bruises shadowed his knees and knuckles. Blood had dried in the corners of his mouth. Nothing looked serious, but out in the wilderness, even the most minor injury held the potential for disaster. And, without clothing, not even a Native inured to the changeable weather could survive. He was in shock, just beginning to shake.

"Lesperance," she said, taking hold of his wide shoulders and staring into his eyes intently, "listen to me. I need to see to your wounds. We're going to have to ride back to my cabin."

"Astrid . . ." he murmured with a slow blink, then his nostrils flared like a beast scenting its mate. A hungry look crossed his face. "Astrid."

It was unexpected, given the circumstances, yet seeing that look of need, hearing him say her name, filled her with a responding desire. "Mrs. Bramfield," she reminded him. And herself. They were polite strangers.

"Astrid," he said, more insistent. He reached up to touch her face.

She grabbed his hand, pulling it away from her face. At least she wore gloves, so she didn't have to touch his bare skin. "Come on." Astrid gently tugged him towards her horse. Once beside the animal, she swung up into the saddle, put her rifle across her lap, and held a hand out to him. He stared at it with a frown, as though unfamiliar with the phenomenon of hands.

"We have to go *now*, Lesperance," Astrid said firmly. "Those wounds of yours need attention, and whatever or whoever did this to you is probably still out there."

He cast a look around, seeming to find a shred of clarity in the hazy morass of his addled brain. Something dark and angry crossed his face. He took a step away, as if he meant to go after whoever had hurt him. His hands curled into fists. Insanity. He was unarmed, naked, wounded.

"Now," Astrid repeated.

Somehow, she got through to him. He took her hand and, with a dexterity that surprised her, given his condition, mounted up behind her.

God, she didn't want to do this. But there was no other choice. "Put your arms around my waist," she said through gritted teeth. When he did so, she added, "Hold tightly to me. Not that tight," she gasped as his grip turned to bands of steel. He loosened his hold slightly. "Good. Do not let go. Do you understand?"

He nodded, then winced as if the movement gave him pain. "Can't stay up."

"Lean against me if you have to." She mentally groaned when he did just that, and she felt him, even through her bulky knitted vest, shirt and sturdy trousers. Heavy and hard and solid with muscle. Everywhere. His arms, his chest, his thighs, pressed against hers. Astrid closed her eyes for a moment as she felt his warm breath along the nape of her neck.

"All set?" she asked, barely able to form the words around her clenched jaw.

He tried to nod again but the effort made him moan. The plaintive sound, coming from such a strong, potent man, pulled tight on feelings Astrid didn't want to have.

"Thank . . . you," he said faintly.

She didn't answer him. Instead, she kicked her horse into a gallop, knowing deep in her heart that she was making a terrible mistake.

And in December, STRANGER
brings the adventure back to London . . .

He protects the world's magic—with his science.
But even the best scientists can
fall prey to the right chemistry . . .

LOOKING FOR TROUBLE

Gemma Murphy has a nose for a story—
even if the boys in Chicago's newsrooms would rather
focus on her chest. So when she runs into
a handsome man of mystery discussing how
to save the world from fancy-pants Brit conspirators,
she's sensing a scoop. Especially when he mentions
there's magic involved. Of course, getting him
on the record would be easier if he hadn't
caught her eavesdropping . . .

LIGHTING HIS FUSE

Catullus Graves knows what it's like to be shut out:
his ancestors were slaves. And he's a genius inventor with
appropriately eccentric habits, so even people who love
him find him a little odd. But after meeting a certain
redheaded scribbler, he's thinking of other types of science.
Inconvenient, given that he needs to focus on preventing
the end of the world as we know it. But with Gemma's
insatiable curiosity sparking Catullus's inventive impulses,
they might set off something explosive anyway . . .

Now was her chance to do some investigating. Surely she'd find something of note in his cabin. A fast glance up and down the passageway ensured she was entirely alone.

Gemma opened the cabin door.

And found herself staring at a drawn gun.

Damn. He *was* in. Working silently at a table by the light of one small lamp. At her entrance, he was out of his chair and drawing a revolver in one smooth motion.

She drew her Derringer.

They stared at each other.

In the small cabin, Catullus Graves's head nearly brushed the ceiling as he faced her. Her reporter's eye quickly took in the details of his appearance. Even though he was the only black passenger on the ship, more than just his skin color made him stand out. His scholar's face, carved by an artist's hand, drew one's gaze. Arresting in both its elegant beauty and keen perception. A neatly-trimmed goatee framed his sensuous mouth. The long, lean lines of his body—the breadth of his shoulders, the length of his legs—revealed a man comfortable with action as well as thought.

Though, until now, Gemma had not been aware *how* comfortable. Until she saw the revolver held easily, familiarly in his large hand. A revolver trained on her. She'd have to do something about that.

"Mr. Graves," she murmured, shutting the door behind her.

Behind his spectacles, Catullus Graves's dark eyes widened. "Miss Murphy?"

Despite the fact that she was in danger of being shot, it wasn't until Graves spoke to Gemma that her heart began to pound. And she was absurdly glad he did remember her, for she certainly hadn't forgotten him. They'd met but briefly. Spoke together only once. Yet the impression of him remained, and not merely because she had an excellent memory.

"I thought you were out," she said. As if that excused her behavior.

"Wanted to get a barometric reading." Catullus Graves frowned. "How did you get in?"

"I opened the door," she answered. Which was only a part of the truth. She wasn't certain he would believe her if she told him everything.

"That's not possible. I put an unbreakable lock on it. Nothing can open it without a special key that *I* made." He sounded genuinely baffled, convinced of the security of his invention. Gemma glanced around the cabin. Covering all available surfaces, including the table where he had been working moments earlier, were small brass tools of every sort and several mechanical objects in different states of assembly. Graves was an inventor, she realized. She knew her way around a workshop, but the complex devices Graves worked on left her mystified.

She also realized—the same time he did—that they were alone in his cabin. His small, *intimate* cabin. She tried, without much success, not to look at the bed, just as she tried and failed not to picture him stripping out of his clothes before getting into that bed for the night. She barely knew this man! Why in the name of the saints did her mind lead her exactly where she did not want it to go?

The awareness of intimacy came over them both like an exotic perfume. He glanced down and saw that he was in his shirtsleeves, and made a cough of startled chagrin. He reached for his coat draped over the back of a chair. One hand still training his gun on her, he used the other to don his coat.

"Strange to see such modesty on the other end of a Webley," Gemma said.

"I don't believe this situation is covered in many etiquette manuals," he answered. "What are you doing here?"

One hand gripping her Derringer, Gemma reached into her pocket with the other. "Easy," she said, when he tensed. "I'm just getting this." She produced a small notebook, which she flipped open with a practiced one-handed gesture.

"Pardon—I'll have a look at that," Graves said. Polite, but wary. He stepped forward, one broad-palmed hand out.

A warring impulse flared within Gemma. She wanted to press herself back against the door, as if some part of herself needed protecting from him. Not from the gun in his other hand, but *him*, his tall, lean presence that fairly radiated with intelligence and energy. Keep impartial, she reminded herself. That was her job. Report the facts. Don't let emotion, especially *female* emotion, cloud her judgment.

And yet that damned traitorous female part of her responded at once to Catullus Graves's nearness. Wanted to be closer, drawn in by the warmth of his eyes and body. An immaculately dressed body. As he crossed the cabin with only a few strides, Gemma undertook a quick perusal. Despite being pulled on hastily, his dark green coat perfectly fit the breadth of his shoulders. She knew that

beneath the coat was a pristine white shirt. His tweed
trousers outlined the length of his legs, tucked into gleaming brown boots. His burgundy silk cravat showed off the
clean lines of his jaw. And his waistcoat. Good gravy. It
was a minor work of art, superbly fitted, the color of claret,
and worked all over with golden embroidery that, upon
closer inspection, revealed itself to be an intricate lattice
of vines and flowers. Golden silk-covered buttons ran down
its front, and a gold watch chain hung between a pocket
and one of the buttons. Hanging from the chain, a tiny fob
in the shape of a knife glinted in the lamplight.

On any other man, such a waistcoat would be dandyish.
Ridiculous, even. But not on Catullus Graves. On him, the
garment was a masterpiece, and perfectly masculine, high-
lighting his natural grace and the shape of his well-formed
torso. She knew about fashion, having been forced to write
more articles than she wanted on the subject. And this man
not only defined style, he surpassed it.

But she was through with writing about fashion. That
was precisely why she was on this steamship in the middle
of the Atlantic Ocean.

With this in mind, Gemma tore her gaze from this vision
to find him watching her. A look of faint perplexity crossed
his face. Almost bashfulness at her interest.

She let him take the notebook from her, and their fingertips accidentally brushed.

He almost dropped the notebook, and she felt heat shoot
into her cheeks. She had the bright ginger hair and pale,
freckled skin of her Irish father, which meant that, even in
low lamplight, when Gemma blushed, only a blind imbecile could miss it.

Catullus Graves was not a blind imbecile. His reaction to
her blush was to flush, himself, a deeper mahogany stain-
ing his coffee-colored face.

A knock on the door behind her had Gemma edging

quickly away, breaking the spell. She backed up until she pressed against a bulkhead.

"Catullus?" asked a female voice on the other side of the door. The woman from earlier.

Graves and Gemma held each other's gaze, weapons still drawn and trained on each other.

"Yes," he answered.

"Is everything all right?" the woman outside pressed. "Can we come in?"

Continuing to hold Gemma's stare, Graves reached over and opened the door.

Immediately, the fair-haired woman and her male companion entered.

"Thought it was nothing," the man said, grim. "But I *know* I've caught that scent before, and—" He stopped, tensing. He swung around to face Gemma, who was plastered against the bulkhead with her little pistol drawn.

Both he and the woman had their own revolvers out before one could blink.

And now Gemma had not one but *three* guns aimed at her.

GREAT BOOKS, GREAT SAVINGS!

When You Visit Our Website:
www.kensingtonbooks.com
You Can Save Money Off The Retail Price
Of Any Book You Purchase!

- All Your Favorite Kensington Authors
- New Releases & Timeless Classics
- Overnight Shipping Available
- eBooks Available For Many Titles
- All Major Credit Cards Accepted

Visit Us Today To Start Saving!
www.kensingtonbooks.com

All Orders Are Subject To Availability.
Shipping and Handling Charges Apply.
Offers and Prices Subject To Change Without Notice.